P9-CLB-852

The Edge

The Edge

JAMIE COLLINSON

ONEWORLD

A Oneworld Book

First published by Oneworld Publications, 2020

A CIP record for this title is available from the British Library

ISBN 978-1-78607-715-8
ISBN 978-1-78607-691-5 (ebook)

Typeset by Geethik Technologies
Printed and bound in Great Britain by Clays Ltd, Elcograf S.p.A.

Oneworld Publications
10 Bloomsbury Street, London, WC1B 3SR, England
3754 Pleasant Ave, Suite 100, Minneapolis, MN 55409, USA

For my family

'It was easy enough to despise the world, but decidedly difficult to find any other habitable region.'

Edith Wharton

PART ONE

1

At 6.15 p.m. on Tuesday 9 May, Adam Fairhead was out on the Los Angeles river, looking for a nice bird. Back in London, he could've made a joke about that, but no one here would get it.

The sun was dipping behind the ridges of Griffith Park, its light fractured by the tall hedge to his right and dancing in soft little shards on the concrete bike path. On the other side of this green barrier – the base of which was littered with the detritus of the river's derelict residents – was the I-5 freeway. Its hum was incessant, but it didn't bother Adam. The scene to his left had a raw sort of beauty, and it was there that his eyes were constantly drawn.

Bliss, he thought, breathing in the aquatically tinged air. Work was definitively over for the day. It was the middle of the night in the UK, and past nine on America's East Coast. He hadn't received an email in over an hour. And this, his favourite walk, allowed him the sense of having taken some exercise – thus earning him a drink – as well as the opportunity to see something wild and beautiful. After a day spent grimacing his way through meetings – with marketing teams, managers, artists and staff – it was just what he needed.

So far, he hadn't seen much of interest. In the wide, shallow flats beneath the Los Feliz Boulevard bridge, there'd been the usual array of black-necked stilts – towering on their improbable, skinny red legs – and a scraggy old great blue heron, frozen, Zen-like, with its dagger bill pointed straight down at the water, ready to stab a passing, unlucky fish.

But these were everyday birds, the regular features of his visits to the river. He was hoping for something more interesting – the furtive green heron he'd seen a week or so back, perhaps. The plover-like bird he'd been unable to identify. Maybe the chattering, frantic belted kingfisher he'd seen the previous evening.

So far, no luck. His recent passion for birding had revealed to Adam, however, that despite lifelong evidence to the contrary, he was actually capable of patience. Birding trips were enjoyable whether they produced much or not. Looking was distracting. The walk wasn't spoiled by thinking about the past, or his mind eating itself over some problem at the office. Birding was quite clearly good for the soul.

Not that he was quite ready to come out, regarding this strange new pastime of his. Not in any professional setting, anyway. Not even to Angelina. She wouldn't understand.

Sofia would have understood. She would have encouraged him, in fact, and probably thought it all quite cool. But he hadn't realized how cool *she* was, and as a result she was long since gone.

He glanced up at the San Gabriel mountains, a looming wall of jagged green, marbled in off-white, blocking off the skyline to the north. Silent and a little forbidding, like sentinels, checking the city's careless sprawl from seeping any further.

At the weekend, he could be back up there. Take another long, solitary trek in the alpine wilderness, quite literally away from it all. The thought gave him an electric thrill. For a hiker, it was a little like having a huge chunk of the Scottish Highlands directly outside London.

His eyes snagged on the highest visible point – Strawberry Peak, a deceptive name if ever there was one. Seeing it doused the thrill a little bit, because he'd recently chickened out of climbing it. 'The Mountaineers' Path' had been too much for him. Standing on its narrow ridge, he'd been overcome by fear. Now, it lingered in his mind, bothering him like an itch he couldn't scratch.

Still, hiking and birding were officially Good Things; healthy new habits that had blossomed with his move to LA. Now, it was simply a case of shedding all the bad ones he'd brought along with him. As it was, he sometimes felt like a half-emerged butterfly, trying to tear himself free of his caterpillar past.

He lowered his eyes back to the river. A homeless man wearing wraparound sunglasses was doing press-ups against a buttress below him. He was topless, his jeans smeared with dirt. His upper body was, Adam had to admit, quite impressive. The late sun shone on his coffee-coloured skin, the muscles big enough to cast shadows on his flesh.

A hundred feet lower down still, beyond the sloping concrete bank of the river, a very fat, bald man was lying in a shallow, sunny spot of green water, bathing happily.

The river was, Adam reflected, a very strange place indeed. Not a river at all in fact, but rather a concrete drainage channel, designed to ensure that excess water from the mountains could be directed safely through the city. Not that there'd been much excess water in Los Angeles in the four years Adam had lived there.

If you looked at the centre of the channel, perhaps blocking out the dirty white banks with your hands, the scene was genuinely bucolic. A wide stripe of rampant, sprouting green vegetation ran along the river's middle, for as far as the eye could see. Smooth plains of blue-green water slipped either side of it, bringing to mind – an English one, at least – lazy notions of messing about on a river.

There was a narrower sub-channel within the flora, and Adam had often imagined slowly canoeing along this, high walls of green blocking off the harsh urbanity either side of him. It would be like floating through a jungle, he thought.

From where he stood now, on the bank beside the freeway, the smell of the water was strong in his nostrils. He always caught this smell before his first sight of the river itself, lingering over the concrete of Los Feliz Boulevard as he approached his walk. A slightly dank, green smell of underwater vegetation. Not unpleasant, and shockingly *wild*, in the midst of the city.

The water couldn't be too dirty, he knew, because it sustained fish and the birds that hunted them. Also, the fat, bald man had been bathing in it every night of the summer – often with friends – and it didn't seem to have done him any harm.

In fact, the river appeared to sustain homeless people – of whom Los Angeles had a great, disturbing many – as well as it did birds. Whether it was the relative beauty of the place, the water to bathe in, or simply the opportunity to make a home somewhere secluded, Adam didn't know.

He was passing one of the smaller camps even now. An ancient shopping trolley had been parked up at a crazy angle beside the bike path. Beneath it was a pair of battered old shoes. A short incline led to a spot where the hedge had thickened into a broad band of foliage, providing a barrier to the worst of the I-5's sound and stink. Here, several filthy, well-worn tents had been pitched. One of them, larger than the others, was made of pieces of stained tarpaulin roped over trees. What looked like a small garbage dump was piled into a gap between it and the fence. Adam resisted the temptation to stare at the settlement. He didn't want to be impolite.

He walked the river as many evenings as he could, whenever he was freed from the tyranny of working dinners, working drinks or working gigs. One of the things he'd come to learn from doing so was that the river's homeless were, as yet at least, unfailingly polite. They smiled, nodded and said hello. They bathed, biked or worked out. The sadder ones made urgent, distraught walks along the bike path, alarmingly overdressed for the hot weather. Not one of them had ever asked Adam for money.

Yet another of LA's many eccentricities, he thought.

A cyclist hurtled past him, a broad, sweating man clad in skintight Lycra bearing dozens of unfamiliar logos. Strange, this logo-wearing,

Adam thought. What distinguished amateur cycling from, say, amateur tennis, when it came to logos? Why bother advertising a load of brands when you weren't being paid to do so?

At the edge of the water, their upper bodies lit orange by the last band of sun, a pair of men were fishing in silence. Adam paused to look at a row of cormorants, perched on a power line, apparently basking in the day's late warmth. He'd almost reached the dilapidated Sunnynook footbridge when he heard a woman's voice.

'Hey!' it said, shouting. 'You.'

Adam turned around, and saw a tall, slim woman crossing the footbridge with her bike. She was dressed in a blue jacket and skin-tight, brightly patterned workout pants, a bike helmet and purposeful-looking sunglasses.

'Me?' Adam said.

'Yes.' She'd almost reached him and was walking quickly, her expression urgent. Adam felt his pulse quicken a little.

'Are you birding?' she said as she came to a stop.

'Yes,' he replied, glancing at his binoculars. He wondered if he'd somehow broken some strange local bylaw forbidding it.

The woman removed her sunglasses. She had quite bright blue eyes, which shone a little with excitement. Adam was taken aback by her prettiness.

'There's an osprey,' she said. 'There.'

She pointed towards a tree, beneath the power line on which the cormorants were perching. Adam raised his binoculars.

'I can't see it…' he said, lowering them again. His pulse was thudding now. 'That tree?' He pointed.

'Hold on,' she said. She placed the bike against the railing, and leaned in towards Adam, looking along his line of sight. She smelled good, he noticed. A light spiciness of hair shampoo, and what he thought might be her own, actual smell, which was equally pleasant. His skin tingled a little where her jacket was touching him.

'No, sorry,' she said. 'There. The one to the left.'

He looked again. Sure enough, a flash of white caught his eye. When he levelled the binoculars, they settled on a perching osprey. A *star bird*, he thought, a wave of excitement rushing through him. A large, slightly shaggy-looking raptor, with light brown outer parts, a lethal bill and huge yellow eyes. Its head was tucked down against its bright white breast as it stared at the water, looking for prey. Adam realized he'd been holding his breath, and now he gasped.

The woman giggled. 'Isn't that great? I thought you'd want to see it. Sorry if I freaked you out.'

'Don't be sorry,' he said, smiling at her. 'It's amazing. That's made my night.'

He raised the binoculars again. 'You have to go an awful long way to see one of those, where I'm from,' he said.

'You're British?' she asked.

'Yes.' He was pleased she hadn't said Australian, which was what most Angelenos accused him of being.

'But they must be there, surely?' she said. 'The European bird is the same species, I think.'

Adam felt a flutter of novice's fear.

'Pretty much wiped them out,' he said. 'There's a few in Scotland and up in north-west England.'

He glanced at the woman, who'd screwed up her face. 'Why would they do that?' she asked.

'Egg collecting, pesticides. Jealousy over trout. That sort of thing.'

'That's awful,' she said, frowning as she picked up her bike again.

'Here,' he said quickly. 'Take a look.'

'Oh…' She reached towards him, but hesitated.

'I don't have pink-eye,' Adam told her, grinning. Many Americans, he knew, had an irrational fear of conjunctivitis.

She gave a quick, sudden laugh, and made a gimme gesture with a bike-gloved hand.

He lifted the binoculars' straps over his head and handed them to her. As she raised them to her eyes, Adam guiltily allowed his own to run down over her body. He was fairly sure this habit had intensified unhealthily in LA, where the temptations of bared flesh were year-round, and workout pants rife.

'Beautiful,' the woman said, handing back his binoculars and smiling. 'It's great that the river can sustain one. Didn't use to be that way.'

Suddenly she had her bike's handlebars in her hands, and was wheeling it away from him.

'Thank you,' he said. 'Very much.'

'You're welcome,' she replied, swinging a shapely leg over her saddle and showing him a perfect, workout-panted behind. 'I didn't want you to miss it.'

Adam watched her cycle off. A shameful notion of looking at her through the binoculars surfaced in his mind, and he banished it. Sometimes he worried he was becoming a creep. All this time spent in self-induced solitude. Maybe it wasn't good for him. Perhaps he was too old to be on his own. Back home, every one of his circle of friends in London had settled down, most of them having children now too. He'd had his own chance, of course, and he'd comprehensively blown it.

But that was then, and this was now.

As he peered at the osprey again, taking in the vicious hook of its bill, and the sharp talons that held it steady as a rock on its narrow branch, he thought of Angelina. Could he settle down with her, he wondered? He pictured the wedding. It would take place in some mansion in the hills, where they usually did launch parties or photo shoots. Angelina would probably use the vows as an opportunity to showcase one of her poems. He might end up one of those people who got married in sunglasses.

No, he thought, sternly. He'd let worry creep in, and that was not to be encouraged. For one thing, it was a sure way to ruin the birding.

As though in agreement, the osprey launched itself lightly from its perch and scythed down to the water in a silent, graceful arc. Just before it hit the surface, it folded itself into a broad arrow, talons reaching forward almost to its head. A split second later it rose once more, wings beating upwards in a shower of silver droplets, the gleaming crescent of a large fish caught firmly in its triumphant grip.

'Yes!' Adam found himself shouting.

'Yeah bro!' someone yelled back. Adam turned to see a bone-thin bum, riding past on a child's bicycle, grinning and pumping his fist, careering off into the oncoming night.

2

On the way home, in a celebratory mood, he stopped off at his local Thai place. The women who worked there – unsmiling yet friendly – welcomed him in, fussing him into his usual seat and asking where he'd been during the week or so since his last visit. He ordered a huge meal of tom yum soup and a sizzling Weeping Tiger, washing it down with two very cold beers.

The evening's remaining hours were spent nestled away in his living room, blinds drawn, lamplight mellow on the varnished wooden floor. In his previous life in London, he'd seemed to be rarely at home. Lately though, his craving for the sanctuary and solitude of his apartment had almost become a concern. The temptations of drink and memory were a constant risk, but social life had started to make him feel anxious.

Tonight though, he had a vivid new experience to ponder. The thrill of the bird and the memory of the woman who'd shown it to him hovered in his mind. He wrote up his impressions of the osprey and read a novel on the couch, limiting himself to two glasses of wine. Occasionally, a creak from the building's wooden frame told him that his landlady was moving around next door. Otherwise, there was just the sound of endless traffic on the Hollywood freeway, or a Harley's pop-and-snarl on Sunset Boulevard.

Just as he was dragging himself off the couch to go to bed, his phone emitted the soft, sinister sound of an incoming video call. He picked it up off the coffee table, frowning at the picture of his mother on the screen. To ignore it would have been too awful. He swiped to accept.

The more recent incarnation of his mother's face appeared on the screen. Short grey hair, square jaw, downturned mouth. A hint of the same cheekbones he had. The eyes above them were closed, opening briefly every few seconds in an inverse blink. Behind her, a nurse moved across the neutral décor of the room she was in.

'Hi, Mum,' Adam said.

'Now then,' she said. Her voice was very clear, at odds with the dopey frown of medicated pain.

'How're you doing?' Adam asked. His heart was beating faster, and he felt anxiety clutch around it. Turning the phone to the side, he drained the dregs of his white wine.

'Could be worse,' she said. 'You?'

'Same,' he said. 'You just caught me. I was about to go to bed.'

Her jaw moved in a gurn. 'Late there, is it?'

'10.30.'

'Right. Thought it might be a good time to catch you. Early here.' The eyelids opened, the eyes within struggling to focus, presumably on his own digitized image. A miniature version of this was at the top right of the screen, and he tried not to look at it.

'How are you feeling?' he asked.

She grunted. 'No change really.'

'It'll be tennis season soon, won't it, the French Open? Are you looking forward to that?'

His mother had been a lifelong tennis fan and competitive player. Adam remembered many a happy, hot summer afternoon, watching her from old, stackable plastic chairs with his father and sister. The heated-rubber smells of the all-weather courts and new balls; the old clubhouse with crates of small orange juice cartons he was allowed to raid. Happiness radiating from his mum if she'd played a good game, spreading to him from snatched hugs between sets.

'I can't watch it any more,' she said. 'Can't concentrate. I've been knitting.'

'Well, that's good,' Adam said. 'What are you making?'

'Dishcloths. Anything else takes too long to finish.' Her eyes focused on him once again, and a thin smile stiffened her lips.

'You know me,' she said. 'Get bored easily. More so now.'

'Still don't like to sit still, eh?'

'No, I don't. Do you want a dishcloth? I can make you one.'

'Maybe when I see you,' he said.

But her attention, like the sweep of a lighthouse's beam, had turned away.

'Mum?' he said after a moment.

Her chin twitched upwards. 'Have you spoken to your sister?' she asked.

'Not for a while.'

'Why not?'

'I've been busy.'

'You'll have to make some effort, you know.'

Adam's sister lived in Malaysia. While there'd been no open conflict between them, one appeared to have grown slowly, like a cancer. It seemed to him that she thought him a fool.

'I'll write to her.'

'When are you going to come to England?'

'Christmas, I think.'

'To London?'

'No, Mum. I'll come to Somerset.'

'What about moving back properly?' she said. 'Have you got it all planned?'

The chance of his move had come at the same time her condition had been diagnosed. He'd told her it would be two years at most, and he'd meant it at the time. 'Well, you must take the opportunity,' she'd said. 'That's what they say, isn't it?' And she'd quoted his father. '"You only regret what you don't do."' His father, though, hadn't been quite as experimental in his approach to life as Adam had.

'They want to keep me here a bit longer,' he said. 'I'm still going to come back, eventually.'

She seemed to flinch, but that was one of the things she did whether there was a stimulus or not. How could he tell what had caused it this time?

His fists were clenched painfully, and he relaxed them. There was a Xanax in his bathroom cabinet, he remembered. Someone at a party had given him one when he'd asked what they were like. Until now, he'd been too scared to try it.

His mother's face had turned downward, like a deactivated radar dish.

'I'll look forward to Christmas,' she said, her voice slurring.

'Mum?' he said.

'Hmm,' she grunted.

'Is there anything I can send?'

'No, love. I'm OK. Lovely nurses here.'

From somewhere behind her, another lady shouted something.

'I've been making dishcloths,' his mother said. 'Want one?'

'It's alright, Mum.'

For a moment, he simply watched her face.

'I'm sorry,' he said.

The screen went black.

3

He'd dreamed of Sofia, and his thoughts were choked with her when he woke on Wednesday morning. From bitter experience, he knew that there was only one solution to this: get straight out of bed and into the day's distractions.

Mornings in LA were beautiful, which helped. He walked through to the living room and raised the blinds, banishing the ghosts of the previous evening. Standing by the window, he took deep sips of coffee and looked out. The world beyond was bathed in a soft, hazy light that hung over the world like a golden veil, softening the lawns and sidewalks and the palm fronds high overhead.

If I could just stand here for a while, he thought. Leave this new day as a canvas yet to be spoiled. But that was impossible. This moment of purity and calm never lasted long, because every weekday morning was ruined by a torrential downpour of emails.

Even if he'd lately resisted the temptation to scan them in bed, on his phone, and thus delayed the panic they induced, they'd still be there, waiting. A row of a hundred or so bolded, pregnant subject lines.

Adam worked in the music business, for a company whose head office was in London. Once, this company had been a fringe affair which had quietly but consistently released records across the spectrum of guitar music. More recently, in the words of its proud, online mission statement, it had 'hybridized' to become a 'full-service, boutique musical solution-provider', offering marketing, distribution, publishing, synchronization and campaign conceptualization to clients who remained – despite their hopeful sense of contemporary digital empowerment – musicians, pure and simple.

Two years earlier, due to a fortuitous combination of market conditions, technology-driven consumption, depth of back catalogue and one or two minor hits, it had suddenly found itself attracting the attention of bigger concerns. After a year or so of tense wrangling, the majority of its shares had been acquired by a large Norwegian tech firm.

This firm had made tens of millions by creating software that enabled them to automate a complex system of international publishing royalty collection. Now, with money pouring back into the business of recorded music, they wanted a piece of the gold rush. Best of all, they were happy to be silent partners – at least as long as the hits kept coming.

The results had been twofold: the financing had become available to set up an American headquarters in Los Angeles, and things, as Adam saw them, had all got rather serious.

Every morning, by 7 a.m. his time, the London HQ had filled his inbox. The Brits were in the middle of their afternoons; that angriest time of the day, when lunch was a distant memory, energy was flagging, blood sugar levels were dropping, and home – or the pub – was still hours away. What could be more fun than sending moody emails to people who'd had the sheer, bloody good fortune to be sent to LA, and now the audacity to not even be online yet?

And, he had to admit, there were signs that he might not be cut out for this bold new era. Adam's forthright management style, dependable enough in his previous role in London, didn't seem quite fit for purpose for professional life in Los Angeles. He'd recently discussed his troubles with a likeable, ageing crustacean of a man who managed musicians for a living.

'Passive aggression, dude,' the man had said. 'It builds up. Email is like leaving notes for your roommate. You gotta communicate.'

Adam told him that he was having problems managing younger people.

The man guffawed. 'Tell me about it,' he'd said. 'Little bastards, aren't they?'

The consultation had thus been only partly useful.

At 7.55, Adam stuffed his laptop into his hiking pack and swung it onto his back. Peering through the front window, he checked his landlady wasn't on her porch, and took the steps down onto the street. It wasn't that he didn't like his landlady. On the contrary, in fact. But the morning was no time for conversation. The earlier he got to work, the sooner he could leave.

At the corner of Coronado Street and Kent, a tall, skinny woman was standing, her legs heavily tattooed below her tiny cut-offs, a miniature dog at the end of a lead. She was staring at her iPhone through reflective aviator sunglasses, but she looked up from it to wish Adam good morning.

The dog stared at him with bulbous black eyes. It lowered its trembling, bony little behind towards the grass, and produced a chain of droppings as Adam approached. He picked up his speed, not wanting to see the woman reaching down to scoop them up. She, he knew from prior experience, wasn't one of the culprits that left their dog shit uncollected on the narrow strip of grass between the stairs to Adam's apartment and the place he parked his car.

Most days, he walked to the office. An optimal existence in LA meant living reasonably close to the place you had to work. The sun was already hot, and he felt its blaze against his high forehead. Luckily, it was a morning on which he'd remembered to smear himself in sun cream.

A man in a California Republic t-shirt was strapping his daughter into the back of a battered black Prius. The girl grinned at Adam, as though recognizing a favourite person, but then said, 'Oh oh!' and pointed at him warningly. Her father grinned and shook his head, and they, too, exchanged good mornings.

These small acts of friendliness were one of many aspects of LA that Adam liked. In London, the rule had seemed to be that only with your very closest neighbours, only the ones you truly couldn't plausibly pretend not to recognize, should you ever exchange a pleasantry. To wish an actual stranger good morning in the street would have come across as borderline psychotic.

Adam turned up the hill onto Sunset Boulevard. The bear on the California Republic t-shirt had got him thinking about them again. Bears had been much on his mind of late, ever since he'd seen a pair of them while driving to a hike in Yosemite. He'd made a recent, solo visit to the national park and carried out a long, solitary trek to a remote peak. He'd planned to think about important things while he did so. What he actually thought about was bears. Seeing them on the way to the trailhead had lent the experience a frisson of fear.

If I was a bear, he thought now, setting off up the hill towards Echo Park, I'd have been kicked out of the bear colony for shagging the other bears' females and starting too many fights. I'd be one of those manky old solo bears that goes mad, and starts attacking humans, and ends up being shot dead by park rangers. Like the one that got Grizzly Man. The one they cut open and found bits of Grizzly Man and his girlfriend inside.

Might it be such a bad way to go, he wondered? The shooting dead by park rangers bit, not the eating Grizzly Man part. If pressed to choose a method of dying, other than quietly in one's sleep, Adam was certain that surprise sniper round would be the way to go.

He'd often dreamed, too, of going and living by himself in the woods. The closest he'd managed was Los Angeles, which admittedly was a lot closer to nature than London had been.

He loved LA, actually. He loved the space and the wildness. He loved the wildlife – the skunks, coyotes, raccoons and hawks that played on the lawns, menaced the accessory-sized dogs and haunted the skies. He loved the food, the ocean and the brightness. The blue skies, white walls, lofty green palms and scarlet bougainvillea. He loved Griffith Park, with its huge, cliff-clinging wilderness, its lonely mountain lion and its Art Deco observatory. He even liked the people who wished him good morning as their dogs took a shit, they strapped their children into their Priuses, or they watered their gleaming, outrageous lawns.

In fact, the only thing he no longer loved, he realized with an icy shudder, was his job. His entire reason for being there.

It wasn't the job's fault, really. Not at all, in fact. It was certainly his. Most people would have killed to do what he did. He knew how to do it quite well, too – he just didn't *want* to any more. He felt too old for it. Sitting in meeting rooms, nauseated by promotional posters, wall-sized Apple screen savers, affected accents and interrogative statements.

He felt it ridiculous and undignified, at the age of thirty-six, to spend so much of his time discussing the rising and falling cool-stock of a set of strangely monikered young people, whose work was becoming increasingly indistinguishable to him. More and more often, he found himself feeling as though he was trapped in a TV satire about youth marketeers.

The question was: what on earth could he do next?

His best friend in LA was a charming Scottish maniac called Craig. Adam found Craig exciting. Craig, in turn, found Adam funny, though largely, Adam suspected, in the sense of laughing *at* him, rather than with him.

'Your problem,' Craig had once told him, 'is that you got your dream too early, and now you want another one.'

Adam thought he might have been able to content himself with the first, if it wasn't for two things. Firstly, his boss, the company's cerebral matriarch and founder, would soon be retiring. This had led to the rise of her right-hand man, Jason – or, in Adam's mind, the Autodidact. An alpha male in new man's clothing; a quoter of modish popular science, at-desk meditator and possessor of a frightening certainty and zero self-doubt.

The Autodidact had joined the company five years earlier, from a larger, rival label. Before then, he'd had a career in finance in the City of London. It seemed to Adam that, since leaving it, he'd been making up for lost time. The independent music world was not known for its fine business brains, and the Autodidact had hit the label like a hurricane, much to the boss – Serena's – delight.

He had repurposed the firm and executed its acquisition, and was thus the man who had brought in the big money. Subsequently, and consequent to this shift in power, came the second problem: the company had become even more successful.

Earlier in his career, Adam had happily worked for an esoteric punk label in London. He hadn't made much money out of it, but he'd been younger then. Life was more exciting. And he'd had Sofia. The imprint's music was good, and suited his contrarian instincts. It had even won a couple of prizes.

Sadly, its lack of vacuity had been brutally punished by an equal lack of commercial success. The label had gone out of business, and Adam had been snapped up by his current employer. And there he'd been for the last nine years, steadily rising up its ranks, until one day Serena told him that his talents might be best spent setting up a North American office.

So that was what he'd done. And in California he'd found a city he loved, and a first real taste of professional success. He just hadn't enjoyed the latter as much as he should have. Recently, via a couple of the Autodidact's strategic signings – or, in his language, 'pivots' – the label had started to compete in the commercial alternative rock market. It had done so by picking up a handful of young guitar bands who'd incorporated the high-octane drama of American electronic dance music into their sound.

This had proved a heady combination. Young audiences were primed to fall for dance's *drops* and basslines, especially if delivered via the recognizable, time-tested format of the four- or five-piece band.

The industry felt the same way. 'These dance guys,' a TV booker had once told Adam. 'It just looks like they're making sandwiches up there.' But even these ageing, harassed cultural gatekeepers knew that electronic music had hit America, and they were afraid they'd miss out. They just felt safer in booking bands who still wielded instruments.

Adam's company had offered them a solution. But it wasn't stopping there. The very latest crop of signings still featured guitars in their live or televised shows, but their use was little more than symbolic.

And the music was unremittingly awful; a sort of lowest common denominator mulch that Adam loathed. It was a soundtrack for the lives of the wilfully generic; sterile, market-ready, laser-targeted. Cynical and sappy all at once. A populist glut that bypassed the arbiters of the mainstream media and appealed directly to the public's worst instincts. It was music for people who never read books and spent most of their lives staring at pictures on social media platforms.

With the conquering of this lucrative niche had come a need for a new breed of staff. People who had once worked at major record labels; people who actually liked the musical mulch. People who would say 'cool', and mean it, when a narcissistic twenty-two-year-old with a silly hairdo said he wanted Mick Hucknall to feature on his album. The price of success, it seemed, was terrible music, and worse people.

The problem with success, Adam thought, resettling his backpack on his shoulders and wiping the sweat from his brow, was that it raised the stakes. It raised *you.* It lifted you too far off the ground, too quickly. It made you dizzy, which was no good, not when you'd abruptly found yourself with much further to fall.

Here, close to the company's top, he felt precarious. There was one person even closer to that narrowing pinnacle. He was the Autodidact, and his kicking legs threatened to break Adam's grip and send him tumbling.

Here in LA, his first dream had died. It wasn't the last life had to offer though, he was sure of that. There was still birding, and walking in the mountains. There were novels to read. There were women and wine. There was even Angelina.

He wasn't sure that counted as love though, at least not yet.

One thing he was sure of was that he had to *keep* the job he no longer loved. If he didn't, he'd have to go back to London, and he sure as hell wasn't going to do that. London was a graveyard for his former life. A city full of angry ghosts. And beyond London was the far-flung west. *Home* was the word that came to him, making him shiver despite the heat. *Home*, and *duty*.

He spent the rest of the short, steep walk trying to decide if bears did actually live in colonies. By the time he'd reached the bridge across Glendale Boulevard, and the final stretch to the office, he was sweating freely. When will I learn to walk slowly? he asked himself. He'd done it again. It was no good walking like a Londoner, not here, in this heat. Now he was going to arrive at the office covered in sweat, again, shirt plastered to his back and already looking like he'd been wearing it for a whole day. He really must remember to slow his pace.

It was barely considered normal to *walk* in LA, let alone to do so at such speed. Adam knew this because everyone he passed on his way to work – from lumbering bums to slow female joggers – flinched as he drew close to them, certain that his looming, speedy approach could only bode ill.

Still, he thought, there was no point slowing down now. Might as well get into the air-conditioning. Maybe he'd have time to nip home after work. Grab another shirt before the evening's horrors.

Tonight, there would be no slow saunter down the LA River. No chance. There was going to be an industry showcase on the office bloody roof.

And there was the office now, towering above him, and everything else in this patch of Los Angeles. Originally an architect-designed, four-storey home, it was situated a little way down Echo Park Avenue, a stone's throw from the park itself. Adam had overseen its purchase, making use of the generous funding injected by the company's new overlords. The house had cost almost three million dollars.

From street level, a double-fronted garage with frosted glass windows rose into a large, forbidding concrete wall. Above this, what looked like a series of massive, pale-grey Portakabins sprouted from each other. The upper floor was made of a symmetric pair, whose frontages leaned out at an angle, each featuring a wide, horizontal window that gazed down at the street like a malevolent robot's eyes.

Topping it all off was a bright steel railing, which surrounded the large roof garden and elevator tower and gave the robot building a spiky, lopsided hairdo.

Behind the concrete wall, hidden from the street, was a steeply sloping cactus garden. Adam occasionally stood at the window near his desk, looking down at its lethal spikes and spines and imagining a doomed escapee tumbling down the bank, avoiding the robot building's lasers only to be impaled on the vicious, indifferent prong of a giant agave.

But the location was perfect for a new breed of American record company. This was the land of vegan outreach centres and doggy day cares. It was the dizzyingly street-postered ground zero of tattoos, beards and cocktails-in-jam-jars. Rising above the stretch of Sunset that formed the heart of Echo Park, giant billboards bore the faces of smiling real-estate agents, or hyperreal photographs advertising the prowess of the latest smartphones. These eye-grabbing images would, if they worked, sell homes and products to the affluent, discerning hipsters that haunted the city's fashionable inner-eastern side.

The only real problem, Adam reflected as the noise of the Boulevard receded, was the unpleasant chain-gym on the corner of the street.

To Adam's mind, the place appeared to be essentially a dangerous cult – something to be feared and hated; in an ideal world, even legislated against. Above its frontage was a large banner, set in a totalitarian font and reading *Pain is Weakness Leaving the Body.* It made Adam shudder every time he saw it.

And even now, having almost made it to work, he was greeted by a platoon of sweaty, psychotic-eyed people in Lycra, their bodies covered in improbable swellings, who seemed to expect him to get out of *their* way as they ran along the sidewalk, despite the fact that he, as a pedestrian, was surely using it in the way civic planners had long intended. Wasn't there some unspoken rule, he wondered, that it was up to whoever was going fastest to go *around*? Was that rule even unspoken?

'WALK,' he felt like shouting. 'SideWALK.' But of course, he didn't. There was something fearsome about the gym's disciples – the hard core of them anyway, as this group certainly were. Adam quickened his step as he passed the little courtyard directly outside the place – a space reserved for the cult's high priests, who exhibited themselves to passing traffic in skintight one-pieces while wielding enormous weights.

Just you wait, their eyes seemed to say as he passed. *One day soon, there will be enough of us. And when that day comes, we will crush you pathetic weaklings under the heels of our futuristic sneakers.*

Adam made his way up the steep external staircase beside the cactus garden, reaching the building's door and digging out his keys. The elevator was tucked into the front right corner of the house, but it was too slow for Adam. Inside, he finally escaped from the sun and the body-cultists. Maybe one day, he hoped, as he closed the door behind him and switched on the air-conditioning, the gym, even just this one particular branch, might go out of business.

He climbed the stairs to the upper floor, slumped into his chair, plugged in his laptop and watched the emails begin to pour in.

4

Among the release specification documents, production timelines, marketing reports, signing announcements, social media calendars and the odd, fraught, philosophical discussion about A & R, Adam's inbox only held one worrying bit of news. The sender was the Autodidact, and the subject line simply **Call**.

Jason was not a man known for calling with good news. Normally, Adam would have got it out of the way as quickly as possible, but another storm was clearly brewing. Scott, Adam's marketing manager, was glancing at him meaningfully, eyes blinking above rigid lips, and generally giving off a strange vibe. The problem with open-plan offices, as far as Adam was concerned, was that vibes could be transmitted all too easily.

He replied to the Autodidact, asking him to call at 6 p.m. GMT, and swivelled his chair around to face Scott.

'Everything OK?' he asked.

'Not really, actually.'

'Go downstairs for a chat?'

'Yeah. That'd be good,' Scott replied.

Adam and his staff sat in one of the two vast upper cabins. The other was used as a warehouse and mail-order shipping area for CDs, LPs and merch. From Adam's desk, he could just see the Hollywood sign, sitting like an unrealized dream beyond the tangle of billboards, scrubby hills and power lines outside the wide rectangular window.

On the lower floors were a kitchen, a communal dining area, a lounge and a narrow, glass-walled meeting room that had been the original owner's wellness space. Adam and Scott made their way down the stairs, the other staff's interest prickling his flesh like airborne electrical currents.

They went into the meeting room and slid the door closed. Scott slumped on the sofa, picking up a cushion and holding it across his stomach. He was a short, wiry twenty-something with lush, chin-length hair that he regularly ran a hand through. His eyes were slightly protuberant, their irises a penetrating blue, and the combination gave him a permanently intense look.

'How was your evening?' Adam asked him.

'Awesome,' Scott said, brightening at the memory. 'My buddy organized a little secret show for Skrillex, like a friends-only thing?'

'Sounds great,' Adam said.

'Yeah, it was dope.' Scott grinned like a pupil whose holiday report had trounced all others. 'Great to hang with the bros.'

Scott appeared to revel in not inviting colleagues to events that his job had enabled him to attend, but telling them all about them afterwards. He wouldn't, Adam knew, ask about his boss's evening.

'Great,' Adam said. 'So, what's up?'

The smile faded, and Scott's blue eyes widened in a show of worry. Adam found it hard to look directly at them.

'There's two things really. First thing is kinda small. But, like, am I gonna be expected to lead the Disband campaign?'

'Well, yes,' Adam said. 'It's one of the biggest things we've got this year.' He paused, frowning. 'And it's good, too. Don't you like it?'

'Sure, I like it. But if the title is like last time, I'm *not* gonna be comfortable working on it.'

Disband's previous album had been called *BITCHMEAT*.

'What's wrong with that title?' Adam asked. 'It's a punk thing. It's just designed to be a bit provocative, isn't it?'

Scott shifted the cushion, cocked his head and pouted. 'It's demeaning to women. Misogyny is a gigantic problem in this country, and I will not be a part of it.'

Adam frowned. 'But three of the four members are women. The title is a comment on this stuff itself, I think. They're a feminist band. How is it misogynistic?'

Scott shrugged. 'If I'd put that album cover on my Facebook, it would have caused an outcry.'

BITCHMEAT's front cover image had been in the style of an internet meme: naked, bloodied women lined up in a slaughterhouse, the title blown up to fill the frame across two lines.

Adam's temper flared, and he tried to dampen it. 'Really, Scott? An outcry, caused by your personal Facebook page?'

'I have a *lot* of industry friends,' Scott said.

Adam took a breath. 'No one is asking you to post about albums you work on on your own Facebook page.'

'I post *all* the albums I work on on my page. That's my thing. I want to help the artists and the company. All except that one, because I felt I couldn't.'

'You've heard that solo track that Crystal released?' Adam said. 'The lyrics are about a culture polluted by the stench of female fear?'

'Yeah,' Scott said. 'But…'

'I can't imagine any artist making anything more obviously anti-misogynist. Maybe you could post that too?'

'Look,' Scott said, exasperated. 'Maybe we can just ask them what the content of the record is gonna be like, and what the title is?'

'Ah,' Adam said. If his temper had been a Californian wildfire, it would have been thirty per cent contained. 'So we should screen the work of women, to ensure that you, a man, are happy to work on it?'

'That's not what I'm saying at all. I'm a feminist, and I'm Jewish. I believe in intersectionality.'

It seemed safe only to address the first of these statements. 'It's exactly what you just said. You do see the irony, Scott, of you, a man, threatening not to work on women's music because of misogyny?'

Scott pulled his best disingenuous look, mouth agape. 'No, I don't. It's not ironic at all.'

Adam leaned forward. 'I'm going to press you on this point, Scott. It could be a textbook example of irony.'

'Look,' Scott said, looking frightened now. 'This is getting like Fox News. Let's just leave it. I'll work on the record. I'm sure it'll be fine.'

'OK.' Adam took a deep breath. This was only the small thing Scott wanted to talk about, and he'd already had a graphic vision of smashing in his skull with the starfish-like conference phone.

'Thank you,' he said. 'And sorry for getting irritable. What's the other thing?'

Scott widened his eyes again. 'So, something pretty weird happened with Meg yesterday.' He put his feet up on the coffee table, pressing his knees together.

'OK. What was it?' Meg was a young marketing manager, who'd been at the company only a year. She'd grown up in northern England, beginning her career at a large management agency in London. Adam's company had been impressed enough with her CV to sponsor a US visa. She was serious-minded and talented, and, with her tall, slim figure, soft Mancunian accent and long blonde hair, she'd quickly attracted male admirers in LA. Several unpleasant incidents had occurred with music industry men trying their luck.

'Well, she was at KCXE?' Scott began twirling the cushion in his lap.

'Right,' Adam said. 'I remember.'

'And she ended up meeting with Fischer, while the session was going on.'

Fischer was an influential DJ on a big college radio station in Burbank, and one of the label's main supporters in the city. The band who were due to play the showcase that evening – The Suffering – had recorded a session with him the previous day. Adam swallowed.

'Well, he kind of showed her some pictures…' Scott's voice was deep and very loud, and he liked to speak slowly.

'What kind of pictures?'

'Well, at first it was, like, pictures of artists he'd taken. He's, like, shooting pieces for the website or something?' Scott screwed his face up, to show he wasn't impressed. 'Some bullshit.'

'Right,' Adam said. His patience was dissolving. He pictured a clear pool beneath a rocky waterfall. When a large, dark shape slithered under the water, he banished it, outraged.

'Then they sort of moved into these, kinda erotic ones? Well, not even erotic, actually. More like obscene?'

'Oh, Christ,' Adam said.

'Yeah…' Scott widened his eyes further. Adam had the strong suspicion he was relishing this.

'They were in that little tiny office of his. Y'know, the one with all the CDs on the walls? So she was, like, close to him.'

'What were they of? How bad were they?'

'Well, at first it was like they were arty male nudes apparently. I mean, this is just what she told me, on the phone. He sort of segued into them. And he was like, "and what do you think of this one? And *this* one? And then *this* one?" And they were getting more and more… explicit?'

'Shit,' Adam said.

'And they were all zoomed in apparently, on some guy, and in black and white. And they were gradually zooming out. And then suddenly she sees that it's actually *him*, in the pictures.'

Adam felt strangely weak. 'My God…'

'And he's there with this erection – apparently it was huge,' Scott widened his eyes further still, 'and he's like "and what do you think of THAT!"'

'What the hell was he thinking?' Adam put his head in his hands and kneaded the flesh of his temples.

'And in the next one, he was actually *coming*...' Scott was saying.

'OK.' Adam looked back up at him. 'Where's Meg now?'

'She's at home. She said she'd work from there today.'

'Is she OK?'

'I mean, she's pretty freaked out.'

'Should I call her, you think?'

'I'd give her some time,' Scott said.

'OK, let's talk to her about it together, after we get tonight out of the way. Is she still coming tonight?'

Scott shook his head. 'She's too traumatized.'

'Of course,' Adam said. 'Well, we'll be a pair of hands down then. Let's make sure everyone else is around to help.'

Scott curled his lip.

'What?' Adam asked.

'Meh,' Scott said. 'You think many people are gonna come? *Really*?'

Under the careful stewardship of the Autodidact, Scott had renounced his love of experimental post-rock in favour of more commercially rewarding projects. The Suffering had thus far failed to impress him on these terms, despite being one of the Autodidact's personal signings. Adam wondered if Jason had inadvertently created a monster.

'I am certainly hoping they will come, Scott,' Adam said.

'I just don't know why we're doing it. It feels like we got bigger fish to fry. The album just isn't very *good*.'

'Let's just make it work please, Scott.'

'I hear you,' Scott said, looking as though he didn't.

5

He sent Meg a text apologizing for her ordeal, and decided to take the Autodidact's call in Echo Park itself. The privacy would be welcome, and it would give him an excuse for the walk. Lately, he'd taken to wandering around the park in the middle of the day, inventing meetings and disappearing for an hour. He was fairly sure his staff hadn't cottoned on, but nevertheless it was becoming risky. He could just imagine a gleeful Scott making a concerned phone call to London.

'Yeah, he's been inventing these… meetings? And all he does is, like, walk around the park? We're getting a little worried.'

He'd given himself time to circle the park's lake before the call came in. Finding himself once more at its northern edge, he paused for a moment and wiped the sweat from his brow. Bright pink lotus flowers had colonized this corner of the water, sprouting so thickly that it looked as though you could lie down on them. Adam peered at their leaves, on which, if he looked hard enough, he could sometimes make out one of the park's fat bullfrogs, sunning itself. Not today, it seemed.

Giant, skinny palms vaulted above the water, swaying gently in the warm breeze. A man with a long neck and a ponytail was doing yoga on the grass, and dotted here and there were women, lying on blankets, a few of them reading, more sitting playing with their phones.

As ever, a small film crew was setting up on a patch of grass. In Los Angeles, Adam thought, you were rarely more than fifteen feet from a film crew.

He raised his eyes, looking above the park's human occupants and scanning the skies. It was possible, with a bit of luck, to see interesting birds above the lake and palm trees. A whole island had been cordoned off for waterfowl. There were egrets and herons, and overhead the occasional hawk. Just now, there was only a small flock of grackles, chattering loudly as they flitted between trees.

His mobile's artificial trill sounded from his pocket. Right on time, Jason was calling. Adam sat on a bench – picking a spot between splotches of bird shit – let the phone ring three times, then answered it.

'Hello, mate,' he said.

The Autodidact's trademark, throat-clearing cough scratched out of Adam's phone, followed by his voice, which still bore traces of his Liverpool accent.

'Hi, man,' he said. 'How you doing?'

'Not bad, thanks,' Adam said. 'You?'

'Yeah, yeah, all good. You in the office?'

'No. Thought I'd step out and get some privacy. How about you?'

'Yep, meeting room as usual.'

'Right,' Adam said. He pictured Jason, most likely standing – unless show-meditating, he rarely seemed to sit down – in the glass-walled room in London, where he could see out over the office. A short man with long, well-groomed hair, he was very muscular from the regular boxing classes he took. With his barrel chest, upright stance and urgent, short-legged walk, he gave the impression of a cockerel, strutting around the hen coop of the office.

'So listen,' the Autodidact said. 'We need to talk Falconz. I spoke to Roger earlier.'

Falconz were, abruptly, the biggest act on the label. An earnest young girl/boy duo from Chicago who made sugary, ecstatic electronic music overlaid with eighties-style, soft rock guitar solos. Adam disliked their music intensely. Their name didn't improve things.

They had taken Adam's favourite genus of raptor, and done something stupid with it. Roger was their manager.

'Ah. OK,' Adam said. 'How'd that go?'

'Well, not good actually, mate.'

'Right. How come?'

'He's talking about finding a bigger partner for America.'

The sweat on Adam's back ran cold. 'Shit,' he said.

'He's worried we don't have the, ah, *capacity* they need on the next album. There's talk about looking for an upstream deal, or even a licence.'

Upstream, licence. These were the euphemisms for when a major label came and stole your artists.

'Shit,' Adam said again, without really thinking.

'Exactly.' There was a chilly pause. 'How've things been with you and him recently?'

Adam hated Roger. The manager's idea of a good conversation was someone listening intently to one of his monologues, and he wore the kind of un-tapered jeans that Adam associated with men who hung around playgrounds. He was very efficient, but stupefyingly arrogant, and delighted in interrupting Adam mid-sentence on conference calls.

'Fine,' he said. 'They've been good.'

'He said he hadn't heard much from you lately?'

'How could he, when he never stops talking…' Adam muttered.

'What?'

'Nothing.' Adam sighed. 'I'd better get a meeting in with him.'

The Autodidact's voice had cooled. 'Listen, man, it took me a lot of work to get us where we are with them. If we lose them in the US it's gonna cost us hundreds of k. And God knows what the Scandies are going to think. Falconz were the main reason they invested, a foothold in the American market. We need to convince Roger we can handle the album. ASAP. I'm a bit worried your attitude might be getting across to him.'

'I've been nothing but respectful to him,' Adam protested. 'He's had a big success and it's gone to his head a little. Plus he's got every major label in his ear. You know how this goes.'

The cough came again, louder and harsher this time. 'Yeah, but you get in his ear too then, for Christ's sakes. We need to be taking him out every night. Buying him steaks.'

'… He's a vegan.'

'Good. I'm a vegan too!' the Autodidact said, with barely suppressed outrage.

'Ah,' Adam said. 'Yes…' The last time he'd been in London, Jason had been subsisting largely on raw coconut water and activated charcoal.

'Surely he knows we've got greater capacity now, if anything?' Adam said. 'Now that we're better funded?'

'It's not about money for Roger,' the Autodidact said. 'It's about leverage from other artists, market share, all that shit.'

'Right,' Adam said, trying to dispel the familiar psychic clouds of boredom that these terms always conjured.

'Whatever,' the Autodidact said. 'If I'm gonna keep everyone in the job,' he continued, slowly now, 'then we need to keep artists like Falconz on the label.'

'But haven't you hired six new people already this year?' Adam asked.

There was a very long pause. Long enough for Adam to have the sense that any remaining happiness was draining out of him and pooling beneath the bench. He pressed the heel of his right foot painfully into the top of his left.

'Look, man,' the Autodidact said eventually. 'Just meet Roger, please. Just try and sort this out. Send him a nice marketing plan for album two. Do whatever needs doing.'

'Will do,' Adam said, kneading the flesh above his nose.

'You're supposed to be the expert on America. I can't do it from here. I'm happy to toss ideas out, of course, but you lot are gonna have to execute them.'

You can toss me, tossbag, Adam thought. 'I'm on the case,' he said.

'Thank you. Let's speak tomorrow for an update.' And with that, the Autodidact had gone.

Adam marched off at a fast walk, too angry to go back to the office. He let out an audible groan as he set off alongside the lake again, and a tough-looking jogger glanced at him as he passed. The jogger was wearing a hoodie over his t-shirt, and yet wasn't sweating. Why? Adam thought. Why oh why am I the only one who sweats?

He'd believed that reaching the point he had in his career, he'd now be one of an inner circle; lead a conflict-free life of smooth seniority. It was destined never to be. It was like being at school again, being unable to join in somehow. Always needing to pop the bubble of other people's pretensions – and his own too. Making himself unpopular, hated even. Preventing himself from ever being truly invited in. Maybe if he could have played the part a bit better, he'd have developed the belief necessary to do it.

And it was a part, now. Back when he'd had passion, everything had gone well. Now that he hated the music he worked on, he worried that people could smell it on him. He felt like a fraud. A man who'd lost his purpose. He was terrified that someone was going to call him out.

So he sat in meetings uttering buzz phrases and aphorisms, longing to escape, approaching the edge of hysteria, little tremors running through him as he suppressed a mad giggle, thinking *Can't they see? Can't they tell?*

He'd been winging it for too long, and it was becoming dangerous.

A shadow passed over the shining grass beside him, and he looked up to see a red-tailed hawk being chased off by a crow. The hawk was a scraggy old bird, feathers missing from its tail and left wing. The crow cawed at it, as though outraged at its incursion, and the hawk beat a quick retreat towards Sunset Boulevard. I know how you feel, Adam thought. Still, it probably wasn't too bad a life, being a hawk. Probably better than being a bear, actually.

Standing in the shadows at the far end of the lake was a homeless lady – one of the park's regulars. Whenever Adam saw her, she was bent over, hands almost touching the floor, her back at a near right angle to her legs. She was extremely thin and dressed in a filthy, deflated brown Puffa coat. Matted black hair poked out from under its hood, but Adam had never seen her face.

As he walked past, a black plastic bag on the ground beside her subsided, and a shrivelled orange rolled out towards his feet. Adam picked it up, walked over to her and dropped it back into the bag. She didn't look up, but her shoulders – hanging low over the grass – were convulsing. Something fell from her face, and shattered like a tiny crystal when it hit the path. He realized with horror that she was crying.

There was a clump of notes in his pocket, and he pulled it out and placed a twenty in the bag, on top of the orange. As an afterthought, he took his handkerchief out of his back pocket and placed it down carefully on the note. He felt suddenly as though he might cry too, so he stalked away, not wanting to embarrass the woman, horribly embarrassed himself.

A phrase surfaced in his mind: 'There but for the grace of God.' No, he thought, that wasn't right. Here by the grace of the Autodidact. And lucky to be so. Far luckier than this poor woman.

The homeless were always there, wherever he looked. People who maybe just weren't very good at life – and he knew all about that. Was it only him who felt himself to be one disaster – a car crash, a lost job, maybe just one paycheck – away from joining them?

6

At 5.30, back at home on his small deck, he'd found some peace and quiet. More importantly, he was drinking a glass of wine. Not the best idea, perhaps, given that there would be much drinking to come – but today of all days he needed it.

A meeting with Roger was on the cards for the following Friday morning. Bright and early, in Hollywood of course. Perhaps it was wishful thinking, but when Adam had called him, he felt he'd detected a note of gratitude and warmth in Roger's voice. Perhaps all that had been needed was this effort to reach out. It wouldn't be the first time he'd had to check his ego in order to make something work. Maybe, after all, everything would be OK.

Maybe he would even enjoy the showcase, he thought, brightening with each sip of the wine. Craig and Angelina would both be there. He'd be surrounded by friends and contemporaries. How bad could a rooftop gig, taking place as the sun quite literally set over Sunset Boulevard, be?

He'd almost drained the wine when his landlady appeared, stepping out onto her own deck opposite him. The apartment was one half of a duplex, hers the mirror image of Adam's. He'd been inside her half only once, and had resisted any subsequent invitation due to the pungent smell of cat urine it harboured.

'Hey,' she said, grinning. 'Drinking some wine?'

He smiled back at her. Stef was fifty, friendly, a hard drinker and a rare cynic among LA's relentless positivity.

'Yep,' he said. 'I'd offer you some, but I've got to go back to the office in a minute.'

'Oh no. What's up?'

'We've got a showcase on the roof. A band playing live.'

'Cool!' she said. 'Anyone I'd know?'

'No, they're tiny. Called The Suffering.' It occurred to him that he might have invited her. 'You could come, actually!'

'Thanks, but I can't tonight.' She lit a cigarette and blew out a plume of smoke over her dry, dying slope of a garden. She had once laid turf on this, but in a mere two nights the raccoons living under the house had gleefully destroyed it.

'I'm on a deadline,' she said. 'We're script-doctoring a comedy that's going to pilot.'

Stef, with a male partner Adam had never met, was a screenwriter.

'Wow,' he said, impressed. 'That's exciting.'

She beamed at him. 'No, it's not. It's godawful.'

'Really?'

'Yup. A total piece of shit.'

In Adam's experience, this was not how most screenwriters talked. Anyone he'd met who was even vaguely involved in movies only ever described everything as 'exciting!', 'awesome!' or 'great!' – usually through a brittle smile. With screenwriting, it seemed, everything was always just on the verge of really happening – and then it never did.

'Well,' he said, 'work is work.'

'Amen,' Stef said, breathing more smoke. 'So, guess what I did today?' she said, suddenly excited.

'What?'

'Had an enema!'

'Wow,' Adam said again.

'I know, right?' She cackled gleefully.

'Any particular reason?'

'My friend was going, and she wanted some company. She paid. No way I was going to! Money *up* the shitter.'

'How was it?' Adam asked.

'Totally gross.'

'I'm not surprised.'

'It still feels a little weird down there, to be honest. I thought I was going to explode. But hey, they say it's good for you…'

Stef's cat, Beans – an ancient, fluffy black creature with a permanent expression of shock – slunk through the doorway and began pissing against the frame. Stef carefully pushed him off the edge of the balcony with her foot, and he fell to the earth below with a resigned yowl. She stubbed out the cigarette, and grinned at Adam.

'Back to it, I guess,' she said. 'Now I just have to flush out this shitty-ass script.' She cackled again, and disappeared inside.

* * *

It was clearly going to be a very bad showcase. With atrophying patience, Adam watched the band's manager attempting to decipher a rented mixing desk. The sound tech had taken a phone call, and was lurking somewhere on the staircase. Occasionally, bursts of distortion tore from the monitor speakers before cutting out as abruptly as they'd started. A bead of sweat ran down the manager's forehead as he stared at the blinking lights, dials and knobs of the desk. It might as well have been some sort of alien, planet-rending bomb that he'd been called upon to defuse.

The members of the band stood around him, hands on hips, tension radiating from them in waves. Everyone except the bare-chested drummer, who happily bashed at his kit, eyes closed and mouth open – rather like someone having an orgasm. This, Adam knew, was quintessential drummer behaviour.

When the manager looked over at him, Adam turned away, leaning on the railing and peering down the avenue towards Sunset. Below him, a filthy-looking man was pushing a very fat woman in a shopping cart along the sidewalk. When they reached Sunset, they continued across it, forcing the cars to stop. A cacophony of horns blared out gleefully despite the sluggish traffic, momentarily drowning out the drummer behind Adam.

He watched as the couple reached the far side of the road, the woman shouting something, perhaps unhappy with the pace at which the man was pushing her. The man wore only a grey-brown vest and denim cut-offs, and his bare flesh was glistening with sweat. Adam had never seen these particular homeless people before.

He felt a tap at his shoulder, and turned to see the band's worried-looking manager standing a little too close to him. Behind him, the huge, taciturn sound tech had appeared and got the desk working.

'Adam, mate,' the manager said. Like Adam, he was British. Unlike Adam, he was only visiting Los Angeles, and thus hadn't developed the American habit of standing at the maximum reasonable distance from any other person during conversation.

'Benji,' Adam said. Anticipating a problem, he felt the skin of his face clench tight around his skull. 'What's up?'

'Bit of an issue with the tacos.'

'Oh? They're quite good, I thought.'

'Well, it's more the smoke.'

'The smoke?'

'Yes. It's blowing into Cyrus's face. It's not going to work.'

'What's not going to work?'

'Him singing, with taco smoke in his face.'

'OK. So I'll cancel the tacos, yes?'

'Well, what will people eat?'

'Benji, it's really quite late in the day…'

The manager glanced back at the singer, a very thin east Londoner who wore a silver bomber jacket and a baseball cap twisted at an angle above his longish, dyed black hair. He stood gazing upwards, as though in direct communion with the sun, and appeared to be striving to give the impression that he had lofty concerns on his mind. He hadn't, Adam knew. Otherwise he wouldn't have asked for a desk lamp to be brought upstairs and pointed at his face so that the 'crowd' would have a 'focal point'.

Benji squinted, his pale, dry face creasing into fine wrinkles.

'Let's just go with it,' he said, finally.

Adam felt a brightening within. 'I mean, I could maybe have someone stand next to the grill, and somehow disperse the smoke.'

'No, no,' Benji said.

'Are you sure? There's a very tall intern who might do.'

Benji had gone.

Adam walked over to the drinks, and poured himself a large whisky. He glanced at his phone. There was nothing from Angelina. But that was OK, he reassured himself. She had told him she was coming. He opened Facebook, which loaded directly onto her page. Ten minutes ago, she'd changed her status to 'feeling blessed'. Adam felt a twinge of panic. Why was she feeling blessed? What, or more importantly *who*, had been the cause of this?

Benji came back across the roof.

'OK, we're all set,' he said. 'Cyrus still feels there isn't enough light on his, ah…'

'His face?' Adam asked.

'Yes.'

'Maybe he could ask the sun to stay out a bit longer?'

'What?'

'Nothing. I'll send the intern down to get another desk lamp.'

The singer had begun soundchecking, his falsetto voice knifing the still Los Angeles air.

'You leave signals for me… in a language I can't read,' he emoted. His voice was quite good, but he apparently needed urgent coaching on his stagecraft. His stance was awkward and hunched, his eyes squeezed shut and his hands flapping in front of his chest like someone who'd been badly trepanned.

'One more thing,' Benji said.

'Yes?'

'That gap, in the railings, behind where the band are. Can we seal that off?'

'No can do. It leads to the fire escape. Our permit is invalid if it's blocked. The fire department were very firm on that.'

'Can we have someone keep an eye then?' Benji asked. 'Y'know. I don't want anyone having an accident.'

'Sure thing,' Adam said. 'I'll make sure someone stands there. There's absolutely nothing to worry about.'

Benji nodded absently, and wandered off again.

The tall intern, a French girl called Camille, smiled at Adam from across the roof. She was a model-cum-electronic music producer, and wore little more than a sports bra and tiny denim shorts to the office most days. Each time he found himself in conversation with her, she would tell him about some famous producer or other she'd met at a party and now hoped to collaborate with. This was the sort of subject he'd once have engaged with avidly and now felt sickly allergic to. The sort of thing to which his mental chorus might object: *Fraud. Ageing fool. What do you know of these things now?*

What he did know was that she was unlikely to make a career with her music, which he had heard, and that the producers who'd shown enthusiasm were likely more interested in sleeping with her than working with her. He didn't think he could tell her either of these things – you either knew them or you learned them – and consequently he'd limited interaction, wherever possible, to friendly hellos.

In his pre-gig nerves, though, the warmth of her smile cheered him, and he grinned back. He'd lost confidence in his own smile. It felt like he was grimacing. Once upon a time, he'd been considered quite handsome, but now, as far as he could tell, the question was definitely out to the jury.

There was another reason for avoiding Camille. At the last couple of events he'd attended, she had seemed to flirt with him, even extending casual invitations to the sort of parties at which she met famous producers. He had given much thought to this, and had come to the conclusion that he must be imagining it. That was a worrying sign in itself.

He felt old. I'm not old, he told himself. Mid-thirties isn't old. People kept telling him so, anyway, but he was never quite sure if they were being honest.

Maybe the delusion of the intern's flirting was a good thing, simply a security blanket provided by age. Certainly, her smile, these days, was good enough for him. For much of his life, and for reasons he'd never clearly understood, Adam had felt stupid, inferior and pointless. Sleeping with new women had always given him a burst of validation. But it had also got him into a great deal of trouble.

Finally, the soundcheck was over. There was a little over half an hour left before the guests would start arriving. The tacos were cooking, the drinks cooling in a chrome trolley filled with ice, and the intern had taken the band off to get food elsewhere. Scott was sprawled on a sofa, explaining the American music business to Benji – his deep, slow voice droning across the rooftop – and the other staff were eating tacos and drinking a first beer. For Adam, it was a time for nervous pacing of the roof, and for more glances at Angelina's Facebook. This, as with any gig, was the calm before the storm.

To Adam's relief, Craig chose this moment to arrive. Sauntering out onto the roof, a trademark mischievous grin already on his face, he threw out his arms for a hug.

'Now then, fuckface,' he said, his pleasant Aberdeenshire voice drowning out Scott's as he surveyed the scene. 'Isn't this lovely?'

Craig was slim, not quite as tall as Adam, and dressed in the standard-issue LA music industry garb of black jeans, black boots and V-necked black t-shirt. His not-quite-ginger hair was cropped short above his pale skin and broad smile.

'Eaten yet?' he asked Adam.

'No, I was going to have a taco.'

'Have it quickly then.'

Adam felt a little shiver of anticipation. 'Why?'

'Because after you've had a line of the potent gear I've got on me, there'll be no more eating for a while,' he said.

Adam forced down a taco, swigging a beer as he did so, and the pair of them took the stairs down to the office.

'Shit,' Adam said as they did so, looking at his watch. 'It's a bit early.' In his head, little red warning lights blinked among the fog of excitement.

'Oh, fuck off,' Craig said.

At Adam's desk, Craig carefully ground up and carved out a couple of thin, absurdly long lines of cocaine.

'Race you,' he said. They lowered their rolled-up notes, like two mosquitoes alighting on skin, and hoovered the lines up hungrily.

'Shit, those were big,' Adam said, grinning and sniffing.

'I don't wanna be coming down here every twenty minutes,' Craig said.

'How much have you got?'

'I might have anticipated that question.' Craig fished a baggie out of his pocket. 'This one's yours. Eighty bucks please.'

Adam forked over the cash, feeling a warm wave of something approximating love for his friend. This awful behaviour was something he had largely left behind him, in London, in the bad old days. But not entirely.

As they walked back across the office, his brain felt softer, lighter. Confidence lit in him like the power being turned on, and tiny fireworks went off in his head.

'Hell yes,' he said, slapping Craig's back.

* * *

Forty minutes later, the roof was almost full. Adam was pleasantly surprised, and wondered if he might have miscalculated the band's appeal. There was still no sign of Angelina, but she was not known as an early arriver.

Craig was gabbing with a female music supervisor whom Adam had met briefly before. She'd seemed to him a forbiddingly high achiever who'd taken only a cursory interest in their brief conversation. In Craig's presence, though, she was already touching her long, dark hair, and smiling through bright red painted lips as he gesticulated, telling her something funny.

Benji appeared. 'This is great, man,' he said, looking around, his expression a touch manic.

'I know!' Adam said. He felt a druggy rush of warmth towards the manager, and slapped him, too, on the back. There was a large, soggy patch of sweat there, Adam noted happily.

Benji grinned. 'What time's sunset?'

Adam glanced at his watch. 'Starts in earnest in forty minutes. Let's get 'em on at 7.45.'

The elevator pinged in its tower, and disgorged another large group of people.

'Bloody hell,' Benji said. 'What's the capacity?'

'I think it's forty or something,' Adam said. 'According to the permit.'

'Got to be more than forty up here already…' Benji said.

'It's a great turnout,' Adam replied, smiling broadly, slapping him on the back again. 'More the merrier, eh!'

His phone buzzed in his pocket. He fished it out, delighted to see Angelina's name on the screen.

'Hi!' she said when he answered. 'We're outside.'

'Great,' he said, quelling the annoyance that she, as usual, hadn't come alone. 'I'll come down.'

When he emerged into the bright fluorescent light of the corridor at the bottom of the building, Adam realized he was really quite high. Must be careful, he thought to himself as he pushed open the door. Pace yourself.

To his relief, Angelina was with another girl, who peered up at him from beneath a wide-brimmed black hat. He kissed Angelina delicately on the cheek – knowing she didn't like public displays

– and shook the other girl's hand. She didn't smile as he did so, he noted. Also, he'd instantly forgotten her name. He had become terrible at remembering names. It was something to do with the heat of the moment of meeting new people.

'Come upstairs,' he said, feeling expansive and welcoming. 'You're just in time.'

Angelina paused at the bottom of the stairs, glancing meaningfully at her towering heels.

'Please tell me there's an elevator,' she said.

'Oh yes,' Adam nodded. 'Of course, sorry.'

He led them through to a hot little sunlit room into which the elevator opened, and pressed the button to call it.

'Do you, like, live here?' Angelina's friend asked, once they were on their way. She had very silky, straight blonde hair. Her expression was a curious one, which he'd noted on a few young women in LA: a sort of slack-faced, lifeless pout that actually looked – presumably accidentally – like permanent disgust.

'No, just work,' he told her, smiling.

Angelina's heels were patent black platforms, which ended in straps around her ankles and gave her an additional five inches of height. Even so, she was still six inches shorter than Adam. Above the shoes were sheer black tights and a black leather one-piece thing that he thought she'd once called a romper. Her Asian-American skin was smooth, and her face sparkled a little from something in the makeup she had on.

He placed a hand on the small of her back, but she moved away from it fractionally as the doors opened.

'Drinks!' he said.

'Wow…' The blonde girl surveyed the scene, mouth hanging open. 'It's, like, really intense up here.'

'It's a good turnout.'

'This is awesome,' Angelina said, carefully eyeing the crowd of chattering industry types.

'Drinks?' Adam said again.

After a brief discussion, they agreed on vodka tonics.

Adam squeezed his way to the drinks trolley and mixed the cocktails, procuring himself another whisky while he was at it. Craig winked at him from where he stood with the music supervisor. She was now the one doing the talking, Adam noted.

'Here we go,' Adam said, passing the drinks.

'Uh, where's the restroom?' Angelina asked.

'Back the way we came.'

'Oh,' she said.

'I'll take you.'

Adam guided her through the growing crowd, Angelina tottering on her shoes. The elevator spewed out another six or seven people before they could get back into it.

Somewhere, distantly, a brighter warning light blinked more urgently in his head. This one, too, he ignored.

Inside the office, Angelina gave him a kiss on the lips. He slipped his tongue into her mouth briefly before she pulled away.

'I'm celebrating tonight,' she said, smiling at him.

'That's great! What happened?'

'That guy Striker, at CAA? He wants to rep me for my poems.'

Angelina had just over half a million followers on Instagram, where she regularly posted pictures of herself, fashionably dressed and in an enviable location – usually looking dreamily and/or moodily at a landscape – accompanied by a couple of lines of poetry, and at least a dozen hashtags. Whenever someone asked what she did, she would compose a very serious face and say: 'I'm an Instagram poet?'

'That's awesome,' Adam told her, trying not to sound brittle. 'Well done. We can celebrate together.'

'So this is where you, like, work?' she said, looking at the office.

'Yes. Do you really need the restroom?' he asked.

'Yes.'

'Let me come in with you.'

'Ew! No way.'

'Come on, I won't look.'

'I have to take this thing off to pee,' she said, glancing at the leather one-piece as though it had somehow colonized her against her will. *Playsuit*, he remembered. That's what Sofia had called hers. It had been made out of a sort of towelling material, and she'd only worn it in their flat.

He shook the memory away.

'Great. You can do that while I make you a line of coke,' he said, grinning back at Angelina.

'You have coke?' she asked, her eyes widening. 'Oh my God. You're *actually* crazy.'

Inside the bathroom, he leaned against the wall as she slipped the romper off, pulled down her panties as she sat, and peed. A pleasant tinkling sound emerged from between her legs.

'I can't believe I let you in here. Stop watching me!' she said.

'Sorry,' Adam replied, grinning.

When she stood up again he moved over to her, putting his hands on her hips.

'Hold your horses, buddy,' she said. 'It's a little early.'

'Read me some of your poetry,' he said.

'Like, now?'

He felt her tense slightly in anticipation, and took a step back.

'Yes, now. That's what we're celebrating, isn't it?'

With a dainty shuffle, Angelina stepped away from the toilet and composed herself. Her smooth brow reshaped into the hint of a frown, below which she widened her eyes to imply an elemental innocence.

'Sadness is like a bright star,' she said. '… Swallowed, by a black hole.'

'Brilliant,' he said, moving over to her again and kissing her. He lowered his lips to her neck and kissed her there, too, then bit gently at her shoulder. She grunted, and her hand slipped into the rear pocket of his jeans, squeezing his right buttock.

For some amazing, bizarre reason, Angelina could be aroused – despite herself – due to her Pavlovian response to biting.

There was a wide, granite surface around the sink, and Adam lifted Angelina up and sat her on it, biting harder at her neck. She pushed him away and leaned back on her hands.

'So, you want a line?' he said.

'Oh God,' she moaned. 'You're a bad influence. Shouldn't we be getting back up there? Aren't you, like, working right now?'

'Soon,' he said. 'I'm taking a regulation break.'

He made her a line, and as she leaned over to snort it, he kissed and bit her neck again, and she groaned in a way that made him hopeful. When she sat up, he crouched and attempted to pull her bra down to kiss her breasts. She moved one hand to them, preventing him, and the other to the back of his head.

Less hopeful now, Adam reached her stomach, kneeling, and sucked the taut flesh. It was too taut to bite. He was like a dog nipping at a beach ball.

She pulled him away by the hair, looking down at him, unimpressed.

'OK,' she said. 'I think it's time to get out of the bathroom.'

'Baby...' he said, but his phone rang out loudly from his pocket, cutting him off. He glanced down at it, all hope abandoned. Angelina was standing, turning, pulling up the romper and checking her nose.

He let the call go to voicemail, but it rang out again while Angelina was reapplying her lipstick. It was Scott.

'What's up?' Adam asked.

'Are you, like, around?' Scott said.

'In the office. Bathroom.'

'Ah, OK. Cool,' Scott replied.

'What's up?' Adam repeated. *Fucking spit it out for once in your life, you...*

'Just wanted to tell you they're about to start. It's pretty crazy up here!'

'I'm on my way,' Adam said. Angelina was still carefully applying the makeup, her back to him. He pulled the wrap of coke out of his pocket and tipped a little onto the granite, his phone tucked between shoulder and chin. 'Any problems?'

'There's a *lot* of people. We might have gone overboard with the invites a little?'

'Should be fine though, right?' Adam said.

'I guess?' Scott said.

'See you in two.' Adam hung up.

Angelina had turned around. She smoothed her clothing, then looked down at him and glared.

For a brief, horrifying moment, he saw himself through her eyes. A man in the wrong half of his thirties, on his knees in a toilet, half crazed with drugs and thwarted desire.

'Bump?' he suggested.

* * *

Back on the roof, they were confronted with a tight wall of backs. Adam tapped shoulders, doing his best Hugh Grantish apologies and making gaps to slip between them, Angelina's hand in his. Her friend reappeared, her displeasure at Angelina having been gone so long apparent even through her permanent look of revulsion. They found Craig by the drinks trolley.

'This is a bloody smash,' he said, grinning. 'You know Philippa?' He gestured to the music supervisor, who was now apparently attached to him.

'Yes, I think we met at your office, when I first moved out,' Adam said.

'That's right. Good to see you again.' She was swaying slightly – with happiness rather than drunkenness, Adam thought – moving her shoulders as she spoke. Her olive skin glowed as if lit from inside. Adam had the impression she'd have liked to throw an arm around Craig. Not for the first time, he wondered what his friend's secret was. He was able not only to sleep with successful, intelligent women in the music industry, apparently at will, but also to leave them saying nice things about him in his wake.

'You remember Angelina?' Adam asked Craig.

'Ah yes, how you doing?' Craig dipped his head, held out his hands and smiled broadly, as though confronted with one of his favourite people in all the world. He kissed Angelina on the cheeks. Thankfully, she introduced her friend herself. This time, Adam held firm to her name – Charlie.

'We're celebrating tonight,' Adam said.

'Excellent news,' Craig said. 'Why's that?'

'I found an agent, for my poems?' Angelina told him.

'Sick,' Craig replied.

'That's wonderful,' Philippa said.

Angelina, sensing status, took the chance to start working on Philippa.

'Have you ever thought about writing poems yourself?' Craig asked Adam. 'You have that poet sort of vibe actually. A bit sad. All alone in the world.' He grinned evilly.

'As far as I'm concerned,' Adam told him, pleased that a Craig-shaped joke had materialized for him, 'there's nothing that can't be best expressed in a dick pic. Happy dick, excited dick, angry dick… And of course, crying dick is easy.'

'Fucking touché!' Craig said, delighted, and slapped Adam on the back.

The first notes of music resonated from the far side of the roof – just loud enough to shock everyone into silence. Pure, metallic spears from a synthesizer that stabbed and darted through the gathered crowd. The guitarist joined in with a simple, chiming riff from his Gibson 355, the two sounds weaving into an ominous melody that seemed to freeze everything. Taking the opportunity, Adam poured a vodka tonic and handed it to Charlie with a smile – his best guess at how to make some sort of connection with her.

Pouring himself a large whisky, he turned to face the band. Angelina had stepped forward, ahead of him and to his right, and he placed his hand on the small of her back. She turned her head, smiled quickly, and didn't move away.

Christ, he thought, whisky and cocaine merging warmly. This is golden. And golden was right. Tonight's particular blend of smog and fading sunlight lit the rooftop in a yellowy glow.

What have I been worried about? Adam thought. Here he was, after all, older maybe, but running his own office, throwing events, sleeping – or, at least, trying to – with a beautiful woman. High. Drunk. Happy. This, surely, was what he'd dreamed of? This was rock 'n' goddamn roll. Maybe, just maybe, he needed to allow himself to enjoy it.

Scott appeared at his side. 'Yooooo,' he said.

Adam's happiness dipped slightly, but he rallied it and slapped Scott on the back.

Scott glanced past him, towards the music supervisor.

'Cool,' he said. 'Philippa came. She's great.'

'She sure is,' Adam said.

'I like her,' Scott said. His blue eyes blinked, once, as he watched her.

'I think you might have missed your chance there, mate,' Adam told him.

Scott's head clicked left a notch, and he frowned, his upper lip curling as he saw Craig.

Someone bumped Adam from behind. The roof really was quite full. 'Where's the security guard?' Adam asked Scott, remembering they'd agreed to hire one.

'He's down at street level,' Scott said. 'I thought it might look kinda cool. Like a more legit event.'

Adam frowned. 'And where's Ernesto, and Beau?' he asked. 'I think we might need some more help up here.'

'They're Instagramming people arriving. Walking past the guard and shit.'

Adam took a deep breath. 'OK. Would you mind asking one of them to come up?' He scanned the roof for Camille, but couldn't see her.

The pang of worry was interrupted by the singer starting up. His tenuous falsetto merged perfectly with the synths and guitar, flowing around them, three streams of sound intertwined. Beneath it all, a slow, chugging house beat kicked in. Adam sniffed, pulling more coke down into his throat, stoking up the euphoria again as the bitter chemical taste spread into his mouth. He sipped the whisky. Shit, maybe even the band weren't as bad as he'd thought.

He moved his hand down to Angelina's ass, and stroked her left buttock. The fact she didn't move it away was surely another sign. This was going to be a great night after all!

As the band reached the end of the first song – a sort of electronic blues that seemed made for this moment, there and then, on a rooftop in Los Angeles as the sun dipped behind the mountains and stroked the gathered people with the warm farewell of its final rays – a round of applause broke out.

As it faded, Adam heard the elevator ping.

What happened next would be much debated over the subsequent days. Despite the drink and the drugs, Adam remembered it painfully clearly. There was a sense of pushing from behind. Craig actually stumbled forward, spilling his drink and laughing.

'What the fuck?' he said.

Someone shouted, 'Look out.' There was another push, harder this time. Adam described it later, to the fire department, as a surge. More people asked 'What the fuck?' more angrily than Craig had. Philippa had turned around, and Adam saw that she suddenly looked afraid.

There didn't seem to be any space between them any more. Angelina was pressed up against his front – not, in itself, unpleasant – and Scott and Craig either side of him. Someone large and unseen was jammed up behind him. A chilly wave of panic spread through the crowd and reached the band, who paused on the verge of playing their second song, glancing at Benji, trapped in a corner behind them.

'Can you move down?' someone screamed from the back.

'There's no room!' an unseen woman replied.

'Oh my God,' someone said.

'Shit,' Scott said to Adam. 'What are we gonna do?'

Adam took a deep breath and forced his way through the path of least resistance, heading for the microphone. Dropping the Hugh Grant, he did his best at projecting authority with firm 'excuse mes'.

He reached the taco stand as another big surge hit him. A petite woman in brown sunglasses and a denim jacket lurched into him, spilling her drink onto his chest.

'Ow!' she said, trying to turn around and see what had hit her.

Adam lifted himself onto tiptoes. He was only ten feet from the band now. If he could just get to the microphone…

The taco chef was pushing someone away from his grill. 'Be careful,' he said. 'You gonna get burned.' He saw Adam. 'Too many people on this roof, man.'

Adam nodded, trying to push his way past a tall, bearded man in aviators. The man pushed back.

'What's your problem, buddy?' the guy asked.

'This is my event,' Adam told him. 'I'm trying to sort out what I'd have thought is the fairly obvious problem.'

The man went quiet, still bristling, as Adam edged around him. Almost there.

Just then, something slammed into him from behind. The whisky in his right hand flew away from him, its contents splashing over the gas-fired grill.

A flame reared up, and, bent by the breeze, ignited a stack of paper napkins on the grill's shelf. Smoke billowed from them, engulfing the patch of roof around Adam and drifting rapidly towards the band.

Someone screamed, and then suddenly lots of people did.

'There's a fire exit, head for that,' a man yelled.

'Oh my God!' someone wailed.

After that, as Adam remembered it, very little was voluntary. Caught in a tight bunch of human bodies, he was carried forward, doing his best to keep his footing. As the smoke cleared, he saw the band's singer, turning, afraid, as the swarm of people surged towards him. He moved through the open gate to the short gangway between the roof and the fire escape. For a moment, he seemed frozen by indecision. Perhaps, Adam wondered later, he hadn't thought it seemly to run? Either way, when the mass of bodies reached him, funnelled as it was into this narrow space, it simply tossed him aside.

Adam remembered the way he grabbed for his baseball cap the moment before he realized that was the least of his worries. It really did go quite slowly. It seemed to take the singer a dreadfully long time to fall the twenty-odd feet to the concrete path below.

When he hit it, it was clear from the way his legs were arranged – bent out each side at crazy angles – that he'd broken both of them. Thankfully, he'd missed the closest prongs of an agave by some distance.

'Everybody CHILL,' the taco chef shouted authoritatively. Adam glanced over to see him pouring a bottle of water over the napkins.

Either side of Adam, the crowd had frozen. People in baseball caps and sunglasses and angular tattoos, chunky jewellery and beards and emphatic haircuts and denim jackets and bright, pristine designer sneakers were leaning over the railing, phones in hand, taking pictures and videos of the writhing singer, their expressions impassive. Another species, Adam thought. A newer one.

A girl with neck tattoos and shaved platinum hair pushed her way to the front, pressing herself against him as she stood on a railing, expertly zooming her phone's camera onto the singer. After she'd taken her shot, it froze momentarily on the device's screen – clear, sharp and perfectly composed. When Adam recalled this image much later on, it struck him that, in very different circumstances, it might have made an excellent album cover.

7

If I could go back in time, Adam wondered, when would it be to? He was lying in bed, the sheets tangled around him, damp with sweat. He thought he might have slept for a couple of hours at best. When he'd woken, the past, as usual, was pressing on his mind. Competing even with the nightmare of the previous evening. For once – the present unthinkable – he took refuge in it.

There were so many choices. So many moments that might have allowed a different path to be chosen. His boss, Serena, had once told him on a train journey to sign a shoegaze band in Glasgow, her frizzy grey-black hair occasionally tickling his left ear, that life was a progressive closing down of choice. Each time you made one, she'd said, spreading her hands wide and moving them together, like a slow-motion clap, you effectively rejected many others, until eventually you were on a defined trajectory. You could always try to change it, to cut across to another one, but it would be harder the further along you were.

Serena had studied Heidegger at university, and Adam was fairly sure that was where this had come from. He remembered a little bit of the existentialist's philosophy himself. *Being and Time.* Anxiety as the state induced by being truly confronted with reality, every comforting delusion momentarily stripped away. If that was the case, Adam's world was certainly getting realer.

If only, like Serena, he could remember all the useful things he'd learned more clearly. The knowledge she had at her fingertips was astonishing, as was her ability to explain and impart it. More than that, it was Serena's capacity for applying this learning to her own life that impressed Adam. It seemed to have made her path a good one. She'd spent her twenties in the London punk scene, presiding over a rotating household of interesting characters in a ramshackle terrace in Ladbroke Grove. In her early thirties, she'd decided to straighten out enough to apply herself to something, and founded the label.

It was terrible, Adam had thought on that flight, squeezed into his seat and considering Serena's words. With every choice you made early in life, you killed off another self, left them to rot by the wayside. Until eventually whatever was left simply ended up being you. What if one of the other yous you'd left behind had been better, more worthwhile, and more deserving of life?

As a child, he'd been fond of Choose Your Own Adventure books. He'd often thought back to them since. If only life was as simple as keeping your finger between the pages, so that you could quickly jump back if the werewolf had got you, someone important had died, or you'd done something horrible to somebody you loved.

The problem seemed to be that he was so bad at knowing when he was happy. Looking back, there'd been many times he'd been truly, genuinely so, and yet he'd never seemed to realize when it was happening. As a result, whenever he had found happiness he'd ended up wrecking it.

Going back in time was something that regularly preoccupied him. The clearest point to hop back to would be the day he bumped into Sofia, in an alleyway in east London, twelve full years earlier. Then, she had still been simply the beautiful, aloof girl from university, whom he only knew to say hello to. All the history they'd made together depended on that random chance.

It had been one of those early spring days in London, wet and newly warm – or at least no longer cold. Strong gusts of wind blowing occasional sprays of rain, and carrying a scent of defrosted rot and damp. As he remembered it, the wind lent a drama to the day, as though the world could be felt turning, the air blasting down the alleyway and blowing Sofia's long, dark hair about her face.

They'd greeted each other, and he'd asked her how she was, and she'd told him things weren't going so well, actually. That in fact, they'd fallen apart a bit. She'd asked if he'd please meet her for a drink.

And that had been the beginning. She wasn't aloof after all. She was original, and dignified, and very fiery. She had olive skin and big chestnut eyes. On his way home after they'd met for a first drink, he'd seen a family of ducks waddling down a street near his flat, and he'd sent her a photo of them. That day had become Duck Day, to them. It was almost five years from that night that he'd gone on to break her heart.

Duck Day wouldn't be a bad choice to go back to. Nor would their second date, when they'd got drunk in two different bars and talked for hours. When she said she'd split up with the man she'd been with for the last four years, and felt broken and run down, and was mildly offended when he'd clumsily told her she looked 'robust'. But it was true that she always did look healthy. She was tall and large-breasted and curvy, and even the dark circles beneath her eyes, natural rather than inflicted, couldn't seem to diminish the healthiness she exuded.

He'd told her about the job he wanted, and looked like getting, running an esoteric punk rock record label. They said they'd both slept with too many people without using protection, and that they planned to be more careful in future. This had meant that when they went back to his flat, they gave each other oral sex instead of going all the way.

He'd felt so lucky he could barely believe it. The most beautiful girl from university, her long legs wrapped loosely around his neck, her heels resting lightly on his back as he went down on her, trying to do the best job he ever had. He remembered how, before they'd gone to sleep, she'd warned him she might be freaked out in the morning. How in the morning she had duly looked wide-eyed and slightly horrified, and he'd thought that would be it, game over, a one-off. But that was OK, because it was such an experience, such a high point, such a woman. And then she'd texted him telling him he was lovely, and he knew it wasn't going to end there, and he was walking on air.

Yes, that might have been a night to go back to.

In July that first year, he'd invited her to go on holiday with him. When he sent the email asking her, and offering to buy the flights, he worried it was too soon into their fledgling relationship to have suggested it. They'd been together for only three months. When she replied it was clear she was delighted.

Adam was too. He wanted a break, and a first holiday with the woman he was falling in love with. He'd got the job he'd always wanted. The future seemed full of promise.

He researched flights he could afford, and came across Almeria. The descriptions of the place, of which he'd never heard, appealed to him; an area of Andalusia that hadn't been fully discovered by tourists as yet. A place of desert, mountains and ocean. Good food if you knew where to look. An ancient Moorish fort, and old western movie sets dotted in the hills.

Sofia paid for two nights in a hotel, and they hired a car at the airport. This was a new experience for Adam, and it made him nervous. Driving into the city on the first night, Sofia navigating, they made a wrong turn and he snapped at her. It was the closest they'd yet come to an argument, and he apologized. Much later, it would seem to him that this unusually long honeymoon period, in which they seemed too respectful of each other to fight, had simply stored up energy for the rows when they did come.

The night in Almeria was hot, and smelled of cooking fish and saltwater. The hotel room was large and luxurious, better than either had expected, and they spread out their belongings and made love.

Beneath the windows, the young people of the town had gathered, sitting on the low walls of a strip of flowerbeds, chattering and smoking, drinking cans of cola. Sofia had bought a Lonely Planet guide to the province, and she lay on the bed, intent on it, circling points of interest and labelling them in her neat cursive handwriting.

Eventually they left the hotel to explore. There were hundreds of young people sitting or standing outside by then, laughing, swinging their legs, confiding in each other and paying Adam and Sofia no mind.

They walked away from the hotel and the kids, heading in the direction of the port and the sea. He wore shorts, and a prized polo shirt that was the most expensive item of clothing he'd ever bought. Sofia wore a pink dress that showed off her smooth brown calves and large breasts. Adam was very skinny, young and still a smoker, his hair shaved close to his skull.

By the port they found an art installation made of hundreds of narrow concrete pillars, no two of them the same length. They took photos of Sofia standing among them, and Adam seated, leaning against one, looking off into the night.

A North African approached from the quiet, pooled dimness by a jetty, and asked if they wanted to buy weed.

'Sure,' Sofia said, shrugging. Adam had long since stopped smoking it, but Sofia did so daily in London.

She paid the man twenty euros, and he took off at a run down the sea wall, disappearing out of view as he reached its corner.

Adam was surprised at how naïve she'd been.

'I don't think he's coming back,' he said.

Sofia shrugged again, smiling and laughing it off. Her big eyes – a little Eastern-looking – turned downward fractionally at their outer edges when she smiled. She had a small overbite that made her as goofy as someone very beautiful could be.

'Fuck it,' she said. 'Maybe I'll get lucky. Even if he doesn't come back, I'm not going to let it spoil the night.'

Adam lit a cigarette and leaned on the harbour wall. After a few moments, the little figure came tearing around its corner again, growing larger as he zoomed down the path towards them. Sweating and breathless, he delivered Sofia a bag of perfectly satisfactory weed.

For the next few days they walked and drove around Almeria, the city and the province. They explored the Alcazaba, the vast fortified complex built by the Moors when they'd ruled southern Spain. Sofia sat for photographs beside cascading channels of water, and they peered up at the arid brown hills and then the gleaming blue sea below.

There were slots in the external walls for archers to loose arrows. Higher up, the Christian monarchs had built a castle atop the structure, after they'd reconquered the city. Here, the arrow slits were in the shape of crosses. Their guide laughed, and told them these had the added advantage of allowing archers to fire left and right.

They camped in a small, hot, dusty site. Their quiet corner was shared with another Brit, a man on his own, in his late thirties – a longer-term resident who seemed lonely and sad. He was chubby, perpetually sweaty, and wore little khaki shorts and greasy, wire-framed glasses. He seemed pleased to have someone to talk to, told them he was a pagan, and spent most of his time in his tiny, low tent, where he drank from a bottle of Martini.

Adam debated the virtues of paganism with him, in a way that bordered on being unkind. Sofia gently admonished him.

'There's no reason to be mean to him,' she said. 'If his beliefs work for him, then let him have them.'

Adam couldn't imagine, then, how anyone could end up in such a state.

In the mountains they found the old movie-set town. Sofia was wearing a white dress with brightly coloured embroidery on it, which made her look, to his mind, rather Mexican. She sat on the altar in a tiny wooden church and posed, despite his worrying that they might get told off.

In the saloon, portly, ageing Spaniards played out a gunfight once every few hours, before disappearing somewhere unseen, returning the place to a ghost town.

Driving through the little white villages and mountain passes, twisting slowly down a road into the foothills, they listened to the pre-masters for a record he was going to be working on. The album's lyrics, a reaction against a period of po-faced seriousness in its genre, were focused on partying and sex. Adam told Sofia that the record was intelligent.

'What makes it intelligent?' she asked him after a while.

He struggled to explain. 'I think what I meant to say is it's a good idea, rather than intelligent,' he said.

She nodded, satisfied.

They took another hotel room in a town in the foothills. Outside it was a wide, tiled balcony that they could barely believe was theirs for a night, and which looked out over olive groves and vineyards. They sat at the mosaic-topped table there, drinking cheap, good red wine and watching the sun dip below the hills, shadow pooling into their valleys.

Inside, Sofia tied his wrists and ankles to the bed with a scarf, a bra and her tights. She blindfolded him and ran her tongue over his body, the anticipation of where she'd go next driving him wild.

Eventually she straddled him, rearing above him unseen, his hands full with her breasts, their large nipples hard and hot in his palms.

Sitting outside afterwards, at one of the few restaurant tables the tiny hotel offered, underneath the balcony they'd sat at and the room they'd made love in, they ate dinner. The conversation found its way naturally to the relationship they'd found themselves in.

'Let's just see how it goes,' Sofia had said, leaning back in her chair, happy and relaxed. 'Even if it doesn't work out, we've had a really good time already.'

Adam had felt a pang of sorrow and panic at the suggestion, however indirect, that he might lose her.

'Well, give it a chance though, won't you?' he'd said, frowning. 'Don't give up on us yet. After all, we've barely got started.'

Less than two years after that had come the last time he'd felt truly proud of himself, the last chance he'd had to stop things going wrong. He'd been twenty-seven – a very special number, in music. But for the stars, not the staff. Twenty-seven was that well-documented turning point; the age at which musicians died, and joined a very exclusive clique.

He'd once seen an interview with Axl Rose on YouTube, in which the rock star had talked about meeting Prince.

'What did you two talk about?' the interviewer had asked.

'We agreed,' Axl replied, 'that twenty-seven is the hardest year.'

Adam had a theory about the twenty-seven club. Things that had been fun at twenty-five became habits a couple of short years later. Youth was slipping away. Undeniable adulthood was near at hand. Things that might have been enhancements to life and to music now became ends in themselves. Relationships were harder to mend, behaviour harder to justify by simply being young. You needed more of whatever your poison was, in the doomed quest to rediscover what had made you fall for it in the first place.

Twenty-seven was the end of youth. Life, after that, became serious.

As his had. And it had felt good at first. His abiding memory was sitting in the passenger seat of a rental car, Sofia driving them through the hot, wild countryside of another Spanish holiday, thinking how he'd been faithful and decent to her, how that was something to be proud of. How there were no lurking fears and regrets and secrets roiling in his head – as there had been in the past, with other women – threatening to break out of his skull and make themselves known.

Pride before a fall, in his case.

Even if he'd gone back in time to a year after that journey, when he'd already made some of those secrets, but not the big, worst one of them. If he could find himself once more, preparing to send the surreptitious text messages that would be the beginning of the end.

Before his thoughts could turn to the woman at the other end of those messages, he sat up in his bed, the LA sun lighting a hot band across his back where it had found its way beneath the blind. He winced, and wiped the sweat from his brow. Yes. That would have been a moment to go back to. To grab himself by the throat and say *Absolutely not.*

Sofia. She haunted him, both in the real world and in his head. In real life, she'd met someone else, had a baby, and begun a successful career as an art blogger. So successful that her first book had recently been published. From the reviews he had read, it was a clever mixture of charmingly written personal history and analysis of her favourite paintings. If he was unlucky, the images from this life – the life she deserved – would pop up on his Facebook feed.

Seeing them made him feel like a man adrift: stuck in LA, as if free-floating in space, lost forever, trapped in the orbit emitted by the family he might have had on earth.

Still, the Sofia in the pictures wasn't as bad as the ghost Sofia – the one in his memories.

He'd realized what ghosts were from a ridge in Scotland. On a hiking trip a few months after they'd broken up, he'd felt sadness like a cold breath on his neck, and he'd turned around to find its source. A long way below him was a path, and he realized it was one he'd once walked with her a few years earlier. Hurt seemed to throb from it, as though somewhere in time they were still walking there. When he closed his eyes he could see her, turning to look at him, smiling, her hair made darker by the rain.

Ghosts are the people you've loved and lost, he knew now. They live on in your head and wake you in the night. They revisit you as they were, reminding you who you were.

Was he a ghost for her, too?

Enough, he decided now. It was time to get out of bed and banish these phantoms once more. The past, sadly, was every bit as bad as the present.

In the shower, he allowed his thoughts to turn to more recent disasters. The night had been a long, evil one. The fire department and paramedics had been quick to arrive. Most of the guests had already scarpered. Angelina had not stayed to offer her support. To Adam's surprise, Benji had proven himself to be capable of quite biblical anger.

The singer had been scraped off the concrete and taken to hospital. Adam had lost count of the explanations and apologies. But the worst would be yet to come. There would be calls to head office. There'd be reputational damage. There would be a very large liability insurance claim. There would be further ammunition for the Autodidact with which to shoot Adam's career down in flames, should he so wish.

He had chosen not to mention that it was his own drink that had set fire to the grill. Now, on waking, that decision alone among the many made during the previous night still appeared prudent.

At ten o'clock it had all been over. The staff went home, the fire department cleared out, and Adam returned to the office and poured himself another drink. In a nihilistic slump, he gave in to his worst instincts, and decided he might as well top the drink off with a final, abject line of cocaine.

Upstairs at his desk, he found Craig, sitting in lamplight, whisky tumbler in hand, FaceTiming a girl in intimate tones.

'Ah,' Adam said, when his friend had ended the call with a blown kiss. 'I don't know whether to be fucked off you've been down here while I've had that to deal with, or happy to see you.'

Craig made a flamboyantly sympathetic face, and offered him Scott's chair. At least, Adam thought, he had someone to keep him company for some restorative drinking. Perhaps even some encouragement.

The pair of them had sat around the desk, the office in shadow beyond the lamp's glow, drinking whisky and snorting lines.

'Could've happened to anyone,' Craig told him. 'That's the line you take. Come to think of it, it's a pity the fucker didn't die! You'd have had a hit on your hands!'

It had seemed more convincing at the time. Now, standing under the shower with his eyes closed, the world seemed to be pressing in on Adam from all sides. He felt bone-weary, edgy and paranoid from the drugs. Things, he realized, were not at all good. Things would certainly have to change.

8

When the working day was finally over, a walk on the river was just what he needed. Among the many resolutions he'd made during the long, grim hours in the office, focusing on the healthy side of his life was perhaps the main one. He would cut out the drugs. He would cut down on the drinking. He would focus on doing his job with quiet, unassuming excellence. His spare time would be spent on hiking and birding, and taking Angelina on actual dates. Perhaps, he thought to himself, they might even go on holiday together, after all this had settled down. These plans had been committed to paper, in a sort of to-do list-cum-Ten Commandments. All he had to do now was stick to them.

Whether Angelina would actually feature in any plans was definitely a question. In response to the text he'd sent her, she'd replied that she was going to be busy for a while, that life was crazy, that she'd be in touch soon. The message was decidedly chilly. Maybe it was some sort of ending. Maybe that was exactly what it *should* be.

He wandered down onto the path beside the river and paused for a moment, leaning on the railing. He didn't think he'd ever been so tired. An early night was what he needed. After all, in the morning he had the critical meeting with Roger to look forward to.

Serena had been understanding. 'It's a big job you do,' she'd said. Then, more ominously: 'It might be that we need to find more ways to help you.' While it wasn't exactly clear what this meant, it sounded better than 'you're fired', and thus Adam had felt it best not to ask too many questions.

They had agreed that there had been failings on his part. One security guard had not been sufficient. Worse, the one they'd had should have been on the roof, stationed at the fire escape. Adam explained the evening's poor decisions using the first-person singular. He had no qualms about this – the buck, after all, stopped with him. Also, his hangovers always induced a self-flagellating mood.

Now, a fulsome apology would need to be made to Benji and Cyrus, the singer. Some very expensive gifts would need to be purchased. A long and fractious argument over a request for an eye-watering, unjustifiable amount of tour financing would now have to be capitulated on. All of this settled upon, Adam had finally got home.

This, he decided, sober and serious, would be the start of a brand-new era.

Something bright and silvery was thrashing in the river, in a small shallow patch at the bottom of the slope. Adam saw that it was a large fish, apparently unable to get itself back into the deeper water.

As he watched, a heron began stalking over towards it, skinny legs moving in a sinister goose-step. When it reached the fish, it peered at it for several moments before stabbing it in the head. Despite the fish's size, the heron managed to swallow it whole. After it had done so, it shook its feathers and stalked back – slower now – to the shadowy bank, huddling into itself to digest its meal.

He'd started walking again when he saw a cyclist coming towards him. The tall figure in a blue jacket gave him a surprising jolt in his chest. It was the osprey lady. He grinned, raising a hand to wave, but she pedalled straight past him.

Before he'd really thought about it, he turned and shouted after her.

'Hey!'

She slowed, her legs angling outwards, and turned in a tight arc before she stopped. She stayed astride the bike, gripping the railing with one hand to hold herself steady on the narrow racing frame.

'Oh, hi,' she said.

'It's me,' he said. 'The birding guy.'

She laughed. 'I can see.'

'Sorry,' he said, flushing. 'Just wanted to say hello.'

He took a few steps towards her, and leaned on the railing again.

'Seen much this time?' she asked. She wasn't wearing the sunglasses, he noticed. Just the bike helmet. She had sharp cheekbones, a feline sort of face. She was very pretty.

'I just saw a heron murder a massive fish, and swallow it whole.'

'Delightful. Any sign of your osprey?'

Adam felt something galvanize in his mind. '*Our* osprey,' he said.

She smiled. 'OK then.'

'No sign at all. Maybe I'll see it, now I've been lucky enough to see you.'

'You think I might be your lucky charm, huh?'

Adam laughed, looked away from her and down to the water. 'Maybe.'

'Well, you can let me know next time I ride past you,' she said.

'Would you have a drink with me?' he spurted out.

She looked at him carefully. 'I guess I might,' she said. 'When?'

'Would tomorrow be too soon?' he asked.

'Yes.'

'Saturday then?'

'That works,' she said.

'OK, deal,' Adam said. 'What's your name, by the way?'

'Erica,' she said. 'And yours?'

'Adam.'

'OK, Adam. So, take down my number.'

He did so, his fingers trembling as he typed it into his phone.

'You can call me on the day, and we'll fix something up, OK?'

'Yes, brilliant,' he said.

'Good. Now turn around.'

'Why?' he asked.

'So I can bike away without you looking at my ass again.'

'Ah,' he started to say, reddening.

'We usually know, when you guys do that. Just for future reference.' She laughed. 'But at least you had the balls to follow up on it. Now turn around.'

He did as he was told, dizzy with embarrassment.

'Saturday,' he heard her call as she cycled away, laughing again. 'Maybe I'll wear my bike pants.'

9

Adam arrived at LEAF, a vegan restaurant in West Hollywood, ten minutes early. He still felt a little hungover and shaky, but he was trying to be optimistic. All he had to do was win Roger over. How hard could it be? He'd been holding meetings with managers for more than ten years, and he'd never once failed to seal whichever deal was in the offing. This, he reminded himself, was firmly within his area of expertise.

LEAF was on the ground floor of a large shopping mall. Its rear windows looked out onto the mall's inner courtyard, of which the restaurant had a small section for outdoor seating. Adam asked for a table for two, outside, and took a seat in a shady spot beneath a potted olive tree.

The menu informed him that LEAF was an acronym for Love Eating, Animal-Free. In a better world, he thought, it might have meant 'Love Eating Animals, and Fish!' One entire page of the large, hardbound menu listed a bewildering array of juices and smoothies. This was exactly the right idea, he thought. Turning over a new leaf, in LEAF!

His eyes drifted over to the next page, which held an equally expansive list of cocktails, some of them quite mouth-watering.

That kind of thinking, he told himself, is not going to wash in this brave new era. A cocktail should not be mouth-watering at 9.30 in the morning. A juice is very much what is required.

He scanned the list again, and settled on a Belly Blaster. Apparently, it consisted of the usual kale and cucumber-type stuff, with some ginger and chilli to make it interesting.

Adam had recently met a man from New York, at a typically LA industry barbecue, who'd given up his career in advertising to set up a juice company. He'd been something of an evangelist.

'Honestly, dude,' he'd told Adam, Rolex rattling loosely on his wrist, his eyes glinting with the fervour of the convert below his Travis Bickle haircut, 'juice can cure *anything*. Depression, sleep problems, bad skin, stomach issues. Anything.'

'What about cancer?' Adam had wanted to ask. 'Or chlamydia?' Instead, he'd said he must try it sometime.

'You should do a cleanse, dude,' the man had told him. 'Get you all fixed up.'

And here he was, about to do so, because this juice's name surely implied such a cleansing – disgusting as it might presumably be. No pain, no gain, Adam thought. Pain is weakness leaving the body.

When the waiter came out – a short, obese man with a goatee – Adam ordered the juice.

'Sounds a bit frightening, doesn't it?' he asked, laughing.

The waiter simply grunted, without so much as a smile.

Christ, Adam thought. People come here to buy twelve-dollar juices, and as if that's not depressing enough they have to order them from this guy. Mr Loves Eating Anything Fatty, he thought, pleased with himself. Mr Lemon Eating Anus Face.

He looked at his watch. Roger wasn't due for another five minutes. Loves Eating Asses and Fannies, he thought, giggling out loud. Literally Enjoys Anal Fingering.

The waiter reappeared and thumped down a tall glass of frothing green stuff, with a straw mired in its middle.

'Lovely, exciting, amazing, fresh!' Adam said.

'What?' the waiter said, sensing something untoward.

'Oh, nothing.' Adam casually waved his hand.

'Anything else?'

'Not until my friend gets here, thanks.'

As the waiter waddled back inside, Adam closed the menu and tried to focus on the task at hand. He had a couple of good ideas for expensive radio teams up his sleeve, a press angle or two to suggest, some blue-sky marketing plans, and even a creative director he thought might make a good job of improving the Falconz aesthetic. We can't afford a Lamest Ever Artwork Fail, he thought, smiling to himself. God, I am literally a marketing genius.

At 9.40 there was still no sign of Roger, and no message explaining why. Of course, Adam thought, the classic power games. Losers Ever Arriving First.

He finished his juice and scanned through emails on his phone. The waiter reappeared and pointedly asked what else Adam would like.

'Another Belly Blaster, please,' Adam said. 'And a large Americano.'

The latest drinks had just arrived when Roger finally did, too. A tall, slim man with a prominent chin, Roger sported a rubbery-looking black zip-up jacket above his shapeless jeans. An extreme sports junkie, he wore the kind of sunglasses favoured by right-wing militiamen, or school shooters. Also like them, he seemed constitutionally incapable of smiling.

Adam stood up to greet him, putting on his own best smile regardless. 'Good morning,' he said.

Roger shook his hand, giving him what Adam assumed to be a long look in the eye from behind the black lenses of his shades.

'Good morning yourself,' Roger said.

Adam sat back down.

'Uh,' Roger said. 'You mind if we move?'

'Ah... no...' Adam said. 'Not at all. This table no good?'

Roger gestured to the waiter. 'Like to move over here,' he told him, pointing at a table at the other end of the patio. He offered no further explanation.

'Sure thing, sir,' the waiter said, obviously liking the cut of Roger's jib.

Adam picked up his drinks and carried them to the new table.

'You already order?' Roger asked him.

'No. Well, just drinks. I was here a little early.'

'Huh,' Roger said. 'Well, sit down, man.'

'Thanks,' Adam said. With a chill, he realized that Roger had literally turned – or switched – the tables on him.

'So. How're things?' Roger asked.

'Not bad, thanks. Busy, in a good way. Very excited about the guys' new record.'

'Oh yeah,' Roger said, scanning a menu. 'Yeah. It's real exciting, that is for sure.' He took a long pause, looking out into the mall's courtyard. 'I heard you had some drama a couple nights back.'

'Yes. Just an absolutely freak accident, horrible. That said, there's been an outpouring of sympathy and interest from the industry. The irony is that it's probably ended up raising The Suffering's profile. We were all worried sick about Cyrus, but the doctors say he'll regain the full use of his legs.'

Roger nodded slowly. When the waiter appeared, he ordered a water.

'You can't be tempted with a Belly Blaster then?' Adam said, gesturing at his juice.

'Huh,' Roger said, bemused. 'No.'

'Breakfast?'

Roger looked at his watch, a large, futuristic affair made of rubbery black plastic.

'I kinda ate earlier actually,' he said. 'I got into a run before my morning conference calls. Feel free to eat though, man. I don't wanna get in the way of your brunch.'

Brunch? Adam thought. It was you who asked for a breakfast meeting, you fucker!

'I feel pretty full from my Belly Blaster actually,' Adam said, trying to sound bright. 'No problem here.'

'Well, let's get into it, man,' Roger said, looking squarely at Adam again.

He's the Terminator, Adam thought. 'Sure,' he replied.

'I'm sure you talked to Jason,' Roger said. 'As you know, you guys did an incredible job last time around, really helped us get to where we're at.'

'Thanks,' Adam said. 'It was—'

'Here's where our heads are at,' Roger interrupted. 'As a team. Y'know?'

Adam paused. 'Sure, yes, I—'

'Falconz are bigger than any of us realized,' Roger said. He paused, raising his chin grandly. 'They're the Coldplay of EDM.'

Adam, who'd used the chance of this latest interruption to take a long pull on his juice, coughed, his eyes watering.

'So we're gonna need a little more *bandwidth*, on the new album. We wouldn't be being fair to ourselves if we didn't look at every option,' Roger continued. 'To get to where we want to be, we're gonna need experience that none of us have – not even me. We're gonna need ideas from people who've had that level of success before. The best minds the industry has to offer.'

'Right…' Adam said, wondering if he was allowed to speak further.

'So, y'know, it might be a partner comes in to invest on the live side,' Roger said, 'and gives us a whole bunch of marketing money.'

'Well, that sounds great. I think—'

'It might be that we do a licence. We don't *wanna* go that way, but a lot of bigger labels want a piece of what we all got. It'd be dumb not to hear 'em out.'

'I see,' Adam said. He suddenly felt very tired, and a little confused. On the other side of the railing, which divided the patio from the rest of the courtyard, a very tall, skinny man with a shock of ginger hair had paused to look at his phone. In his other hand, he held a dog's lead, and Adam followed the course of the expensive-looking leather cable to see a husky, standing obediently beside its master. The dog was wearing a red bandana and aviator sunglasses.

'… We're gonna have options,' Roger was saying. 'A lot of them. And we owe it to ourselves to look at them.'

Adam glanced back at the dog. The aviators appeared to be genuine, gold-rimmed Ray-Bans, and he was fairly sure the bandana had a Marc Jacobs logo.

The dog's owner tutted, typing furiously into his cell phone. His own sunglasses matched the dog's, Adam realized.

'Everything OK, man?' Roger said.

'Yes, absolutely,' Adam replied.

'You look a little distracted.'

Adam looked at Roger, and briefly considered telling him about the dog in sunglasses. No, he thought, sadly. That is not the kind of thing Roger will find amusing. He will probably consider it a sign of poor character that I'm questioning the animal's right to protect its eyes.

'Not at all, I'm just thinking about what you're saying. As you know, Falconz are very, very important to the label. I believe we can hire in the people we need to make the next album a full-scale hit. There are independent radio teams out there producing number ones at Top 40 and Dance, and we can hire those people, no problem. They have genuine track records. I also have an idea about a—'

'Those people can't compete with major label in-house teams,' Roger said. 'It's about leverage. It's about "Here's Adele. Now play Falconz."'

Adam felt the Belly Blaster churning acidly in his stomach.

'It's, like, who's our Lucian Grainge, you know what I mean?'

Adam frowned. 'Lucian Grainge is the head of Universal Music Group,' he said, unable to keep the edge of protest out of his voice. 'He's the most powerful man in the entire music business.'

'Exactly. That's the kind of person you guys need.'

'To work… for us?'

'Like a president.'

'… Right.'

Adam sipped his coffee. The man with the husky was on the phone now, talking quietly but quite angrily into it. As Adam watched, a slinky little Italian greyhound in a sky-blue coat ran into view and paused beside the husky's rear, looking up at it and panting. The husky raised its tail.

Maybe there's some sort of dog meeting in this mall on Friday mornings, Adam thought. Like a play date for dogs. He risked a glance to his left, into the courtyard, but couldn't see anyone obviously in charge of the miniature greyhound.

'This is the kind of thinking we need to be doing,' Roger said, triumphantly.

'Yes indeed. I quite see what you're saying,' Adam said. I'm not good enough at my job, and we should hire someone who gets paid tens of millions a year basic to come and run our office of nine children and release fringe indie rock.

'So do you, ah, have any offers on the table?' Adam asked.

The man with the husky had turned his back on it, and was now cupping his hand over his phone and hissing into it furiously. As Adam watched, the greyhound raised itself onto its back legs, exposing a bright purple, damp-looking penis, which looked very much like a lipstick. Adam choked on his coffee. He glanced at Roger, but saw that the manager's view was obscured by a large urn, which had been planted up with a proliferating rosemary bush.

In the background, Roger was still talking. Roger-dodger-kiss-my-todger, Adam thought, uselessly. Loud Enervating Asshole Fuckface. He forced himself to turn away from the dogs.

As he did so, he was aware of sudden, furious movement. He glanced back, and saw that the greyhound was energetically humping the husky, its eyes wide and unblinking, swelling with ecstasy. The husky stood as casually as it had before, its fur rippling very slightly with each thrust, but otherwise behaving as though nothing was happening.

'Adam,' Roger said. 'Hey, Adam.'

'Sorry,' Adam said, looking back. 'It's just—'

'Listen, man. I know this is hard news. I know you're having a few issues of your own right now.'

'What?' Adam said. 'What issues?'

'The artist community is small, man,' Roger said, as though relaying an unfortunate truth. 'Interconnected. I think people are a little worried about your office's *capacity*. Especially after the other night. Issues of safety, you know what I mean?'

Adam shook his head, trying to think. *Capacity?*

The husky barked, once. Involuntarily, Adam looked at it. The greyhound was thrusting faster, its hindquarters a blur. The husky barked again, and its owner turned, and said 'WHAT?' so loud that even Roger now looked over.

Just as he did so, the man screamed and dropped his phone. 'OH MY FUCKING GOD,' he shrieked, 'SOMEONE IS RAPING MY DOG!'

'Christ,' Roger said, standing up. He picked up his glass of water and attempted to throw the contents over the greyhound, which neatly sidestepped the liquid, taking the husky's rear with it as it did so, and looked Roger in the eye, unblinking, as it carried on its business.

'Who owns this freaking animal?' Roger said. He glanced at Adam, then back to the greyhound, noticing the line of sight.

'Adam,' he said. 'Did you *know* this was happening?'

A loud, female scream came from the other side of the courtyard. A woman – who looked a little like Steven Tyler of Aerosmith – came hurtling past the central fountain. 'Francis,' she screamed. 'Francis, NO!'

'FOR THE LOVE OF GOD SOMEBODY PLEASE HELP!' the husky's owner shouted.

Just then, the greyhound convulsed in three separate, shuddering spasms, and dropped back down to all fours, wagging its tail and looking proudly up at its owner, who clattered to a halt in a blur of high heels, angular shopping bags, giant purse and strong perfume.

'Oh my God,' the husky's owner sobbed, dropping to his knees by his dog, tears streaming down his face. 'Oh my fucking God, he came inside Jonathan.'

By the time a mall cop in a blue uniform had arrived on a Segway, Roger was making his excuses and fitting a Bluetooth headset to his ear. He left the restaurant without shaking Adam's hand.

Shit, shit, shit! Adam thought. Losing Everything ASAP. Fuck!

When the waiter arrived with the check, Adam sent it back and ordered a margarita.

10

Thankfully, Friday afternoons in Los Angeles were usually plain sailing. By the time Europe, then Britain, then the East Coast and then the Midwest had all knocked off an hour early to go drinking, it was still only about 3 p.m. Adam sat behind his laptop, gratefully numbed by booze, listening to 'Never Let Me Down Again' by Depeche Mode on repeat.

He glanced over at Scott, who was listening to his own Spotify playlist, as usual. Like the universe, Scott's playlist was always expanding.

Maybe I can just leave, Adam thought. Offer no explanation. Go to the river and try to see the osprey. Get away from here.

His thoughts were interrupted by a chat window appearing on his screen. It was Scott.

Yoooooooo, it said.

Hi, Adam replied.

What's up? Scott typed.

Adam frowned, unsure how to respond. Hadn't Scott contacted *him*? Had he sensed something was wrong, and was actually expressing concern for Adam's well-being? That really would be a turn-up for the books.

He considered simply turning to Scott and talking to him, but the idea filled him with dread.

What's up yourself? he settled on.

Easy Friday vibes, Scott typed. *Chillin'. Couple things I wanted to bring up.*

OK, Adam typed.

I guess we should talk to Meg, before the weekend?

Shit, Adam thought. Yes. *Shit,* he typed. *Yes.*

Also, Hype just ran this piece on The Suffering, and the showcase…

OK, Adam typed. *Send me a link. Actually no, just summarize it. If that's easy enough.*

It's pretty good. Super positive on the band. Dean Shprits just read it and hit me up. He's gonna put us in a big playlist next week. Show us some love. You know. Support Cy.

That's great.

Yeah. I mean, the album is totally awesome. We just needed an angle. Kinda weird to say but, we kinda got one now…

Adam frowned, an itchy heat rising in his neck. *You said the album wasn't good?* he typed.

No I didn't? Scott replied.

Yes, you did, Adam typed. *You were quite emphatic on that point.*

The song in Adam's headphones finished. A few feet away, Scott bashed at his keyboard. The air between them had tensed.

I don't remember that, the message came.

Adam sighed, restraining himself. *What else does the article say?*

It's a LITTLE negative about the label. But it just says artists need to be nurtured, that type of shit.

OK. I'll read it later.

Cool cool. So you wanna talk to Meg?

Yes.

Scott whipped off his headphones and stood, performed a couple of stretches, and then sauntered across the room. When he reached Meg's desk, he perched on it, cocking his head sympathetically. She pulled off her own headphones and looked up at him.

'You alright?' Scott said.

'Getting there,' Meg replied, sadly.

Adam walked over, trying to adopt a pose that wasn't awkward, wondering what to do with his hands. In the end, he shoved them in his back pockets.

'Shall we go downstairs for a chat?'

'Why not?' Meg said. 'Sounds good.'

'Shall we send the intern out for coffee?' Scott asked.

The Friday intern, whose name was Michael, was sitting six feet away from Scott and wore no headphones. His cheeks flushed, and he turned his eyes down to the keyboard of the spare, ancient laptop he'd been allocated.

'Michael,' Adam smiled. 'Would you mind? Get yourself something too of course.'

'Coffeeeeeee,' Scott said happily. 'I'll do a cappuccino. Skim milk though, dude.'

'Sure,' Michael said. Adam handed him a twenty, and made a mental note to give him some vinyl later. He vividly remembered his own long years as an intern.

In the meeting room, Scott took up his usual position on the sofa, a cushion in place on his lap. He glanced expectantly between Adam and Meg, who took a seat in the corner.

Adam was rather nervous of Meg. He thought very highly of her, but had found it difficult to build a rapport. Neither of them was the type to do so around their shared nationality. And in her new life in LA, she'd thrown herself into politics, becoming involved with several organizations and quickly winning friends among their ranks.

She'd recently begun to voice radical opinions in the office that Adam found difficult to resist challenging. On the occasions he had, it had not gone well. She reminded him of his younger self in that regard. Made him see how annoying he must have been to older colleagues who'd been unable to resist challenging him and had been equally frustrated by his youthful certainty.

And did he perhaps envy her a little? She was joining in, meeting people, making a life, while he, with his hikes and birding, had become almost solitary.

And his nerves were worse today. He was stiff with anxiety, and he felt ashamed. The very notion of being in charge, in the face of this problem, seemed inhuman and ridiculous.

'That's a cool badge,' he said, as an icebreaker, gesturing at a plain white jigsaw puzzle piece pinned to Meg's denim jacket.

'Oh yeah, that. Thanks,' she said. 'Gonna be wearing it a whole year.'

'Really?' Adam asked. 'Why a year?'

'It's a white privilege badge. It's like a challenge, to remind yourself every day.'

Scott nodded sagely.

'Ah…' Adam said, the icebreaker having revealed itself to be more like thin ice. 'Well, we wanted to discuss what happened on Tuesday. I'm sorry it's taken a while, what with everything that happened at the showcase…'

'Sure,' Meg said. 'It would have been good to talk sooner, but I get it.'

'Yes, understood, I apologize for that,' Adam said. 'I think ideally we'd have another woman in here actually, but everyone's out. Would you rather wait?'

'No,' she said, waving a hand. 'Honestly, that doesn't matter.'

'I'm really sorry, Meg,' he said. 'For what happened, and also for not dealing with it faster. It's not good enough.'

The selfishness of his recent distractions instantly and horribly clear, he meant the words, and they came with a tremor in his voice. He cleared his throat.

'Thank you,' she nodded, relaxing fractionally.

'I'll call Fischer, and tell him what happened was unacceptable. I'll also speak to his producer.'

'Alicia?' Scott said.

'Yes,' Adam said. 'Alicia.'

'Actually, I think Alicia might be moving off the show,' Scott said. 'I heard from my BFF Sarah over there that she might get that job.'

'Alicia is still the producer now, yes, Scott?' Adam said.

'Sure.'

'Well then, I will talk to Alicia.'

'All that's great,' Meg said. 'I just think maybe we need to go a little further?'

'OK. Further like how?' Adam asked.

'I dunno. Like, couldn't we name and shame him? We could call him out on social media. I'd be happy to go public. Use my real name.'

Adam considered this. 'Well, we can't name or shame him on the label's social media without a much wider discussion with HQ. If you want to, we could certainly ask. I'm sure Jason would have some… thoughts.'

'I didn't necessarily mean the label's socials,' Meg said.

'Right,' Adam said. 'Well, obviously it's entirely your decision if you want to call him out personally. If you're sure you feel comfortable. It might get quite ugly.'

'Yeah…' Meg nodded.

'We'll do everything we can to support you, of course. I'll make an official complaint immediately. And obviously we're not going to be able to work with him any more after this.'

'OK,' Meg said. 'I'll think about it. Thank you.'

Adam glanced at Scott, who'd gone rigid with apparent alarm.

'We can't do that,' Scott said. 'On socials. Can we? I mean, we can't drag the label into anything.'

'We're not,' Adam said. 'Meg is considering making a public statement on her own behalf. The fact she works here is incidental.'

Meg looked sharply at Scott. The atmosphere in the little glass room seemed to be curdling.

'But that *would* involve the label. The label's name is gonna be all over it. And there has to be some sort of… due process?' Scott said.

'Yes. Me calling Alicia is the due process. Anything else is Meg's personal decision. I don't think it's any of our business.'

'But it's gonna cause a shitstorm around the company,' Scott said, moving to the edge of the sofa and glancing between them. 'Surely we need to consider this properly? Discuss it with the team? We should talk to Jason.'

Adam's pulse beat faster. 'This has nothing to do with Jason,' he said.

'Jason is the boss,' Scott said, fixing his gaze on Adam.

Adam felt a wave of rage that came very close to overwhelming him. He wanted to scream, grab Scott's perfect hair in one fist and beat him with the other. He might be my boss, you little prick, he wanted to shout, but I am yours.

'Well, this dickhead involved the label himself,' Meg said, her voice rising in volume, 'when he showed a label rep pictures of his dick. I mean, if I went out to my email group with this they'd have a field day. I could maybe give an interview? To an ethical outlet?'

'I am not going to tell you what to do in that regard,' Adam said, trying to keep his voice steady.

Everything was blurring – rage towards Scott, the need to demonstrate his own authority, his instincts for righteous drama and for chaos. Amid all this, the most important element – what was simply the right thing to do – was becoming obscure. The alcohol's pleasant numbing effect had long since worn off, leaving a dull headache in its wake.

Meg had flushed, and was trembling. She turned to Scott.

'Actually,' she said, her voice turned to ice, 'I don't need anyone's permission to call out a creep. And I'd suggest you don't push the theory that I do.'

Scott flinched, looking afraid. 'Sorry,' he said.

'Meg,' Adam said. 'Take the night to consider things. Talk to someone you trust about it, then do what you think best.'

Meg's face looked stiff, but she didn't cry. 'I feel like if this is the shit I'm gonna have to deal with every day in this industry, I might as well go back to bartending.'

'I can't really imagine this happening again,' Adam said. 'It seems like some sort of awful one off.'

He realized his mistake as soon as he'd spoken.

'This is the third time something like this has happened,' Scott said emphatically, leaping at the chance to redeem himself.

'Ah yes,' Adam said.

The precociously young manager of a famous rapper had sent Meg explicit, wildly inappropriate texts on two separate occasions, he remembered now.

Maybe it was LA, he thought. For all its veganism and alternativeness, it was still, at times, an unreconstructed place, apparently forever stuck in 1983. It was a place where the rich lived in the hills, literally looking down on everyone else. Where people drove purple BMWs, and you could meet a hippie who'd try to hard sell you real estate.

'How was that situation resolved?' Adam asked.

'I think Jason gave Meg some tickets?' Scott said.

Meg reddened. 'The tickets were nothing to do with what happened,' she said. 'He apologized and we made friends.'

'Well, obviously this is a bit different,' Adam said. 'That was a friend going too far. And this was in a daytime professional situation with no, ah, reasonable excuse or claim to have misunderstood or—'

'Exactly!' Meg said.

Adam breathed deeply.

'Don't start regretting your whole career over this idiot,' he said. 'You are brilliant at your job.'

'Thanks,' Meg said. 'I don't regret it. Actually, the only thing I regret now is not punching him in the dick.'

'I can understand entirely,' Adam said. 'I'll start with Alicia. We need to make an official complaint. Let me see what I can do.'

'Maybe there's, like, a support group or something, for this sort of thing?' Scott said, sinking his chin low between his shoulders in an 'I dunno' shrug.

'Yes,' Adam said, trying to keep the anger out of his voice. 'Why don't you look into that, Scott? I'm sure you want to help too.'

'Well,' Meg said. 'Maybe I could take some personal time next week?'

'You mean some holiday?' Adam was still confused about American terminology for this – language recently enshrined in a seventy-two-page staff handbook.

Meg looked at him, eyes flashing. 'You mean I have to use my own allowance?' she said, her voice rising alarmingly.

'No, no,' he said. 'Take some time. Take… three days?'

Scott frowned.

'OK, thanks,' Meg said. She took a deep breath and sighed.

'Well, let's leave it there then,' Adam said. 'We can pick it up again whenever you're ready.'

'OK, sure,' Meg said.

Scott was looking meaningfully at him. Adam knew that he'd be hoping for a post-meeting debrief in which he could question his boss's decisions.

'Right, let's call it a day,' he said.

* * *

At Arturo's, a new bar in Echo Park, which Adam favoured for its dim lighting and relative lack of pretension, Adam and Craig found a booth near the big rear window. The wooden deck beyond it was bathed in pink evening light, some of which leaked into the pints of IPA Craig slammed down.

'Just this one pint,' Adam said. 'I'm running on empty.'

Craig grinned, and held a finger out horizontally.

'This is the edge,' he said. With his other hand, he made two fingers into a pair of legs, one of them dangling dangerously over the ledge he'd made and trembling. 'And this is you, you silly cunt.'

'Funny, isn't it?' Adam said. 'That only on our little island can calling each other that be a sign of true friendship.'

'Australia too. The Americans don't know what they're missing out on,' Craig said. 'Now come on. Cheer up.' He held his glass out, and they clinked and drank deeply. Adam sighed with relief.

'So, how's your lady friend?' Craig asked.

'Haven't heard from her since the gig. Think she only wanted me for my contacts.'

'How'd she leave it?'

'Something about her being crazy, and needing some time.'

'Ah, screw it. She was a red frog.'

'What?' Adam said.

'You know, in nature. A red frog. It's basically telling you "I am freaking deadly. Do not eat me!" That's her. She was telling you.'

'But I did eat her?' Adam said. Well, nibbled her anyway, he thought.

'Yes, but you spat her back out.'

'Well, I'm not sure that's exactly—'

'Good fucking riddance,' Craig interrupted.

'What about Philippa?' Adam asked.

'Ah, she's a lovely woman. A real star. We're going to be great friends.'

'I do miss Angelina,' Adam said, eyeing his drink.

'No, you don't,' Craig said. 'You only think you do. Stop being so English and wet.'

'Fuck off.'

Craig cackled. 'Anyway, I've got some good news.'

'Go on,' Adam said.

'You and me are off to Joel Liebowitz's pool party.'

'Joel Liebowitz…'

'Oh fuck *you*,' Craig said with passion. 'Don't tell me you don't know who he is. You do read *Billboard* occasionally, don't you? You know that's essential for you to do your actual job?'

'Yes,' Adam said, dishonestly. 'Occasionally.'

'The top fifty most important people in electronic dance music?'

I don't like EDM, Adam thought. A distant memory surfaced. 'Oh,' he said. 'Of course. He's the super-agent.'

'Thank God for that,' Craig said, taking a deep, relieved swig of his pint.

'I dunno,' Adam said. 'Won't it be…'

'What? Full of beautiful, influential people who could help you with your *career in the music industry*?' Craig said.

'When is it?'

'Thursday.'

'Where?'

Craig rolled his eyes. 'The hills, obviously. In Joel's new super-agent's super-house.'

Adam sipped his beer thoughtfully.

'You know there's about ten thousand people who'd murder their own puppy to go to this party?' Craig said. His cheeks, Adam noticed, had actually reddened.

'The thing is, Craig,' Adam said, 'will it actually be any fun?'

Craig leaned back in his chair, the pink light settling over one side of his face. His eyes had taken on something Adam hadn't seen in them before. A colder look.

'Don't be such a child,' he said. 'It's work, but work can be fun too, can't it?'

'It used to be.'

'If you're so tired of it all, what are you doing here?'

Adam didn't reply.

'Do you think it'd be different in any other job? Everyone has to network if they want to make it in life. And you can have a lot of fun along the way.'

'I dunno,' Adam said. 'It all feels a bit shameful.'

''Twas ever thus,' Craig said. 'A girl took me to an art gallery recently to look at a Rembrandt. The fucker painted himself endlessly, apparently, and he did so in the same style as all the greats that went before him, to make it absolutely clear he counted himself among 'em. And in one of the descriptions, it says he married a woman with art world connections.'

'I see your point,' Adam said.

'The guy was a furious networker. And this is in puritanical Holland. So stop acting like it's something new and everything's gone to shit and it's all so absolutely dreadful.'

They sipped their beers. 'Let me ask you this,' Craig continued. 'Your dad. What did he do for a living? If he's retired, that is.'

'My dad's dead,' Adam said. 'He died of a heart attack ten years ago.'

Craig's eyes closed briefly. When he opened them again, his annoyance had lifted away like vapour. 'I'm sorry, Adam.'

'It seems a long time ago now. He was a lawyer. If your question was going to be "was your dad's job any different?" the answer is no. He was always at it, networking.'

'I see,' Craig said. 'But you're not sure, understandably, that you want to be like that?'

'I'm not sure I can be. He was better at it than I am. More dignified. Work seemed to matter to him more than it does to me.'

'The heart attack was due to overwork?'

'The heart attack was due to smoking and drinking.'

'Right,' Craig said, raising his pint to his lips. 'Did I ever tell you about my accident?' he asked when he'd sipped again.

'No.' Adam looked at him.

'A van knocked me off my Vespa, when I was still in Glasgow. Went over me, after. It almost killed me. I was twenty-five. Was in hospital for six months.'

'Jesus, I'm sorry too,' Adam said. 'Don't you worry about it now? Health, I mean, with all the partying?'

'No. Less so than before. When you've bounced back from that shit, it puts it in perspective.'

'Did you think you were going to die?'

Craig grinned, showing teeth and winking. When he made this grin – which he often did – it gave him a rodent-like appearance that was perversely appealing.

'To be honest with you,' he said, pulling a fresh cigarette packet out of his jeans, opening it and knocking it on the table to raise its contents, 'not once. Not because of anything special about me, I don't think. Just because you don't, do you, when you're twenty-fucking-five?'

He looked across the bar to the front window, beyond which a couple of other smokers were standing.

He knows exactly who he is and what he wants, Adam thought. The bastard. I used to have that. All I know now is that I want to stay here. To not go back. To confront the past only in my memory. To disentangle myself from it, somehow.

'And I don't believe in all that shit about everything having a meaning,' Craig continued. 'But it all has a significance, doesn't it? Seems it has with you. And in my case, it made me want to take over the world and party like a motherfucker.'

He stood, cigarette and lighter in hand. 'So that's what we'll do on Thursday. No arguments.'

'OK,' Adam nodded, raising a smile.

* * *

Half an hour later, he was walking down the hill towards Silver Lake, a little drunk and melancholy. He thought of his dad, picking at memories like painful little scabs.

There was an argument they'd had, in the kitchen of the house he'd grown up in, which his parents had lovingly stripped of a lurid green paint, applied in the sixties, to restore to its Victorian glory.

Exasperated at something Adam had said, his dad had stood by the kitchen sink, tall and formidable as ever, but unusually emotional.

The fight had suddenly gone from him, and he looked as though Adam had hit him.

'You don't have any respect for my values or beliefs,' he'd said, 'so what's the point? I've tried to show you the best way to live as I know it, but you don't think I know anything about anything.'

That's not true, Adam wished he'd said. Even more so now. He dearly wished he was more like his father, and he dearly wished he'd been able to tell him so.

As it was, he'd been dumbstruck and horrified by this awful moment of vulnerability. It was like a chasm cracking open in a trusted stretch of road.

The sun had sunk low and red above the Boulevard, but the evening's cool was yet to set in. Adam stepped through the pools of shade cast by the tall dirt banks that rose up either side of the street. High up in these, in the hollows between the trees, more homeless people lived, looking down on the sidewalks, doing whatever it was they did when evening fell.

In the novels of one of his favourite writers, vampires lived in the trees in Los Angeles. The reality was the inverse, Adam thought now. Actually, it was people who'd had the life sucked out of them that ended up living up there.

11

In this age of grand stupidity, birds seemed increasingly clever to Adam. In fact, across the whole history of human folly, they had carried on doing pretty much the same thing.

The revelation of what it meant to watch them had come to him shortly after he'd moved to LA. A favourite relative had visited, an eccentric uncle whose taste in books and wine Adam admired, but whose birdwatching habit he'd always considered faintly amusing. They'd driven to Santa Barbara to visit a distant cousin – a gentle, diffident widower who lived in an upscale apartment block on the edge of town. The three of them drove around the rolling green hills together, Adam staring up at the airy crags that jutted from their tops like exposed bone.

'There's a little wetland, by the beach,' the cousin said. 'You might be interested.' He had the habit of giving a short, self-effacing chuckle after everything he said.

'Oh, goody,' Adam's uncle, enjoying playing the Englishman abroad, had said. 'Yes please.'

The place turned out to be a car park for a beachside restaurant. Blond, muscled, tanned boys paraded in swimwear, throwing and catching an American football. Little groups of girls walked slowly between cars and the beach, arms folded over bikinis, expressions of practised boredom on their faces. A row of palms separated the parking lot from the sand itself, on which were beach volleyball courts. Most of the vehicles were new and expensive – Lexuses,

BMWs and Audis. Even the driftwood on the sand looked upmarket, as though waiting to be turned into tasteful beach-house furniture.

At the south side of the lot was a bank overlooking a small slough, backed by a swathe of very tall trees. Adam stared out at the scene. There were a few white birds in the water, and something with a very long beak and legs, pecking at the sand. He prepared himself for a tedious hour, and wondered if he could leave the relatives to it and go and have a drink.

His uncle ran his green Swarovski binoculars over the trees and water. Adam glanced at their host, who shrugged.

'Very interesting,' his uncle had said, finally.

'What do you see?' Adam asked.

'Well, it's quite a scene,' the older man said. He chuckled, as if everyone was in for a treat.

'I guess you need the binoculars,' Adam replied, becoming irritated.

'Not necessarily. Not if we wait a few minutes, and get a bit of luck.'

'So what's going on?' Adam demanded.

'Well. Down here we have a curlew.' He gestured at the bird on stilts, which prodded the ground with its ludicrous bill. 'Those are mergansers. A type of duck. There's a great egret.' He peered at Adam over his glasses. 'The thing that looks like a white heron. You know what a heron is, don't you?'

Adam nodded.

'And several snowy egrets, those smaller ones. In the bank below us are night herons. They're waiting for dusk, which is when they do most of their fishing.'

Adam peered down below him. Sure enough, there were five or six squat, furtive-looking herons lurking in the bushes. Their eyes were red, their backs a smooth grey over white flanks.

'Jesus,' Adam said. 'They're sort of, *evil* herons.'

'Night herons,' his uncle repeated, peering through the binoculars again. 'On that power line, over the river, that's a kingfisher perching. It's not fishing at the moment. Just watching out. Twitchy little fella.'

'Ah yes, I see it.'

'And in the trees are great blue herons. The type you'll have seen before.'

He pointed, and Adam made out tall, grey shapes in the branches, perfectly still, their U-bend necks and stiletto beaks tucked into the trees.

'And watching over the whole scene, at the heart of this story, is the thing in that tree, there,' his uncle said, passing the binoculars. 'That's why some of the other birds aren't moving around much.'

Adam was surprised at the clarity and scale through the viewfinders, and had to look away again to find his bearings.

'Don't adjust the focus. Just run them up that tree,' his uncle said.

Adam did so. After a moment, the image was filled by a pair of sharp yellow talons, the legs above them like thick, scaled cable. Adam steadied the binoculars and lifted them another fraction.

'Oh wow…' he said.

Sitting in the tree was a muscular raptor, its breast striped grey-white. Its bill was also tinged with yellow, its wide base culminating in a sharp hook. Its eyes were what struck Adam. They were huge black orbs – big as a human's, it seemed to him – rimmed with more yellow.

'What is that?' he asked.

'A peregrine falcon. It's the fastest creature on earth, actually.'

'Does it eat other birds?'

His uncle chuckled. 'Oh yes, very much so. It's like a sparrowhawk on steroids. That's what it's planning now, most likely. Rich pickings, here. The herons probably know it's there. That's why they're all in their trees. It'll eat most things given half a chance. Keep watching.'

And Adam had. A few moments later, a small flock of white birds had flown left to right across the slough.

'Now, perhaps,' his uncle said.

The peregrine exploded from its branch, flew for a fraction of a second, and then changed shape in the air. Its wings tucked away, it became a short, stout dart that fired itself at one of the white birds, stabbing down onto it from above.

'It's a tern,' his uncle said, his voice tight with excitement. The peregrine smacked into the smaller bird with a lethal-looking thump, and Adam saw feathers puff outwards into the sky.

'Got 'im,' his uncle said.

The little world before them erupted. The shorebirds took off, scattering in every direction like woodchips under an axe. The ducks vectored overhead, calling out in alarm. The herons stamped and shook in the trees, their evil cousins in the bushes beneath Adam's feet shuddering and flinching. A wave of animal fear pulsed outwards from the slough, strong enough for Adam to feel it.

'Like someone shouting "shark" on a busy beach,' his uncle mused.

Above, the peregrine made a lazy circle, a limp white shape hanging in an inverted U beneath it, and dropped out of sight behind the trees.

'Kills it in the air, you see,' his uncle had said. 'If the impact doesn't do it, then one slash with those talons...'

Behind them, cars pulled out of spaces, boys laughed, and a glum man walked past with a dog.

'Holy shit,' Adam had said.

His uncle laughed gleefully – a man with a convert.

Ever since that moment, Adam had become aware of the underworld – or rather *overworld* – that existed around him at all times. An endless life-and-death story; a high drama for all to see in the skies and the trees, but ignored by most of the humans going about their lives below. Crows angrily dive-bombing trees, because sitting within their branches was a raptor, or an owl that might want their dinner. Mockingbirds systematically quartering their domains, so territorial they'd drive away cats – or crows. Finches, warblers and flycatchers risking dangerous displays of their beauty to attract mates or to take insects on the wing.

Hawks and vultures that lived as opportunists and scavengers, watching the ground for rodents, lizards and carrion, or waiting for the chance to grasp an unlucky pigeon. Being constantly harassed and driven on by fierce, more agile corvids.

The apex predators that ate them all, cruising high above, watching from their cliffs or trees, staring down and seeing everything, waiting for a chance.

It made a mockery of human life, Adam had realized. It made it seem petty and vain, as though mankind was just a backdrop for this higher drama.

It was a glimpse of this other world that he hoped to see on Saturday morning, when as usual he woke early. Lie-ins seemed to have been permanently wrecked for him by age and worry, but this, at least, meant that mornings were there to be used.

The sun wasn't fully up when he descended the stairs to the street, and threw his binoculars and a jacket into the back of his Mercedes C-Class. The early-morning world was deep blue and cold, the strip of grass beside the sidewalk glistening with dew. LA's nights could be unexpectedly chilly. It was, after all, technically a desert.

He had the freeway almost to himself. Plunging down the 101 towards Downtown, he bore left, skirting Chinatown and picking up the Arroyo Seco Parkway towards Pasadena. This was a beautiful stretch of road, lined by palms, cliffs and hills, undulating upwards towards the rearing mountains in the background.

His destination was Ernest E. Debs Park, a hulking green foothill that rose up to the right of the freeway in a jungly mass. It wouldn't be open as yet – its main gates still locked to vehicles – but Adam knew where there was a snick in the fence higher up. He parked by the last house on a steep, zigzagging lane, behind the Jeep Wrangler that was always there, and sneaked into the park.

The streets around Ernest E. Debs were visibly middle class, but lower down, Monterey Park, Montecito Heights and Highland Park all had their share of troubles. Adam had read that two young Hispanic girls had been murdered by a gang-banger and hidden in the park's deep undergrowth. It would be a logical place to hide a body, he thought now, as he crept through the chain-link fence. The park's steep sides were covered in verdant bush. There were deeply wooded areas, cliff faces and scrub. It was about as wild as a city park could be, which was exactly what made it an excellent spot for birding.

He climbed up a steep bank, an unofficial trail cut into it by the park's other out-of-hours users. The sky was paling above him, and as he levelled out onto a plateau, a man was doing t'ai chi on a grassy flat, close to the brim of a slope. Behind him, Downtown's skyscrapers were sharp and hard against the flawless sky, and a mild orangey glow could be seen broadening above the horizon.

Adam turned into the pine trees and entered a forested nook, which contained a large pond known as the peanut lake. It was surrounded by tall reeds, and Adam stopped and removed his binoculars from their case, running them slowly over the plants, which seemed a likely spot for a rail to be lurking. In a patch of sunny water a few feet from him two terrapins had surfaced, their red-spotted heads protruding from the water, still as mired driftwood. The green smell in the air reminded him of the LA River's, and he thought of Erica, and his date that evening, his heart lurching a little.

He set off around the lake, heading for the higher paths that led out onto the park's steep ramparts.

Another new woman. Still dating as he pushed his late thirties. It wasn't what he'd have pictured, he didn't think.

He sometimes wished, as he pottered around Los Angeles, that he could show Sofia these places. Soon after he'd lost her, in one of their final communications, she'd told him she missed their walks.

And it was true that their relationship had revolved around walks in parks. In fact, it was almost as though it had been processed and driven by long rambles, usually around Victoria Park and the Regent's Canal. Here, on hungover Sundays, other couples drifting happily on bicycles or sprawled among ravaged copies of the *Observer*, decisions could be made, plans formed, disputes resolved.

This was the time before Victoria Park – built as a royal park for the poor, a lung for the choking, industrial East End – had been cleaned up for the Olympics. There was graffiti on walls, dog shit on the grass, no bright red, happy pagoda for tourists to marvel at. The canal was a faded place of abandoned warehouses, their windows pocked by thrown stones. Squats, tower blocks and beautiful, scruffy old terraces whose sleepy appearances belied their savage increases in value.

Adam would have loved to show Sofia the parks of Los Angeles. To point out what he knew about the city from Griffith Observatory's airy, cool stone promenade, or to tell her that the lumps in the green water of the peanut lake were not in fact mired pieces of wood, but the heads of terrapins, which would flinch, duck, and dive away into the deep, dark recesses if you got too close to them.

Victoria Park's lake had been beautiful, too. Towards the end of that life, he'd often stood in front of it, looking over to the island reserved for waterfowl, and dreamed of wading over and setting up a camp there, escaping from a world besmirched by his own stupidity.

They must have walked a thousand miles across that park, in the five years they'd been together.

'Maybe we should sleep with other people,' Sofia had said one day, as they set off along a path between stretches of damp grass. It was autumn, a time of year that emphasized how beautiful she was. The chestnut eyes and dark brown hair, the olive skin. She was an autumnal symphony herself.

'Why?' he'd said.

'Because we're not having sex any more. Something has to change.'

'We do have sex,' he'd protested.

'Once every two weeks, and when we do it's not good any more.' She'd been frowning – he could see that she wouldn't be easily distracted from this oft-deferred subject.

'Why don't you want to have more?' she asked. 'It's fucking insulting.'

Because I'm sleeping with someone else, would have been the truth she deserved.

'I promise we will. I've just become a bit lazy, I think,' he told her instead. 'I'm sorry.'

'Lazy?' she'd said, the frown deepening as she considered this. 'But it shouldn't be an effort. It's not a chore.'

'I know,' he said. 'What can I do to make it better, for you?'

He'd felt a change in the atmosphere at this – like an escape hatch opening up. She was almost shy, suddenly.

'Well,' she'd said. '... I don't know.'

'Tell me,' he said, looking her in the eye.

She glanced away. 'I'd like it if you'd rough me up a bit.'

That night, drunk on whisky, he had done his best at this, though he suspected it had been rather too polite for Sofia. Mainly, it had involved a surprisingly erotic form of play wrestling that had seen them crashing noisily into the living room furniture.

After half an hour or so of this, they'd given up, exhausted. They'd just settled down by the sofa to watch a DVD when there'd been a very loud knock on the door of their flat.

'Hello?' Adam had called.

'Police,' had come the shouted reply.

He and Sofia looked at each other. 'Oh shit,' she'd said.

'Hold on,' Adam shouted, putting his clothes on, shaking with shock and the aftermath of his physical exertions.

'Open the door *now*, please,' a male voice boomed.

Adam got to the door and swung it open. There'd been two cops. A middle-aged man with grey hair and glasses beneath his hat, and a tall, broad woman, her face rigid with concern.

Sofia appeared at Adam's shoulder.

'Can we come in, please?' the woman asked.

'Sure, yes.'

'We've a had a report that there was a potentially violent situation here,' the man said.

'Oh God,' Sofia laughed nervously. 'We were just playing around. I'm really sorry. It's all fine.'

'OK, love,' the female officer said to Sofia, pushing past Adam. 'I want to separate you two, so is there somewhere we can go?'

'Yes,' Sofia said, 'we can go into the kitchen, but honestly this is all just a misunderstanding.'

The woman guided Sofia through the lounge, past a half empty bottle of Scotch and an overflowing ashtray – wife-beater style, Adam thought with a pulse of worry – and into the kitchen.

'OK, sir,' the man said. 'If you can stay here with me, please. Tell me in your own words what's been happening tonight.'

'Well, to be totally honest,' Adam said, aware that he was slurring slightly, 'earlier on we went for a walk in the park…'

A puzzled look came over the policeman, who was presumably already sensing a lack of menace in the flat.

'… And Sofia – that's my girlfriend – was telling me she was a bit dissatisfied with our sex life. I asked her what I could do to improve things, and she said I should rough her up a bit. So we were getting a bit drunk just now, and I thought "no time like the present".'

'Right,' the cop had said, dubiously.

'So I was roughing her up a bit, basically,' he said.

'And she asked you to do this?'

'Absolutely. It's not really my thing, if I'm honest,' Adam said, smiling politely.

'OK. Wait here please, sir.'

The cop walked through the lounge, glancing at the whisky and heading into the kitchen. There was some discussion in low voices, and then the two officers reappeared, Sofia behind them, apologizing.

'Well, it seems you're both telling the same story,' the man said. 'So please just keep the noise down now. You've given your neighbours a real scare.'

'I'm very sorry, officers,' Adam said. He felt a flush of warm, drunken affection for these two hard-working, harassed officers of the law. 'Thank you,' he said, waving from the door as they gave him a final, puzzled look and headed for the stairs. 'Thank you very much indeed!'

Here, now, in Los Angeles, seven years later, Adam broke from the treeline and started along a narrow path which led up the spine of the park's eastern flank – a catwalk high above the city.

Eyes on the skies, he scolded himself. Enough of all this bloody thinking.

He set off up the slope, the sun rising ahead, the day's heat flooding over him in a wave. A man in a wide sunhat walked past and nodded good morning.

At the top of the slope was a viewpoint with benches, a line of trees rising up from the hill's crest. Adam turned, and saw something moving in one of them.

Feathers, he realized with a sharp thrill. Tiny feathers descending from a branch, like a plume of smoke in a rewound film. He followed them upwards and saw a small bird of prey standing on a flat branch, another bird trapped under its foot, being eaten. Below it, an iridescent blue scrub jay was hopping about, waiting for scraps.

Adam raised his binoculars.

The raptor was a merlin – a small falcon that looked almost exactly like a peregrine in miniature. Like a small man, Adam knew, it compensated for its size with sheer aggression. *Pugnacious*, was the word from his field book that sprung to mind.

It was tearing at the flesh of the smaller bird under its foot, the feathers slowly twisting downwards in the still morning air. The prey was already too mangled to be identified. A murder victim. An innocent, whose day had barely begun when this monster had torn it from the air.

The jay hopped and bopped a foot or so below, its blue feathers shining in the sun. Very brave, Adam thought. Corvids were a tough family – the gypsies of the air. When the merlin was full, it took off from the branch and flew away, fast and straight like a squat little bullet. The jay leapt up to the branch it had vacated, and began hungrily cleaning up what was left.

12

Adam arranged to meet Erica the osprey lady at Khwām Suk̄h, a Thai place in the little six-block chunk of Hollywood designated as Thai Town. Like many of LA's finest eateries, it was unpromisingly located in a strip mall.

These short, squat blocks of uniform shopfronts could be found all over the city. Set back from the street across a small parking lot, they usually contained a launderette, a massage parlour, a liquor store and a restaurant or two. If you knew how to cook, and wanted a cheap space to sell your food, a strip mall was the ideal location.

Angelenos, Adam knew, would admirably suspend their snobbery if it threatened to get in the way of discovering a *great new spot.* They thought nothing of driving to insalubrious locales to park in front of a bum-magnet liquor store and eat Cuban food in a crammed storefront.

Khwām Suk̄h was one of the more famous examples – its walls and tables were covered in clippings of newspaper and magazine reviews, and reports of celebrity visits: 'Drew Barrymore's Thai Tip!' 'Quentin Tarantino's Spice Shangri-La!'

To Adam, it had seemed the right balance of unpretentious and fashionable, and when he'd called Erica she'd seemed pleased by the suggestion.

He dressed in blue jeans and a white shirt, and took a cab to the restaurant, arriving a few minutes before their agreed meeting time of 7.30. There were no reservations at Khwām Suk̄h, and he didn't want an awkward wait. He'd just secured the promise of a table when Erica walked in.

He felt a bodily thud of nervous excitement as she did so. Out of her bike clothes, she was beautiful rather than pretty. She wore black heels and jeans and a deep red, shimmering top with a mandarin collar, embroidered with gold stitching at the hems of its short sleeves. Her black hair was tied back, and she flashed him a smile as she saw him.

'Hello,' he said as she approached. The word seemed to drown in the chatter around him.

When she reached him, he realized the heels had made her as tall as he was, and he didn't need to lean down to kiss her on the cheek. He noted how good she smelled, how her height was somehow satisfying.

'Hi,' she said, looking around at the eating, murmuring couples at tightly packed tables, the low-lit cosiness of the newsprint-covered walls.

Adam suddenly felt very awkward. 'How are you?' he asked.

She laughed, breaking the tension. 'I'm well, thanks,' she said, dipping her head to ape his formality.

A young waitress with a bouncing ponytail gestured, and led them through the restaurant to a table by the windows.

When they sat, Erica looked at him expectantly, and the nerves stiffened him again.

'It's good to see you,' he said.

'You too,' she replied. 'Did you have a good Saturday?'

'Very good, thanks. I went birding.'

'That's great,' she said. 'Where?'

'Ernest E. Debs Park. Do you know it?'

She was looking over his shoulder, distracted. Don't be boring, he told himself.

'I don't,' she said.

'It's near Highland Park. It's a good spot. There's an Audubon office nearby.'

'Right,' she said. 'Interesting.'

She clearly wasn't very interested, and a stab of annoyance penetrated his anxiety.

'It's a strange place,' he said. 'Lots of birds. They have peregrines. And today I saw a merlin. But because of where it is there's also some gang problems apparently. Two girls got killed and mutilated and then hidden in there.'

Erica frowned. 'Jesus,' she said.

'Sorry.' Adam took a deep breath. 'I'm rambling… I'm actually a bit nervous.'

She looked at him and smiled. 'Because you're suddenly on a date?'

'Yes,' he said. 'I mean, I knew I was going on a date.'

She leaned forward a little. 'Oh, you did?'

Abruptly understanding that she liked mischief, he felt himself to be on firmer ground. 'Yes,' he said. 'But this place seemed so sort of…'

'Datey,' she said.

'Exactly. And then you looked so beautiful when you walked in.'

She glanced downward, briefly, then looked back at him. 'Thank you,' she said.

The waitress reappeared with a notebook. 'Drink?' she asked them.

Adam gestured to Erica.

'I'll have a Singha, please,' she said.

Adam ordered one too, relieved. You never knew, in LA, if the person you were with was going to say, 'Just water.' It seemed to be a plague.

'So this isn't your usual spot for dates?' Erica asked him, smiling again. 'You don't take all the girls here?'

'Absolutely not. To be honest, I haven't really been on one for a while.'

'You surprise me.'

'And you?'

'I haven't either. It can be a pretty weird scene in LA.'

'It sure can,' Adam said. He had an excruciating flashback to the office bathroom, on his knees, brain popping on drugs, Angelina looking disgustedly down at him. *I* can be weird! he thought, quashing a churn of horror.

'But I bet that accent gets you places, huh?' Erica said.

'Not as much as you might think,' he said. 'People always seem to think I'm Australian.'

She laughed again, unfolding the menu and scanning it. 'Poor guy. Getting confused with a simple colonial.'

At the table beside theirs, another waitress seated a very pregnant woman and her tall, slim husband. The woman huffed as she sat down, and gave Adam and Erica a smile.

'About ready to burst,' she said.

'Oh,' Erica said. For a moment she looked girlish, unselfconscious. 'I'm happy for you!'

'Thanks,' the woman said. Adam noted that her husband's legs barely fitted under the small table. He looked pale and tired.

If I'm ever to be a dad, Adam thought, I'll be so old by the time it happens.

Before he had too long to spend with this thought, the beers arrived. They said cheers, and Adam drank gratefully. He looked at Erica and felt a glow spread in him.

'So,' she said. 'Decided on food?'

'I haven't looked yet.'

'I'm gonna have the catfish, it's my favourite here.'

'Are you a regular?'

'Not really, but I've been a few times.'

'Aha,' he said. 'This is where you take all the boys.'

'Actually no,' she said. Her own smile was almost reluctant now, he thought, as though she knew she was letting herself be charmed and thought it a little silly of her. Some guy with an English accent she couldn't help liking, no matter how dumb that was.

Adam looked at the menu. 'Where is the catfish?' he asked.

She pointed. 'It's *really* hot. Definitely an acquired taste.'

There were three little images of chillies beside the dish, apparently the most awarded to any meal on the menu. Adam's theory on hot food in America was that it was never truly hot, because everyone was too scared of getting sued to risk injurious levels of spice.

'I'll try it too,' he said.

Erica frowned. 'I sort of feel like that came off as a challenge or something, that I said I was gonna get it,' she said. 'Honestly, it's *really* spicy.'

'I'm pretty sure I can handle it,' Adam said. 'I've been hardened by years of east London curry.'

'Of course,' she said. 'I spent some time in Cambodia, and they use a lot of spice there too. I'd say I learned to handle it then, but I think it's probably genetic, to be honest.'

'What were you doing there?'

'Oh, you know. An American girl from a safe little town goes to see somewhere a little more interesting.' She waved a hand. 'All that.'

Yes, he thought. He could picture all that.

'Well,' he said. 'Sounds as though we can both handle the catfish.'

Now she smiled properly, angling her face up at him. He felt a sudden joy at having this woman opposite him. She was big and lithe and as frighteningly beautiful as a wild animal.

'Fine,' she said. 'Don't say I didn't warn you.' She swigged her beer and watched him.

When she wasn't talking about herself, he noticed, she was much more confident. He wanted to ask how old she was. There were laughter lines around her eyes, and there was something about her that spoke of hard work. The handbag she'd placed on the seat beside her was Prada, though, and the heels had looked expensive.

'So, now we can start asking each other questions, right?' she said. 'Is that how it works?'

'Since neither of us seems to have had much practice recently, I think we can make up the rules.'

'OK,' she said. 'But let's ask each other some questions.' She leaned on her elbows, moving closer to him. Her scent reached him again, and her hair shone under the dim lighting. 'We can start with the usual stuff. What do you do?'

'I work in music.'

'That's exciting,' she said. 'Doing what? Producing?'

'No, working for a record company.'

'You find the artists, put out their albums?'

'*We* do that,' Adam said. '*I* do some of that.'

'You like it?' she asked.

'I'm actually not so sure any more,' Adam said.

'Oh no. A crisis of faith, huh?' she said, smiling. 'Let me guess, the entertainment guy wants to do something more meaningful? All that?'

'Nothing so admirable, I'm afraid. I think I'd basically like to be retired.'

She laughed. 'Right. And what would you do then, play golf?'

'No chance,' he said. 'Actually, I'd probably wander around looking for birds. Read a lot. Stop for drinks. And lots of hiking.'

'Doesn't sound bad,' she said, and took a swig of her beer. 'I like hiking too.'

'Something in common then,' Adam said. 'And you? What do you do?'

'I'm a doctor.' Again the reluctance passed over her features, and she watched to gauge his reaction.

'That makes a lot of sense,' he said, nodding.

'It does? Why's that?'

'Well, you seem very smart. And also, I have the impression you're someone who's worked hard.'

She widened her eyes and mouth, briefly, showing white teeth. 'I'm not sure how to take that,' she said. 'Do I look worn out?'

'No,' Adam replied. 'Like I said, you look really beautiful.'

For a moment, neither of them spoke. Adam took a long pull on his beer.

'I've just realized that I'm quite uncomfortable with privileged LA types,' he said. 'I mean the ones that don't really seem to have worked for what they have. That sort of financial class system here. And I think I did work hard.'

'You don't now?'

'Maybe I do. Anyway, what I mean is that it was intended as a compliment.'

Robust, he thought, remembering what he'd said to Sofia on their first date.

'Anyway,' he said, smiling at her.

'Enough on work,' Erica said. 'Tell me about your last hike.'

'Ah. You would ask me that.'

She leaned forward again, intrigued. Her beer was almost empty, he saw, and sipped his to catch up.

'Is it a good story?' she said.

'It's embarrassing. There's this mountain called Strawberry Peak. Do you know it?'

'Of course. It's the fun peak.'

'Right. You know the mountaineers' route?'

'Yes. That's the fun *part*.'

'Well, I sort of chickened out of it,' he said.

'What, at the scramble before the summit?'

'No. At the scramble on the way to the scramble before the summit.'

'Oh no,' she said, giggling. 'At that little hump near the water tank?'

Adam saw himself, standing astride a very narrow, spine-like path, a thousand-foot drop either side of him, clouds blowing over a giant granite mass ahead as he approached a yet more sharply rising ridge – like a shark's fin made of rock. He almost shuddered just thinking about it.

'Yes,' he said.

Erica drained her beer and looked up, nodding at an unseen server behind him.

'Well hey,' she said, holding up two fingers for more beers. 'If we make it to a second date, maybe I can show you how to do it.'

The fear of the mountain path and the excitement at the second date talk were hard for Adam to distinguish from each other.

They ordered shared starters, fishcakes and satay. As they were eating them, the restaurant's owner – a very fat, smiling woman in glasses – approached the pregnant lady beside them.

'Oh my God,' she said, touching the woman's belly. 'Honey, you look like you gonna burst!'

'I know,' the woman said, rubbing her tummy.

'When you due?'

'Five days ago,' the woman said.

'I got something for you, darling,' the owner said seriously. 'You gotta try my special soup. You wanna go into labour? My soup gonna fix like THAT—' She clicked her fingers.

The pregnant lady and her partner looked at each other. 'Is it spicy?' she asked.

'No, no, darling. Not spicy. Just herbs, vegetable and coconut milk. It's delicious.'

'You know what?' the woman said. 'Screw it. That's what I'll have.'

'Good choice,' the owner said, grinning widely and squeezing off between the tables.

A younger, skinnier waitress replaced her, and asked Adam and Erica for their orders.

'The catfish, please,' Erica said.

The waitress frowned. 'You sure? *Very* spicy.'

'I've had it before, thanks.' Erica smiled at her professionally.

'And you?' the waitress asked Adam.

'The same please,' he said.

The waitress frowned again. 'You had before too?'

'No, but I'm used to spice,' he said.

'Maybe you try something different?' she said. 'No refund you don't like it.'

Adam looked her in the eye. 'The catfish, please.'

The waitress frowned, and darted away.

Erica grinned. 'Cheers,' she said, and held up a fresh beer, which sweated promisingly in the low yellow light.

When the mains arrived, Adam had almost forgotten what he'd ordered. He was too busy enjoying finding out about Erica. That she was from Charleston, South Carolina; that she'd studied at UCLA, and that she lived in Atwater Village, a bohemian suburb not far from Silver Lake. She didn't want to live on the west side, she said. Nice to visit, but too sterile. The east had more going on.

Her ancestors were Danish, her parents alive, together, retired and involving themselves in local politics back in her hometown. She loved reading fiction, especially short stories. Plenty in common, Adam thought happily – despite her being a cyclist.

On her return, the waitress placed two oval-shaped plates of steaming fish before them.

'Catfish,' she said, and glanced at Adam.

'Thanks,' Adam said. 'It looks delicious.'

They removed their chopsticks from their paper sleeves and rubbed them together, grinning at each other.

'Bon appétit,' Erica said.

Adam began eating, focusing on his chopstick abilities, which were inconsistent at best. The fish was delicious, he thought. After a few seconds, all he could feel was a pleasant heat, a smoky flavour from the chargrilled flesh.

The couple beside them had also received their food. The woman's soup had been proudly delivered by the owner – a big bowl of creamy white liquid, studded with vegetables and speckled with mild-looking green herbs. The proprietor had stood above the table momentarily, after placing it down, hands clasped in happiness as she'd told the woman to enjoy it.

'Yum,' Adam said, tucking into his fish. 'The food here is great.'

'Sure is,' Erica said. 'So I guess we should talk a little more about you. Though it's kinda refreshing that we didn't already.'

'If we have to,' Adam said, raising a large chunk of food to his mouth.

'Where are you from, originally?' Erica asked. 'Where in England, I mean?'

Adam chewed the mouthful of catfish, and prepared to swallow so that he could speak. It was only as he tried to that he realized there was a problem. Something strange was happening in his throat. It seemed abruptly to be constricted.

A cough rose up, and he raised his napkin to his mouth and stifled it.

'Adam?' Erica said.

He held up a hand as if to excuse himself.

'You OK?' Erica asked.

Adam tried to say yes, but all that came out was a croak. He stifled another cough and sucked in air. It was only when he had a lungful that he realized there was another problem. His mouth felt like it was slowly setting on fire.

Shit, he thought. Shit shit shit. The catfish was still in his mouth. He dearly wanted to cough. He covered his mouth with the napkin once more and did so, and a little more air seemed to flow in his throat. When he tried to swallow the food again, though, he still couldn't. It was as if the napalm-like fish had scorched away the muscles in his throat.

His mouth now was in agony. He looked down at the table, realized his eyes were filling with liquid. A single tear ran down his right cheek.

Finding his water glass through the blur, he picked it up and poured some of the icy liquid into his mouth, along with the food.

After half a second's relief, the burning sensation roared back to life with renewed anger. It was as though he'd poured petrol on the flames.

'Adam?' Erica sounded worried. Adam looked at her, but his eyes were too full of tears to see her face properly.

'Your face…' she said. 'You've gone totally pale.' She paused. 'Except for some weird splotches, actually. I think we need to get you something to…'

Adam opened his mouth wide, like a suffocating fish. He realized, too late, that he'd forgotten the napkin, and that he was thus displaying a mouthful of half-chewed, soggy food to Erica. He sucked in as much air as he could, and then closed it again.

'Hey,' Erica was shouting, evidently to a member of staff. 'Could we please have a glass of milk?'

For a brief, elastic moment, things seemed better. Adam blinked away the tears, clearing his vision and taking in the beautiful, concerned woman who was peering at him across the table. He wondered if perhaps it was now safe to swallow the food.

Then, taking him utterly by surprise, a vast, propulsive cough surged upward from his chest. Incapable of containing it, he jerked forward, doing his best to keep the pulped fish in his mouth as the cough blasted out.

He blinked away more tears, and saw that he had failed. A small, dark, oily mark blossomed on the pristine red of Erica's top, as near as dammit to the pinnacle of her left breast.

'Oh,' he croaked, reaching a hand across the table to wipe it away. Thinking better of this, he froze.

For a moment, there was silence. Erica lowered her eyes to her top and raised a single slim finger, using its manicured, painted nail to surgically remove the fleck of fish.

'OK,' she said, screwing the finger into her napkin. 'Next time you bring a date here, maybe you can try the pregnancy soup.'

* * *

'Well,' Erica said, in a small, dim bar a little way down Hollywood Boulevard. 'That was quite a meal.'

She was laughing at him, which seemed to be the best he could hope for.

The barman approached them, and took a second look at Adam. 'He OK?' he asked.

'He's fine. He ate something a little too hot for him.'

The barman frowned. 'He's not gonna, like, throw up, right?'

'No,' Erica said. 'Trust me, I'm a doctor.'

'OK,' the barman said. 'What'll it be?'

'A margarita,' Erica said.

'Two please,' Adam said through his ruined mouth.

'Regular, or jalapeño?' the barman asked.

'Jalapeño for me,' Erica said. 'Regular for him. With extra salt on the rim.' She looked at Adam. 'Heal up that mouth of yours.'

'I'm so sorry,' Adam said.

'If I didn't laugh,' she said, looking down at the stain on her top, 'I'd cry.'

'Do you think it'll come out?'

'I hope it will. You can cover my dry-cleaning bill either way. Now, where were we?'

They talked for another hour, drinking second margaritas more slowly than the first, tucked up together at the bar as Adam answered her questions. There was so much to explain by the time you were approaching forty, he thought. It was completely exhausting. Also, in his case, much of his history didn't seem very promising.

After the second drink, Erica looked at her watch.

'You have to go?' he asked her.

'I do, sadly.'

'Can I walk you to your car?' Adam asked.

'We can walk a little way before I call an Uber,' she said.

Adam paid the bill and they set off down Hollywood Boulevard, strolling close to one another.

'What were you really doing in Cambodia?' he asked her.

'I worked in a hospital there for a year.'

'That must have been quite an experience.'

'It was wonderful, largely.'

'I love the way you speak,' he told her. 'For an American.'

'Words, or accent?'

'Both,' he said.

'Ha. You can take the girl out of the South.'

'So,' Adam asked her. 'Did I qualify for the second date?'

'Ah yes, the hiking date to Strawberry Peak?'

'Yes,' he said.

'How could I say no?'

Adam took her hand and they sauntered, a warm glow spreading in him from the margaritas, the rescued date and, he thought, probably the radioactive catfish burning a hole in his stomach lining.

After a moment, Erica took her hand back and tapped at her phone to order the car.

A shuffling black bum with a beanie hat and short grey beard approached them.

'Hey, man,' he said to Adam. 'Spare a little change?'

'Sorry,' Adam said.

'Are you a racist, man?' the bum asked as they passed him.

Adam laughed, outraged. 'What?' he said.

The bum, who'd paused behind them, glanced down at Erica's behind.

'Man,' he said. 'You with a white chick, but she got booty like a black chick, so you can't be all bad.'

Erica looked up at Adam, mouth wide with shock.

A Prius pulled up a little way ahead. 'Erica?' someone called from inside.

Erica watched the bum wander off.

'Thanks a lot, buddy,' she called after him. 'You really know how to make a girl's night.' Her face had stiffened with anger.

'Ignore him,' Adam said. 'He's just pissed off.'

'I know,' she said. 'But that's not really a good reason for making comments about my ass.'

She looked at Adam, her blue eyes blazing. 'Sorry,' she said.

'It's fine.' He couldn't help smiling at her.

'It's not funny,' she said.

'That's not why I'm smiling.'

'Erica?' the voice in the car said again.

She sighed, the tension going out of her shoulders, and kissed Adam quickly on the cheek. 'I guess this is me,' she said.

'When can I see you?' Adam called after her.

She glanced over her shoulder. 'Saturday,' she said. 'That work?'

'Perfect,' Adam said.

And then she was swinging her legs into the back of the Prius, the car door closing after her. Adam stood and watched as its brake lights faded into the night.

13

In the meeting room, the conference phone was spurting out the harsh tones of caffeinated British voices. The American staff, crammed onto the sofa and several chairs in the confined space, still coming to terms with Monday morning, frowned, leaning in towards the phone and trying to decipher the cacophony of laughter, raised voices, sarcasm and occasional anger.

'OK, OK,' the Autodidact said, silencing the room at the British end. 'Americans, you with us?'

'Yep,' everyone said at once.

'Good. Where's Abi?' Adam, finely attuned to the intricacies of the weekly marketing conference call, could tell that this question was directed to the London meeting room rather than the assembled global staff. Abidemi was the office manager, responsible for taking minutes.

Someone in London muttered a reply to the effect that Abi was not currently available.

'Right,' the Autodidact said. 'Probably downstairs sending out phishing emails from the office server.'

Adam grimaced and avoided his colleagues' eyes. At the other end of the line, a few male voices sniggered uncertainly.

'OK, well, let's crack on then,' the Autodidact said.

'Right then,' said a cheerful Irish voice at the British end. This was Jennifer, a talented Oxford graduate whose role was head of operations. Due to the Autodidact's belief that titles were cheaper than raises, most people were heads of something.

'Shall we talk about the latest on the branding side?' Jennifer continued.

'Yeah, er, we're making some pin badges,' a deep male voice said. This was Steven, head of marketing. 'And we're gonna do our own tents, in time for the summer festivals and that.'

'Cool,' Kristen in the LA office said. 'Like, what do they look like?'

'They're black,' Steven said. 'With a small white logo on the door.'

Excellent, Adam thought. Black tents will stay nice and cool in the sun.

'Great. Let's talk *Shades*?' Jennifer said.

The Autodidact cleared his throat, but didn't speak.

'Jason?' Jennifer said.

'What?' the Autodidact replied.

'What's the latest?' Jennifer said.

'What do you mean what's the latest?' the Autodidact said, sounding more Liverpudlian. 'This isn't for me to run. It's meant to be run by the people of colour among the staff.'

'Yes, but…'

'But what?'

'Well, it was your idea? And no one's really leading it.'

'Jesus fucking Christ,' the Autodidact said.

'It's just not very well organized,' an unidentified female voice said.

'OK, OK, OK. Does everyone know about this?' the Autodidact said.

'No,' Scott said, breaking the silence in the LA meeting room, frowning deeply at the conference phone. He leaned closely over it, with one hand planted in his hair. Nothing was worse, for Scott, than not knowing something before the majority of his colleagues.

'OK, so I guess I'll give a bit of a prologue,' the Autodidact said.

'Pre-logue!' a few male voices chanted – the Autodidact's loyalists.

'So the idea is that it's a total disgrace how white-led everything is in the indie-rock scene,' the Autodidact said. 'We're starting to build a genuine BAME roster, and this is about a project being completely run and decided by the BAME members of staff.'

'But it was your idea?' Brian, the British head of radio, had known the Autodidact long enough to taunt him.

'Yes, it was my bloody idea,' the Autodidact screeched. 'And I've taken more shit for it than anything else ever.'

'Well, am I going to be taking it into stations?' Brian said, abruptly prim. 'Because if so I want approval over the edits.'

'Noyouwillfuckingnotbetakingit!' the Autodidact raged. 'A person of colour will be taking it in.'

'But that's my job!' Brian said.

'Maybe you should appoint a project manager?' Jennifer suggested to Jason.

'Fucking hell,' the Autodidact said. 'It's not for me to appoint one. They should be appointed by a person of colour.'

There was a long moment of silence. 'Fuck's sakes, where's Abidemi?' the Autodidact said. 'Someone call the fucking fraud team.'

A few people in the background laughed nervously. As far as Adam could tell, Jason thought of these jokes as a sort of ironic meta-humour. An edgy, comic commentary on the ugly behaviour of bad bosses – of which he so clearly wasn't one. It wasn't an argument Adam would have wanted to defend in an employment tribunal.

'Are we really gonna go forward with White Slavery?' This was Ed, head of retail, whose gruff West Country tone was easily identifiable.

'Why would we not move forward with it?' the Autodidact asked.

'Well, she can barely play her instruments,' Ed moaned. 'Me and Brian went to see her on Saturday. She was holding a guitar and playing one note on it over a backing track, and chanting sections from the Labour Party manifesto. Over and over again. It was embarrassing.'

'So you think we can afford to send people to music lessons, or wait around while some other twat signs these bastards?' the Autodidact said. 'It's all artifice, this game. No one gives a shit about how well you can play guitar. None of these fuckwits have done their ten thousand hours.'

'What?' someone asked.

'Gladwell,' the Autodidact said, sagely. 'Anyway, White Slavery's music seems to me to have potential to go exactly the right way.'

'I agree,' Scott said, seizing the chance to support Jason in his best, weary-expert voice. 'We just need to be smarter about the projects we pick up. Think more tactically and less… emotionally. She looks great, too. It's gonna be very important that she's on her own album cover and in all the videos.'

'Exactly,' Jason said. 'But not in an exploitative way. She dresses like a total LDN hipster with an ethnic twist, so that's perfect.'

There was a long pause as the Autodidact let his words sink in.

'But mainly,' he continued, 'she's a black female civil rights activist making indietronica, and we've got hardly any female artists, which is a disgrace in itself.'

In both conference rooms, there was silence. Adam felt an unbearable tension spread within him. His leg, in response, began jiggling furiously.

'OK,' Jennifer said, calmly. 'I think Sasha should lead *Shades* then. Is that OK, Sasha?

'Sure,' came the distant reply.

'So you guys get together for a meeting about it later. The title is just provisional, so if anyone has any better ideas that'd be great.'

'I like *Spectrum*,' someone said.

'*In Full Colour?*' said somebody else.

'Maybe something to do with vinyl and that?' Steven said. 'Maybe, like… *Black on Black?*'

'*What?*' the Autodidact said.

Someone in London giggled.

'Sasha and her team can discuss that later,' Jennifer said. 'If you guys could get a tracklist together too, that'd be brilliant.'

'Send that to me when it's done though, yeah?' the Autodidact said.

'OK,' Sasha said.

'Anyway, let's move on,' the Autodidact barked.

The conversation headed into the calmer waters of digital metadata delivery. Aaron, the hirsute Monday intern, appeared outside the conference room and mouthed 'Coffee?' Scott made a prayer gesture, and Adam held up a thumb and mouthed 'Thanks'.

His mind drifting from the numbing detail of digital song registration, Adam idly opened Instagram on his phone, leaning back so that no one could see his screen. He felt an instinctive loathing for social media – for its shoutiness and his increasing inability to understand how it worked – but it often seemed to be the only way to find out what anyone was doing.

Scrolling down his feed, he very quickly entered the familiar mood of anxious absorption. Craig had posted a picture of himself, standing on a rooftop in pale morning sunshine, arm around a well-known techno DJ. From the look of the buildings behind him, Adam could see that he wasn't in LA. Detroit maybe? He ran his eyes down to the hashtags, trying to decipher them.

#berlin, they told him. #partylife #music #lovingit #sick

Berlin? Adam thought. What the fuck? Weren't they supposed to be going out on Thursday? He made a mental note to message Craig later. In fact, he thought, maybe I'll message him *in* Instagram. That's probably faster these days. If he could only remember how to get into the messaging bit.

A little lower down was a post from Sofia, whom Adam had mistakenly followed a few months back in a spirit of short-lived optimism about doing so. The picture was of her book – a beautiful, bright hardback, elegantly designed and perfectly typeset, her name writ large upon it. Above an array of art- and writing-related hashtags, she'd posted excitedly that the book was going into its third print run.

An image came to Adam of his favourite, birding uncle, sitting across from him amid the dark wood of a London pub, shaking his head as Adam told him what had happened with Sofia.

'Well,' his uncle had said, lowering his eyes and raising his pint to his lips. 'You had it made there, pal.'

Fuck, Adam thought now. Fuck fuck fuck.

Lower down still was a picture of some long, brown, attractive female legs. They were crossed at the knee, embedded in sand with the bright blue-white of the ocean beyond them. In the foreground, the picture was cut off high up on the thighs, just before the point Adam assumed a swimsuited crotch would appear. The photo had been posted by Meg, with a single hashtag.

#headspace

In a strange way, it cheered him. Good on you, he thought. Rather there than here.

For a short while after that, none of the posts interested him. People he barely knew, at weddings or on holidays, posing like rappers or fashion models. Bizarre little videos that looked like they'd been shot accidentally then covered in hand-drawn digital ink. These were interspersed with pictures of flying birds or improbably luminous, enhanced landscapes. Places that taunted him by being somewhere he wasn't while trapped in the curdled air of the meeting room – the digital equivalent of the desert island postcard on the jail cell wall.

Could it only be him who thought that all this stuff had made the world a worse, more confusing place? That a culture in which people had stopped buying newspapers and books, and instead ingested this inane nonsense all day, had better be careful about where it was going? The real world was being forsaken for this flattened virtual one, where disembodied voices regurgitated received wisdoms or insulted each other horribly. And he, of course, was part of the problem – why couldn't he stop looking at this stuff?

Yes, he thought. Life before social media had definitely been better.

The worst aspect of it was that it had made the previously unspoken pecking order hideously tangible. Like everything else in life, it was now a simple matter of data, of looking at the numbers. This was a world fit only for the most craven, cold-eyed social climbers, who could measure their influence in hard statistics. A worldwide school playground, where the in-crowd would only speak to each other.

Suddenly, taking him by surprise, Angelina appeared on his feed.

She was standing atop a rock formation in Joshua Tree, the image filtered to black and white. A flowing black dress revealed her legs and shiny, black leather ankle boots. She gazed off into the distance, brushing a strand of hair from her upturned face. Adam scrutinized the picture, feeling a pang of jealousy and unhappiness.

Below the image was one of her poems:

I want to fly
Above the world
To see your beauty
In its context

There were more hashtags than words, and a series of emojis of prayer hands, cherries, flowers and hearts. The post had 5,348 likes. Adam took a deep breath, anxiety clutching his chest.

'Adam,' a voice was saying. 'Adam?'

Shit, it was the Autodidact.

'Yes?' Adam said.

'What are your thoughts on this?'

No no no no no! Fatal error! He'd walked straight into the conference call trap, again! The Autodidact had pounced on him like a hawk on a hapless pigeon.

'Sorry,' he said, trying to sound casual. 'Got distracted by an email there.'

The Autodidact impersonated this sentence in one of his funny voices – a sort of rapid, low-pitched jabber – like a schoolboy parodying someone with special needs. In the meeting room in London, men and women alike roared with laughter.

Adam's innards burned with anger and hatred. He glanced at Scott, who was smirking at the conference phone.

'I was saying,' the Autodidact continued, 'that the *project* seems to be paying dividends.'

Ah, Adam thought, the heat slowly draining from his neck and cheeks, receding into a ball of rage in his gut. The Project. The Autodidact's gradual, craven commercialization of everything Adam had once held dear.

'Yes,' Adam said, weakly. 'It's certainly working well for us here.'

'I think we can all recognize that there's real knowledge out there in the industry at large about what we're capable of doing now,' the Autodidact said. There were murmurs of approval from the London team. In LA, Scott leaned closer to the phone, nodding frantically, his expression serious once more.

'Big artists are telling us they want to sign, that we feel like the right home for them.' The worst artists, Adam thought. The artists who make music for people who own selfie sticks.

'We *have* to acknowledge that the project is working,' the Autodidact said, with real passion.

Oh dear, Adam thought. This was the climax of the marketing meeting, he knew, the Autodidact's grand summing-up: his state of the nation address.

'And there's more to come,' he was saying now. 'With The Passion rolling over for a tummy tickle and Lunar Patrol showing some arse, I think we've got two solid, first-eleven players lined up, capable of delivering decent coffee-table albums.'

Adam's head swam with metaphors. He glanced at the sofa-full of Americans, who were frowning into the middle distance, deeply puzzled. All except Scott, whose nods had become a series of orgiastic thrashings, like a woodpecker on good cocaine.

The Passion made the kind of mind-numbing, generic house music that soundtracked self-conscious hotel pool parties. I am going to have to work on The Passion, Adam thought.

'If we can get their album right,' Jason was saying, 'I truly believe we're going to have a global megahit on our hands.'

How would you know when it was right? Adam wondered. It would be like trying to judge the quality of liquid shit.

'As for concerns about credibility,' the Autodidact continued, 'with albums from White Slavery, Hot Knives and Chapels coming this year, I do feel like we're already some distance ahead on the intellectual curve, at least when it comes to this very conservative contemporary music scene.'

There was a pause here, and Adam wondered hopefully if that was the end of the meeting.

'These more commercial projects have much bigger reach, though,' the Autodidact continued, 'and I do take some pleasure in feeling like we're creating the soundtrack to a very meaningful and profound phase in the lives of young people.'

Scott, lips pursed in solemn agreement, slowed his nod to match the Autodidact's rhythm, his movements now like that of a nodding donkey pump in an LA oil field.

Christ, Adam thought. His mind felt completely numb.

'Adam,' the Autodidact said. 'Anything to add?'

'Nothing at all,' he said in his best encouraging tone. 'Very well put.'

'Great, man,' the Autodidact said. 'Can you stay on the line actually, and we'll have a catch-up?'

'Sure,' Adam said, feeling sick.

After the LA team had filed out, heading for the kitchen to make oatmeal and more coffee and hear about each other's weekends, Adam closed the sliding glass door to the meeting room.

'Hold on,' the Autodidact said. 'I'm just going to get Serena.'

Serena. The boss. The dear, departing boss.

'Hi, mate,' Serena's warm, south London accent rang out from the phone. Adam felt a flush of affection.

Save me! he thought. 'Hello,' he said.

'Alright?' Serena sounded bright and cheerful. Maybe it's good news? Adam allowed himself to wonder.

'So listen, couple of bits,' the Autodidact said.

'OK,' Adam said.

Outside the meeting room, Scott walked past slowly, flip-flops scuffing the floor, a bowl of cereal in one hand and a coffee in the other. He glanced into the meeting room, and looked away quickly when he saw Adam was watching.

'So I dunno how that meeting with Roger went,' the Autodidact was saying. Adam felt a cold hand clench around his heart. 'But he's gone very cool on us. I'm sensing the presence of a larger predator. I think we need to take some radical action.'

'Right,' Adam said.

'They're playing Red Rocks next week, right?'

'Yes,' Adam said.

'Were you planning on going?' Serena asked.

'No, I wasn't.' Adam saw where this was going. 'But I can.'

'Someone should be there,' the Autodidact said. 'Neither of us can make it.'

'It's my wedding anniversary that day,' Serena said, apologetically.

'And I've got a mentoring session,' the Autodidact said.

Jason spent a couple of evenings each week mentoring the troubled youth of Hackney Wick. Adam had encountered one or two of them at gigs, during trips to London. From what he'd been able to tell, Jason's teaching had primarily resulted in their acquiring several of his favourite business buzz phrases and his own supercilious expression. Adam sometimes wondered if the Autodidact was trying to create an army of replicants.

The sessions also gave him a good excuse to avoid travel and act largely through other people. To wear them like a glove, Adam thought. Oh God. Is the Autodidact wearing me like a glove?

'Yes, well, I should probably have planned to be there anyway,' Adam said. 'Just lots going on here as usual.'

'Sure, sure,' Serena said.

'I'll book a ticket,' Adam said.

'You need to get in there with the guys themselves,' the Autodidact said. 'Direct action. Bypass Roger.'

Oh Christ, Adam thought. 'Got it,' he said. 'Yes, that makes total sense.'

'Good man,' the Autodidact said. 'And there's one other thing,' he continued. 'Serena, do you want to...'

There was a pregnant pause. Adam closed his eyes.

'Yeah, so, you know how we were talking about you needing more help there, with it being such a big job and everything?' Serena said.

'Ah, yes, I suppose so,' Adam said.

'Well, the good news is that Isa wants to come back.'

A feeling of icy dread came over Adam, the flesh on the back of his neck crawling. He shivered. Isa. A strikingly clear series of images of her rose into his mind and blazed there. Turning to him with a complicit smile, naked, her golden-black skin damp with sweat. Her compact body and slim bare legs. The tattoo on the back of her left shoulder...

'Ah...' he said. '... OK.'

'To be based out of your office,' the Autodidact said. 'In LA.'

I know where my fucking office is, you fuckface! Adam screamed inwardly.

'Is that a good idea?' he said.

'Well, it's a bit of an experiment,' Serena said, in her optimistic tone. 'But we think it'll strengthen the office. Give you an extra set of hands. Give us more—'

'*Capacity*,' the Autodidact said, with barely disguised glee.

'But...' Adam said. 'But what about her master's?'

Isa had left the company to go and study for an MBA.

'She didn't like it,' Jason said.

'Jason stayed in touch with her. He's managed to get her back into the fold,' Serena said.

This can't be happening, Adam thought.

'OK,' he said, slightly dizzy. 'When is this going to happen?'

'Two weeks.'

'Wow. Who... who will she report to?'

'Me,' the Autodidact said. 'She's going to report directly to me.'

'Jason's been reading a book called *Remote*,' Serena said, voice swelling with pride. 'It's brilliant. All about how to manage staff in different places. It's by the guy who founded Bandcamp.'

'*Basecamp*,' the Autodidact snapped.

'Shit, yes. Sorry, mate,' Serena said.

'That... sounds great,' Adam said.

'Yeah, it's brilliant really,' Serena continued. 'So many ways to make this work these days. Technology. All that... You should read it too!'

'Yes,' Adam said. 'I'll add it to my list.' Straight to the top, above Ten Methods for Killing Yourself in a Way That Will Upset Absolutely Everyone.

'OK, well, let's keep talking about it all,' Serena said, evidently relieved to have broken the news. 'Keep the discussion going.'

'It wasn't really a discussion though, was it?' Adam ventured.

'Well,' Serena said, as though mildly hurt. 'We just think it's going to really strengthen the office there. It's such a big job you do.'

'Yes,' the Autodidact said. 'A very big job. Let us know how you get on at Red Rocks. Operation Bypass Roger.'

'Will do,' Adam said, and rang off.

He walked out of the meeting room and quickly down to the lower floor storage cupboard, closed its door behind him, and began viciously and repeatedly kicking a giant, four-foot roll of bubble wrap, which remained there primarily for this very purpose.

14

'Adam.'

He'd just reached the foot of the steps to his apartment when he heard a voice whispering his name.

He glanced around, confused, but there was no one in sight. He started up the steps, but the voice whispered again, more urgent this time.

'Adam!'

'Stef?' he replied.

'Yeah. Down here.' Adam looked at his feet, and saw that Stef was peering out at him from between two of the wooden steps. All he could see was a pair of big, quite pretty grey eyes. He flinched in surprise.

'Pretend you don't see me,' she stage-whispered. 'Act natural.'

'... OK,' he said.

'Maybe sit on the step. Smoke a cigarette.'

'I don't smoke,' he said, sitting down.

'Oh yeah,' Stef said, from somewhere near his bum.

'What are you doing?' Adam said quietly.

'I'm trying to catch the guy who's been stealing the mail,' Stef said, her whisper containing real excitement. 'I think he comes around this time, when I'm usually out.'

'Right,' Adam said, looking down the street.

'I think it might be the crazy neighbour. You know, the one with the genocide signs?'

'Yes. That might make sense.' He glanced at his watch.

'I was gonna put a trap in there,' she said. 'Like a razor or something. But you can get into trouble apparently.'

'I imagine so,' Adam said, wincing at the thought. He liked to retrieve his mail by sliding his fingers into the slot rather than unlocking the box. 'How long are you going to stay in there?'

'Not too much longer,' Stef said. 'He might have seen you come back. And I need to crap.'

'Lovely,' Adam said. 'How's the writing going?'

'Bad. But the insurance claim on the car came through. I *love* insurance claims. I make way more money out of them than I ever did from writing,' she whisper-cackled.

Adam laughed, as quietly as he could. 'What are you going to do if the thief appears?'

'I have pepper spray,' Stef said. 'I'll take him down.'

'Is that legal?'

'I think it is, if I tell the cops I was scared for my life.'

'Brilliant,' Adam said. 'Well, I'm going to go inside now.'

'OK. If it goes down, come back out and help me get the guy.'

'Will do.'

Adam went up the steps and let himself into the apartment. There was half a bottle of white wine in the fridge, and he emptied the best part of it into an oversized glass and slumped onto the sofa.

On the coffee table was the book he was reading: James Ellroy's *LAPD '53*, a collection of photographs of cops and crime scenes from that year, interspersed with Ellroy's illiberal laments. There were tough men in suits, pinky rings and college ties. Bodies sprawled across dirty sidewalks. Fifties Fords and Buicks with bullet-pocked windows. He opened the book and flicked through it. One of the dead women looked a little like Stef, he thought. A creak under the house announced that she was moving around now, perhaps giving up on her vigil.

He swigged the wine, feeling it loosen the tension in his shoulders and neck, its glow spreading within him. Perhaps, instead of lying around drinking and reading books, he should start looking for another job, he wondered. But doing what?

Sometimes, on these lonely nights in, he thought of writing to Sofia. Maybe that way he could exorcize her. He picked up his phone and clicked through to her Instagram account. There was a new photo at the top of her feed, of her with her family. She was seated, her baby son on her lap, smiling out at the camera with her parents standing behind her. Her mother had placed a hand on Sofia's shoulder, and was beaming with pride and happiness. Her father's shock of unruly, curly black hair hadn't thinned at all since Adam had known him. If they'd had a child together, he remembered now, and if it had been a boy, they'd talked about giving him her father's name.

God, he thought. How many dreams die on any given day? Writing to her was a stupid idea. What would he say? Sorry, of course. But that would be no use to her now. It was a selfish idea, because what he wanted out of it was her forgiveness, or maybe even just *her*. He wanted to talk to her about his memories, and find out if she still recalled them too. He wanted to ask if she remembered walking on the South Downs, behind her parents' house, during their first spring together. If she remembered the photo he'd taken of her as she moved through a patch of bright purple wildflowers, one hand in the air as she raised it to push back a strand of her long brown hair.

Or the time one summer, with his parents, when they'd driven high up the River Barle to Cow Castle, on Exmoor, for a picnic. Adam had carried the heavy basket half a mile or so from the car, and they'd lain on a blanket together by the sun-splashed water and gorged themselves on red wine, sandwiches and cake. He and Sofia had stripped to their underwear to swim, and he'd been able to feel the mild shock in his parents when they saw her tattoos: a line of William Blake's poetry on her ankle; a delicate spiral down her left side.

There was a ducks' nest on the far bank, and Sofia had swum close to it with a piece of bread, intending to feed them. When she'd thrown it in, the mother duck and her brood had all leapt out and swum off down the river, quacking in alarm. Back on the bank, as Adam and Sofia dried off in the sun, the ducks had become so tame that Adam had been able to pick one up, the moment caught in a photograph.

There'd been five years between Duck Day and the day he lost her.

He wanted to know if she, too, remembered the heat and light of their falling in love. If she remembered the things they'd said to each other. Her dream of making documentary films. Her fear of abandonment, because her father had left communist Hungary to commence the long process of moving his family to England.

If she ever thought of their fucking, for long entranced hours in his basement room, or in her childhood bedroom in Lewes, or in her parents' king-sized bed.

He wanted to know if she'd felt the giddying pauses in her heartbeat that he had, on receiving a text from her during the day. If she'd also had a bright, warm light – like a personal sun – blazing at the back of her mind because they'd had each other.

The thrill of it all. The sheer delight he'd felt, sitting at his desk and reading a text from her that told him how much she'd appreciated the grace and delicacy with which he'd orchestrated several moves on her, among their tangled sheets, that he was pretty certain were illegal in several states of the US. Or at an email telling him that 'basically I put on and lose weight regularly, but you are expected to love me regardless'.

He wanted to tell her that if only they'd met later, he'd have been better, he'd have been good. But he wasn't better, was he? He was what he'd always been, it seemed. He was lying on a couch, feeling himself to be in trouble, drinking, tight up against his agony.

After he and Sofia had been together a couple of years, his parents had taken them to Russia, where his sister was living. It was the last trip he'd ever make with his father. A few months later, he'd collapsed and died.

They all took a sleeper train from St Petersburg to Moscow, and Adam and Sofia shared a wood-panelled cabin with his parents. Sofia took the bunk above his dad, and when the train got under way, they opened a bottle of Burgundy to celebrate. Sofia, typically clumsy, had spilled her glass over the knees of his father's clean, pale slacks.

'Well,' his father had said, laughing it off in a way Adam had admired and even envied a little. 'I suppose you two had better make a swift exit while we get them into the sink.'

Leaving his parents in the tiny cabin, Adam and Sofia had stood with his sister and her boyfriend in the gap between carriages, drinking and smoking and laughing. The night air had roared past, sucking away the smoke. Sofia had spilled a glass of Baileys over his sister's top.

Then, the future had stretched ahead of them, like the endless-seeming rail tracks to Moscow. Sometimes he wondered if they were all still there, somewhere on time's tracks, flying through the night, excited by the still-free future, preserved as if in amber by the smoky, breathless air of that black space.

In Moscow, he'd stood beside a large brass plaque that had been indented into a public square. Surrounding it were staring homeless people.

'You turn your back and toss a coin over your shoulder,' his sister had said. 'And make a wish. If it lands on the plaque the wish comes true.'

Adam had done so. The coin had indeed landed on the large brass circle. The homeless people allowed it to settle before they ran and snatched over each other to grab it. The wish Adam had made had not come true.

They didn't, did they? he thought now. Not unless you made them.

He had cut what he and Sofia had grown together off at the stem. He had killed off his better selves, and was left with this one. A bit less skinny, a bit sadder, a bit older.

How, he wondered, can you go about liking yourself, when you've been such a total cunt?

An image of Isa surfaced in his mind, spread out before him in a squalid hotel room. He groaned, stood up, and went back to the fridge to open a fresh bottle.

PART TWO

15

On for tonight? the text from Craig said. *It's warm out, and daddy wants a brewski.*

Thursday had come, and Adam, too, was ready for a drink. Meg was back in the office, and he hadn't dared ask her to turn off the loud hip-hop she was playing. The charm of the rap Adam had grown up on, and had once loved ardently, seemed to have vanished. The zeitgeist now was for generic beats, autotuned vocals, and the blandly diaristic lyrics of unpleasant men rambling endlessly about money and sex.

In the end times, he thought, this will be the soundtrack. When all that's left of civilization is the charred, smoking ruins, the only sound will be one of these songs, playing from a dying, discarded mobile phone.

'She like that dick up on the whip,' the rapper on the latest song was saying, 'so I call her hood rat.'

Adam frowned, trying to focus on the Expedia page he had open and the flights to Denver he was reluctantly searching for. Another song had started, a Trumpian anthem about moving commas around in large sums of money.

Meg, seated at her desk, nodded her head and shimmied her shoulders to the song.

'Sick,' Scott said, raising two fingers in the air, pressed together to create a gun-like shape.

'I know, right?' Meg said.

Sick-making, Adam thought. He checked the flight details and hit the button to purchase them, then picked up his phone.

Def on, he replied to Craig. *Bar first?*

Hell yes. Donnie's. 7 p.m.

Donnie's Distillery was a sports bar on Santa Monica Boulevard, West Hollywood, which for some reason Craig seemed to favour. Adam wasn't sure if it was ironic, or whether even Craig occasionally needed a break from the tyrannical cool of the music industry.

They were seated in a small plastic booth, surrounded by a mixture of tourists and hard-bitten local drinkers. TVs seemed to be everywhere, playing a bewildering number of American sports. A waitress, whose large, prominently displayed breasts Adam had tried and failed not to notice, had served them a pitcher of beer along with two cold plastic glasses.

This was a different side of LA – geographically and culturally. It was tourists, boob jobs and beer pitchers. It could've been the bar Sarah Connor was attacked in in *Terminator*.

'So the party,' Adam said. 'It's at his house? I assume that's completely epic?'

'Oh yes,' Craig said, sipping his beer. 'He's made a *lot* of money.'

'Jesus,' Adam said. 'Maybe I should have been a booking agent.'

'You're not cut out for it,' Craig said, staring at a screen somewhere above Adam's head. 'You have to go to festivals and hang around the agents' compound arguing about who should suck whose dick.'

'Yes,' Adam said. 'Yes, there's always a payoff, thank God.'

'You should've been a *manager*,' Craig said. 'Like me. That way you wouldn't have to sit in a bloody office all day.'

'Yes – what exactly do you do all day?' Adam asked.

'Arcane manager stuff. Dark arts.'

'You sit around in your pants looking at Instagram, don't you?'

Craig laughed heartily. 'I seem to be largely sitting on planes these days.' He swung his legs out of the booth. 'Back in a mo.'

Adam gazed blankly at a sports screen, spinning a beer mat on the table. After a moment, the waitress reappeared, her large, tanned thighs squeezed into a pair of tight cut-offs above knee-high leather boots, the smell of her fragrance swirling in the booth's air. She had very big lips too, Adam noticed. He wondered if they'd been somehow enhanced, how you were supposed to tell these things.

'You guys doin' OK?' she asked.

'Yes thanks,' Adam said.

Craig reappeared as she departed, and appraised her from behind. 'Jesus wept,' he said.

'Quite,' Adam replied.

Craig turned to him, a devilish light playing in his eyes. 'Go to the toilet right now,' he said. 'The cubicle.'

'Why? What have you done in there? If it's some sort of spectacular turd then I don't want to see it.'

'Go. Now.'

Adam stood, and wove his way through a group of people playing with a basketball game and some others whooping and cursing around an air hockey table. At the long bar, a row of individual drinkers stared up at the TV screens.

There was no one in the toilet cubicle. Adam entered it, closing the small door – it had a large gap at its bottom and top – and found Craig's iPhone atop the cistern, a long line of cocaine on its screen.

'Ah,' he said to himself. 'Lovely.' His resolutions drifted into the mists at the back of his mind.

Peering over the top of the cubicle door, he rolled up a twenty, turned, and snorted the line with a flourish.

Back at the table, Craig was grinning up at him.

'Good?'

'Very good, thanks. Lucky someone left their phone in there for us to do lines off.'

Craig's smile vanished. 'That's my phone!'

Adam laughed, and handed it to him.

'Wanker,' Craig said. At the pool table beside their booth, two tall young men and a chubby blonde girl in denim shorts were playing a game. The girl was leaning over, lining up a shot, her bottom advancing towards Craig, who watched it calmly until it touched the edge of their table.

The girl looked around and giggled. 'Sorry,' she said.

'Anytime,' Craig said, winking at her.

The girl shook her bum at him, appealingly, and took her shot.

'Shit,' Craig said, sipping his pint. 'I love Hollywood.'

'So the party,' Adam said. 'Is it gonna be the usual thing where no one lets loose?'

'Not for us it won't,' Craig said. 'Lots of industry cunts though, I'm sure.'

'What's he like?'

'Mad as a badger.'

'Anything I should know?'

'Whatever happens,' Craig said, looking at Adam now, 'keep the fucking chang away from him. He's only just out of rehab.'

* * *

Their Uber wound upwards through the steep, narrow streets above Sunset, twisting and turning towards the highest echelons of the Hollywood Hills. The houses here were big, and very expensive-looking. In their front gardens were signs warning of private, armed-response security firms. Among the Priuses on the long, often gated driveways were the odd Ferrari, Porsche or Aston Martin. It was as though a white village in southern Spain had been razed to the ground and a cluster of paranoid millionaires' fantasy homes built in its stead.

Looming above, through the moon-roof of their car, was the Hollywood sign.

'Have you been here before?' Adam thought to ask.

'To the hills?'

'To this house.'

'No.' Craig's eyes glinted. 'This is a new high in my social achievement.'

The driver dropped them at the bottom of a long, narrow driveway, with tall hedges either side of it. The gates were open, and they set off up the steep slope. It took a full minute's walking for the house to come into view, and when it did they both stopped – for breath as much as to take a moment to admire it.

'Jesus Christ,' Craig said.

The house was built on a broad, high ridge – the last line of buildings before a steep, scrubby slope that led up to the sign itself. The entrance was on its upper level, but they could see that another, lower floor had been built into the dip beyond the ridge. It was massive: a modernist construction of glass, steel and concrete, gleaming in the late sunlight.

'How much, you reckon?' Adam said.

'Ten, twelve,' Craig replied.

'How old is he?'

'Thirty-five.'

'Bastard,' Adam said.

They walked up to the front door and rang the bell.

It was another full minute before it opened. When it did, a short man in a white dressing gown, swimming trunks and big black sunglasses stood before them. His hair was very short and neat, as though cut that day. He smiled, showing brilliant white teeth, and threw his arms wide.

'Craig,' he said, as they embraced. Appealing voice, Adam noted. Warm and resonant, like a radio DJ's.

'Joel!' Craig said. 'This is my friend Adam. The label guy I told you about.'

'Sure, sure, great to meet you, man,' Joel said, embracing Adam too. 'Sorry about the attire, guys,' he said, glancing down at himself. 'We're in the pool. Come out back.'

They followed him through the house, where he'd left wet footprints on the way to let them in. The floors were tiled in deep red marble, veined with gleaming white. Positively villainous, Adam thought.

In the cavernous lounge, a huge painting – evidently a Picasso – was hanging on the far wall.

'Holy shit,' Adam said. 'Is that—'

'Real? Sure,' Joel said. 'Not mine, though. I look after it for the original owner. He's in Hawaii these days, surfing. Great dude, man.'

'Wow,' Adam said.

'I know. If only, right? A little way out of my reach, that's for sure. Come on through, guys. There's a bar by the pool. It's a help yourself thing, if that's cool?'

'Sure is,' Craig said, turning to Adam with his trademark rodenty grin.

Beyond the French windows were a mid-sized, kidney-shaped pool and a large Jacuzzi. A separate pool house sat at one end of it, bigger than most of the flats Adam had lived in in London. On the far side of the water was a portable chrome bar, with two ice buckets and dozens of bottles. Fifteen or twenty people were milling around the edges of the water, in which two very thin, tanned girls were splashing and laughing.

'Welcome, guys,' Joel said, turning and spreading his arms. 'Get yourselves a drink! Let's hang!'

'Sick,' Craig said. 'Can I get you something?'

'Not for me, thanks,' Joel said, smile widening beneath the impenetrable shades. 'I'm off the sauce. Started enjoying myself a little too much for a moment there.'

'Well, you look great,' Craig said, edging towards the bar.

'Thanks, man!' Joel said. 'I feel *so* good.' He let the robe drop to the floor, revealing the sort of stocky physique that Adam thought of as very American, and jumped into the pool, dive-bombing the shrieking girls.

Adam and Craig made their way around the tiled edge of the water, nodding at the other guests. Everyone else seemed more subdued than Joel, the atmosphere among them one of mild tension. No one appeared to be drinking very much.

In LA, Adam knew, social life was working life. Barbecues, drinks, dinners and lunches: all were opportunities that must not be squandered – especially when they were hosted by someone very important. The fear of faux pas at the heart of the power-hang had induced a sort of meta-socializing, where people mainly talked about how much they were enjoying hanging while the hanging was actually happening.

For Adam, barbecues and parties were things you did with friends, occasions at which you could drink rather heavily without fearing the consequences. The very notion of friendship was different, in LA, among the people he met at events like these. The concept was closer to what he thought of as acquaintance.

'Whisky?' Craig asked him, making himself busy with the drinks. One of Craig's many charms, as far as Adam was concerned, was that he seemed comfortable in any circumstances.

'Please,' Adam said.

One of the girls had climbed out of the pool, and she approached the bar, throwing a towel over her shoulders. She was pretty in a big-eyed, girlish way. Her pupils were widened, Adam noticed, and she seemed to have trouble focusing, a loopy expression on her face.

'Hey,' she said. 'I'm so thirsty. What're *you* drinking?' Her accent was what Adam thought of as valley-girl – all elongated vowels, and a sing-song intonation that made any statement sound like a question.

'Whisky,' Adam said, smiling at her.

The girl was dripping on his shoes, but he resisted the temptation to step away from her.

'Ew,' she said. 'Is there, like, vodka?'

'Yep,' Craig said. 'How'd you take it?'

'Tonic!' the girl said, like a child ordering a long-promised ice cream. 'And lots of ice!'

'Coming right up,' Craig said.

'What're you *doing* later?' the girl asked Adam. Her jaw was working, he noticed, realizing that she was on some form of ecstasy.

'You mean after the party?' Adam said.

'Yah,' the girl said, eyes rolling in her head.

'Probably going back to Silver Lake,' he said.

'Where's *that*?'

'It's about ten minutes east of here, on the freeway.'

'That sounds *far*.'

'It's where I live,' Adam replied.

'Well,' the girl said, smiling vacantly as Craig handed her the drink, 'get back to Hollywood safely after.'

Joel appeared, dripping wet in his snug swimming trunks and the sunglasses. Droplets of pool water were now running down the lenses.

'Hey,' he said, his smile still in place. 'Let's get a photo!'

'Cool!' the girl said.

'Wait wait wait! Let me get in there too,' the other girl in the pool said. She began moving through the water, her efforts to do so rapidly appearing like a strange, strenuous dance.

'Want me to take it, Joel?' a serious-looking man asked, standing close to them in a leather jacket, white t-shirt and black jeans.

'Please man, yeah,' Joel said.

'Use my phone,' Craig said, handing it to him.

Joel put one arm each around Adam and Craig. The loopy girl went to Craig, the other to Adam. She slipped a cold, wet arm beneath his shoulders, dripping all over his left side. Her nipples, he couldn't help noticing, were protruding quite sharply through her bikini top. He wondered if other men were able to train themselves not to notice things like that – whether they even needed to.

A droplet of pool water ran down the back of his shirt, and he grimaced as the flash went off.

The girl turned to him as the group broke apart. 'Beware,' she said quietly.

'Pardon?' Adam said.

'*Beware. Of Joel,*' she said, and jumped back into the pool.

'Alright!' Joel shouted happily. 'This is Lynx, by the way.' He gestured at the man who'd taken the picture.

'Nice to meet you guys,' Lynx said, his serious expression remaining in place.

'Hey – guess what Lynx's brother is called,' Joel said, grinning fiercely.

'Go on,' Adam replied.

'*Eagle!*' Joel said.

Adam wasn't sure whether to laugh, so he smiled politely.

'Guess what Lynx's *mom* is called…' Joel said.

'I can't possibly,' Adam replied.

'Moon!' Joel said, delighted.

'Now,' he continued, for some reason directing all of this to Adam. 'Guess what Lynx's *dad* is called.'

'Tiger?' Adam said.

'Terry!' Joel said, and laughed uproariously. 'Fuck, man. I love you fucking Brits!'

'Yeah,' Lynx said, in a tone Adam couldn't quite identify, and lit a cigarette.

Craig was playing with his phone, and when Adam glanced at the screen he saw that he was uploading the photo to Instagram. Sure enough, Adam's phone buzzed in his pocket, presumably telling him he'd been tagged in the picture.

'It's great hanging, guys!' Joel said. 'Hey, you want the guided tour?'

'Sure,' Adam said, 'love to.'

'C'mon, guys, bring your drinks. Let's do this,' Joel said. Slipping on a pair of flip-flops and his robe, he set off back into the house. Adam wished he'd take the sunglasses off, so he could see the eyes behind them.

'This is Italian marble,' Joel said, scuffing a tile with a flip-flop as they re-entered the lounge. 'The guy I bought the place from built the bathroom suite with it too. Imported a shit ton of the stuff all the way from Europe. But it was too heavy for the floor, so the whole thing collapsed onto the hillside,' he said, laughing. 'BOOM. Discount, motherfucker.'

He turned and tossed them a grin. 'I mean, I love the guy to death, but he's a little screwy, know what I mean? I'm like, stick to the surfing, bro.'

'What did he do, before the surfing I mean?' Adam asked.

'Movie guy,' Joel replied. 'Big deal back in the day.' He pushed open a door, which revealed a large bathroom. The suite was made of normal, if expensive-looking, porcelain, as far as Adam could tell. Above the toilet was a vivid painting of a naked tattooed woman. Its colours were so lurid that Adam felt an odd reluctance to look at it properly. After a moment, though, he couldn't help it. The woman was seated on a toilet herself, legs spread with two fingers between them, displaying her vagina while she pouted at the viewer.

'Nice,' Craig said.

'Through here is my home office,' Joel said, leading them into what was apparently a separate wing – a sort of long, wide, glass-walled corridor of a room, with views either side of the hill. On a side table was a large watch-winder, with three Rolexes behind the glass.

'Serious stuff,' Adam said, peering at them.

'Those're my babies,' Joel said.

He turned to face them, leaning back on a wide mid-century desk, his teeth shining in the dimming light as the sun dipped under the hills behind him. Above his head, through the window, Adam saw that there was one more house on the hill: a sort of Disney vision of a Georgian mansion, with window shutters giving it a more homely, American effect. Joel, Adam realized, was only second to the top of the hill.

'God,' Joel said. 'It's interesting not drinking at parties.'

'Must be,' Craig said. 'But just think how beautiful tomorrow morning will be.'

'Exactly.'

'What happened,' Adam asked, 'to make you stop?'

Craig shot him a look.

'Well,' Joel said. 'I was at the EDC festival, in Vegas. I usually rent a house up there, throw an after-party for the artists. It's become kind of a tradition. Everyone loves it. Shit gets real wild.'

'I've heard,' Craig said.

'This year got a little too wild. One of the DJs wanted me to order up some women… You know,' he grinned.

'Uh oh,' Craig said. He was peering at a framed photograph, which appeared to show a very young Joel, playing bass on a stage with blissed-out eyes and a cigarette in his mouth.

'Yeah,' Joel said, grin widening. 'Bad Joel. Horrible Joel.'

'And what happened?' Adam asked.

Craig glanced at him again, tickling Adam's contrarian instinct. He didn't like the idea of pussyfooting around the super-agent.

'Instead of hookers I got the goddamn vice squad,' Joel said. 'It was a mess.'

'Wow,' Adam said.

'Yeah,' Joel replied. 'They were after the madam, not me. Tapped the fucking call or something. But the house wasn't exactly clean. Luckily I have a great security team.'

Craig laughed. 'Shit. Dramatic stuff.'

'It gave me a little pause, shall we say,' Joel said. Then, adopting a more contrite tone: 'So now I'm trying to nurture the better side of myself. I have to celebrate the things that are good about me, rather than everything that's worst.'

Aha, Adam thought. Therapy! The dreadful truth of platitudes.

'Who lives up there?' he asked, gesturing up the hill behind Joel.

Joel's face stiffened, becoming squarer.

'This heiress chick. Owns half of West Hollywood. Bars and restaurants, at least one hotel, I think.'

'Right, yes. You don't like her?' Adam asked.

'She's fine. It's her fucking house husband I can't stand. He's like this creepy hipster cowboy. He and I are sort of at war.'

'How come?'

'He's just one of those guys that's a little too good to be true, do you know what I mean? All the women up here think he's super hot. He has this long fucking hair he's always playing with. Teaches the local kids soccer, always playing Mr Perfect. Which is easy when you do jack shit all day because your wife keeps you.'

'Right,' Craig nodded.

'And when we first moved in, I happened to mention I was learning to surf, and the guy was all over me, talking about his vintage boards, how we should get in the water sometime, tossing his long fucking hair around like he's talking to a girl. And eventually he insists on lending me this board, some ancient wooden thing he says Brian Wilson used to own. Perfect board to learn on, according to him.

'So, I stuck it out by the pool and said thanks, and he's all horrified like "you're not gonna keep it out here, are you?" Apparently the sun would destroy thc wood or the varnish or something. And there's usually someone staying in the pool house. So it ends up in here. It was leaning against that wall, in fact.' He pointed to where Craig was standing.

'And one night, after a really long day, I took a highly annoying call in here from another agent who'd recently fucking stolen one of my artists, and after I put the phone down I just kicked the surfboard in two, like this…' Joel stood up, kicked a muscular, tanned leg out from under his robe, and made a karate-movie 'ya!'

'Holy shit,' Craig said.

'And then my maid, God bless her idiotic little soul, leaves the two pieces of the board out in the street on recycling day. Sure enough, Mr Perfect comes along with a fucking topknot and his track pants, dribbling his fucking soccer ball, and sees the board and flips the fuck out. I had to pay him ten thousand dollars, and he still won't speak to me. Which in itself is no bad thing…'

Joel raised his left hand to his chin and gazed down at the wooden floorboards of his study, before turning his eyes to the house above his on the hill. 'Ten thousand dollars,' he said quietly. 'Every time I see the guy, I want to fucking kill him.'

There was a long, chilly pause. Adam glanced at Craig, who seemed to be avoiding his glance.

'But the worst thing about that house,' Joel continued, brightening fractionally, 'is they overlook my Jacuzzi. And I *really* like to fuck in my Jacuzzi.'

Craig laughed. 'Well,' he said. 'Maybe they enjoy the show.'

'Right?' Joel laughed. 'So, guys.' He looked at them, expectant. 'Enjoying hanging?'

Adam glanced at Craig again. 'Definitely. Amazing,' Craig said.

'Well, cool,' Joel said. He rubbed his hands together, as if waiting. My God, Adam thought. He wants to throw himself off the wagon!

'So, you guys partying tonight?' Joel asked.

'Keeping it low-key,' Craig said casually.

Joel's smile dimmed fractionally. 'Cool, well, the night's young, man. Get a couple drinks, let's see what happens.'

'Definitely,' Craig said.

'Yes,' Adam agreed. 'Great. It's very good of you to invite us.'

Joel threw an arm around Adam. 'Of course, brother,' he said. Then: 'Family.'

This, too, was standard procedure at the power-hang. People you'd spent all of ten minutes with, and would probably never contact you again, abruptly referring to you as *family*.

After letting go of Adam, Joel headed back towards the door. 'Feel free to look around the rest of the house, boys,' he said. 'I better go check on the girls.'

And with that, he departed.

'Fuck me,' Adam said, peering at the Rolexes again.

'Whatever you do, don't give him any drugs,' Craig said.

'What are you so worried about?' Adam asked him.

'My boss. Told him I was coming up here tonight. He's friends with Joel. Told me under no circumstances was I to take drugs into this house.'

'Aha,' Adam said. 'I always forget you have a boss.'

'Fuck off,' Craig said. 'Let's find somewhere to do a line. I'm almost fucking sober myself.'

A corridor beyond the living room led to the open door of a generously proportioned bedroom. Adam was about to suggest they'd found the right spot, when they saw a pair of slim, pretty feet with painted nails poking out from under the bed. Whoever they belonged to groaned when she heard them coming in.

Back in the corridor, they glanced at each other. 'Weird,' Adam said.

'Fucked,' Craig agreed. 'Pool house? Think I saw a side entrance from the house.'

Sure enough, they found a door in the place they'd expected. Craig opened it slowly. Inside, an old lady was lying on a bed watching a huge TV, her bare feet – comparing unfavourably to those in the bedroom – raised on a pile of pillows.

'I'm his mom,' she said, without looking at them. 'When you see him, can you ask him to confirm he will take me back to the desert on Saturday? I'm tired of this.'

'Sure,' Adam said.

Craig closed the door on her.

'Fuck it,' he said. 'Bathroom.'

After they'd locked themselves in, Adam looked at the painting above the toilet while Craig carved out the lines.

'We need to be quick,' Craig said.

'I've never seen you so flustered,' Adam replied. The painting was quite erotic, he decided, but in a very regretful way. He opened the bathroom cabinet. Inside were rows and rows of medication in small tubs, most of them with warnings about controlled substances on them.

'Holy shit,' Adam said. 'This guy is a fucking basket case.'

Beside the medication was a saline nasal spray – the cokehead's best friend.

'Here,' Craig said. Adam snorted his line, and they high-fived.

'Christ,' Craig muttered. 'Worse than being in a bar, trying to get high in here.'

When Adam opened the door, Joel was standing directly outside it. His smile, beneath the jet-black shades, was by now quite frightening.

'What's up, guys?' he said.

* * *

Three hours later, a hard core of them were in Joel's bedroom. The woman who'd been under the bed had now emerged. She was very pale and thin. A small Star of David was tattooed on her inner right wrist, and she'd only spoken to tell them she had a headache.

Just then, she was leaning over a large mirror in the centre of the bed and snorting a line of cocaine.

Adam looked at his watch. It was 12.30 in the morning.

Joel was leaning against the headboard, holding court, telling a story about one of his artists pulling a gun on a festival promoter.

The loopy girl from the pool was lying across the foot of the bed, wearing only her bikini top and a towel, saying 'oh my God' to Joel's story. Lynx, standing by the open window, was smoking, and the other pool girl was cupping her cell phone to her ear, ordering more drugs.

Craig, seated by the dressing table, had gone quite pale.

Adam looked at his phone. He appeared to have several notifications from Instagram, and he opened the app to view them. One, a message from Angelina, made his overworked heart beat even faster.

'Hey playa!' it said. 'We should meet up next week.'

She had liked the photo of him standing by a pool with his arm around a super-agent, the Hollywood Hills rising pinkly behind them in the sunset.

'My *chest* is *hurting*,' the loopy girl said.

'Don't worry, baby, eventually you just go to sleep,' the pale woman – apparently Joel's significant other – told her, sniffing.

'No,' Lynx said from the window. 'Eventually you die.'

No one, apart from Adam, appeared to find this comment remarkable.

'Hey Adam,' Joel said, grinning at him like a hungry vampire.

'Yes?'

'Your drink's empty, man. C'mon, let's get you a refill.'

Joel leapt off the bed and put his arm around Adam, leading him out of the bedroom and through the lounge doors towards the bar, which stood in silence now beyond the gleaming pool. The water was very still, the angle of the external lights making its surface appear pure white, as though it was filled with milk.

'What're you having?' Joel asked. His voice, post-cocaine, had gone a little gravelly. It really was quite pleasing on the ear.

'Whisky, please.' Adam scanned the bar for Scotch, and once again failed to see any. 'On the rocks.'

Joel picked up a bottle of bourbon and poured him the drink, moving around the bar like a professional mixologist.

'What are you having?' Adam asked him.

'I'm sticking to the Diet Coke for now, man,' Joel said, his grin a touch rueful now. 'Already kinda fucked up on one resolution.'

'Well,' Adam said. 'Everyone needs a blowout every now and again. Everything in moderation.'

Joel stopped moving and looked Adam in the eye – or, at least, aimed the shades directly at him. 'Thank you, man,' he said.

Adam nodded awkwardly.

'So, you guys, your label. What do you do again? It's, like, indie rock, right?'

'Not so much any more, actually. We're focusing on more commercial electronic stuff, especially here.'

'Right,' Joel nodded vaguely. 'What kinda thing? Anyone I'd know?'

'Falconz, perhaps?' Adam said. 'They're our biggest artist now.'

Joel frowned. 'Right, yeah… Those guys are coming back?'

'They sure are,' Adam told him, trying to sound bright. 'Bigger than ever. They're the Coldplay of EDM.'

When they reached the bedroom door, Joel turned to face Adam.

'You're a good guy, man,' he said. 'I'll remember what you said.'

Before Adam had a chance to ask him which part of what he'd said, Joel was back in the bedroom, arms raised.

'What's *up*?' he asked his assembled guests.

Adam resumed his place in the corner and sipped his whisky. Craig was snorting a line of coke. The remainder of the tableau was much as it had been.

After a minute or so, a strange mood came over him, and he excused himself to go to the toilet. Once inside, he locked the door, and slumped down on the seat to pee. He resisted the urge to take his phone out of his pocket. Fuck you, he thought, regarding Angelina. The sentiment immediately struck him as a little unfair. Searching for something more positive, he thought of Erica.

Saturday. Less than two days from now. Less time than it took to recover from the sort of hangover he was working towards. Before he had time to question the decision he'd abruptly made, he sprayed half a bottle of Joel's saline spray into his nostrils and crept out of the bathroom, then the house. He had to walk a fair way down the hill before his phone found a signal again, and when it had he ordered an Uber. It was 1 a.m. It could have been worse.

Erica, he thought. I want to go on another date with Erica. I want to feel clean and good and I want to be with her.

'Long night?' the driver asked Adam, glancing at him in his rear-view mirror.

'Could've been,' he said. 'But I escaped.'

16

Friday morning didn't start as badly as he'd feared. He woke with his alarm and spent a few minutes lying still, trying to gauge his hangover on his personal Richter scale. Six, he thought. Maybe, just maybe, a five – though he hadn't moved his head very much just yet.

By the time he'd drunk three cups of coffee, showered and eaten a banana, he decided it was hovering around four. Not bad, considering.

Next, he ran the Shit Report. This was his regular, psychological debrief after a heavy bout of drinking, during which he cast his mind back over the night before for any embarrassments, failures, indiscretions or general bad things. The Shit Report often involved him talking to himself – mainly internally, but sometimes, on very bad days, out loud.

Today's list was far from his worst. Cocaine, obviously. The blight of his adult life. A departure from a party without saying his farewells. No biggie. An Irish goodbye, as the Americans called it. Craig was quite partial to those himself, so he'd doubtless understand. Plus, they'd all be feeling too guilty and awful themselves to worry about Adam.

Knocking a super-agent off the wagon? Not a shred of guilt there, he found. It would make a good story. And anyway, it had been Craig's fault really.

It was a relief to have been only a side note in the night's story, rather than its headline. Things were not too bad. The hangover was even developing into the other, rarer variety he experienced, characterized by a sense of warm benevolence, freedom from care, and a desire to be generous and kind to his fellow men.

It was in the spirit of this optimism that he decided to call his sister Elizabeth. It would be late in Kuala Lumpur, but she was a night owl.

She took a long while to answer, but sounded fully awake when she did.

'Hello,' she said. 'This is a surprise.'

'Hi,' Adam said, brightly. 'Yes, thought we were overdue a catch-up.'

'Nothing terrible's happened then?' she said. Her speech was brisk and firm, a touch sardonic.

'No. Not that I know of.'

'What time is it there?'

'8.45,' he said. 'In the morning.'

'Coming up to midnight here,' she said.

'Yes. Sorry.'

'It's fine,' she said. 'It's nice to hear from you.'

To Adam's relief, she sounded as though she meant it.

'Have you spoken to Mum?' he asked her.

'Two days ago. Didn't seem to be any change.'

'Yes, same when I spoke to her.'

'When was that?'

'Hmm,' Adam said. 'Ten days ago.'

'Weird. She didn't mention you'd called her.'

Adam chose not to correct this small misassumption. 'Well, that's hardly surprising…'

'Suppose so,' Elizabeth said. 'Though she's weirdly good at remembering who she's spoken to. What did she say?'

'She asked when I was coming back.'

'To visit, or permanently?'

'Both.'

'She asked me the same,' Elizabeth said.

'What did you say?'

'I said I'd be back for Christmas.'

'And what about the permanently part?' Adam asked her.

'Not sure. I've had a job offer actually,' she said.

'Really? Where?'

'Russia again. There's a growing demand.'

'I bet,' Adam said. 'Everyone's terrified that Putin'll sabotage their election, or invade the Balkans.'

'The Baltics,' his sister said. 'Thankfully for the Balkans, they're short on geopolitical significance.'

Adam flushed with shame. He'd known this very well, but the fear he felt of making himself seem stupid to his sister was, as ever, self-fulfilling.

'It also remains unclear how Putin is able to physically prevent US presidential candidates from visiting swing states,' his sister said. 'Perhaps I'll get the scoop.'

'Maybe you will,' Adam said, too chastened to attempt to spar. 'Well, congratulations.'

'And you?' Elizabeth asked.

'I told Mum I'd be here a while longer.'

'You don't sound very happy about it.'

'Don't I?' he said, surprised.

'No.'

'Well, I'm not really enjoying my work very much.'

'Right,' Elizabeth said. 'That's different to sounding happy about being where you are, though.'

'Yes,' he said, frowning.

'And what's happening at work?'

'I think that, essentially, I don't really like the music very much any more.'

'Hmm,' Elizabeth said. 'Well, it is a business after all. But I know you've always found that side of things very boring.'

Adam didn't say anything.

'You know, I was quite envious of you when you started this job. You loved it so much. I've never experienced that, to be honest.'

The idea of his sister's envying him had never occurred to Adam. He wished she'd told him at the time.

'Well, sadly things have changed a bit now,' he said.

'Perhaps you should seize the chance to do something else,' Elizabeth said. 'I assume you're talented at it, and now with all that under your belt…'

'Yes,' he said. 'I've been wondering about it. What about you? Will you take the job in Russia?'

'Yes,' she said. 'I reckon so.'

'Is it Moscow?'

'Yes.'

'And after that?'

'I might go home, you know.'

Adam felt an unexpected twinge of something like envy himself.

'I've been thinking about Russia,' he said. 'When I came with Mum and Dad.'

'And Sofia,' Elizabeth said.

After he'd lost her, his sister hadn't spoken to him for a month.

'Yes. Remember Dad, drinking vodka shots with that ex-KGB guy, in the bar we all liked near your flat?'

His sister laughed. 'Yes. Don't think I'll ever forget that. Nor will I forget Mum's nagging at him: "Be careful, you're not used to vodka."'

'He hated that,' Adam laughed.

'I know.'

'He held his own, though. Mind you, I think it's easier to drink vodka in large quantities than other spirits.'

'I don't agree with that at all,' Elizabeth said.

These confident dismissals of Adam's statements were his least favourite thing about his sister. They were put into sharper relief by his life in LA, where no one spoke to each other like this. His optimistic spirit dimming, he decided it was time to go to work.

'Anyway, that sort of thing didn't do him much good in the end, did it?' Elizabeth said.

'No,' Adam replied. He closed his mind to the darkening memories, turning to the window and the bright sunshine outside. 'You should come to LA,' he said. 'Come and visit.'

'Yes,' she said, neutrally. 'Maybe when I'm settled back in Moscow.'

'OK, sis. Bye for now,' he said. 'Stay in touch.'

* * *

The Friday feeling was restored somewhat by his saunter to work. The day was still cool, and a red-tailed hawk was flying low above Sunset, scattering the pigeons from their overhead cables. He paused several times to watch it, and to snap pictures on his phone.

His hangover, he knew, would worsen steeply after lunch. But for now at least, the world seemed imbued with a sweetly melancholic beauty. Presumably it was this delusion that could be witnessed in late-stage alcoholics as they became mawkish with drink. Still, it felt good to Adam as he strolled up the hill.

The office was empty when he got in. He set up his laptop and stood for a silent moment before the window, peering out at the flawless sky and the towering palms.

He'd just decided to go and make more coffee while his emails downloaded, when he noticed a large piece of paper standing in the centre of Scott's desk, propped against the wall. It had been neatly printed in a flamboyant serif font, on the special cream cardstock that the company had used for The Suffering's showcase invitations. Within an elegant, floral border, it read:

B (Broad appeal)
O (Originality)
S (Synch)
H (Hunger)

'Jesus fucking Christ,' Adam muttered, anger quickening his pulse. Scott, like a lovesick schoolboy, had printed out the Autodidact's latest A & R decree and displayed it above his desk. As far as Adam was concerned, he might as well have declared war.

The entire company had been subjected to this recent dogma via an email to Global Team. No longer would signing artists be about gut instinct, the Autodidact had said. No longer would it be about excitement, fans among the staff, passion, or any other such strange and immeasurable concept. 'Is it any good?' he had declared, should be the last question you ask yourselves.

Going forward, A & R would be about BOSH.

Broad appeal: how wide was the market for any given project?

Originality: how fresh was the music this artist made?

Synch: would the music sell to advertisers?

Hunger: how badly did the artist want it?

This, to Scott, was apparently dynamite. A credo by which to live. Having put away the childish things he'd once professed to love, he was now a fully paid-up subscriber. Scott was a disciple, a true believer; a recruit to the Autodidact's radical new cause.

As far as Adam was concerned, that made him a Judas. And besides, how on earth would they explain this to any visiting artist?

'What's that, guys?' 'Oh, it's our A & R policy. We do the whole thing by box-ticking. How many can we cross off for you?'

Adam carefully picked up the manifesto, pulled down his trousers and underpants, and wiped it between his buttocks. The card was quite difficult to bend, but he put in the effort. Having only recently showered, his bottom was clean, which made the gesture merely symbolic. But it was the thought that counted.

When he'd finished, he considered drawing an immense, erect penis on the edict too, but decided that might be a step too far. After all, it might not be the best time for something like that to get back to the Autodidact.

For quite a long moment, he felt much better. It was only afterwards, when propping it back up, that he realized how crumpled the previously very uncrumpled, lovingly created sheet of card was.

Scott, Adam realized with a small tremor of panic, would certainly notice this. He was someone who owned a purpose-made, Plexiglas-covered display board, onto which he'd fastened the ticket and, later, the backstage laminate, for every single gig he'd ever attended. Adam reeled at the psychology of a person who'd begun this project at the age of twelve. As someone who'd destroyed his Guns N' Roses CDs on discovery of Nirvana, he couldn't conceive of anyone having a personality so continuous, and so consistent.

One day, he thought, I will get my hands on that board, and I will draw the biggest, most lovingly crafted cock that has ever been drawn.

The A & R edict dragged him back into the here and now. Soon, Scott would come to work. It would be glaringly obvious that someone had taken his special notice, done something strange and aggressive with it, and then put it back in place. With a touch of genuine shame, Adam realized that the only person who'd do something like that was him.

Heat rose up from under his shirt and flushed into his face, the panic coming over him in a wave. He glanced around, and noticed the stack of LPs beside his desk. Picking half of them up, he placed them on his desk, put Scott's special card on top of them, and placed the other half on top of that. Pressing down on the stack, he felt sweat break out on his back and under his arms.

He'd just removed the top stack when the door downstairs opened. Shit, he thought. The card was now very flat, but very creased, as opposed to crumpled. It had an aged appearance now, like a flower petal – or a gig ticket – tenderly pressed. Fuck it, he thought. Deny everything.

Hastily, he put the notice back in its place and sat down in his chair, resting on its arms and sticking his legs out to affect a relaxed, unflustered pose.

Ernesto, the studious in-house press officer, appeared on the stairs, his hair neatly parted at the side and his shirt as pristine as Scott's notice had been not so long before. Ernesto was one of the few members of staff who seemed to find Adam's management style entirely reasonable. In fact, it seemed to Adam that Ernesto actually looked up to him.

'Hey,' he said as he emerged into the office.

'Good morning!' Adam replied, more loudly than he'd intended.

'Someone's in a good mood,' Ernesto said, smiling. 'Want me to make coffee?'

'Please,' Adam said gratefully.

Ernesto nodded and began to turn back to the staircase, but something had apparently caught his eye. He glanced downwards from Adam's face, his expression clouding over momentarily.

'Ah,' he said, as though he'd noticed something he thought it best to mention. He hesitated, and then apparently thought better of it, setting off down the stairs. Adam could have sworn that the young PR's cheeks had reddened slightly as he did so.

Ernesto having disappeared, Adam glanced down now too. A bead of sweat ran down his temple as his worst fear was confirmed. His belt and flies were undone.

He tried to think of conclusions, other than the obvious one – that his boss was an office masturbator – that Ernesto might reach as to what he'd been doing.

None of them gave him much hope.

* * *

Finally, coffee at his side, his face hidden from Ernesto's glance by his laptop, he saw that an email had come in from Isa, with the subject line **LA.**

Seeing it crystallized an oncoming headache. When he put his fingers to his brow, he could feel a small vein in his temple pulsing under his touch.

His hangover was clearly reverting to the common or garden variety: dread and exhaustion topped off with a dose of persecution mania.

He opened the email, into which the Autodidact and Serena had both been copied:

Hi Adam
It's been a long time, I hope you're doing good. I'm really looking forward to rejoining the company and moving out to LA. Jason suggested we have a Skype call to talk about it. I've got a fair few questions. Would today work for you?
I could do it at 5 p.m. my time if that works.
All best,
Isa x

This is really going to happen, Adam thought. Bubble wrap, I'm coming for you.

A small part of him dying, he replied:

Yes, it's great news. 5 p.m. is fine. Call me then.
A

He looked at his watch. 5 p.m. in Britain would arrive in ten minutes' time in Los Angeles.

Scott appeared just as Adam was awaiting the call.

'Morning,' Adam said to him.

'Yoooo,' Scott said.

'Good evening?' Adam asked.

'It was great. Hung out at Casa Nueva and saw James Blake. That place is so awesome.'

'Excellent,' Adam said. *My evening was lovely too, thanks very much.*

Scott sniffed, loudly, twitching his head upwards as he did so. Adam watched from the corner of his eye. Scott didn't seem to have noticed anything wrong with his manifesto. He put his headphones in, opened up his Spotify playlist, and began tapping away at a chat window and sniffing every few seconds.

Adam, who had been raised not to sniff repeatedly – let alone loudly – in public, flinched each time he did so.

At 9.15, Adam's Skype rang out, a picture of Isa smiling and squinting on a bright beach appearing on his screen. 'What fresh hell is this?' he muttered, and clicked to accept, putting his headphones in.

Isa's head materialized on the screen. She didn't look any older than when he'd last seen her, more than two years previously. Her hair was still straightened, framing her large cheekbones and alert, wary eyes – the face he'd once known so well. He tried to read her expression, looking for the hatred he was sure she felt, but she'd always been good at making herself hard to read.

He had a vivid flashback to the last time he'd seen her on Skype. They'd been having quite explicit screen sex. Now, the sudden recollection made sweat break out on his brow.

'Hi, Adam,' she said, flashing a quick smile.

'Hello,' he replied.

'How's everything going?'

'Good, thanks. Busy as ever.'

'I'm sure…' Isa said. Adam was fairly certain he detected a note of sarcasm, emphasized by the short pause.

'So,' she said. 'How's life in LA? Do you like it out there?'

'Yes, I do. Most of the time it's a great place to live.'

'It's funny,' she said. 'I can't quite picture you in LA.'

'Why not?'

'Oh, I don't know. You're so neurotic and English. You don't really do the whole laid-back thing, do you?'

'I suppose not,' Adam said. 'But there's plenty of neurosis in LA. Anyway, it sounds as though you'll see me out here for yourself soon enough.'

'Yes,' she nodded. 'I'm very excited.'

'Me too,' Adam said. 'What happened with the degree course? Everyone said you were really pleased to get onto it.'

'It wasn't for me. Full of posh boys trying to get bigger jobs in finance or whatever.'

'Right…'

There was silence for a moment, and Adam tried to think of something to say.

'How's everything else?' he asked. 'How's your brother doing?'

Isa had been born and raised in east London, by first-generation Jamaican immigrants. She and her older sister were very successful, but she had a younger brother who was troubled. He'd been the cause of many a hushed, urgent telephone call on the office staircase in London.

A slight frown tightened over her face, and despite the digitization and the thousands of miles, Adam felt a distinct chill emanate from her.

'He's fine.'

He hadn't intended the question to injure her, and wished he hadn't asked it.

'Good,' he said, glancing away from the screen. 'So where shall we start?'

'Well,' Isa said, with a professional smile, 'Jason tells me you're in charge of the HR there. I'd like you to run me through it all, please. Health plans, office policy and all that sort of thing.'

Adam took a deep breath. 'OK,' he said.

'I'd also like to discuss exactly where I'll be sitting in the office, and what the layout is, given the circumstances.'

'Yes,' Adam said.

'And Jason told me you might be able to help with some practical stuff too.'

'What sort of stuff?'

'Well, I've been to LA a couple of times. I know the place a bit. But I'll need a car, and a place to live obviously. So I'd like some advice about sorting out my social security number and driver's licence and that sort of thing.'

'Right.'

Isa had leaned a little closer to the camera. The smile was widening on her lips, and she was looking straight at him, unblinking.

'So if we can talk through all of that,' she said, 'that'd be brilliant. And I'd appreciate it if you could send me a follow-up email with all the info you have in writing, too. I'm sure it's a lot to digest.'

'OK,' Adam said, unable to hide his annoyance any longer.

'C'mon, mate,' Isa said. 'Jason told me you'd be only too happy to help.'

Unable to stop himself, Adam put his head into his hands and closed his eyes, sighing deeply. In his headphones, Isa gave a low, satisfied chuckle.

Revenge – it seemed to say – is very sweet indeed.

* * *

When the call was finally over, thinking the worst of the day's horrors behind him, he prepared to enter his own little world – as far as it was possible to do so while sitting in an open-plan office. But what to listen to? With an odd, depressive feeling, he realized he was out of ideas. For a few days previously, he'd been mining the gloomy, metallic thrills of Public Image Limited, but the prospect suddenly seemed too bleak.

The old favourites? Wu-Tang Clan's *36 Chambers*, or Nirvana's *In Utero*? No, something more elemental, something beyond words to take him out of himself, out of the office. Classical music then? Something he'd been trying to learn about, aware that there were, out there in the world, masterpieces of Shakespearian scale with which he was completely unfamiliar. But where to start? Wagner? Schubert? Which recording? Oh God.

Roger's phrase regarding Falconz surfaced in his mind. Coldplay. Did Falconz actually sound anything like Coldplay? What did Coldplay actually sound like?

Fuck it, he thought with a mirthless grin.

A quick Spotify search revealed many Coldplay albums. *A Rush of Blood to the Head* was a familiar name, and there, a little way down its running order, was another – 'The Scientist'. Adam had heard the song over and over again during a spell doing office temping in the early 2000s, but his recollection of it now was murky. He double-clicked on it, and the opening notes rang from his headphones.

What happened next was very strange. In fact, several things started to happen at once. Firstly, a horrible, creeping, irresistible truth began to make itself clear. Namely, that Adam *liked* this song. It was simple and beautiful and clever, and he wanted to hear more of it.

Secondly, a black, black abyss of shame and self-loathing yawned open in his mind. Oh God, he thought. Oh for Christ's fucking sakes. For fuck's fucking sakes, I like Coldplay now. I'm old and terrible and pathetic and I fucking like Coldplay!

Chris Martin's really quite likeable voice soared with unpretentious earnestness over elemental piano. Drums joined in. Simple, meaningful phrases washed through Adam's mind. His hangover having reached peak melancholy, they carried the dreadful weight of timeless wisdom. No one *had* said it was going to be easy – yes, that was right. But equally, nobody had said it would be so *hard*, either. Adam turned the song up very loud, automatically, burying himself within it.

As far as he remembered, Chris Martin was only a couple of years older than him. In his early twenties, he'd achieved this song. What had Adam achieved by then? Nothing important. The gloom gushed from the abyss. It was probably too late now to achieve anything!

Chris Martin was singing about going back to the start, which was exactly where Adam wanted to go. He was being moved quite profoundly by a Coldplay song. His shame was complete. Everything he'd ever believed in was lying in tatters. Oh God, he thought again. Oh God oh God oh God. Why is this happening to me?

But something else was happening too. Around him in the office, at least two of his colleagues were smirking at each other. They glanced up from their machines, frowning and grinning with faces that seemed to ask 'what the fuck?' As he looked up, they glanced at him quickly before looking away.

Me? Adam thought. Am I the source of some sort of joke? The colleagues were looking back at their screens, doing the rapid sort of focused typing and pausing that could only signify the sending and receipt of instant messages.

It won't be about me, Adam told himself. Get over your own ego, for Christ's sake. Not everything is about you. No one cares. You are not the centre of the universe – not even of this office. You are suffering from persecution mania. And you are listening to Coldplay and enjoying it. Something is very wrong with you, and colleagues' smirks are the least of your worries.

But there was another glance from Ernesto, and another from Kristen. Adam risked a glance of his own to his left. Sure enough, Scott was looking at him too. He wasn't smirking, though. In fact he looked annoyed.

Whatever, Adam thought, who cares. Whatever they're waffling on about to each other will be unimportant and tedious. A strummed guitar joined in on the song, broadening its depth and texture, giving it an added layer of emotional urgency.

He was aware of Scott standing up behind him, and then he felt a tap on his shoulder. The song hadn't finished. He wanted to listen to Coldplay and escape and now... Absurdly angry, he tore off his headphones and looked up at Scott.

To his surprise, the same Coldplay song was playing very loudly in the office.

'Dude,' Scott said, as though addressing someone who'd done an atrocious fart. 'You're connected to the Bluetooth. Can you turn that shit off?'

* * *

When lunchtime finally arrived, he almost ran from the office, emerging onto the sunny street breathless with relief. Before he'd a chance to decide otherwise, he walked straight to the local pub and drank a pint of IPA.

Deciding he'd stay for lunch, he had another pint to wash down the burger he'd ordered. Like countless other old-world customs, cars and sports, this style of beer had become stronger and blunter in its American mutation and was thus an efficacious hair of the dog. And an American burger – in its typically stupendous portion – was a reliable way to soak it up. Ever since he'd given up smoking, a big lunch had been one of life's greatest pleasures, but today he'd only got halfway through the thing before his appetite had gone. Giving up, he stumbled back out into the dazzling light of Sunset Boulevard, feeling slightly euphoric from the beer.

The call to Alicia – Fischer's producer – had to be made. It seemed unlikely that the day could get any worse, or more embarrassing, and at least edging off the hangover had a numbing effect on his nerves.

Back at the office, he enclosed himself in the meeting room and dialled the studio's number. Calls like this were best made without too much advance planning.

'Alicia Silverman's office,' a brisk female voice said.

'This is Adam Fairhead, can I speak to Alicia, please?'

'Can I ask what it's regarding?'

'Yes. I want to talk to her about a sensitive issue that arose out of The Suffering's session with Fischer last week. I represent the band's label.'

'OK, please hold.' The line instantly switched to hold music. Middle-of-the-road, inoffensive indie rock – music for people who were doing something else while they listened to it.

After two minutes, he began to feel hot prickles of irritation. It was five minutes before the voice came back.

'Hello?' it said.

'Hi,' Adam replied.

'Oh,' the voice said, as if disappointed that he was still lurking on one of her lines. 'You wanted Alicia, right?'

'Yes,' Adam said. 'And believe you me, she's not going to be very happy if you keep me waiting any longer.'

'Hold on,' the voice said. More hold music chimed blandly out.

'OK,' the voice said, returning more swiftly this time. 'I have Alicia.'

'Good,' Adam said.

'Do you have… ah…'

'Adam Fairhead?' Adam reminded her.

'Yes.'

'I *am* Adam Fairhead,' he said.

'Oh,' the voice said, its surprise making a nice change to the practised boredom. 'OK. Hold on.'

One day, he might actually have to get an assistant, Adam thought, so that other people's assistants weren't so confused by him making his own calls. LA underlings, he well knew, were all drilled to within an inch of their lives to have their counterpart's boss on the line first. He imagined siccing his future assistant on the owner of this disembodied voice, with a variety of sharpened, bloodied office implements.

'Adam?' Alicia's voice was throaty and clipped. Pure New York. A tiny, fearsome woman, she spent her life balancing the deranged whims of musicians against the towering ego of her presenter.

'Hi,' he said.

'So this is about that thing last week, with the girl and the photos?'

Adam took a breath. 'Yes. Fischer told you then?'

'No, actually someone from your office contacted my production assistant.'

Adam's skin prickled, and his vision swam with anger. Scott…

'Right,' he said. 'Well, I'm calling to lodge an official complaint.'

'OK, well, that's noted,' Alicia said.

'Noting it isn't going to be enough. What happened was unacceptable, Alicia, and we need an official response from the station.'

'You'll be getting an official response in the mail.'

'What does that mean?'

'Our lawyers wrote to you already. Regarding the threats that your staff member made.'

'Threats? What do you mean, threats?'

'Apparently, she threatened to make public accusations about Fischer.'

Adam was pacing the rug in the narrow meeting room, circling the low white coffee table.

'That doesn't mean he didn't do what she says he did. That's all that counts here,' he said.

Alicia sighed. 'Look, Adam. I get that she's freaking out. I'm a woman. He didn't mean anything by it, though. She showed interest in his pictures. She actually asked him about his photography.'

'Of bands, Alicia.'

'His photography, Adam. He's very clear on that. He showed her a bunch of his shots, including some that he considers to be pieces of art.'

'You're fucking kidding me?'

'I'm not.'

Adam prodded his right temple, where the throb had broken out again. 'How can you say this stuff, Alicia?'

'Don't let's go there, Adam. You and I have always had a good working relationship...' She sighed, and when she spoke again her tone was deadened, as though she was reading from a script.

'In the current climate,' she continued, 'the station simply wanted to ensure there was no inflammatory public accusation here, not before they've had a chance to investigate.'

'Have you seen these pictures, Alicia?'

'No, I have not. I have never expressed an interest in his photography.'

Adam remembered something. 'You're leaving the show soon, aren't you?'

'Yes, Adam.' She paused. 'Can you think why?'

'Right,' Adam said. He sat down on the couch, empty of ideas.

'As I understand it, one of your executives has spoken to the girl – what's her name again?'

'Meg. Which executive?'

'Some guy in London, I don't know his name. Anyhow, I am registering an official complaint at my end, and she knows that. It'll be handled. In the meantime, the letter from our lawyers is intended to make sure it's handled properly.'

'Right,' Adam said again.

'I'm sorry we've found ourselves in this difficult situation, Adam.'

'Me too,' Adam said. He hung up, and slid the meeting room door open.

'Scott, come down here, please,' he called.

Scott's slim, muscled calves and flip-flops appeared on the backless stairs, and when he reached the bottom he scuffed his way into the room wearing a 'what now?' expression.

'Shut the door,' Adam told him.

Scott did so. Both of them remained standing.

'You called your friend at KCXE and warned them about Meg, didn't you?'

'I called to tell them about the *problem*,' Scott said, as though weary of pleading for reason with a madman. 'I have my own relationship with the station. Also, I knew that Jason wouldn't like the way it was potentially gonna get handled.'

'And you called Jason, too?'

'He called me. We were catching up. We do that. I'm not gonna lie to him.' Scott shrugged. 'I don't have a poker face.'

Adam felt dizzy with anger.

'If you ever go behind my back again regarding a professional matter,' he said, 'you and I cannot keep working together.'

'Right.' Scott slid the door open and scuffed out of the room.

Adam waited until Scott was out of view, and slumped onto the couch.

His head pounded with betrayal, confusion and rage. This bitter cocktail, it seemed, was the price he must pay for his life in Los Angeles.

17

He'd moved in with Sofia in the spring of 2008. Her flat was in an old red-brick mansion block in London Fields, built in 1901 as housing for the poor. A century later, by modern standards, the space within each flat was decidedly luxurious. A group of incoming middle-class types had bought out the freehold, and the block's courtyard was lined with potted plants, olive trees and a leafy gazebo.

Over the next year, Adam and Sofia lived as contently as he ever had. The punk label had gone bust, but he liked his new job working for Serena, and he was earning more money. He was still working on records he believed in, and which seemed to give his life purpose. Sofia was less happily employed at an art restoration company, located as far away as it was possible to be while remaining in London. She was up and gone each morning before Adam got out of bed, and home after he was.

She poured her passion into her own art, taking him to gallery shows she wanted to see, making notes on the pieces in her neat, attractive handwriting. She began filming herself in the living room, splicing images of paintings with her own thoughts on them. She was very good at speaking to the camera, and her enthusiasm was infectious. The videos were uploaded to YouTube, apparently for her own pleasure and with little fanfare. These were the seeds of the career that sprouted after he broke her heart.

The flat was cosy and run-down. In winter, the smell of wet towels lingered by the front door, which was beside the bathroom. Adam used one of the bedrooms as a study. He, too, had been passionate, and working late from home had been a point of pride.

When had it started to go wrong? Possibly as early as a few months in, when the fights had finally started. By then, Adam's fear was less of losing her, and more of her jealousy destroying them. He had foolishly thought that jealousy would exist in inverse proportion to the overall value of a person. That Sofia, in her beauty and loveliness, would have no need for it.

In hindsight, of course, he saw that he was the worst person to be with for anyone who suffered it.

Sofia's jealousy came like storms. A period of heavy tension, cloying air and dread, followed by a flashing outbreak of anger.

One night, this souring of her mood had occurred shortly after they'd made love in her room. Adam was lying on the futon that was pushed into a corner. The walls were painted in faded pale green woodchip, probably unaltered since her landlord had bought the place.

Adam had loved the bedroom nonetheless. There was a wardrobe stuffed with Sofia's clothes, a built-in dressing table with a mirror over it. Placed on this was a bust made of wicker, on which she hung her jewellery.

That night, she had been playing an early Missy Elliott album on her midi system, and had gone quiet as she was dressing.

Adam had already come to know the stiff, unhappy look that had set over her face. The room's usual comfort had been stripped away, and he felt trapped in its newly heavy weather.

'What's wrong?' he asked eventually.

With other women, this question had been only the first step in the grim trudge to revelation. With Sofia, the journey was often mercifully faster.

'I'm pissed off about your ring,' she said.

She spoke in a pretty, clear RP that gave away no trace of Hungarian. In fact, the only incursion into her accent was that of the estuarial south, when she said words such as 'salt'.

Adam wore a simple silver ring on his left hand. His last girlfriend had bought it for him in South East Asia. Inside it was engraved 'Love Ya Big Daddy'. The ex, a life-hardened South African, had never been comfortable with sentiment.

Adam loved the ring in small part for the memory it held, in far greater for the object itself. Sofia hated it as a token of a former lover, someone whom he'd loved and had left him. This subject, like others, had been often deferred.

'Please let's not go through this again,' he said. 'I've told you, I love you. I'm so happy with you. There's nothing left over about her.'

Her frown deepened, but she made no reply. Not that he'd said anything very inspiring to her. Was ever a phrase spoken in argument that wasn't calcified with overuse? Perhaps only the insults were ever original.

'It's just a ring,' he said into her silence. 'It's just a possession that I really love.'

'With a fucking dedication from her scratched into it. "Love Ya Big Daddy."'

When angry, the clear tone of her voice cooled and hardened, like flowing water turning to ice.

'It's been over two years since we broke up, for God's sake. It's all over and done with, ancient history. Please let's not go into all this again,' he repeated.

He couldn't tell Sofia quite how great his love for her was. That knowledge wouldn't come to him until it was far too late.

'But you thought you were going to marry her,' Sofia said. She was at her dressing table now, crouched, tidying loose items into a cardboard box. Every now and then she pushed a strand of hair back behind her left ear. Her pout was natural, the result of a face with full lips showing unhappiness. Women in LA would have killed for a pout so perfect.

This was the price of intimacy, Adam had thought. You told the truth, and it could be as dangerous as a lie. Intimacy was cruelly objective, it allowed a view of the worst in people as well as the best.

Above Sofia's head, on her wicker jewellery stand, was a fine gold chain. Hanging from this was a small, open-ended cylinder, also gold, etched with swirling patterns. It was by Gucci, and from Sofia's ex.

'What about your necklace?' Adam asked, his own anger boiling up.

'It doesn't say anything in it, and I don't wear it every day.'

'Do you want me to stop wearing the ring?' he asked.

'No. I want to get rid of it. I've bought you a new ring.'

Adam frowned, the anger ebbing. 'Well, thank you,' he said. 'That's really nice of you. I'd love to wear yours instead. I'll put this one away and never wear it again if you like. It's having a ring I love, not where it came from.'

'No,' she said, looking at him. 'I want to get rid of it.'

A heavy despair settled in Adam. 'What do you mean get rid of it? Get rid of it how?'

'It doesn't matter how,' she said. 'If you love me and you're over her, you'll let me do it.'

'That's unfair,' he said. 'You can't just take someone's possessions, the things from the past that mean something to them, and throw them away because of something you feel.'

'If it's just an object then it doesn't matter. I'll give you a new one, so if what you say is true, you shouldn't care.'

Adam, lying on the bed, felt drained and lifeless.

'If you keep that one it's never going to be OK,' Sofia said.

This went on for an hour, until eventually he gave in.

Sofia took the ring, put on her shoes and left the flat. She returned a few minutes later.

Adam, too, was now stiff with unhappiness. 'What did you do with it?' he asked.

'It doesn't matter,' she said. Her own mood, perhaps inevitably, had now softened.

'It does matter,' Adam said. 'You owe me that. I did what you asked and I want to know what you did with it.'

'I put it down a drain in the street,' she said. She looked as if she'd cry. 'You'll never find it. It's gone now.'

'Did you really?' Adam asked. 'Promise me you're telling the truth.'

'Yes,' she said. 'I am.'

Rage flashed and cracked within him like sheet lightning. Fucking bitch, he thought. You fucking bitch.

In Asia, when he'd been given the ring, it had slipped from his finger in the sea while he was swimming. Distraught, he'd slumped on the beach in panic while his girlfriend's helpful, optimistic friend had dived for it. Lost, he'd thought. It's lost.

After ten minutes the friend had emerged from the water, standing, dripping and golden, hand raised in triumph, her fingers clasping the bright silver ring. Relief had hit Adam bodily, like a drug, and left him alight with happiness for the rest of the day. He'd told himself never to be so careless again with something he loved.

Now it was down a drain in Hackney, and he would never see it again.

'And when do I get the new ring?' he asked Sofia.

She moved over to him, kissed him and stroked his head. 'Not now. It's not the right time to give it to you. Let's wait for a better moment. I'm sorry,' she said.

You fucking bitch, Adam thought. And hadn't he actually sworn revenge?

Over the years, he often thought of that ring, and where it had come to rest. Was it still lodged in a sewer, somewhere beneath the flat they'd shared all those years ago? Losing its shine, the words etched into it gradually fading away, the metal itself thinning and degrading. Or had it moved, made a merry journey, found itself carried off by the subterranean currents to end its long, sad journey elsewhere?

Who was he kidding, he'd think. It was where she'd thrown it, lodged among the shit in a place they'd once lived and been happy, and every other trace of them was now gone.

By anyone's standards, particularly those of the age he found himself in now, all of this had happened a very long time ago.

Was it normal, he wondered, to be haunted by it for so long? How was he ever to be rid of her?

18

Erica's place in Atwater Village being north-east of Adam, and thus on the way to the mountains, they arranged that he would collect her.

He pulled up outside at 8 a.m., with a queasy curdling in his stomach. Butterflies at the prospect of the date had mixed with raw fear at the memories of his last attempt on Strawberry Peak.

Erica lived in a smart grey bungalow on a wide, pretty street. Most of the houses had gleaming lawns, but Erica's front garden had been gravelled over, with brick circles built within it to house tall cacti. Good on you, Adam thought. LA's lawns were one of his pet hates. The vampires of garden design in this parched city.

On the driveway beside the house was a Mercedes – the same model as Adam's.

Erica appeared in the doorway of the house before he'd had a chance to call her. She wore a small pack on her back, lightweight hiking shoes, a long-sleeved, figure-hugging top made out of some space-age fabric, and the brightly patterned workout pants he'd first seen her in. On her head was a black Nike baseball cap.

She smiled as she approached the car, and Adam grinned back, a swell of jittery anticipation rising in him.

She shrugged the pack off and opened the back door of the car, placing it on the seat beside his.

'Hi,' she said as she swung into the front. Her scent filled the air, and Adam leaned over and gave her a peck on the cheek.

She peered at the car's interior, and ran an approving hand over the dashboard.

'Snap,' she said.

'You have excellent taste,' he replied, peeling away from the kerb.

'So,' she said. 'Ready to conquer the mountain?'

'I think so,' he said.

'*Think* so? That's not the right attitude. You need to know so.'

'Ah yes, the American way. I should visualize success. Bring my A game.'

'You got it,' she said. She switched the radio on – her fingernails were painted a dark red colour, he noted – and moved the dial to a classic rock station, then leaned back in her seat and shot him a grin.

After a few minutes, they escaped from the stop-and-start grid of Glendale's streets and were released onto the 2 – Adam's favourite freeway. Erica seemed happy to be on it too; as the gradient changed beneath the car and the rock songs' riffs tripped from the speakers, there seemed to be no pressure to speak.

The 2, Adam thought, was as beautiful as a road could be. A long, wide ramp that fired them out of the city in a truly kinetic experience – like driving into the sky. It was impossible to speed up it, to see the mountains swelling in the windshield without feeling excited, and feeling better. Even the churn in his stomach seemed to be settling.

As they drove north, and up, they exchanged hiking stories and favoured trails. It quickly became clear that Erica had tackled far bigger hikes than Adam had. Possibilities began to yawn open in his head. Bigger hikes with her. Long days on airy mountain trails.

They turned off the freeway and made the short run eastwards to the Angeles Crest Highway. This winding, vertiginous road was considered one of the finest in the country, a route through the mountain range that very quickly placed you in an entirely different world. The closest comparison, Adam reflected, would be a mountain road in Andalusia. But with more muscle cars and bikers, and the futuristic towers of Downtown LA rupturing from the vast flatness a long way below and to their right.

'I like the outfit,' Erica said, regarding him.

Adam was wearing blue Rohan trousers and a long-sleeved checked shirt. On the back seat of the car was a wide-brimmed Tilley hat that made him look ridiculous. He'd considered not bringing it, but fear of skin cancer had won out.

'Thanks,' he said, laughing.

'It's quite British. It's what I imagine someone very sensible might wear, if they were taking out some Boy Scouts for the day. In the seventies.'

'I can't seem to escape from it,' Adam said. 'I still dress like I'm hiking in Scotland.'

'It's cute,' Erica said. 'Though I'm glad I saw you for a city date first.'

'The shirt has high UV protection,' Adam said proudly.

After a moment he glanced at her again. 'I like *your* outfit.'

'Well thank you,' she said. 'I remembered that you liked these pants.'

After forty minutes, they were at five thousand feet. There were alpine forests vaulting above them on the steep, higher slopes of the San Gabriels. This place never failed to amaze him. From that giant, seething city to this raw mountain landscape in less than an hour, he thought. Less time than it took many Angelenos to commute to work. Beyond the car, and the occasional Harley-riding biker or early-rising muscle car driver, there was the silence of a thousand square miles of wilderness.

As they approached the small parking area for Strawberry Peak, Adam's stomach began to roil again. Images of his last attempt came back to him – the ground rising steeply and thinning beneath his feet. The sense of airiness around him, of a long drop. The vague outline, to his right and higher in the sky, of a steep, sharp mass of dark granite, looming above him like an airborne dreadnought.

'You've gone quiet,' Erica said as they pulled in. 'Nervous?'

'A bit.'

She put a hand on his leg and squeezed. 'Don't be. There's really no need. There's no actual danger up there. It's all about the line of sight. It's deceptive. Makes you think there are cliff edges where there are none. You can follow me if you like, when we get up there.'

He nodded.

'Remember, Adam,' she said. 'It's never as bad up close as it looks from afar.'

19

There was one other car in the small, dusty parking lot, but no sign of its occupants. They swung on their packs, picked their way along the smooth rock of a dry waterfall, and soon they were on their way.

The route to Strawberry Peak, for those taking the mountaineers' path, began in a ravine called Colby Canyon. In winter months, when there wasn't a drought, this canyon featured a wide, shallow stream, collecting into rocky pools in places, and fed by cascading waterfalls that had carved smooth-walled funnels into the canyon's sides.

When Erica and Adam entered it, it was tinder-dry. The canyon's high walls offered some shade, though, and at that time in the morning the air was cold rather than cool. Adam's hands felt bony, his skin taut and his limbs brittle. His left leg was stiff and slightly painful.

He followed Erica as they climbed the side of the canyon in switchbacks, and soon emerged onto its upper, eastern lip. Below them, quite suddenly, was a long drop down to the canyon floor – far enough to make Adam feel a moment's dizziness.

'It's gonna get hot now,' Erica said. She walked steadily and rhythmically, picking her way along the parched, narrow path.

The mountainside rose greenly above them, and the ridge – and Strawberry Peak's summit – soon came into view: a daunting, vertical pile of dark grey rock.

'Doesn't look so bad from here, right?' Erica said, tossing him a smile.

'It looks steep,' Adam said.

'It *is* steep. But it's not dangerous.'

'I believe you.'

After an hour's hiking Erica suggested they stop for a break. Adam fished his Ziploc bag from his pack and placed it on the ground. The sun was high above them now.

'My God,' Erica said. 'What did you bring?'

'Sandwiches,' Adam said.

'And a boiled egg?'

'Two. In case you wanted one.'

'Oh, thanks.' Erica laughed. 'And what's in that can?'

'It's mackerel.'

'You're so weird!'

Adam grinned. 'It goes with my outfit.'

'You're like some guy in an ancient British nature documentary. In your funny hat.'

'The Tilley hat is the greatest ever made.'

'But your ears are tucked in!'

'There's one downside,' he said. 'Anyway, what did you bring?'

'Energy balls.' She produced a shiny metallic bag covered in fluorescent yellow text and containing lots of brown balls, flecked with white.

'That's like something from a truck stop. The hiking equivalent of trucker speed.'

'It's just coconut and oats and some peanut butter. They're organic!'

'You can keep your balls to yourself,' he told her.

She was rummaging in his pack. 'Oh my God,' she said. 'Did you only bring bottles of sparkling water? On a hike? You're *so* weird!'

He wanted to lean forward and kiss her, but wasn't quite confident enough. He was trying to convince himself when the sound of a lizard flicking away through the scrub, somewhere near his right hand, distracted him.

They fell into a happy silence as they both ate, and each drank a great deal of water.

'I guess I'm also a little weird with snacks,' Erica said as she packed up.

'In what way?'

'I'm kinda careful with sugar. As a kid I wasn't allowed it. My parents sent me to school with raisins. I got laughed at. None of the kids wanted to swap.'

'Oh dear,' Adam said.

'So I used to steal the sugar bowl and take it under my covers at night.'

'And now you eat energy balls.'

'Exactly. With natural sugar only,' she said. She stood up, swung her pack on. 'OK. Let's get going. It's still a long way to the top.'

'Yes ma'am,' Adam said.

The path steepened, and the air became hot and dry. From this point on, he knew, there'd be no cover. He was sweating freely, and he could see beads of liquid on Erica's bare shoulders too. Her ponytail bounced above her slim neck as she walked. Adam watched her long legs, the planes of her calf muscles as she strode, the sheen of sunscreen that made them glisten.

She moved along the rocky path with a catlike grace, barely making a sound. Tall, sleek and slim, and impossible to tear his eyes from.

'Tell me more about growing up,' he asked her, wanting to hear her speak more. He was breathing hard now, his legs aching as they climbed the steep, zigzagging path to the ridge ahead.

She glanced over her shoulder. 'I loved horses. I had one. I was a showjumper.'

'Wow.'

'Yeah.'

'What happened to the horse?'

'I left for college, but my parents kept him until he died. They have some land. It isn't expensive really, in South Carolina. Not compared to here, anyway.'

'What sort of politics are your parents into?'

'Oh, they're Democrats,' she said. Then after a moment: 'What about you?'

'I veer around the middle,' Adam told her.

'Hah,' she said. 'Interesting.'

They were silent again, apart from their panting. When they stepped out onto the ridge beside a small, flying saucer-like water tank, they came across the occupants – Adam presumed – of the other car in the parking lot. They were a couple, or at least a man and a woman. Mid-twenties, Adam thought. The girl was sporty and skinny. She had her hands on her hips, and kept moving, birdlike, in light little steps. The man was chubby and bearded, and carried a wooden stick.

They greeted each other with nods and muted hellos.

'Going to the top?' the woman asked.

'Yes,' Adam said. Now that they'd stopped, the nerves had taken hold of him again. From here, he knew, they'd turn off the main path onto the mountaineers' trail.

'You guys too?' Erica asked.

'Yeah, exactly,' the girl said. She was swinging her pack on, as though keen to get going.

'Hope we all make it,' Adam said.

'Oh yeah, you will,' the woman said. 'It isn't bad at all. I've done it before.' She seemed keen for them to know this, Adam thought.

'Well, enjoy,' he told them.

'You guys too.'

The couple disappeared past a bluff of rock, around which the path made a sharp turn.

'Well,' Erica said, smiling. 'That's the hard work done.'

'Yes,' Adam said.

He saw that she'd noticed his nerves. 'I'm not making it up about it being safe and easy,' she said. 'You've scrambled before, right?'

'Yes, on a very frightening ridge in Scotland.'

'And you were fine?'

'The advantage then was that once you were on the ridge, you either had to keep going or call mountain rescue. It turns out my fear of embarrassment narrowly outweighs my fear of very big drops.'

'Well, that's perfect,' Erica said. 'You don't want to embarrass yourself today either.'

'No, I don't. I'm actually having the best day I can remember,' Adam said, truthfully.

'Good,' Erica said. 'Because now we're at the fun part.'

The mountaineers' path was easy to miss. In fact, Adam had initially done so on his solo attempt. It didn't seem like the sort of place a path would be, because it ran straight up the side of a steep bank of rock, away from the better-used main trail.

They climbed onto it and began tracing their way up the dusty path, picking their way between bristling, dagger-like Spanish Bayonets – the botanical equivalent of a porcupine in defence mode – and scorched, sharp branches of deadened trees.

'There was a big fire up here,' Erica said. 'The Station Fire, they called it. It started in La Cañada and burned a quarter of the forest.'

'How did it start?' Adam asked her.

'Arsonist,' she said. 'It usually is, from what I've read.'

The path climbed steeply to a mass of vertical boulders, narrowing to a fine point above them. Once again, it reminded him of the spine of a fish. The angle up and over this obstacle was greater than forty-five degrees, and this was where he'd turned back previously.

'This part is easy,' Erica said. 'Maybe fifty feet. There's a ton of hand- and footholds.'

She turned back and grinned at him, clinging to the rock with hands and feet.

'Ready?'

'As I'll ever be.'

They began hauling themselves up the rock. Adam's heart was beating very fast. His knees were trembling, and his palms broke out in a sweat.

Great, he thought. Here I am, clinging to rock, thousands of feet in the air, drops either side of me, and the two things I need most are steady legs and dry hands.

Speed, he thought. That is the answer. The actual climbing was technically very easy. His long body enabled him to lever himself up the rocky pile very quickly. Before long, his head was by Erica's bum.

'Woah there,' she said. 'I don't wanna kick you off this thing.'

He paused, looking upwards. Erica glanced back at him.

'Adam,' she said. 'It's OK to look down.'

He did so. The ridge was wider than he'd thought. He was placed in the centre of the rocky mass, with large boulders either side of him, blocking off any real chance of a fall. He took a deep breath.

'It's all in the eyeline,' Erica said. 'It deceives you all the way up. What looks like a sheer drop never actually is one.'

Soon, they emerged onto a wide, flat ridge – Strawberry Peak's shoulder. Adam sucked in breath and turned slowly. The mountain feeling – that of standing on top of the earth, looking down as though from a plane – suffused him. Around them were the thousand square miles of wilderness.

'Wow,' he said.

'Beautiful, huh?'

'It's amazing up here.'

Erica was gazing along the path ahead of them, which now ran straight along a steepening ridge to the top.

'I think that couple must have missed the turn,' she said.

'Maybe they were taking the other path,' Adam said. 'The main one.'

'She said they were going to the top. It'd be a very long way around to do it from the other side. Wouldn't make any sense.'

'Maybe we should have said something.'

'Yeah. But she didn't seem to want any advice,' Erica said.

'Yes,' Adam said. 'I got that feeling too.'

They set off along the ridge. Ahead of them, the scramble to the summit rose as a vertical bank of rock. Adam tried to ignore it, focusing on the softer views around his feet, or below them in the valleys.

His eye was caught by a small raptor, zooming through the air below them and banking hard, dropping and climbing, apparently playing, rather than hunting.

'What's that?' he asked Erica.

'It's a sharp-shinned hawk,' she said. 'An accipiter. Looks a lot like a Cooper's hawk. Took me years to learn how to tell the difference.'

'And how did you? Learn, I mean.'

'My dad. Hours out watching with him. Standing in hides with nothing happening, talking to weird old guys with telescopes. I thought I was hating it at the time, bored out of my mind. But I love it now. Those were some of the best times of my life.'

'That's how I feel about hiking,' Adam said. 'Every summer in Scouts, slogging up hills in Scotland in the rain. Slumping into stinky minibuses afterwards, steaming and exhausted. Thought I was hating it too, and now I do it for fun.'

'Exactly,' Erica said, smiling as she watched the aeronautic bird.

When it had disappeared, she pulled her water bottle out of her pack and drank from it, looking at him.

'You haven't said anything about your family,' she said.

'My father died ten years ago. Heart attack. My mum has quite advanced dementia and is in care in Somerset, where I'm from. I have an older sister. She's a journalist, in Malaysia.'

Erica frowned, and broke eye contact. 'Right. I'm so sorry,' she said.

'There's no need.'

'Don't you miss your mom? I mean…'

'There isn't really a whole mum to miss.'

'But still, I mean…' She fell silent for a moment. 'I'm sorry, I'm being pushy.'

'Not at all. I should see more of her. So should my sister.'

'You're all so far-flung…'

'After Dad died, there didn't seem as much reason to do all the usual family tradition stuff. He was quite good at that. Gregarious. Without him we became a bit unmoored.'

'You're not close with your sister?'

'We are and we aren't. She's eight years older than me. She's very clever, and she makes me feel a bit stupid.'

She thought for a moment. 'So your parents, they were older when they had you?'

'Yes. I was unexpected.'

'Cute.'

'Do you have siblings?' he asked her.

'A younger brother. He likes football – the American type. And hunting and fishing. He's a doctor too, back home in SC.'

'Smart pair,' Adam said.

'I suspect he's a Republican, so he's maybe not that smart,' she said. She turned back to the trail, and began picking her way along it once more.

A little while later, the ground turned rockier, until they found themselves making their way across big boulders. All too quickly, they'd reached the foot of the big summit scramble.

'So?' Erica said.

'You were right,' Adam replied. 'It doesn't look quite as bad up close.'

From where they were standing, Strawberry Peak's summit looked like a massive, upturned ship's hull built of giant granite lumps. At least, Adam thought, it wasn't quite as narrow as it had appeared from the bottom.

'We go pretty much straight up,' Erica said, gripping the rocks and lifting herself onto them. Her calves strained a few inches from Adam's eyes. When her feet were beyond the height of his head, he followed.

The climb wasn't quite vertical, but it was near enough. As Erica had said, there were plenty of hand- and footholds. The stone was cool and dusty under his hands. His heart was beating so fast that he wondered if it was sustainable without something terrible happening in his chest.

Eyeline, he kept thinking. The bank of rock felt as though it was narrowing, space – exposure – closing in on him from either side. Before each upward pull, he was sure that he'd find himself abruptly on a cliff's edge, a yawning drop below. Then, fear overwhelming him, he'd drag himself up to find the mountain swelling out further, more routes between the boulders that would keep him away from any drop.

Erica had paused, scanning for a direction. A big rock above her was jutting out sharply, blocking the way.

Fuck, Adam thought. His heart beat even faster. Fuck fuck fuck. I don't like this. Stopping was much worse than going. She must have taken us the wrong way, he thought, panic rising. There's no way around that rock…

'To our left,' Erica said.

There didn't appear to be very much at all to their left. Just a few sharp rocks, and then space. Beyond that, a valley with a tiny thread of road within it, as though seen from an aeroplane.

'Trust me,' she said.

She levered herself up a narrow gully, gripping one of the sharp rocks and pulling herself up onto what looked like an edge. She squatted there, her buttocks and thighs spreading above his head, stretching the material of her leggings across them.

It was almost lewd, he thought, gratefully distracted by a surge of desire.

Buttocks, he thought. Focus on the buttocks, and they will keep you safe. The lovely soft buttocks are not like the horrid sharp rocks.

'Wha… what's up there?' he managed to ask.

'It's fine, it widens out below us quite gently. We need to move back around to the right. Are you OK?'

'Let's keep moving,' Adam said.

'OK,' she said, and disappeared behind a wide rock above.

Adam began climbing again, his limbs trembling. The same process recurred over and over. Raw fear, then the revelation that it hadn't been quite justified. Even when he looked down, he could see an easily climbable route back to the base of the scramble.

After thirty minutes, he suddenly pulled himself over a large, shining granite lump, to what looked like a steep path, rather than a climb. Erica was standing on it, grinning.

Adam moved onto the sandy path and lowered himself, chimp-like. He could feel that his eyes were wild.

'How much more?' he said.

Erica laughed – a big, natural laugh that rang across the rocks.

'Just this path now.' She pointed. 'That's the top.'

'Fuck,' Adam said. He pushed a grey pointed tree branch out of his way, snarling at it when it sprang back into place and poked him, and set off after her. There was one more, short scramble, which he barely paused to take in, and then suddenly they stepped out onto the dusty, rocky flat of the summit.

Adam threw his hands in the air and whooped.

Erica stood watching him, a wide, astonished smile lighting up her face as he twirled and whooped and yelled.

'Yes!' he shouted. 'Yes, yes, yes!'

'Woah,' Erica said, laughing again. 'You're really pretty happy!'

'This feels amazing,' he said, wiping his brow and taking in the view. 'Holy shit.'

'Well done,' Erica said. 'I'm quite impressed, actually.'

She stood, hands on hips, pack dropped to the ground behind her, regarding him with a half-smile.

Adam studied her for a moment, then marched over to her and kissed her.

For a few moments after this initial boldness, he felt as awkward as a teenager. He couldn't seem to remember what he was doing. It was a long time since he'd really kissed someone, he realized. Or cared about the act, anyway. He seemed to be giving her a series of slightly elongated pecks on the lips, his mind devoid of other ideas.

He'd once considered himself a good kisser, but the horrible thought struck him that maybe he no longer was. Prickly heat rose up from his neck, and he stiffened up. Was kissing like dancing, he wondered? Was there very little chance you'd stay good at it forever?

Thankfully, Erica moved a hand to the back of his neck and slipped her tongue into his mouth. Adam relaxed, pressing his own fingers into the small of her back, moving his tongue over hers. They avoided falling into a rhythm, and he began to remember how it worked. After a moment, he was simply enjoying the texture of her tongue on his. He'd forgotten how intimate it was, to really kiss. How it could be an enjoyable act in itself, rather than a simple formality to observe before others could begin. How falling into a kiss was like experiencing gravity afresh. How strange and lovely the soft pink universe was that you fell into…

Erica drew back, smiling and squinting in the sunlight. She took his hand in hers.

'Are you happy?' she asked.

'Very,' he said.

And, he realized with something like relief, he really was.

* * *

There was a back route down from the mountain, and, Adam fearing the scramble in reverse, this was the one they took. A long, sweeping path that led through wild meadows, shady forest and back across the rocky north face of Strawberry Peak. It took them four hours, during which time Adam experienced a bliss he'd thought forever lost to him. They talked when they wanted to, and the rest of the time walked lightly and happily in silence.

Soon after dropping down to this path from the summit, they came across the couple. They were standing at a junction of the easier summit path that Adam and Erica had just descended, the back way they would now take, and a third path leading to a well-known starting point a long way from their own. The man was prodding the earth with his stick, calm and quiet. The woman was agitated, taking her quick little steps. She glanced around them in different directions, evidently trying to locate herself.

'Have you come from the top?' she asked them.

'Yes. Did you miss the turn?'

'Shit,' she said. 'Yes.' She turned to the man. 'I'm so sorry. I've done it before and I was sure I'd find it.'

'It's fine,' the man said, trying to calm her. 'Do you happen to know what's up this path?' He gestured along the ridge, away from the peak, with his stick. Adam saw that he was trying to be kind, to compensate and suggest something new.

Erica answered his question.

'I'm so sorry,' the woman said again. 'Let's just carry on to the top from here.' She looked as though she might cry.

* * *

Back in the city, Adam dropped Erica off.

'So,' Erica said. She looked at him as though trying to decide something.

He wanted very badly to be asked in, or to suggest they meet that night. But fighting this was a fear of messing it up, of having too much of a good thing. He wanted to take each moment with her carefully, to prevent himself from getting it wrong.

'Call me soon,' she said, finally, and grinned as she climbed out of the car.

20

It was the week of the trip to Denver. Despite this, and the usual Monday general meeting being once more upon him, he found himself in an excellent mood as he arrived at the office.

At nine o'clock the staff started to file in. Adam installed himself in the meeting room and flicked through the latest copy of *Billboard*. Market shares, streaming income, men with hairdos and showy suits getting new jobs at the few remaining majors. God, he thought. No wonder I don't read this more often.

A picture a few pages further in caught his eye. It took Adam a moment to place its subject. Joel Liebowitz, he realized. Almost unrecognizable out of his poolside garb and sunglasses, smartly dressed in a black suit jacket and crisp white t-shirt, grinning at the camera. The eyes, finally revealed, were shiny and clear with bright blue irises. Actually, Adam thought, they had about them an odd – and certainly unexpected – look of innocence.

Behind Joel was a tall slab of frosted glass, etched with the enlarged logo of Euphonic, the ascendant US live music promoter. Despite recent revelations regarding the right-wing political sympathies – and donations – of its shadowy Texan owner, the festivals it owned had seen record attendances already that year.

Joel, it seemed, had been appointed CEO.

Adam peered at his photo, trying to gauge – inconclusively – whether or not he'd kicked the drugs.

By 9.30 the staff had cooked their oatmeal, made coffee, discussed basketball results and weekend activities and begun to drift into the meeting room. Scott was first to come in.

'How was your weekend?' Adam asked him.

Scott sniffed violently. 'It was awesome,' he said. 'I was at RPPD in San Diego? The festival?'

'Ah yes,' Adam said. 'That's one of Euphonic's, isn't it?'

Scott frowned, apparently perturbed by this rare display of industry knowledge from his boss. 'Yeah,' he said.

'How was it?' Adam asked.

'It was *awesome*. Really, really great,' Scott said, eyes widened in emphasis. 'I really, really enjoyed it actually.'

My weekend was lovely too, Adam thought, nodding serenely.

'Think I'm getting sick, though,' Scott said. 'It was really dusty down there on the site. Think it must've been that.'

Scott, Adam knew, was pathologically incapable of admitting, to himself or anyone else, when he was hungover.

'Right, yes,' Adam said. The famous viral dust of San Diego. Not the mammoth quantities of MDMA you've been shoving down your throat.

Kristen, head of North American radio, walked in and sat down. She slumped onto the couch, still wearing her oversized sunglasses. Her platinum blonde hair was tied back severely, the vest top she was wearing allowing her gothic, metal-style sleeve tattoos to show.

A thirty-something with a background in alternative rock, she'd only been with the company three months. The Autodidact's bold new age of commercial crossovers had required a different sort of staff. The era of waifs, strays and loveable weirdos was over. Now, Adam had begun poaching people like Kristen from the corporate music world.

She seemed to vacillate wildly between hard partying and a fanatical health regime, and Adam was never quite sure which mode she'd be in. In Scott's words, she 'coked at the weekends and kaled during the week'.

'How you doing?' Adam asked her.

'Soooo wiped,' she said.

'Hectic weekend?' Scott asked her.

'Just a *lot* of yoga,' she said. '*So* needed. Totally killed me though.'

'What's your spot?' Scott asked.

'Reaching Crane,' she said. 'In Echo Park?'

'Cool,' he said. 'I like Yologa, in Culver City?'

'I heard about that place. Do you know Atrium Yoga, in Silver Lake?'

'Sure, I've been there a couple times when my spot was closed. What about Silver Monkey? It's in the Valley, but God, *so* worth it.'

'Yep,' Kristen said. 'My BFF works there actually.' She paused, eyeing Scott. 'Do you know Golden Path Yoga, in Hollywood?'

Scott frowned, disturbed. 'No...'

'It's pretty new?'

'That's cool.' For an elastic moment, Scott looked crestfallen, and this alien little ritual appeared to be over. Then he rallied.

'What about Flow Yoga, in Atwater?' he asked. 'It's *awesome.*'

Just as Adam was imagining how it would feel to headbutt the giant bubble-wrap roll – a completely new urge – Beau walked in. Adam brightened. Beau was from Montana, which apparently made him less alien, to Adam, than his LA-bred colleagues.

'Morning, Beau!' Adam said.

'What's up?' Beau grinned.

'Do any yoga at the weekend?' Adam asked.

'Hell no,' Beau said, smiling broadly. 'Too damn busy having fun.'

'Good lad,' Adam told him.

When all the staff were gathered, the meeting was opened with general business.

'I have something actually,' Kristen said. Her default expression was one Adam had recently heard referred to as 'resting bitch' – the same lifeless pout that Angelina's friend had favoured.

'Go ahead,' he said.

'So, like, my wellness practitioner has told me I have to drink kombucha every day. For, like, my stomach?'

'OK.' Adam nodded.

'It could be workplace stress-based, apparently.'

Scott frowned, then sniffed violently, twice in quick succession.

'So... Can we, like, install a kombucha tap?'

Adam sipped his coffee. There seemed to him to be only one possible answer.

'Yes,' he said. 'Absolutely.'

'Great,' Kristen said.

'Excellent. Anyone else?'

The staff, crammed into the room on moulded plastic chairs, shook their heads.

'Great,' Adam said. 'Then the only other thing, I think, is that we're going to have a new member of staff in LA.'

'Really?' Scott said, alarmed.

'Yes. Isa Dixon is going to come out here to join us full-time.'

'Who's that?' Kristen asked.

Before Adam had a chance, Scott leapt in. 'She used to work in the London office,' he said, 'then went off to do an MBA.'

The team, each of them too ambitious to greet this news with any real enthusiasm, feigned it.

'What's she gonna, like, do?' Kristen asked.

'Business development,' Adam said.

'*Really?*' Scott curled his lower lip.

'Yes. Under the Au—' He stopped himself just in time. 'The, ah, auspices, of Jason.'

'Honestly,' Scott said, 'Isa is a *very* good friend of mine, but I'm just not sure there's a role for her here.'

'Well, a role is being made for her,' Adam said.

'That's great,' Beau said, first to warm to the idea. 'I like Isa a lot.'

'Do you even *know* Isa?' Scott asked.

'Sure I do,' Beau said. 'I hung with her in London. She's a lotta fun.'

* * *

Isabella Dixon had already been at the company for three years when Adam joined it. She was five years younger than him, and Adam's position was senior to hers. It had seemed to him that she'd disliked him on sight. In the first marketing meeting they'd been in together, he'd found her staring at him, and when he smiled at her she didn't return the gesture. In fact, he didn't think she'd smiled at him once for the first few months they worked together. The experience was upsetting, and worsened by the fact that Isa seemed to have friendly, even flirtatious relationships with several other men in the office. After a few attempts to improve things, Adam had more or less given up.

Isa was short and slim, her hair cut into a fringe that framed her watchful eyes. She'd studied English Literature at Durham, and could switch between London slang and high eloquence in a heartbeat, something she used to tactical advantage daily in meetings. Her Nike Airs and bright streetwear made her stand out from the indie-rock garb worn by her colleagues. Later, she admitted to Adam that she didn't like guitar music at all, rather hip-hop, and that for her it was about the right company for her career, not a genre. Adam had never encountered someone outside of a major label who spoke like that, and he admired her for it.

In fact, other than with the handful of male colleagues she flirted with, she didn't seem popular among the staff. The label tended to attract a type – nerdy boys and the occasional girl, people who spoke quietly and didn't usually interrupt each other. Isa was not like them. Her voice, which moved with her guise between a strong east London accent and Queen's English, was loud and clear; and she thought nothing of interjecting or cutting a colleague off, most often with a better idea than the one they were having.

Serena loved her, and the boss's open approval only made her more unpopular among the rank and file. To Isa, this was water off a duck's back. Worrying about it wouldn't have been worth the energy she could put into advancing herself.

Isa made it clear that she thought of herself as very valuable, and later, Adam wondered if he'd come to desire her in part because of this.

One day, after three months of her virtually ignoring him, an instant message window had appeared on his screen. It was from Isa.

Hi mate, it said. *Did u complain about me?*

Adam, in charge of the marketing department, had an office to himself. Nevertheless, his pulse had thudded anxiously.

No, he'd typed. *What do you mean?*

He wasn't surprised by how quickly the reply appeared – he'd already been impressed by Isa's rapid, loud typing in the main office.

Serena says I need to work better with you.

Well, I didn't ask her to do that, Adam said.

OK good, Isa said. *What do you do down there all day anyway? Is it nice having an office all to yourself?*

While Adam was considering his reply, another message had appeared.

U a big shot?

And so a flirtation had begun between them, too.

It was difficult to say exactly when this had become serious, more meaningful than Isa's others. Adam assumed at first that it simply meant she'd accepted him, and he hoped they'd become friends. It was a relationship commenced, and largely conducted, over instant messages. These would start early in the morning, usually regarding some minor work issue – Isa sarcastically and superfluously asking the big shot for his opinions and ideas. As the day wore on, they gradually grew in intensity, and later explicitness.

Instant messages evolved into texts. One night, coddled drowsily in the back of a warm car, heading from Geneva to the French Alps, Sofia gazing sleepily from the window opposite his, Isa had texted to ask when he was back in the office.

Good, she said when he'd replied. *I think I actually miss you.*

I don't believe you, Adam told her.

It's tru. When you get back, we should go out for a drink…

It wasn't anything, he told himself. He was aware now that he would like to have sex with Isa, but he didn't think of it as something that might actually happen. A few days after he'd returned, though, the instant messages took on a new sense of purpose.

So, she'd asked him towards the end of one of these days. *When are we going for a drink?*

They had gone to an old pub in Soho after work, and got quickly drunk. After a couple of hours, Isa had run a hand between his legs and felt his cock through his jeans.

'I'm going to the gents,' she said. 'You can follow me in.'

Giddy with drink and transgression, he did so. Isa was standing in a cubicle, its door open, bright and impossibly exciting amid the drab concrete floors and dirty white Formica of the stalls. She stared at him brazenly as he approached.

When he'd reached her, she closed the door behind him and they pulled at each other, kissing urgently. He felt a moment's reviving shock at the different feel and taste of her as they did so, the shape of her face against his – how emphatically she was not Sofia.

They kissed for several minutes, until Isa pulled away and sat down on the closed toilet lid. Adam leaned back against the stall, breathless and trembling, as Isa began fishing for something in her handbag. Now's my chance, he thought. I could just leave now. But then he saw a wrap appear between the intricately painted nails of her left hand, and she looked up at him, smiling, holding his gaze. She moved her other hand to her brow, and pushed a loose strand of hair back. When she had, her hand lingered, not so far from Adam's crotch.

He took hold of it and placed it back there. Isa dropped the wrap back into her handbag, and undid his belt and flies.

It was only a blow job, he told himself. It was a bit of naughty fun. A one off. She was expert at this, twisting her hand around his cock beneath her mouth, her warm saliva slipping down to his balls. She looked up at him as she did so, holding his gaze and occasionally smiling as she paused and worked his dick with her hand. She swallowed his come without compunction.

Afterwards, he apologized that he'd done nothing to satisfy her.

'Don't worry, darling,' she said. 'It's my favourite thing.'

A one off, they'd agreed. But it hadn't been. A seal had been broken, a bottle of evil spirits opened. There were more messages at work, more texts outside of it.

They lingered late in the office after hours, waiting for the last colleague to go home, or to the pub. In his tiny, cluttered nest of an office – years of demo CDs and promotional material piled up around it, like layers of sedimentary rock containing the fossils of Adam's recent past – they began to have sex several times a week.

Eventually he had taken her home when Sofia was away. In the spare room – his study – there was a mattress made up with bedding. They passed a drunken night on it, carrying out a series of sordid acts until they fell asleep, exhausted, in the early hours.

In the morning, Adam was crippled by his hangover. They stayed tucked into the soiled bedding, eating whatever was in the fridge and watching DVDs, Adam reeling from the bleak glare of his sin. Isa, too, had a significant other, but she didn't seem to feel as guilty.

He hadn't realized it at the time, but Adam had destroyed a world.

The messages during office hours were now spent planning sex. They met outside of work, when Adam could make excuses. They fucked in toilets in Bethnal Green pubs and after-hours bars in

Hackney, and in a more upmarket bathroom in an expensive restaurant.

And before long, something else had crept into their messages, too. Something more sinister, and far more dangerous. Isa didn't just want sex. She wanted him to love her, too.

What do you think about me? she'd ask. *Why do you like me?*

It was clever of her, because of course he had to think of the answers.

She continued to flirt with other men in the office. Adam had come to possess her, as he'd wished, but only in part. He became jealous, and confused this with love on his part, too. And so he started telling her what she wanted to hear.

He convinced himself that all of this did in fact amount to love. That this sort of sex was exciting, rather than empty and regretful. That it meant he was more compatible with Isa than he was with Sofia. He thought that maybe Isa was what he needed, because he wasn't ready for the life he'd been preparing for with Sofia. He was too wild, needed to carry on being so for a while longer yet.

One day, Sofia told him that her mother had said he was *slow*. What was he waiting for, she'd asked, before marrying her?

Somehow, most of the time, he hid away inside himself all the darkness he'd created. When he lay awake at night, though – something that happened more and more often – the full consequence of what he was doing would settle over him like a shroud.

He lay frozen beside Sofia, watching her, wondering what was wrong with him, fearful that the horrors in his head would somehow escape for her to see. How could she not know? he wondered. How could all this be happening within a skull beside hers, buzzing around like a swarm of trapped, repellent flies, and she have no idea? Why could she not see him for what he really was? He was vile, and he knew it.

He tried several times to break it off with Isa. He left her weeping at a bar, and again in the office one night. She was very clever though, and she loved him. The combination made her persuasive. And he was weak. Each time he tried to give her up, he feared he was making a mistake. He was addicted to the dose of self-worth she gave him every time she offered herself.

And so he carried on the affair.

21

Monday ticked towards its inevitable end. Adam had planned to leave the office early, to pack for Denver and take some time for himself. Before he could, he was due on a conference call for one of Kristen's projects.

They walked down to the meeting room together and sat opposite one another.

Kristen tapped the number into the conference phone, and before long, each of the thirteen participants began announcing themselves.

These phone calls had measured the passage of Adam's professional life for the last fifteen years. He was on at least ten of them each week, and they rarely deviated from the same template: running through every aspect of a campaign, listening to updates from PR, digital marketing, booking agents and artist managers. Usually, someone would talk for too long. Another person would sound shamelessly bored and disengaged, and everyone else would wonder how they got away with it. Without fail, someone would be caught out not listening and stutter an excuse when their name was called.

Fifteen minutes into the call, it became clear that the PR team in New York had no idea about the very expensive radio campaign the label had invested in. Thus, a core element of the record company's duty – ensuring everyone had lots of ammunition and no excuses – had gone unfulfilled.

Kristen flushed. 'I'm pretty sure I sent you an update,' she said, frowning and tapping at her laptop.

There was an awkward silence. 'Um, we didn't get anything,' one of the PR team said.

'Maybe it went into junk?' one of his colleagues suggested.

'... Yeah,' Kristen said. 'I'll make sure I get it over to you ASAP.'

When the call was over, Adam attempted to carry out his own duty.

'It's fine obviously,' he said, 'but when we're spending this much money it's really important to make sure everyone has the news about it early on. They'll already have been making their pitches...'

Kristen glared at him. 'Yes,' she said. 'I know how to run a fucking campaign. I am just full to capacity right now and some things are gonna get missed.'

Kristen worked a rigid 9–5 day, and spent at least one hour of each of them on Facebook. Adam took a deep breath, and reminded himself that it simply wasn't worth arguing with her. Apparently satisfied with her performance, Kristen left the room.

Adam walked down to the garage and gratefully sealed himself within the car. The day's travails were over, and he was determined not to let the evening be poisoned by them. As he turned onto Sunset, he caught a glance of Strawberry Peak's summit rearing above the city. A sharp thrill lit through him. He saw the mountain every day, haze permitting, but now its meaning had been transformed for him.

It was no longer just the top of a mountain that had beaten him, that he had wanted to go back to and conquer. It was somewhere he could see from his daily existence in LA, on which he'd had one of the happiest experiences of his new life. He had kissed a beautiful woman on top of a mountain – something he'd never done before. He'd thought the chances of such things had vanished along with his youth. Now, each time he glanced at it, it showed him there was still hope.

Traffic was already bad on Sunset, and he tuned the radio to a current affairs station, thinking of the first glass of wine, of the evening he had to himself before his trip. After a while his thoughts turned to Erica. Images of her, but things she'd said, the way she was, too. The afterglow of being close to her.

His phone rang as he turned into his street, cutting off the radio and shattering his reverie. The Autodidact's name popped up on the car's screen. It was late in the UK. Jason's dark shadow could apparently menace him at any time of day.

Adam clicked to accept.

'Hello,' he said into the still air of the car.

'Hi, man. How you doing?'

'Good, thanks. You?'

'Not bad, mate, yeah. Wanted to catch up with you about a few staff bits.'

'OK. Anything urgent? It's late there, isn't it?'

'Tell me about it. Loads going on, man.'

'Right.'

'So,' the Autodidact said. 'Wanted to let you know that we've let Heather go.'

Adam wracked his brain. 'Heather?'

'Brummie woman we had doing reception,' Jason said. 'She's transgender.'

'Ah yes, I remember her. What happened?'

'She was setting up her own label with some friends. They approached two of our smaller dudes and told them not to tell me.'

'Artists?' Adam asked.

'Yeah.'

'Wow,' Adam said. 'How stupid of her.' There was no way Jason had called him at midnight to tell him this.

'Exactly.'

'How did she take it?'

'Dunno. I got Serena to do it. I've got too much else on currently.'

'Right,' Adam said.

'What about your office, everything alright there? Got to be so careful these days.'

'Everything seems fine.' Adam paused. 'Though it would have been nice if you'd spoken to me after you talked to Meg. I found out when I rang the radio station to complain.'

'Dunno what you expect, mate,' the Autodidact said. 'It's absolutely mental here, and then I hear from Scott that you're telling people to go public with complaints against radio stations, before we've even heard about it.'

Adam's heart began pounding. 'That's not what happened,' he said.

'Whatever. I've just had to take another call from a member of your staff because they're upset over something. It's starting to worry me.'

'What do you mean?' Adam asked.

'I just had Kristen on the phone.'

'Kristen?'

'She was quite emotional. She says you've been harassing her over a radio campaign or something?'

Adam thought for a moment. 'Words fail me,' he said.

'And that you pulled a face when she asked if we could get medical kombucha for the office there?'

Something broke open inside Adam. A little mental flood-gate, from which poured white hot psychic liquid.

'And you believe all that?' he said.

'... Well,' the Autodidact said.

'Anything else?'

There was a long pause, the gentle hum of static. Adam pulled his car over outside the apartment.

'Just make it happen with Falconz tomorrow,' the Autodidact said eventually, his voice brittle. And with that, he rang off.

* * *

'You look like I feel,' Stef said as Adam climbed the steps.

She was sitting at the little table on her balcony, smoking a cigarette.

'I'm fucking livid,' Adam said.

'Bad day at work?'

'Yes,' Adam said. He stood on the landing between their two apartments. He was short of breath, and he paused, leaning on the wooden banister.

'Come and sit down.' Stef nudged the chair opposite hers with her foot. She, too, looked unusually glum.

'What's up in your world?' he asked her as he sat.

'Everyone hates my movie,' she said, breathing out smoke. 'I thought maybe this one was a winner.'

'I did too,' Adam said. Stef had been working on her own script, a dystopian tech thriller about smart homes. It had seemed a good idea, but what did he know?

'Thanks,' Stef said. 'You got any wine?'

'Yes. White or red?'

'Let's start with white.'

Adam went and fetched a bottle from his fridge, along with two glasses. He didn't trust hers to be clean and free of cat emissions.

'Don't give up on it,' he said when he'd poured the drinks. 'Don't they say it takes dozens of rejections to get the acceptance?'

'My manager hates it,' Stef said, and smiled ruefully. 'That's a pretty bad sign.'

'Right.'

'Do you wanna talk about your work?'

'Not really,' he said. Stef's cigarettes were lying on the table between them. For the first time in years, he wanted one. But that was the last problem he needed to lumber himself with again.

'Gimme the outline,' she said. 'An elevator pitch. It'll do you good.'

'My job just seems to have become endless bullshit,' he told her. 'I'm caught between the difficult little fuckers I have to manage, and the megalomaniac I report to in London. And the music isn't as good any more.'

'Yet you're doing something most people would kill for,' Stef said, lighting a cigarette. 'And getting rewarded for it pretty well.' She nodded at his car.

'Yes,' he said.

'And believe me, kid,' she continued, 'the music isn't as good any more for any of us. If you think this is bad, wait until you're really middle-aged.'

Adam laughed, sipping his wine. 'The problem is that I know it's my fault. I have a dream job I worked very hard for, and I don't understand why I'm so pissed off with it.'

Stef drew on her cigarette and watched him.

'I am the problem,' he said, 'and so I don't really know how to fix it.'

'This is where we get into clichés,' Stef said. 'But maybe just try and remind yourself that things aren't so bad. Shit, they could certainly be worse. Have you looked at the jobs most people have?'

Adam nodded.

'I did therapy for a while,' Stef said. 'Hated it. Didn't do any good. The one useful thing the woman told me was "don't take anything personally". I find that works if you can stick to it – which is easier said than done.'

'Yes, right,' Adam said. He was trembling a little, and hoped she hadn't noticed. 'Thanks. That did do some good.'

'I'm glad,' she said. 'The wine is doing *me* some good.'

For a moment, they sat in silence. Stef stubbed out her cigarette and pointed down to the road.

'You didn't see the fence,' she said.

Adam glanced down to the bottom of the sloping garden. Stef's sun-bleached, decrepit fence was hanging towards the sidewalk at a forty-five-degree angle.

'What happened?' he asked, smiling.

'It's not funny,' she said, smiling back and blowing smoke at him. 'A little Mexican skater kid was walking along having a fight with his girlfriend on his cell phone. It finished just as he reached my fence, so he punched it.'

'Must've been some punch,' Adam said, taking a deep swig of his wine. 'Did he stop?'

'He tried to run away, but two guys in a pick-up got out and cornered him.'

'So you'll get him to pay for it?'

'No,' she said. 'Poor little fucker was terrified. He was, like, sixteen, and I felt bad for him. He was already in the middle of a very bad day. He said sorry and I told the guys to let him go.'

'Good on you.'

'Yeah. Then I went inside and got the script news. Also, I don't have any money to fix the fence.'

'It can't be that hard to mend, can it?'

'It's all rotten, I think. The two guys from the pick-up said it'd be expensive. But I think they were kind of annoyed I made them let the kid go.'

Adam looked at his watch. 'It won't get dark for two hours,' he said. 'We can mend it, can't we? We might as well try.'

'Really?' she said.

'Yeah. You've got that massive toolbox. Let's get it out and see what we can do.'

'OK,' Stef said, grinning at him. 'You're on.'

The fence posts were indeed rotten. They found that by using a great deal of very long nails, however, they could reattach the posts and boards in a sturdy enough fashion. By the time they'd finished, it was upright at least. After Adam had used some garden twine to strengthen their bodge job, it actually felt fairly strong. They'd finished the white wine, and were both much happier.

'Good job,' Adam said in his best American accent. They high-fived.

'I'll help you varnish it one weekend,' he told her.

'You're the best,' she said, lighting another cigarette. 'Let's open the red.'

* * *

When they said goodnight, Stef stumbled into her apartment, leaving her cigarettes outside on the table. After Adam heard her locking up, he crept back and slipped one of them from the pack. There were two left, he noted – he wouldn't have liked to steal her last.

There was a box of matches somewhere in the kitchen, and after he'd rifled around in a few drawers and found it, he carried them through to his bedroom. Lying on the bed, he lit up. The smoke tasted odd at first, and he struggled not to splutter when it kicked the back of his throat. No way, he told himself, as though even alone it would be embarrassing to do so.

And then suddenly he was exquisitely, shockingly light-headed. He sank back into the pillow, flicking ash onto the floor and watching the smoke curl liquidly into the air above him, slowly flattening out into the old, familiar blanket.

The head rush was delicious. High, he thought, marvelling at the power of the drug, all drugs. A choice that was made, the consequence of which sucked one into escape with the irresistible force of a vacuum.

He recalled the last time a cigarette had affected him so profoundly, when he was fourteen, and at a richer boy's house; among a little group he wasn't quite popular with. They'd smoked in the sparse wood between the big house and the fields that ran from it to the horizon.

The cigarette – only a Silk Cut, he seemed to remember now – had felt fat and taut and clean in his hand, then his mouth. A marvel. And as they'd climbed back over the fence into the garden, the head rush had kicked in. He remembered giggling, holding on tight so as not to fall, all the awkwardness and nerves suddenly, fleetingly vanishing from him.

Now, he smoked the cigarette as slowly as he could, softening the room around him into a cocoon, allowing his mind to flicker back into a former, long-gone self.

22

He slept heavily. When his alarm jolted him awake at seven o'clock, he flipped it over to turn it off, and saw he'd received a text from Erica. The thrill woke him fully, and he sat up in bed and rubbed his eyes to read it.

Hey! What time's your flight?

Noon, he replied. *Why?*

He wondered if he should get up and into the shower, but she began typing almost as soon as his own message had gone.

I have the day off, her reply said. *How about you buy me breakfast and I give you a ride to the airport?*

I would love that, he replied.

I'll pick you up at eight? Send me your address.

Adam did so, and showered and dressed in a whirl of nervous excitement.

* * *

She arrived on time, waving and smiling from her car. Adam put his duffel bag on the back seat and got in beside her.

'Hey,' she said, smiling. She wore red heels, slim black trousers that showed her ankles, and a little black blazer over a grey silk shirt. Her hair was up in a ponytail, and her expression was mischievous.

'This was an excellent idea of yours,' he said.

'I'm glad you think so. I hope I didn't mess up your schedule.'

'Not at all,' he assured her. 'You've made my morning.'

She pulled out, glancing at her mirrors. The inside of her car smelled good. A strong desire came over him to sit in it with her all day, driving around the city and seeing what they could see.

'You look very smart,' Adam told her.

'Well, it's a doctor's day off,' she said. 'Which means I still have to go to a meeting later.'

'I'm sorry.'

She shrugged, turning the wheel to guide them smoothly onto Sunset.

'Are you excited?' she asked. 'About Denver?'

'Yes,' he lied, reluctant to spoil the happy mood in the car. 'Red Rocks is incredible, apparently.'

'So I've heard. Lucky you.'

At the junction of Sunset and Benton Way was a towering, rotating sign advertising a foot clinic. On one side of it was a happy-looking foot, smiling and dancing and waving a hand. On the other was a sad, injured foot, its eyes red, leaning on a crutch with one of its toes in a bandage. Adam had met someone at a party who'd told him that they drove past the foot every morning and believed that whichever side they saw first would decide the way their day went.

'Man,' the guy had said. 'I hate to see that crackhead foot.'

Ever since, Adam had found it difficult to resist the superstition himself. This morning, the smiling foot was facing them squarely. Erica took the turn before it had rotated away. He sighed happily, and leaned back in his seat.

When they reached Hillhurst, Erica turned north towards Los Feliz. Halfway up the street, she performed a smooth U-turn and stopped outside a place called Recess, with a patio outside a smart, low-rise building. A valet, the sleeves of his white shirt already rolled back over large forearms, welcomed them and took the car.

In the courtyard, which was cool and bright in the new day's light, only a few tables were taken. Two young mothers with their babies, a few older women with little dogs on leashes at their feet.

'You wouldn't believe how busy this place gets at weekends,' Erica said.

'It's lovely,' Adam replied.

'Here's the plan,' she said. 'You go order, I'll get us a table.'

'Perfect. What are you having?'

'Pancakes and a coffee. And I think I want to drink a Bloody Mary.'

Adam raised an eyebrow at her.

'I wouldn't usually,' she said. 'A little fun on my day off.'

'You're preaching to the choir,' Adam told her happily.

It was still only 8.30 when they were seated with their coffees. Beyond the courtyard's edge, Hillhurst looked bright and clean in the morning light. Traffic moved along it briskly, and a storekeeper was sweeping the sidewalk across the street from where they sat. The old ladies were quieter now, digesting their breakfasts, sipping coffees and looking out into the street, absently scratching behind their dogs' ears.

'Cheers,' Erica said, when the drinks arrived.

'This beats doing emails,' Adam said.

'Will you get in trouble?'

'I'll do them on the plane.'

The Bloody Mary was delicious, and he told her so.

'I'm a connoisseur,' she said. 'This will sound very pretentious, but there's one out in Topanga at this bougie hippie place that I think is the best in LA. They take it so seriously that they put a piece of dyed purple cauliflower in it, though I'm not sure that affects the taste.'

'You should start a Bloody Mary Instagram,' Adam told her. 'It'd be a hit.'

'I'd rather stick to drinking them,' she said.

'I'm just so happy you're a drinker,' Adam replied.

She tossed her hair back and laughed, her beauty ringing out at him from across the table. He felt an odd pang of fear in the face of it. Already, he didn't want to lose her.

The food arrived, and more customers began to fill out the courtyard. There were lots of women in yoga pants and trainers, several more people with little dogs.

'Can I ask you a personal question?' Adam said.

'I guess so.' Erica looked straight at him, intrigued.

'When were you last in a relationship with someone?'

'Huh,' she said. 'A year ago.'

'Right. Is it OK that I asked?'

'I think so,' she nodded.

'What happened, with the guy?'

She sipped her coffee and looked over his shoulder.

'Well, he was also a doctor…' She paused.

'And?'

'He got a transfer to a hospital in the Bay Area. He asked me to go with him, but I could tell he didn't want me to. I don't think he wanted to settle, all that.'

'Right,' Adam nodded.

'Why did you want to know?'

'I just think you're very lovely,' he said. 'The train of thought started there.'

She smiled again, and sipped the Bloody Mary through a straw.

'I see,' she said. 'Histories, huh?'

'Yes.'

'And how do you feel now you've asked your question?'

'Very good,' Adam said.

* * *

In the car, he put his hand on her thigh and squeezed it gently. He meant the gesture to be affectionate, to tell her how good it felt to be with her, but the boozy drinks had generated an undertow of sex and this physical connection strengthened it. She gave him a quick, urgent look before turning back to the road.

There was something more than just sex, too, that he was sure was mutual. He felt oddly raw and emotional.

'Adam,' she said.

'Yes.'

'I wish we had more time.' She was watching the road, speaking quietly but clearly. 'You know?'

'Me too,' he said.

'Well,' she said. 'When you get back.'

They glanced at each other. Her mischievous look had returned, and she smiled, breaking the tension.

On the freeway, driving south towards the airport, the car was filled with a happy silence. It seemed to Adam that they were floating along the tarmac in a cloud of desire and happiness. He looked at Erica's feet in her heels, her slim ankles and wrists. He wanted to tell her to turn the car around, so he could stay in LA.

'Thank you for driving me,' he said when she pulled up in the terminal.

'You're very welcome.'

'That was an adventure.' He wanted to shower her with praise, felt it wise to restrain himself.

She leaned across the seat and kissed him.

A moment later someone knocked on the car bonnet, and they both looked up in surprise. A large, unshaven airport cop was glaring through the windscreen.

'Alright, folks,' he said, already looking away. 'Move it on.'

Adam climbed out, pausing at the door to look at Erica.

'Call me,' she said. She glanced at her cell phone, tossed it into a cupholder and turned off her hazards, already gauging the traffic ahead.

Adam closed the door, and felt a thud of longing as her car disappeared around a curve in the airport's beltway. He picked up his duffel bag and walked into the terminal.

23

At least, he reflected as he slumped into his window seat on the plane, Falconz were nice people.

His Platinum status with the airline had won him a Comfort Class seat, but not First. No matter. He'd boarded early, removed his book and headphones from his bag, and stashed it safely directly above his head. Plane seats, for Adam, induced instant drowsiness. Especially today, after the unexpected liaison with Erica and a strong drink first thing.

Normally, it would simply be the sudden draining of stress, he thought: the stress of getting to the airport, going through security, and not knowing whether the preponderance of large wheelie cases would mean his bag would not end up directly above his head.

But today, all of these obstacles had been surmounted. Now, all he had to do was stay awake until the drinks trolley appeared.

He wished he felt more excitement for the trip, and for Falconz. Sadly, though, being a nice person wasn't always the best qualification for being a good artist. Successful, perhaps, but not necessarily good.

In Adam's time in America, he'd noticed that this new breed of musician had begun to dominate. There seemed to be a whole legion of artists like Falconz, who applied to music the sort of steely diligence and frank ambition that they otherwise might have to careers in financial services, or extreme sporting feats. It was hard to think of them as artists, people who made the sort of imperiously original work that changed lives.

In Adam's experience, the distinguishing characteristic of artists who made that sort of work was how troubled they were. Difficult, sensitive souls who made the world a more beautiful place, but whom it was often terrible to be. In fact, they were often the sort who, if it weren't for their talent, might have ended up resident on the LA River.

It was a long time since he'd worked with one, he reflected, peering out of the plane window. If he was honest with himself, it was getting on for a decade since he'd last truly loved a musician's output and felt privileged and excited to work with them.

That artist had been a maverick north London rapper, who radiated a sort of manic, attention-deficit charisma, and whose work Adam had loved deeply. The rapper's ability to deliver fiery, extended vocal performances, littered with casually brilliant metaphors and burning with restrained anger and passion, had seemed to Adam to approach the transcendent. To Adam's joy, a strong personal bond had developed between them, too.

'You might be a white man from Bath,' the rapper had told him, 'but you do know your shit.'

He was the same age as Adam, but had been raised in a broken family, partly by an aunt who brought a succession of 'uncles' into the house and cooked crack cocaine in her kitchen.

'I used to wonder what they was doing in there, mate,' the rapper had told Adam, on the train to a festival in Belgium. 'All this steam coming out under the door.'

He'd been stabbed twelve times, in two sets of six. While he and Adam worked together, his forearm had been deeply slashed with a Stanley knife by an older man who wanted the rapper to make a career for his talentless son.

Adam had listened one night as he'd hosted a pirate radio show, regularly pausing the music to insult another artist he'd fallen out with. The show had ended with the studio being attacked by this newly minted rival and his crew.

When Adam finally got hold of the rapper, and asked if he was alright, the reply came: *All good mate. They slashed me but on my back they dint get my face.*

The artist was famously mercurial. He never stayed with a label for more than one record before he fell out with them explosively. But Adam had managed, somehow, to release four.

I love you mate, the rapper texted him once. And Adam told him he loved him too.

Sometimes he wondered if it might have been more exciting to work with very famous artists. To go to a big label and encounter some of the people with the towering egos that were, apparently, often necessary to reach the dizzying upper echelons of success.

He'd had the chance, too. For a year or so, he'd worked in the production department of a much bigger label, assisting an A & R man with the daily travails of mixing and mastering singles. The label's artists regularly appeared on prime-time TV shows, and Adam had once accompanied one of them. In his youthful, emphatically hip-hop morph of baggy jeans, giant t-shirt and silver chain, he had stood out like a sore thumb. He had not been happy at the label.

One of the defining recollections of this brief stint was being driven to a studio by a junior A & R man on one of his first days.

'What do you think the difference will be between working at an indie and working here?' Adam had asked him, somewhat innocently.

'Well,' the A & R man had said, sniffing, and glancing at Adam as he drove. 'I think it'll be a lot more debauched.'

But the music had been bad, and he'd gone back to the smaller world of independent labels. He'd wanted to stick to his principles, work on esoteric records he loved, try to make successes of them for the artists that made them. Somewhere, though, something had gone wrong.

Now, the majority of his time was spent working on Falconz. They were good, untroubled people. With them, it was only the music that was the problem.

But there was, of course, a more frightening alternative. Namely that Falconz, and their ever-expanding, numbing swathe of contemporaries, were actually good, and that Adam simply couldn't tell.

Perhaps he'd become too old to get it. As a youth, he'd observed a joyless, jaundiced cynicism in older music fans with a sort of disgust. Nirvana, several of them had told him, are just ripping off Pixies. So why bother with them? It was clear, then and now, that they'd been missing the point – completely failing to hear the beauty and originality in music they'd been confronted with.

Was that what was happening to him now? Certainly, he found himself more and more often wanting to tell younger people about the antecedents of what they were listening to. Whenever he gave in to temptation and did so, they nodded noncommittally and kept listening to the new thing, the one *they* were into, that was happening *now*.

Fuck off, Grandad; that was what he'd used to think, whenever someone did it to him.

But might there not be some grain of truth in the idea that music was getting worse? That mavericks and visionaries and gut instinct, loose cannons and colourful characters and passion, were being replaced by data, sanitized corporatism and laser-targeted marketing?

Adam, as a young man, had loved that there were tribes. Rockers, ravers, indie kids, metalheads, clubbers and hip-hop crews. You distinguished yourself by your clothes, your music and your friends. Other tribes were the enemy. There to be ridiculed, run from or occasionally fought. Back then, it was normal to love and hate with equal passion.

Now, social media and a new breed of smarter, insidious brand sponsorship seemed to have dissolved the tribes into a sort of globalized, homogeneous hipster template – replete with tattoos, beards, the same haircuts and a standard set of tastes. No one dared to say they hated a given genre now – outside of Christian rock, perhaps, or Nazi punk. The tribes had been unified under the good word of a handful of music websites. Now, everyone liked the same, few, officially sanctioned artists from each main genre.

Hipsters had the internet. The albums Adam had dug out of record stores, had made the dread decision over which to select, to spend his meagre pocket money on, had dared to carry to the counter under the cold stare of pale young men riddled with obscure knowledge, had taken home and studied – often recoiled from – had worked to understand and often to love, had haunted and terrified and electrified him, were now torn up in a digital frenzy of recycling, before everyone moved on to the next thing.

When Kurt Cobain had died, Adam had to wait two days for his *NME* and *Melody Maker* to arrive and tell him, in any detail, what had happened. Nowadays, Wikipedia could demythologize a band in less time than it took to listen to a song.

And with the brands had come a total loss of romance towards independence. Adam hadn't heard the phrase 'selling out' mentioned in almost a decade, and never once by anyone younger than himself. Now, if your favourite rapper worked with Maroon 5, more power (and money) to him. It was *better* to be on a major label. That made you the real deal – not just some chump who could only get signed to an indie.

Yes, he believed, it was surely possible to make an argument that music was getting worse. That the Led Zeppelins, Beatles, Stones, Bowies, Nirvanas, Outkasts and Wu-Tang Clans just didn't come around as often any more.

And however depressing it was to believe this, to have become one of those old men, it seemed worse to be dishonest, to pretend to be excited.

Maybe music was simply a young person's game. Certainly, the sense of befuddlement that he'd noted, gradually settling in his once-passionate, non-industry friends, had recently come over him too. He had started to occasionally mispronounce artists' names, to confuse second and third albums. Worse, to not care very much when he did so.

Every day, millions of oddly named, semi-talented people uploaded their music to the internet, and the industry tried to sift through the manure to find the gem. It was a cacophony out there, and Adam's ears were ringing.

And that, he thought, staring at the baking runway tarmac beyond the window, might well be his undoing. This befuddlement must be hidden at all costs. Particularly from the Autodidact.

He'd worked himself into some anxiety when his phone beeped in his pocket. When he removed it, he saw he had an alert on Instagram.

Reluctantly, he opened the app. How best to discourage, or even close down, this additional method of contact? he wondered. The message was from Angelina.

Will u b in Denver for red rocks?? it said. *If so c u there* ♥

A reply wasn't immediately forthcoming. He didn't want to be rude, but neither too encouraging. Go away, red frog, he thought. No. Not fair. It was hardly Angelina's fault.

Sure thing! he wrote eventually. *Hopefully see you there!*

The phone still in his hand, he thought of Erica. Before he could decide not to, he sent her a text.

You're lovely. I can't wait to see you again.

The thought of her made his stomach flutter like a teenager's. If only she was beside me now, he thought. If only we were going somewhere together. Images of a hot place, of a beach and sunshine and Erica's smiling face, rose into his mind and blazed there. Lying on that beach and talking to each other. Faces close together, happily drunk, bodies laced with sand and salt water.

Her face, but also the rest of her, he thought, onwardly. Her bedroom, undressing together as they kissed. Moving his lips down her long neck and to her breasts and her stomach and everywhere else.

He wanted to hear her speak more. The edge of mischief she had. The way she said exactly what she meant, and the way that revealed a mind that he liked very much. The precision of her speech. Her laugh and her smile.

His penis and his heart swollen in equal proportion, he replayed the morning's memories of her, letting them work their powers. Grinning stupidly, he put the phone back in his pocket.

The plane had started to fill up. Adam watched the procession of travellers moving slowly down the aisle towards him. Young women in baggy sweatpants, almost like sleepwear, he thought – flight pillows attached to their wheelie cases, larger-sized iPhones in free hands. Young men in LA Dodgers baseball caps, many in shorts and vests, even flip-flops, several with big, gleaming Rolexes. Older men with comfortable slacks and smart polo shirts, moustaches, cell phone belt-clips, briefcases and the harder-earned, subtler types of Swiss watches.

A man entered the plane who caught Adam's attention, some primal warning tingling in his spine. The first things that stood out about him were the long, greasy hair beneath a baseball cap, and a square, rapidly chewing jaw below mirrored aviators. He looked a bit like an eighties one-hit-wonder gone to seed, Adam thought, or a movie cliché of a trailer park top dog – a slightly sweaty, unwashed look about him. As he boarded the plane, he glanced about himself in quick, proprietary looks, an amused twitch around his mouth.

Adam watched as he made his way down the aisle. The man's jeans were stonewashed, riding low on his hips and high on his boots, over which they flared a little. The boots themselves had a squared-off toe. But the t-shirt was what really stood out. It was yellow, and too short for the man, exposing an inch or so of brown, shiny-looking flesh divided by a line of vertical fur. On it, the word 'MINE' was printed, with an arrow beneath it pointing to the man's left.

'Jesus,' Adam muttered to himself. The guy wasn't even travelling with someone, as far as he could tell. He shivered, glancing about and trying to gauge how many seats were still free. There were plenty.

Anyway, the law of plane seat averages meant he shouldn't be worried. It simply never happened. It could be a beautiful, slim, smiley girl, or a gigantic, waddling, snacking teenage boy, and neither dream nor nightmare was ever ultimately realized. Usually, it was one of the older, smartly dressed men, who would make a typically warm, interested, American form of small talk and perhaps leave him with a business card – and that was just fine.

Adam watched as the man drew closer. He held a cheap-looking leather holdall in his right hand. The elbow above it was slightly bent, the forearm muscled and tattooed. The bag bumped the shoulder, fingers or elbow of every passenger in the aisle seats on the left side of the aircraft as the man passed. No one seemed to get annoyed. It baffled him. From above, Katy Perry's voice had begun battling the tinniness of the speakers.

The man paused beside the toilets. He ran his eyes along the seat numbers, and Adam's heart began to sink. Please, he willed. No.

The man swivelled his head towards Adam. His eyes were invisible behind the shades. He grinned, leaned up to the luggage bin – the ribbon of stomach expanding now to a full abdomen that was both a dirty brown shade of tan and, also, somehow very shiny – and jammed his bag on top of Adam's.

He sat down heavily, opened his legs wide, and flexed his shoulders. When his left forearm made contact with – and displaced – Adam's right, he swivelled his head again and gave Adam a long look, the smile, this time, noticeably absent. There were tiny scratches on the frames and lenses of his sunglasses.

Cunt, Adam thought. His blood beat in his ears. He pictured how he must look – indeed how he knew himself to look, from photographs – a tall, slim, self-conscious man in his smart shirt and his jeans and desert boots, sitting crammed into his seat by another man who appeared to be airing his balls and wearing a t-shirt that claimed Adam was 'his'.

How dare he? How dare this man swagger through life, a sardonic grin on his leathery fucking face and a catch-all mockery on his chest?

Adam picked up his book, seething, opening the page. It took three or four minutes before he realized he wasn't reading. All he was doing was hating, and scanning his eyes uselessly up and down the text.

The man beside him moved his left leg inward, back within the obvious confines of his own personal seating area. For a beautiful, endorphin-flooding moment, Adam believed that the man had realized how boorish he'd been, was making a gesture. This small victory would have been enough. Adam would have forgiven him anything. Anything to be able to rid himself of this hatred, which he already knew was toxic, was dissolving his insides.

The man slipped a hand into his left pocket and pulled out a pair of white Apple headphones. As soon as he'd done so, his leg sprang back to its forty-five degree angle, knocking heavily into Adam's.

Adam's blood felt thick – atheroma-like anger was coagulating in his arteries. The base of his spine pulsed – an entirely new symptom of his rage.

Music began to spritz from the man's cheap plastic earphones. Actually, Adam thought, it was merely the calcified skeleton of whatever the actual music was. He tuned into it, trying to identify the song. 'Sail' by AWOLNATION, he realized with a venomous shudder.

Utter fucking cunt. He looked down at the man's left arm, reappraising the tattoos. He'd decided the guy was some sort of country fan, but the generic, tribal-type ink that covered his wrist like a gauntlet suggested otherwise. This guy didn't even have the decency to believe in something.

A hot snake of anger writhed inside Adam. A terrible knowledge had come over him. He knew he would do, now, what he always did. He'd suffer in silence, and simply soak it all up. This hatred would turn into an ulcer in his stomach, pulsating and acid-filled, while the man beside him breezed through life in perfect bliss.

The plane took off. Normally he'd be dozing already, a small part of his otherwise dormant mind listening out for the drinks trolley, the potential missing of which was the only remaining anxiety. Turbulence, deficient video screens, babies or naked feet: all of these were of no concern to Adam. Even the violent and comprehensive reclining of the seat in front of him by its occupant was no longer the problem it once had been. Airmiles. SeatGuru. Forward planning. These formed the trident with which to battle poor-quality travel. Those, and plenty of gin and tonics.

But not today. Today Adam took to the air pickling in his own hate. The man beside him was thumping the hard-looking heel of his boot into the thin floor of the aircraft, shuddering Adam's seat – in fact Adam's entire, enclosed little world – each time he did so. The muffled scream of the engines at least obliterated the music for a while.

A man like this was never questioned, Adam thought. Never confronted. Never taught anything. His expression as he'd sauntered down that aisle had been derisive, appraising the other passengers as if they were simply playthings. Adam remembered reading a newspaper article about a psychopath, who'd described himself as 'like a cat among mice'. This man was a psychopath, he was sure. Who else would spit in the face of social-mindedness as he had? Who else quite simply did not give a fuck about the people around him?

The only people who would teach a man like this something would be other men like him, when he occasionally fought them in shitty tourist bars. It saddened him to think of this person being from LA. It made him think of the Strip, of the strip clubs, the middle of Hollywood and the sixteen-ounce margaritas. All of these were usually cordoned off for Adam, his mental floodlights illuminating only the other, better side of the city.

Potentially, this man was Denver's fault. After all, that's where he was going, this alpha male type who hadn't even bothered to wash. He didn't smell bad, exactly. He just smelled strong. Strong enough to actively remind Adam that humans were animals. Livestock, jammed into a humming metallic tube. Strapped in and trussed up, fed and watered in their restraints. The vision made Adam shiver.

The man turned his head again, slowly, curious at this sudden movement. Now Adam caught a glimpse of his eyes, which were narrowed behind the shades. They were hidden once more as the man looked directly at him, confronting him with a distorted vision of his own face, reflected in the shades' lenses.

This image of himself made him feel even worse. He looked more male, more manly – or rather, mannish – than he'd expected, somehow. More so than in his mental self-image. Not for the first time, Adam wondered if he had some sort of reverse body dysmorphia, by means of which he always believed himself to look better than he actually did. In the shades' scratched lenses, he looked redder and more careworn than he expected.

Christ, he thought. You're not so far from him, are you? You're the same species after all. Just another ageing male bristling at the incursion of another. You're one of him too! In fact, if he's the alpha male, that makes you the beta.

At this, he felt a glum wave of depression rise up in him like nausea. He frowned and fought it back. It must just be the shades, he thought.

Before the man turned back into his seat, Adam saw once again the arrow, printed onto the shirt in bold, unblemished white. 'MINE' the shirt said above it, as it prodded at Adam. 'MINE.'

A flight attendant was pushing the trolley down the aisle towards them; a large, grey-haired lady who smiled warmly at the passengers.

Adam saw himself through her eyes, and gritted his teeth until they ground.

It took an age before she made it to them, an age in which Adam felt himself to be bathed in searing exposure. He felt as bad as he might if he'd been naked.

'Drinks?' she asked. Adam first, he was in the window.

'Gin and tonic, please,' he said.

'You sure you don't need this fella's permission for that?' the woman said. And she, and quite suddenly the man, burst into laughter.

Adam squirmed, his smile-grimace wobbling as he waited for his drink.

'And you, honey?' the stewardess said to the man.

'Beer,' the man said.

'Well, I got Sam Adams Seasonal, Coors Light or Heineken.'

'Take a Coors.'

The woman moved off. The sound of her cart, of her colleague, of the orders she received, receded from Adam's ears.

All that remained was the thumping of his blood, the red mist filling his vision, which tunnelled onto the sweating drink before him.

It was just like being at work. He was going to sit there and stew in his own anger and get heart disease and a stomach ulcer because he was too weak to say anything. It was just like being on the Tube in his old life, some macho idiot standing in front of the doors, braced against the handrail, giving Adam a hard look to signal it was him that must squeeze around.

It was like the three woke-looking hipsters in Echo Park who had laughed after their unleashed dog chased a mother goose and her goslings across the grass and into the water. As in all of these instances, he would do nothing, nothing except brood on his failure for the rest of the day, beating himself up and fantasizing about what he should have said or could have done.

The little mental floodgate burst open again, and tore off its hinges.

'Excuse me,' he said, turning to the man. His voice came out as little more than a whisper.

'Excuse me,' he said again. 'Excuse me.' His voice was much louder now, but noticeably trembling.

The man turned, pulled his headphones out with one hand.

'What's up?' he said.

Adam swallowed. 'Please move your leg,' he said.

The man glanced down. 'Sure,' he said, and did so.

Adam stared at him.

'Anything else?' the guy asked.

'Your arm. You should share the armrest.'

'Fine,' the guy said.

'Good,' Adam said. 'And your music is very loud.'

The man frowned, as though mildly hurt. He turned away and raised his earbuds.

'I'll turn it down,' he murmured. 'All you got to do is ask.'

Adam slumped back into his chair. He took several deep breaths, and after a moment he closed his eyes and smiled, sinking into the seat as if floating in a cloud of light. His relief was like a pressure valve, draining his overworked arteries. He felt like a man who'd just delivered a keynote speech to a standing ovation.

He drank half of his gin and tonic in one gulp, and reopened his book.

24

'Welcome to Denver, Mr Fairhead. Cookie?'

At the Whalley Hotel in downtown Denver, he was being checked in by a tall, pale young woman with glasses and a long black dress.

'I beg your pardon?'

'Oh,' the receptionist said, giggling. 'Sorry. We offer all of our guests a cookie. They're fresh. Want one?'

'Why not,' Adam said.

The girl slid the plastic key cards for the room across the desk, along with a little paper bag.

'Enjoy,' she said.

Adam thanked her, crossed the lobby and called the elevator. When it arrived, he stepped into its small, bright red interior and pressed the button for his floor. An elegantly dressed older lady stepped in after him, smiled and selected the floor below his.

In place of the usual ping, the elevator apparently had a different electronic voice for each stop, making chirpy references to what were evidently American films or TV shows that Adam was only vaguely familiar with.

In his room, he had an hour to kill. He stood before the mirror in the bathroom and regarded himself. In this kind, dim light, he didn't look as careworn and red as he had in the lenses of his neighbour's glasses on the flight. Cheered, he took off his clothes and lay on the bed.

His thoughts drifted, and settled on Erica once more. Automatically, his hand moved to his penis. The urge was lacking, though; he didn't actually want to masturbate. Strange, he thought. It was the first time he could remember feeling this lack in a similar situation, on any other of the many occasions he'd found himself lying naked on a new hotel bed.

His phone chimed, and vibrated on the glass of the bedside unit. He picked it up quickly, thinking the text might be from Erica, and was disappointed to see Roger the manager's name on his screen.

30 mins. Suite 3, penthouse level.

Why was everything with Roger so ominous? Adam wondered.

He showered, and ordered a Martini from room service. When it arrived, he had to drink it quite quickly before heading back to the chirruping elevator.

* * *

'Welcome, ladies and gentlemen,' Roger said. He was standing before a vast panel of glass that ran the length of the luxury suite. Behind him, the few skyscrapers of Denver's token downtown were dwarfed by the snow-topped Rocky Mountains beyond.

The speakers of a specially rented sound system rose almost to the ceiling either side of him, their black, silhouetted forms somehow menacing – as though a pair of robot bodyguards were flanking the manager.

'Tonight,' Roger continued, 'you are all gonna drink the Kool-Aid.'

Adam swallowed. My God, he thought. He's finally fucking lost it.

And it was true that Roger's eyes – free, now, from his sunglasses – looked frightening. Red-rimmed, unblinking, the pupils shrunk to little black dots and the orbs themselves appearing to protrude. On the first album, Adam recalled, it had taken a lot longer for Roger to reach this stage of intensity. The new record wasn't even out yet.

He scanned the room, looking for something to drink. An *actual* drink would have been nice. All that had been laid out on a coffee table was a few bottles of mineral water.

Roger, meanwhile, looked at each of his captive audience, eyeing them like the leader of a small, armed band of musical resistance. He had insisted that the key players fly in for the gig. As well as Adam, there were four other attendees: a smart blonde radio promoter in her mid-forties – visibly annoyed at her summoning; a slim, earnest PR guy; a very young woman who dressed like a goth and specialized in digital streaming; and Falconz' booking agent, a stocky, aggressive man in a sports jacket whose enthusiasm for the band was second only to Roger's.

'Let me tell you a story,' Roger said, softening his voice momentarily. 'The other day I found myself in a techno rave. A kid that I'm mentoring in the office wanted to take me to see one of his DJs at a warehouse party downtown. Now, I'm not much of an underground dance guy, but I thought – hey, why not? So I went. And it was just… amazing.'

He paused, scanning his seated audience. 'It was dark in there. Disorienting. Strobe lights, smoke. Dancing figures. People seemed to emerge from nowhere… The music… It was so heavy, so intense. So… big. Every element, every layer of it was so clear and so loud. The bass. I could feel it… pounding… deep in my gut.'

Roger closed his eyes, and thumped a fist into his stomach. The radio promoter flinched.

'So when I got back to my hotel, I was in a daze. I poured myself a glass of bourbon. The sun was already coming up, but a question was tearing at my mind, and I put on the first Falconz album. I had to know, you see. I needed to compare it to this experience of a different world, to make sure the music we work on has the same level of power. To make sure I hadn't been trapped in… some sort of a bubble. And guess what?' He paused, drew in a deep breath, trembling a little.

Maybe he's realized? Adam wondered. Maybe it's suddenly struck him that it's just emotional incontinence in musical form?

Roger raised his eyes once more. 'I was *even more* blown away,' he said, voice cracking with passion. 'And that's when I realized: Falconz are geniuses on a whole different level… Beyond electronic music. Beyond rock. Beyond *music*, even. What we are witnessing is just the beginning. Falconz are one of the key creative forces of their generation, working in any medium.'

Adam coughed. The radio promoter glanced at him. *Run!* he felt like shouting.

Roger had paused, eyeing each of them again in turn. The radio promoter – a highly regarded industry veteran – was wearing a pair of pristine, patent-blue heels. Her legs crossed before her, she'd allowed one of these to dangle from a toe. Now, she began waggling the heel rapidly, a frown deepening on her face.

Adam risked a glance rightward, along the row of seats. The agent and the PR guy were nodding, reflecting on Roger's words. Only the goth remained impassive.

'Falconz,' Roger continued, 'are bigger than all of us. Tonight, you are gonna see one of the greatest shows of your lives. I personally guarantee it. But before you do…' The manager's latest pause was long enough for the radio promoter to frown more deeply, and glance at Adam again. '… You are gonna hear some brand-new Falconz music.'

With a flourish, Roger stepped aside and clicked a small black remote in his hand. Adam tried not to wince as the air in the room was abruptly filled with a very loud sound.

Falconz' music was a strange, sickly blend of soppy emotiveness and sugary euphoria, concocted with bland synths and wooden, electronic drums. Each song featured, half submerged in these other elements, an uninterrupted, masturbatory guitar solo, played by the band's male member – Bret – with the utmost sincerity. It was, Adam reflected, gazing into the middle distance and trying to look enraptured, all one big sense of release from a tension that hadn't existed in the first place. A constant gushing of big chords, noodling guitar and rigid beats, topped with ear-scratching, sped-up vocals that brought to mind a lovesick cartoon chipmunk.

Listening to Falconz was a bit like spending a long time, sober, with someone who was very high on ecstasy: pleasant enough at moments, but ultimately utterly mind-numbing.

The playback lasted thirty minutes. Afterwards, Adam's ears were ringing.

They all clustered around Roger, sipping mineral water and uttering superlatives. Monica, the radio promoter, was the first to leave the room.

'Hey Adam,' Roger said, taking him aside.

'Yes?'

'I think she's gonna need some more work.' He gazed at Adam meaningfully.

'Right,' Adam said. 'I'll, ah, talk to her.'

'Good man,' Roger said. 'The show will knock her out. But we gotta be sure, man. Everyone working this record has to believe.'

His mad eyes lasered into Adam's.

* * *

'Everybody listen up,' the tour manager boomed as he entered the dressing room. 'Be in Ryan's world at 10.05. NO LATER. That's 10.05. Thank you.'

'What's Ryan's world?' Adam asked an assistant.

'Oh, he means get their earpieces in. Ryan runs all comms from that point on.'

In the warren of rooms and tunnels backstage, there was a hive of activity. Falconz themselves, along with Roger, hadn't yet appeared from their private inner dressing room. That was fine by Adam. He was perfectly content drinking beers from one of the coolers dotted about, chatting to the many technical staff, or the members of a Denver gospel choir who'd been roped in to provide backing vocals. It was, he reflected, all a very long way from punky little gigs in sweaty east London venues. Was he mad to have preferred those?

But Red Rocks, he had to admit, was an impressive place. Nestled between monumental outcrops of crags and cliffs of rock that was, true to its name, a ruddy clayish colour, it sat at an elevation of six thousand feet. It seemed improbable that a venue like it could ever be opened now, in the modern era of chronic health and safety. On the way up from the city, Adam had seen a storm blow over, forked lightning spearing down from the sky. Luckily for Falconz, it had disappeared almost as suddenly as it materialized. Apparently, lightning within two miles meant an instant shutdown.

The backstage area was carved out of the rock itself, the walls formed from it; long, curved spurs reaching out across the floor. It was like something from a *Star Trek* episode, Adam thought. Kirk and Spock in an alien concert venue, enjoying some interplanetary culture before everything inevitably went pear-shaped and they wound up back on the Enterprise.

In the centre of this backstage warren was a wide, flat wall, covered in small plaques, one each for every artist who'd played there. Adam paused in front of this, sipping a can of beer, reading. Stravinsky. The Beatles. Neil Young. U2. Depeche Mode in their *Violator* heyday. God, what he'd have given to beam back to any of those.

Somewhere around the corner from where he stood, voices were raised in greeting, and the air seemed to take on the heightened electrical charge that always surrounded successful musicians. Adam turned, preparing his smile as the two members of Falconz, Roger a step or so behind them, turned the corner and came into view.

Clad in black jeans, Adidas trainers and t-shirts, both of them were beaming. Bret – stocky, sleeve-tattooed and dark-haired – and Marissa – a petite woman with short blonde hair and a fleshy, instantly likeable face.

'Fuck yeah!' Bret, the more vocal of the pair, raised his hands and grinned. 'So glad you made it, man.'

'What's up?' Marissa said, and gestured for Adam to lean down and kiss her on the cheek.

Adam hugged them both, while Roger looked on from behind them, his arms crossed over his chest.

'When'd you get in, man?' Bret asked.

'A few hours ago,' Adam replied.

'Thanks so much for coming,' Marissa said. 'It really means a lot.'

'Oh man,' Adam said. 'No way I was missing this. It's such an honour to be here.'

He felt queasy with his own dishonesty, as though he'd sipped something poisonous.

'First time at Red Rocks, right?' Bret asked.

'Yes,' Adam said.

'Well,' Marissa said, glancing down the corridor, 'we'll do our best to make sure it's a special one.'

'It's going to be amazing,' Adam said. Sentences like these came to him reflexively, backstage at shows. He was a fount of enthused cliché.

'So, are you guys all set?'

'Think so, man,' Bret said. The pair looked at each other with a quick, nervous smile.

'This place is something to live up to,' Marissa added. 'And we got a lot going on up there tonight.'

'Yes, I've already met the choir,' Adam said. 'You guys will be brilliant, you always are.'

'Thank you, Adam,' Bret said.

The pair of them looked at him gratefully, in a perfect example of the genuine charm that had won hearts and minds everywhere they went.

Adam felt like an imposter, a fake. You were invited here, he thought. And you're lying to their faces.

'Well,' he said. 'Break a leg. I can't wait.'

Bret slapped him on the back, and they hugged him again before disappearing into the centre of a group of serious-faced men and women wearing clip-on walkie-talkies or earpieces, calmly but firmly updating and instructing them, circling the pair in a small orbit of bodies.

'All set?' Roger asked Adam.

'Yes indeed,' Adam nodded.

'Good man,' the manager replied. 'I'm watching from front of house. I'll see you there.'

Adam waited until Roger had disappeared around the corner, the corridor abruptly empty and silent. At his feet was a large white cooler. He raised its lid and stuffed two cans of beer into each jacket hip pocket, and stood. Fuck it, he thought, reopening the cooler, and shoved a fifth into the inner one. They were small cans, after all.

25

The show passed, slowly, in a blur of flashing lights, big-screen visuals and musical bombast. Generically ethnic dancers twirled on the screens, amid chopped-up, artificially enhanced images of waterfalls, mountains and forests. It was a sort of nature porn, Adam thought. Harnessing the wide appeal of the nature documentary, or the Apple screen saver, and marrying it to the bland excitement of a baseball match's interval. Quite clever really.

Behind him, a row of stony-faced technicians worked faders on various desks for lighting and sound. They reminded Adam of lizards, unmoving, heads extended towards the stage, eyes intent on it.

At least Falconz' was a coherent artistic universe. The music sounded as though it could soundtrack a Disney movie, forever stuck in the moment in which a small, native boy wanders into the forest for the first time, and, wide-eyed, is introduced to the animated animals who will become his friends. They even had a line of fire dancers, who emerged every now and again wearing different costumes and orgasmic expressions and spun their flaming sticks around like something from a Thai full moon party.

The gospel choir was underused, and the black-clad singers did a good job of not looking bored for the long periods in which they stood onstage doing nothing. Bret and Marissa were raised on twin platforms, Marissa singing her heavily digitized, pitch-shifted vocals between bouts playing synths, twiddling knobs and leaping, waving her hands and occasionally bashing an electronic drum kit.

Bret spent the entire show contorted over his space-age, angular guitar, cycs closed, thrashing his head and occasionally moshing as he tapped and bent the strings in his endless solos. His efforts were painfully at odds with the thin, bloodless sound the guitar produced. A long way back in the mix, it sounded as though it had been generated by a game console.

But it scarcely mattered amid the general audiovisual onslaught. There was so much gear, so much pomp. So many people onstage. Christ, Adam thought. So *American*, somehow. It's no wonder we couldn't win the war without these fuckers.

He kept his face aimed at the stage. Whenever Roger turned to look at him, he shook his head, doing his best stunned disbelief face. He was fairly sure Roger hadn't counted the three beers he'd drunk before he'd escaped for a brief toilet break, or the two he'd finished subsequently.

Spread across the hillside, surrounding the small pocket in which Roger, Adam and the other staff stood, eight thousand people danced, yelled and sang. Most of them seemed to be girls in their early twenties, with flowers in their hair and glitter on their faces. Largely white, healthy-looking and ecstatic. Here and there, muscular boyfriends were dotted about, sporting backwards baseball caps and basketball jerseys, some of them with the girls on their shoulders, arms aloft.

It was all rather sexless, but that was no surprise. Adam had once found himself at a party full of twenty-two-year-olds around a visit to the Coachella festival. In the living room, the boys – who'd looked much like those here at the concert – had called each other 'bro' and racked long, fat lines of cocaine from enviable stashes, breaking off only to do shots. In the bedrooms, their girlfriends had gathered on the large, chintzy beds, dressed in oversized hoodies and jogging pants, staring at Facebook and gossiping about acquaintances who happened not to be present.

There'd been no pairing off into bedrooms or kissing in the corners. Not even any flirting. None of the pregnant, charged atmosphere that Adam remembered from the house parties of his own youth.

On the third, final day of the festival, three dead-eyed young men from Orange County had arrived, all of them in singlets, well muscled and with an air of affluence – a frightening little posse of USC kids. They brought with them a Tupperware box, with a giant rock of cocaine inside that Adam thought must have been approaching a kilo in weight.

To be young in Southern California, he'd realized, was to be virtually a different species.

He turned from the stage, taking in the jubilant crowd again. Was everything in music actually just taste and style? Was there no objective difference in value between Falconz and the bands he'd loved? Were the kids he'd become one with at the gigs of his youth, throwing themselves into the air or surging towards the stage and yelling with abandon, no better than these face-paint-wearing airheads? Had all those bands been, on some level, just as bad as this, and he simply blind to the fact?

Adam felt, with a pang of loneliness, that he was the only person in this sea of happy humanity that considered himself to be in a sort of hell. It was as though he was trapped in an endless advert for a mobile phone brand. Forlornly, automatically, he searched his mind for the advert's potential slogan. *Make every day a journey?* It would do.

This is not what I wanted, he thought. Somewhere, without really meaning to, *he'd* sold out.

After an hour and a quarter had passed, he could feel he was on the final stretch. The thought, and the onset of drunkenness, cheered him a little. A few more drinks, a bit of chatter, back to the hotel. Home, he thought. Oh God, take me home.

He was wondering whether he could get away with another toilet break, and perhaps a slug of backstage whisky, when he felt a tap at his shoulder. He looked around to see Angelina, leaning over the railing above him.

'Hey,' she yelled, smiling. Her teeth, in the light from the stage, were glowing neon white, her skin shining with her trademark, glitter-infused face product. She looked younger than he'd remembered.

'Hi,' he shouted back.

Roger glanced at him, frowned, and turned back to the show.

Adam moved closer to the railing. Lonely as he was, he couldn't help but be pleased to see her. A thin, pale security guard with a curly Afro was standing at a gate that allowed access from the public seating areas to the sealed-off section in which Adam and Roger stood. He glanced at Adam's all-access pass, which dangled on a lanyard around his neck.

Angelina and Adam leaned into each other, and she touched his head with hers as he moved closer.

'How are you doing?' he shouted into her ear.

'Good,' she yelled back.

'Who are you with?' he asked.

'Just some friends.' She gestured behind her. The pouty girl from the rooftop showcase was a few feet along one of the rows, watching him, and apparently accompanied by a sweating, dancing boy, who was intent on the stage.

'Want to come back here?' Adam asked her.

'Yeah!' Angelina said.

Adam felt a further brightening at how pleased she was to see him.

He turned, and tapped Roger on the shoulder. The manager nodded, upwards, with his chin.

'Can I have another pass?' Adam said. 'My friend Angelina is here.'

Roger frowned again. 'Is she cool?'

'Supercool,' Adam assured him. 'She's a very successful Instagram poet.'

'Oh shit,' Roger said, peering at Angelina. 'I know her. She takes those awesome photos in the desert.'

'That's her,' Adam said.

Roger reached into an inner pocket and removed another laminated pass. Adam, with a perverse pride, could feel the manager's interest perking. Professional, but sexual too, he realized. The Terminator, it seemed, was human after all.

I'm impressing Roger, he thought. Why do I care about impressing Roger?

Angelina bounced through the gate, jerking her head and shoulders to the swingless drums.

'Hi!' she yelled at Roger.

Roger stooped down to her, shaking her hand. Adam was shocked to see him smiling widely, more pleasantly so when, instead of trying to win over this latest industry contact, she moved back to Adam, and began dancing very close in front of him. Every few seconds, her buttocks grazed his crotch, creating a warm, tingling sensation.

Roger glanced back over his shoulder, twice, the smile having vanished but the interest very much alive.

Angelina's shoulders were bare and smooth. She wore skintight black jeans, a black vest top and patent ankle boots. The backdrop of Adam's thoughts seemed to sink away, his mind tunnelling its focus. Before long, he had an erection.

The show ended with fifteen confetti cannons blasting their contents out over the screaming, feverish audience. Like giant cumshots, Adam thought, light-headed with booze and pleasure at the ordeal's end. He, Roger and Angelina all threw their hands in the air and clapped, Adam taking the opportunity to make some comedy anguished howls now that he knew there was enough sound to mask them.

A photographer appeared onstage, and Bret and Marissa turned their backs on the audience and threw their arms around each other's shoulders, the camera flashing, capturing the vast crowd of people behind them, a mass of heaving bodies between the iconic, jutting red crags.

Then, all of a sudden, Adam was following Roger down the long, steep, graffitied tunnel to the dressing rooms, Angelina's hand in his, warm and dry, his erection half subsided.

His unformed thoughts were of a bit of harmless fun, the familiar mental mist blooming in his head, hiding the potential consequences comfortingly away. He had thrown himself into the drunken current of the night, to become as free and as lost as a twig in a stream. This giving over of himself was something he'd once loved – perhaps still did – and had certainly become automatic.

In the largest of the dressing rooms, Marissa and Bret were whipping out earpieces and whooping. Adam hugged them both, hands pressed into their sweat-drenched backs, both of them apologizing for their state as he did so.

Somebody passed Marissa an iPad, the screen of which showed the picture taken from the stage.

'Holy shit,' she said, looking at it with misty eyes. 'Tonight was really something.'

Angelina was introduced, whisky and vodka were poured. Roger had become separated, drifting off in a discussion with the venue manager on the other side of the room.

All around them stood affluent-looking, older-type hipsters. Men in black, designer versions of Thai fishermen's trousers, hair tied into topknots above thick-rimmed transparent glasses. Women in leather and denim cut-offs and minimal vest tops. Pendants, Rolexes, oversized rings and angular tattoos abounded. These were the people making a living from their dreams.

Monica, the radio lady, appeared more alive now. She stood towards the far wall of the cavern-room, laughing, throwing her blonde hair back and wearing a large black belt over her red dress.

I should work on her, Adam thought. But I have no idea how. Anyway, the show seemed to have done the trick. He felt a mild sense of betrayal, as if she'd gone over to the other side. It was the end of *Invasion of the Body Snatchers*, and he was the last, doomed human left alive. He decided to call Monica during the week, for form's sake.

And anyway, wasn't he here, making the scene, doing his job? People greeted him, hugged and high-fived him. It always came as a shock to Adam to find himself, technically at least, one of the most important people in the room.

Bret, in a pause between hugs and congratulations, glanced over at Adam, then at Marissa. A look came over his face – equal parts conspiracy and glee.

'Yo,' he said to Adam and Angelina. 'Follow us.'

The four of them slipped from the room, heading down the corridor, past the plaques and around the corner, where Bret paused. Marissa still had the iPad in her hand.

'Hold up,' Bret said, raising a hand and peering back around the wall of rock in the direction they'd come from. He turned to them, a mischievous grin lighting up his face.

'I think we lost him,' he said.

'Who?' Adam said.

'Fucking Roger, man. Jesus fuck, he's driving me nuts.'

Adam laughed. 'Really?'

'Dude,' Marissa said, shaking her head. 'It's like being on tour with your dad.'

'Seriously,' Bret said. 'If he comes after us now we're gonna have to go back to the hotel and party in a room.'

'One he isn't allowed into,' Marissa said, evidently meaning it.

Adam couldn't control his grin.

'Is he that bad?' Angelina said. Her hand had moved to the small of Adam's back as they watched the corridor.

'Oh my God,' Bret said, eyes widening. 'He's so intense. You have no idea.'

The little group fell silent, peering around the wall and watching.

Just then, like the actual Terminator in the police station scene, Roger himself appeared at the far end of the corridor. Automatically, all four of them flinched back around the corner.

Marissa and Bret turned to them, eyes wide.

'Run,' Marissa whispered.

The group set off down the corridor at top speed. A little way down, a tough-looking woman in a yellow security jacket was seated beside a doorway.

'What's in here?' Bret asked her.

'Exit,' she said, gum visible in her mouth.

'Shit,' Marissa said, looking nervously the way they'd come.

'Go,' Bret said. They all set off again, rounding another corner, coming to what appeared to be a separate set of dressing rooms on the far side of the venue from the ones they'd left.

Bret tried a door, which was evidently locked.

'Damn it.'

Adam, on the edge of hysteria, was struggling not to laugh. Operation Bypass Roger, he was thinking. Mission successful! Haha! In your face, Autodidact! And in yours too, Roger, you mad-eyed robotic bastard!

Angelina tried a door, which opened onto a darkened storage cupboard.

'Yes,' Marissa said. 'In in in!'

They piled in and closed the door.

Bret ended up furthest inside. He banged into a metal shelving unit as the others moved into position, and a loud clanging rang out.

Marissa, closest to the door, hissed, 'Shhh!'

Angelina was pressed up tight against Adam – tighter, in fact, than he suspected she needed to be. His heart was pounding with fear and exhilaration. He felt like a schoolboy. It was hard to decide what the implications of all this might be. Harder still, in the moment, to care.

After half a minute, footsteps could be heard in the corridor outside.

Marissa turned to them in the darkness, the white of her bared, clenched teeth and eyes visible within it.

The footsteps paused, not far beyond the door.

'Guys?' they heard Roger say.

A door handle was rattled, then went silent.

Marissa flashed them her comedy fear-face again, and gestured for Adam to lean his weight against the door beside her.

Sure enough, after a moment the handle turned. It rattled, stopped. Adam had just begun to release the pressure when it rattled again, more violently now. After a moment it stopped again.

Adam turned, and doubled over towards Bret, panting, certain he could control his laughter no longer.

Angelina placed a hand on his back.

The door handle rattled a third time. Adam whipped around, lending his weight to Marissa's again.

'Bret?' Roger said from outside. 'Marissa?'

Was it Adam's imagination, or did he sound almost sad? A pang of sympathy took him by surprise, but quickly faded away. Fuck you, Roger, he thought, with a surge of potent glee.

A few more door handles were tried, and then the footsteps were heard once more, receding down the corridor.

'Holy fucking shit,' Marissa whispered, her suppressed giggle coming out as a wheeze.

'That was scary!' Angelina whispered.

'Has he for sure gone?' Bret said. He was contorted into the corner of the room, half behind the shelf, trembling.

'I think so.'

Cautiously, Marissa opened the door.

'OK,' she said, looking back at them. 'Coast is clear. Let's find somewhere to do some fucking drugs.'

A fire escape at the far end of the hallway allowed them to climb to the next floor. Here, a large conference room took up most of the space off the corridor they found themselves in, but there were also a number of small, comfortable dressing rooms, all of them unlocked.

They crammed into one of these, piling onto a leather couch. There was a small drinks fridge beneath the dressing table, and Bret opened it, looked up at them and grinned.

'Score,' he said, and began passing out cans of beer.

Adam was at the far end of the couch, Angelina sitting on its arm beside him. He moved his hand beneath her top, running his fingers over the small of her back, where she was sweating slightly. She pressed her leg tight up against his shoulder.

Harmless fun, he thought, distantly.

'It's good to meet you,' Bret said to Angelina. 'I'm a fan.'

'Really?' Angelina sounded girlish. 'That's so cool.'

'Yeah, man,' Bret said. 'We'd love to get a song in one of your Instagram videos.'

Videos? Adam thought. What fucking videos?

'Oh my God,' Angelina said. 'Done.'

'Sorry about all that,' Marissa told her. 'Sometimes we just seriously need a break from the guy.'

She'd begun pouring cocaine from a small plastic baggie onto the surface of the iPad.

'So he's really driving you nuts?' Adam asked.

'Man,' Bret said, 'I love him, I guess, but he's just so full on! It's like he's just watching us the whole time. This is the last fucking tour he's coming on, I'll tell you that much.'

'We have to hide from him every time we wanna party,' Marissa said. 'And it's not like it's every night. We have one night a week to kick loose a little on tour, the rest of the time it's full-on work.'

She began carving up lines with a silver credit card – which, Adam noted, bore the business name Falconz, Inc. and had an expensive-looking gold trim – while Bret rolled up a note.

'To be honest,' Adam said, surprising even himself, 'he's actually a very good manager. He certainly keeps me on my toes.'

'Really?' Bret asked, as sceptically as someone so well raised could be.

'Yes. And to be honest, having a manager who discourages partying probably isn't the worst thing in the world.'

'That's fair,' Marissa said. Her serious expression gave way to a mischievous grin. 'But fuck, it feels good to escape and do some drugs.'

'Amen to that,' Adam said. 'That was the most fun I've had at a show in a long time.'

'Thank you, man,' Bret said. Luckily, he'd failed to notice that Adam hadn't been thinking of the actual set.

'Guests first,' Marissa said, passing the iPad along to Angelina.

'Ah, thank you,' she said. Balancing the machine on her knees, she leaned down and pushed her black hair aside – exposing a long, shapely neck – and daintily sniffed her line.

When she passed the iPad to Adam, he held it out for Bret. 'You guys first, I insist,' he said.

'God bless you, sir,' Bret said. With practised efficiency, the pair of them snorted the large lines of powder.

Finally, the iPad was on Adam's knees, the note in his right hand, his mouth wet with anticipation.

Just then, the door opened. Framed in the light from the corridor was the tall, slim, ramrod-straight frame of Roger.

He looked down at Adam, then at the iPad, his eyes red-rimmed and gleaming like hard, bright little stones.

'What're you guys doing?' he asked.

Adam glanced down. 'Ah,' he said, gesturing at the cocaine. He looked back up at Roger and put on his best smile. 'We're just looking at pictures of cocaine on Marissa's iPad,' he said.

For a moment, there was utter silence. Then, suddenly, everyone was laughing. All except Roger, who simply turned and left the room.

* * *

It was 4 a.m. before Adam and Angelina left Marissa's hotel room. The question of where Angelina was staying didn't seem to need raising. She was burbling happily as they walked the darkened corridor towards the elevators, Adam frowning, trying to keep track of the way, of how high and drunk he was, of what Angelina was saying. Everything seemed to be at a slightly strange angle, as if he'd been slapped hard on the side of the head and hadn't quite recovered.

'We're gonna start a band,' she was telling him.

'Cool,' he said. 'What's it going to be called?'

'We don't have a name yet. It's been about finding the right vibe between people.'

Finally, the elevators. Adam pressed the button, impatient.

'Are you going to sing?' he asked.

'*Loooost in Spaaaace!*' the elevator said as its door opened.

'No, but we're gonna use my poetry as lyrics. I'm gonna do production.'

'Production?'

'Yep,' she said. 'And creative direction.'

'Cool,' he said.

In the elevator, one wall had been decorated with a photograph of a piece of street art which could only be described as a sort of multicultural space scene.

'What does that say to you?' Angelina asked, giggling.

'The same thing all street art does. That the reason it's on the street, and now in an elevator, is because it's not good enough to be in a gallery. That hopefully, one day soon, some men will come and pressure jet it to oblivion.'

'You're so negative,' Angelina said.

As the door pinged, a question rose to the surface of Adam's mind.

'How's it going,' he asked her, 'with Striker, your agent guy?'

'Oh,' she said, pouting. 'I dropped him. We had different priorities.'

Different priorities? Adam thought, trying to unpick this.

The doors opened onto the silent, darkened corridor that led to Adam's room.

Once inside, she turned to kiss him, and he pulled off her clothes without ceremony. When he removed her boots, he could smell the dull tang of her feet. He was ringing with drugs and drink, all thought obliterated. There was just desire, and Angelina. A faint worry about whether he'd get hard enough to fuck her. And a new dynamic between them, too. Previously, Adam had always been the one chasing her. She had mainly been a frustration. She had never made him come, and he had never before penetrated her.

He had met her at a gig, when she had heard him say something about his job, and she'd reached out and pulled on his nose and grinned and said, 'Hey you,' and he'd found himself charmed.

When she was naked, now, before him, he pulled off his own clothes and kissed her, on the mouth, then her neck, then her breasts and stomach. Before long he was going down on her, her legs spread wide, soft whimpers coming from somewhere a long way above him. There was something soothing about being there, in the closed world between her legs, after all the fevered socializing of the long night beforehand. A while later, Angelina's identity began to blur and fall away. It could have been any woman, every woman. She could be Erica, he thought, feeling as though he was dreaming.

He pushed his tongue further into her, past the metallic tint to the salty juices beyond. He let Erica's image form in his mind, the idea that he might soon be with her sending a purer desire surging through him.

When Angelina finally tugged at his hair, he collapsed onto the bed beside her reluctantly, crashing from the pleasant dream-state back into the gloomy, crushingly familiar surroundings of a generic hotel room. Despite the blackness that was blossoming in his mind, he was painfully hard.

Angelina rolled over to face him.

'I'm thinking of getting a tattoo,' she said. 'You think I should?'

'No. Tattoos are for sailors and the criminal underclass,' he told her.

'You're *so* negative.'

'Please suck my dick,' he said.

As she did so, he stared up at the ceiling, fevered images of things he'd done and things he'd wanted to flickering in his head.

'Turn over,' he told her after a while. 'On your knees.'

He spat onto the fingers of his left hand and rubbed his saliva into her pussy. She was still very wet, though, and he pushed the tip of his penis into her.

Her head rose before him, and she sucked in a breath. In the light of the bedside lamp, he saw the lips of her vagina fold inwards as he moved his cock into her, gripping it. He pulled it back out a fraction, gazing at the gleaming smear on his dick, looking down and searching for excitement to light in him. Instead, oncoming guilt announced itself, like the sound of a distant, unexpected vehicle approaching in the night.

Angelina flicked her head, her hair falling back over her neck. Her back shone with sweat.

'Fuck,' she said, her voice high and thin. 'Fuck me.'

When he had, and Angelina had fallen asleep beside him, the sky paling beyond the imperfectly drawn curtains, he reflected how strange it was that you often came to possess something when you no longer wanted it so badly.

26

On the birding trip to Santa Barbara, taken with his uncle and led by a hired guide whose demeanour and appearance were that of an off-the-grid, trailer-dwelling misanthrope, and whose manic excitement for birds had stoked the flames of Adam's burgeoning enthusiasm, they had screeched to a halt in the middle of a narrow lane between mudbanks.

'Hey,' the guide had said, mischief in his voice, ponytail whipping around and brushing the back of his army surplus jacket as he turned and gestured. 'Take a look in that hole.'

Adam peered out of the window at a large, lateral cavity in the bank – almost a crack, rather than a hole. All he could make out was darkness.

'With your binoculars, man,' the guide said.

Adam raised them. As ever, it took him a few seconds to orient himself within the sudden magnification. After a moment, he made out a pair of large yellow eyes, widened as though in alarm, peering out from the hole at him. They blinked, once.

'What the fuck is that?' Adam had said, forgetting, momentarily, that his uncle was sitting beside him.

'That's a burrowing owl, dude,' the guide said, chuckling, his elongated, surf-bum vowels alight with pleasure.

'Wow,' Adam said.

'Oh yes,' his uncle muttered, leaning across Adam with his own, more powerful binoculars.

'How did you know it was there?' Adam had asked.

'Found him the other day,' the guide said proudly. 'Seemed like a good spot for one to be hanging out.'

Now, thirty thousand feet above the Rockies, the afternoon after the morning before, Adam pressed his head against the cold glass of the plane window and pulled the thin blanket over his head.

I am a burrowing owl, he thought. Safe and warm in my dark little hole.

'Sir,' someone said. Adam swivelled his head and peered out from within his blanket. The steward was looking at him from beyond the empty seat beside him.

'Drink?'

Adam waved him away, too hungover to contemplate his gin and tonic, or even a Bloody Mary.

As the trolley rattled onwards, Adam turned his head back to the window. I am not a burrowing owl, he thought, sadly. I am a far less noble creature. A snake, perhaps. No, meaner; a cuckoo, or a magpie.

The comfort of the owl guise vanished, he tried to disentangle his thoughts.

Never mind Falconz, and Roger, he decided. It was what it was, it would be what it would be. Looked at a certain way, it was mission successful. He'd got in direct with the band. Four hours of elated, loved-up chatter. Bonding time. Yes, Operation Bypass Roger had been a success.

But he shouldn't have slept with Angelina. Not when all he really wanted was Erica.

Once, this wouldn't have bothered him at all – on the contrary, in fact. He squirmed at the realization that, once upon a time, he'd have been recalling the night before with relish, as some sort of victory. Not any more, it seemed. He had absolutely no appetite for that now.

But he hadn't broken any commitments, so why did he feel so guilty? He picked at the feeling until he understood. It was because he was still out of control, he realized. Didn't that demonstrate that he hadn't mended himself at all, and probably never would? This was exactly the sort of mistake that had once cost him everything.

'Would you just fuck any nasty pussy that appeared in front of you? Would you just fuck *anything*?' he heard Sofia say, her voice quiet with rage.

Now, he knew quite suddenly, he was going to love Erica, and last night he'd slept with someone else. He'd poisoned it before it had even started.

This old mistake, this tiresome old habit. He'd never found anything in life as exciting as the first time a new woman removed her underwear in front of him, and it had cost him dearly.

Once, on a happier, longer flight than this one, he'd found himself in conversation with a man at the bar. When Adam had suggested that his well-spoken accent must have been popular in Los Angeles, he'd revealed that he too was originally from Bath. It turned out they'd been to school together, separated at the time by the yawning, icy chasm of two academic years.

They were still separate. The man was an investor, and he drank his vodka tonics and acclaimed a new type of champagne designed to be drunk with ice. Adam drank his unadorned Scotch and decided it would be easiest simply to listen.

The man told Adam that he'd loved school, but hated university. Adam wondered how that was possible. After the miserable years of school, where all but a few other outcasts had seemed to loathe him, university had been everything he'd dreamed of. He'd recast himself from his unpopular, unhappy clay into something more interesting and appealing.

And girls had liked him. There were so many brilliant girls, he hadn't wanted to squander any of them. He was in awe of them. Not just their bodies. Sex was as much about the mind, if it was to be worth having. It was a shared undertaking, a leaping off the ledge, hand in hand. It was fresh, unspoiled intimacy he craved. The type that came before jealousy and boredom, and the seeing the worst of each other. The type that came before someone took your possessions and threw them down a drain.

And so he'd become used to craving novelty.

He'd never have guessed how much guilt he was storing up for himself. Now, he was the unhappy projector of a whole mental slide show of women, whom he'd hurt then and who hurt him now. The women he couldn't shake off, whose ghosts he lived with daily.

It hadn't really mattered until he met Sofia, in an alleyway in east London on a newly warm, blustery day in April. He wished he'd understood how lucky he was, how valuable she was. She should have been enough for him, and for a while, at least, she had been.

He remembered a meeting during a business trip to New York, late on a Thursday afternoon in spring, at a publicist's office downtown. He'd been with Sofia a little over two years.

The publicist had given him a strong cocktail. The light outside was still bright, and one of the two assistants was stepping away from him across a patch of blazing sun, having delivered the drink. Her hips sashayed beneath her short dress, outlining her buttocks, and her heels clicked on the floorboards.

Her dark hair was clipped up at the back, and at that moment it seemed eminently grippable. When she reached her desk, she turned and looked at him, unsmiling. She was attractive in the way only a New York girl can be, sexiness emanating from self-regard and style rather than prettiness. Adam felt a surging desire to possess her, to transform her from this aloof, pristine being into someone ablaze with the same animal desire for him that he was feeling for her.

Later, in the car back to his hotel, he'd breathed hard in relief. He didn't do that any more, he suddenly realized. It had been two years, and he hadn't cheated. It was over. He loved Sofia. She was the only woman he wanted. He was proud of himself.

But it didn't last. He did love Sofia, but eventually he wanted something different, another kind of sex. Excitement had been drained by the repetitive orbit of daily existence, desire flattened by the weight of small tasks and irritable exchanges.

At first the transgressions came in one offs. Like a smoker falling back into the trap, they satisfied him at first, made him feel as though he was still desirable, could still do it – whatever *it* was.

There was a handful of them. A young, excitable Canadian intern who pursued him, was in awe of him, and with whom he slept at a friend's house. A pretty, soft Irish woman he took back to his flat, and who left, horrified, the next morning, when she saw a bottle of Sofia's perfume on his shelf. A strikingly beautiful, short-haired French girl on a business trip to Paris, who left his hotel room to obtain condoms by simply calling out to open apartment windows until someone tossed some down.

Each time, he woke up feeling sick with guilt, promised himself it would never happen again. He moved in with Sofia, and for a while it hadn't. He seemed to have got away with it. And then he'd met Isa.

It hadn't seemed to matter, really, until Isa.

27

On Thursday morning, Adam arrived at the office to find Scott standing by the coffee machine, intent on his phone. It was a hot day, and he was wearing flip-flops and shorts, his wiry brown legs on show.

'How you doing?' Adam asked him.

'Awesome,' Scott smirked.

Whenever Adam asked how he was, he seemed to take on the demeanour of a teenager talking to a proud grandparent, as though Adam was someone who would dearly want to hear his latest news but could wait until Scott had dealt with more important matters.

'Thanks for making coffee,' Adam said.

Scott was staring down at his phone, grinning. After a moment, he creased his face into an exaggerated smile and tittered nasally. When he'd finished, he looked back up at Adam.

'What's that? Sorry, it's just…' He looked down at the phone again, paused, then lifted his chin and laughed his deep, booming laugh.

'… Sorry,' he said again. 'Jason's texting me. He's just…' Another message arrived, and Scott threw his head up skyward once more and laughed even louder, like a barking seal.

A wave of hatred washed through Adam, and an image came to him of setting about Scott with a spiked sealing club. He took several deep breaths.

'So,' he said when Scott had finished. 'Anything much happen while I was out?'

'Not much,' Scott said. 'Oh, Philippa called for you. That music supe?' He curled his lip.

'OK, thanks.'

'Yeah,' Scott said darkly.

His defences already weakened, Adam was unable to resist this barbed lure.

'Why are you pulling that face?' he asked. 'When she came to the rooftop thing you said Philippa was great?'

'I *never* said that,' Scott said. 'I just think she's kinda nasty.' He gave an extra-aggressive sniff, and turned back to the coffee pot.

'Nasty?' Adam said.

'Yeah. She was all over the place at that party. With that Craig guy.'

Restraining himself with difficulty, Adam counted to ten, and swallowed his outrage.

'Anyways,' Scott said. 'I told her you'd call back.'

Adam shut himself in the meeting room. Philippa would have to wait. The first task of the day was to update the Autodidact and Serena.

He dialled into the conference system from his cell phone, in case Scott was listening from outside.

'Hey, man,' the Autodidact said. The character of the echo at his end told Adam's finely tuned ears that he was in the London conference room.

'Hi,' Adam replied.

'Hi, mate,' Serena said, loudly. As ever, she was apparently attempting to inject good humour, and, as ever, Adam was grateful.

'How are you both?' Adam asked.

'Great, thanks,' Serena said. 'You?'

Just then, beyond the glass of the meeting room, the door to the office opened, and Isa walked in. She gazed about herself, and then noticed him. It seemed to him that her face brightened, and she waved. Adam grinned and returned the gesture. Isa Dixon. She stretched her arms out, cocked a hip and flicked her head back, posing as if to say 'I've arrived!' She was, he realized, already displaying a resplendent LA music industry morph: black Nikes and matching black designer sportswear. She would fit in perfectly, he thought – her arrival in Los Angeles was as natural as a migratory bird's.

She stood and looked at him for a long moment, smiling. It looked as though she meant it, too. Could it be he'd simply forgotten how to read her? Was he almost pleased to see her?

'Adam?'

'Sorry, yes, I'm here. Isa's just arrived.'

'Good,' the Autodidact said.

'Great!' Serena enthused. 'Ah… It's gonna be so much fun there.'

Isa was walking up the stairs to the mezzanine, and Adam heard Scott's voice, then hers, chattering excitedly.

'Yes,' Adam said.

'So, how'd it go?' the Autodidact asked.

Adam spoke slowly, trying to pick his words carefully. 'Well,' he said. 'Overall, it went very well. Marissa and Bret and I ditched Roger, and I spent a long night with them at the hotel room.'

'Wow, perfect,' Serena said.

'OK,' the Autodidact said, more suspiciously. 'How was Roger?'

'Probably not entirely happy. Bypassing him, as you put it, might not have gone down very well.'

'… Right,' the Autodidact said.

'But the guys were sick of him and wanted a break. Turns out he's been breathing down their necks. I had the chance to express a lot of enthusiasm direct.'

'Can't ask for more than that…' Serena said. Then: 'I expect?'

'I'll call Roger today,' the Autodidact said. Adam raised two fingers and jabbed them at the phone, pulling his demented monkey face.

'Sounds good,' he said, making his voice as mild as possible.

'Alright, well, chat soon then,' the Autodidact said.

'Yep,' Adam said.

'Shall we stay on actually, Adam?' Serena said. 'Have a quick catch-up?'

'Why not?' Adam said.

There were footsteps on the concrete floor at the other end of the line, then the swoosh of the door being slid shut.

Adam pictured Serena sitting in the long rectangular meeting room in the London HQ, looking out through its glass wall across the busy office floor, and perhaps beyond it, through the large industrial windows to the trees of Victoria Park.

'So,' she said, her voice still full of warmth. 'How are things?'

'All fine, I think,' Adam said. 'I'm a bit worn out. Good to have Isa here, though. At least, I think it is.'

'Yeah, do you think that'll be alright?'

'God knows,' Adam said. 'I'm sure it'll be fine.'

'Listen, Adam,' Serena said. 'You've done something really great, setting up that office. We are grateful.'

Quite suddenly, emotion soaked through Adam like water into a sponge.

'Thanks,' he said.

'You should think about what you want, out of all this.' Serena said. 'That's sort of what I did… It helps to think about what's going to be best for you.' There was a long pause. 'What *do* you want?'

What do I want? Adam thought. It was an excellent question. To live in a sex colony castle in the Scottish Highlands, somewhere near a golden eagle's eyrie. To wander about naked, to drink whisky, to fuck and to be internationally recognized for something or other. To surgically attach a small bag of cyanide beneath Scott's nose.

To see Erica, he thought.

'To be honest,' he told Serena, 'I haven't really thought about it.'

'Exactly. Too busy with the office and all that. You should. Have a think about it.'

I want your wisdom, Adam thought. I want to give you a hug.

'Thank you very much indeed, Serena,' he said. 'I really appreciate that.'

* * *

Just before lunchtime, the sing-song digital pulse of a Skype call rang out from Adam's laptop, which was raised, dais-like, on its stand. Scott turned around to glance at it as Adam ran over. When he reached it, he saw with horror that the image of his mother had appeared on the screen. Scott having seen it too felt like a shameful intrusion. Adam snatched up the computer, along with his headphones, and went downstairs to the meeting room.

When he clicked to accept, the broad, lined face of a nurse appeared.

'Hello,' Adam said.

'Oh, hello,' the nurse said, frowning at the screen. 'She wants to talk to you. That OK?' Her accent was broad West Country. Home, Adam thought automatically. Duty.

'Yes, fine,' he said.

'I need to warn you, she's not in the best of moods. Thought it might help if she could speak to you, but you never know. It's fine to end the call if you need. Better for her too, potentially, so don't worry if you have to.'

Adam nodded.

'That alright?' the nurse said. 'Sorry, can't get on with these little bloody screens. We always use the iPad at home.'

'Fine,' Adam said. 'Yes. Of course.'

'Right,' the woman said. The room appeared behind her, the camera zooming unsteadily in to his mother in her chair.

'I'll have to hold it for her,' the nurse said.

'What do you want?' his mother asked. Her eyes were open quite wide, something he hadn't seen for a while. She looked wired, like someone on an upper.

'They said you wanted to speak to me,' he said.

'Since when does that make a difference,' his mother said. 'Want that quite often. No one fucking cares.'

He was unused to hearing her swear, and the word sounded odd and unnatural in her voice.

'Mum,' he said.

'Language, Christine,' the nurse admonished.

'It's true. Neither you nor your sister.' She blinked rapidly.

'I'll try to call more often. I'm sorry, Mum. I know it's not good enough.'

His mother's expression had gone neutral.

'I was going to send you both some presents,' she said.

'That's very kind of you.' He was about to remind her that sending items to Malaysia by mail was an arduous process.

'But I haven't been able to get anything for Sofia,' his mother said.

'Mum,' Adam said. He blinked back sudden tears. 'I'm not with Sofia any more. Remember?'

His mother screwed up her face, fighting through the mists.

'Yes,' she said. 'Stupid.'

'You're not stupid, Mum.'

The eyes flashed. 'I know I'm not stupid. You're bloody stupid. Throwing her away.'

'It was stupid,' he said, his voice trembling. 'Yes.'

'Just like your father. He was a bastard too.'

'Dad wasn't a bastard,' Adam said. 'Why would you say that? I wish I was more like him!'

The nurse, out of view, coughed, and the image on the screen wobbled as she did so.

'Once, I found out he was taking that awful secretary he had on a so-called business trip with him, when he'd told me it was one of the junior partners.' His mother's brow creased deeply as she took hold of her memories.

Adam sighed. 'Nothing had happened though, had it, Mum?'

'I made sure nothing happened. Told him she had to go or I would.'

'He was just worried about your reaction. There was every reason to take the secretary.'

'Believe that and you'll believe anything. Awful ditzy bitch.'

'And that was the only time you ever suspected anything, wasn't it?'

His mother's eyes had closed. She'd drifted again.

'It hasn't been like that with me, Mum,' he said. 'I only wish I was more like him.'

'What,' his mum said. 'Dead?'

'Mum… Please.'

'When can I go back to the house?' she said, looking up at the nurse, a sudden look of raw fear on her face.

'Christine,' the nurse said. 'Adam, do you want to?'

'The house is gone, Mother,' he said. Like so much else in life. 'We had to sell it. You know that.'

When she spoke, it was in an awful childlike whine. 'Why?' she asked. 'Why?'

'There wasn't enough money. There was a mortgage. You'll remember. Please don't worry.'

The face on the screen twisted with anger. 'You fucking bastards,' she screamed. 'Why did you sell my fucking house?'

'We'll leave it there, Adam,' the nurse said firmly. Another was already tending to his mother. 'Try again soon. Be well.'

The screen went black. Adam closed his laptop, and walked through the office to the storage cupboard and the giant roll of bubble wrap. He found he lacked the energy to kick it, so he simply slumped down against it and sobbed.

* * *

Isa wanted to go for lunch, which didn't seem a dreadful idea. She picked Crew, a cavernous bar and restaurant across Sunset from the office; one of the high-capacity, modishly decorated places that arrives in a hip area well after the hard work is done. To Adam, it inspired feelings of guilty refuge, as might a colonial embassy in a conquered foreign town.

Nevertheless, it was convenient, and the beer was good.

'So,' she said as they walked across Sunset, 'here I am.'

She turned and flashed him a quick smile from beneath a pair of stylish tortoiseshell Persols. He noticed that in the flesh she did look a little older than he remembered. Her face was thinner, and there was a dusting of grey in her hair that lit up brighter in the sunshine. But she had a new, dignified air about her, too, and it suited her.

'Yes,' he said. 'You sure are.'

She laughed. 'Are you OK with it? Me being here?'

'I suppose I'll have to be.'

'Oh, Adam,' she said. 'Don't be like that.'

At the restaurant, they were seated in the large atrium at the far end of the building. Once, it had been a cinema, this the area in which its screen had towered.

'I'm sorry if I came on a bit strong on the call,' Isa said. 'I know you thought I was trying to wind you up…' She grinned. 'I probably was a bit. But it's a big move, isn't it? I was nervous about everything.'

'Yes,' Adam said. 'It's all a bit overwhelming at first.'

They fell into a discussion about the problems of relocation. Driving licences, credit history, finding an apartment, jet lag.

'And getting a place here is just as expensive as in London,' Isa said.

'I don't suppose you're getting a housing allowance?'

'No chance. Jason was all sweetness and light when he was trying to get me to come back. Then as soon as I agreed, it was a different story.'

'Right,' Adam said. 'I'd assumed you and he were very tight.'

Isa was one of the few members of staff Jason had rated when he'd joined the company. He'd tried hard to stop her from leaving.

'We are tight,' she said. 'But mainly in a way that seems to work best for him. And he's started dating one of my best mates now, which is a bit weird. Whatever, though. I've always wanted to be out here for a bit, and now I am.'

The waitress arrived, a tall, dark-haired woman with an upturned nose.

'Can I get you anything to drink to get started with?' she asked.

'The beer's really good here,' Adam said.

'Bit early for me, I think,' Isa said. 'Drinking at lunch makes me feel sleepy these days.' She looked at the waitress. 'I'll just have a water, please.'

'Excuse me?' the waitress said.

'Water?' Isa asked.

The waitress flushed. 'Sorry…'

'Oh right, yes,' Isa said, laughing. 'Ward-ah. Can we have some ward-ah, please?'

'Oh OK, sure,' the waitress said, relieved.

'And a pale ale for me, please,' Adam said.

'Coming right up,' the waitress told them.

'These Yanks, eh?' Isa said when she'd gone.

'It's a foreign country,' Adam said. Isa had picked up a beer mat and was spinning it between her hands with their freshly painted nails. It suddenly struck him that she was nervous.

'I hadn't realized you wanted to leave London,' he said.

'You forget things, mate,' Isa said. 'I always wanted to come to the US for a bit. I used to prefer New York, though.'

'What about your family?'

She glanced away, and suddenly looked brittle. 'I might as well tell you,' she said. 'Michael got into some trouble.'

Michael was Isa's younger brother, whom Adam had only met a handful of times. He was very big and tall – earning him the nickname 'Biggie', outside the family home at least – and usually dressed in darker streetwear than the bright colours Isa had once favoured.

Although he'd been very quiet, he'd seemed friendly enough to Adam, but according to Isa he had an anger problem.

'I'm sorry to hear that,' Adam said. 'Is he OK?'

'He's in jail,' she said. 'And it looks like he'll be there for at least another two years.'

Adam began to ask what had happened, but stopped when he saw the pleading look in Isa's eyes.

'I really don't want to go into it just now,' she said. 'Just wanted to tell you. I was well ready for a break from it all anyway. It was so much drama.'

'I can understand that,' Adam said.

'And please keep it quiet in the office, obviously,' Isa said. She took a deep breath, and suddenly gave her trademark low chuckle. 'Talking of the office, Scott's running around like a little bloody baron, isn't he?'

'Tell me about it.'

'I'd only been there two minutes, and he started telling me his vision for what I could bring to the team!'

They both laughed. 'It's good to see you,' she said.

'And you too,' Adam replied, realizing, to his surprise, that he meant it.

The drinks arrived. Adam swigged his beer, the alcohol merging with unexpected relief, and something like affection. She doesn't want revenge, he thought. Why would she? It was all years ago. Why hadn't he thought of the idea of simply being friends?

She was, after all, funny and clever. He'd almost forgotten that. When he'd first got to know her, he'd found her ability to switch between characters exciting and attractive. One minute she was the icy, educated, cut-glass debater, the next the raucous east London street kid. After a while, the charm had worn off, and he'd begun to believe that he didn't actually know the real Isa. She could switch between playful and serious in an instant, but both seemed to him to be masks. It appeared now that she'd finally settled into herself.

Maybe if I'd just been friends with her in the first place, he thought.

Isa raised her glass, clinked it against his and took a long sip.

'It's *really* good to see you,' she said.

Before long, she was telling him of her boredom with the London music scene, and her disappointment with the degree she'd started. Adam listened and sipped his drink.

'What exactly are you going to be doing now, workwise?' he asked her eventually.

'Didn't Jason say?'

'Not exactly.'

'Lots of meetings with big dogs apparently,' she said. 'Agents and managers and that, people Jason wants us to work with.'

'Ah yes, our newer type of friends,' Adam said.

'Exactly. All this fucking macho big player stuff. I've got to go meet some EDM agency tonight, from Vegas. They keep texting me about partying together later.' She glanced at the screen of her phone, on which several texts had arrived over their lunch.

'Well, I suppose it might be a fun night out.'

'But I think they mean drugs,' Isa said. 'I don't really do it any more, gear and that. Also, I don't know how to get stuff here.'

'You could call my friend Craig,' Adam said. 'He works in music too. Seems to have all the contacts.'

'OK great, why not,' she said, looking unenthused. Adam sent her the contact from his own phone.

There was silence for a moment.

'Isa,' he said.

She looked up at him, watching him carefully.

'I wanted to say, I'm really sorry…'

Her eyes flashed warningly. 'Mate,' she said, quietly shutting him off. Her smile had vanished, along with any façade. 'Don't even think about going there.'

Yes, this was her, he thought. This was the real Isa.

'Right,' he said, nodding and looking down at his empty plate. 'Of course.'

After they'd finished, he told her he had to make a call, and walked down to Echo Park. The sun was hot, and he sat on a bench, the emotion and the beer mixing potently, more memories breaking off and rising from the depths.

He had come to hate Isa. After he'd lost Sofia, they fell into a relationship that lasted a year. Having sprung from this poisoned well, it was doomed from the start. Adam had lost his home, and moved out into a small flat in a grim high-rise with a friend from college. Suddenly he was thirty, with little money, lots of bad habits and a big weight of sadness resting on his heart like a stone. There seemed little choice but to give himself over to the darkness.

The things he'd thought he needed, and that Isa had offered, the wildness and excitement he'd been frightened to lose, suddenly acted on him like poison. The scales removed from his eyes, what Isa offered had seemed sordid and disgusting. The path he'd been on had been the right one after all, and now it was lost to him forever.

He hadn't given Isa a chance. She had been what he thought he'd wanted, had emphasized the part of herself she thought he was attracted to. She was sad, too. He hadn't left Sofia for her, hadn't chosen to be with her. The relationship was formed purely by default.

But the masks they'd worn for each other stuck. They dragged each other downwards into an abyss: parties, drink, drugs and depraved sex. Threesomes with other men and women. Jealous rages.

Images of this life popped flashbulb-bright in his head, and he reeled from them, as though they'd happened to someone else. It had all been so wretched and awful.

Between these grim episodes, the sad semblance of a normal relationship. The first time he tried to take her home to meet his mother, the train became stranded in the ice outside Reading, and they had to turn around and go back to London. When they finally did meet, his mother had been unable to disguise her disappointment.

'She's perfectly nice, Adam,' she'd told him. But he could see the question written on her face: was she worth what you did to your lovely girlfriend?

He'd come to blame Isa. She was a living reminder of everything he'd lost.

After he'd finally broken it off with her, he came back to the flat one day to find her in his bedroom. His flatmate had let her in. The room was dim, lit only by the dozens of red tea lights she'd placed around it. Music was playing, something he liked, and there was a bottle of red wine and two glasses.

She was standing before the built-in wardrobe, hands clasped before her, doing her best to look demure.

'There's dinner, too,' she'd said. 'Please give us a chance, after everything. It's my fault, I haven't shown you my good side. I can be a real girlfriend, I promise. Please give me another chance.'

Something molten and dreadful had eaten at his numbness, but he held it at bay.

'No,' he said. 'It's too late, I'm sorry.'

And he'd told her to leave.

It hadn't been her fault at all, he saw now. She had loved him, and he'd thought he loved her too, for a while. All that pointless hatred of her he'd allowed to grow within him. It was like an illness, dissipating now, lifting off him and making him feel better.

Yes, they could have saved each other a great deal of trouble if they'd simply been friends all along.

28

He messaged Erica before he left the office, telling her he was back, and that he'd love to see her whenever she had time.

Back at the apartment, he lay on the couch, a large glass of white wine sweating on the coffee table. He'd almost nodded off when the phone rang, but Erica's name on its screen jolted him to alertness.

'Hi,' he said.

'Hey,' she replied. It sounded as though she was driving. 'You wanna go hiking?'

Adam looked at his watch. 'Now?' he said. 'The sun sets in an hour or so.'

'I know. This is a short hike, near my place.'

'Then yes. That sounds perfect.'

'Good. I'll get you in about ten minutes.'

'Great,' Adam said.

There was a pause. 'Do you wanna stay over at my place, after?' she said. 'I have an early shift, so you'd have to be up with me.'

Adam felt giddy with nervous pleasure. 'Yes,' he said, swallowing. 'I'd love to.'

He shoved some things into a bag, brushed his teeth and headed for the door. When Erica pulled up outside, Stef was sitting on her terrace, smoking a cigarette.

'Well, check you out,' she said. 'Did you join the Mercedes owners' club?'

The window of Erica's car rolled down, and she stuck her head out, waving.

'Woah,' Stef said, leaning over the wooden railing to get a better look. 'She's hot.'

'I know,' Adam said, locking the door, smiling.

'I won't wait up!' Stef called after him.

He waved to her as he swung his bag onto the back seat of Erica's car.

She was wearing her long Lululemon workout pants, a t-shirt and lightweight Nike trainers, and no makeup. She glanced down at herself as he sat.

'Luckily I had some gear in my locker at work,' she said.

'You look beautiful.' He leaned over and kissed her.

'Thank you,' she said as they pulled away. 'How was Denver?'

'Tiring,' he said. 'I'm really glad to be back.'

She parked on a quiet street a little way north of Los Feliz Boulevard and beneath the eastern flank of Griffith Park. Adam had often seen this green, imposing hill, which rose up, stern and sphinxlike, beside the I-5 freeway and the river, as though guarding the park from the filthy traffic.

'Are we going up there?' he asked her, pointing.

'Yep. It's called Beacon Hill,' she said. 'Perfect for sunset.'

In the evenings, the good ones at least, LA turned golden once again, the sharp lines of the day softening with the light. They walked along a shaded street, past the tall, tucked-away mansions of Los Feliz. The cars parked here were expensive, the houses, as in any affluent area of Los Angeles, wildly varied.

Here was a wide colonial-style mansion, there a large Spanish villa; a little further on, the gleaming glass cubes of another modernist fantasy. The road stopped at a chain-link fence, a narrow gate which led onto a steep dirt track. A sign beside the gate warned that they were entering a wilderness area, to watch out for rattlesnakes and mountain lions.

God, I love LA, Adam thought. Half a mile from the freeway, thirty feet from someone's house, and we're stepping into a different world. A city riddled with escape hatches into wilder, better places.

'Ready?' Erica asked. He leaned forward and kissed her again, running his hand under her hair, onto the back of her head. After a moment she pulled away, smiled at him and took his hand.

The dirt track became a path, and very soon the houses were out of view. They climbed steeply, the trail winding around the folds and flanks of the hill. Before long, they could see a driving range gleaming beneath them, and to their right, beyond it, the I-5, the river, the nestled houses of Atwater Village and Glendale. To the north, the mountains rose, their ridges softened and their bulk dark green in the evening light. Adam located the summit of Strawberry Peak, and felt its newly familiar thrill.

Above them, Beacon Hill stood out, proud and aloof from the coiling traffic below it.

'It's beautiful here,' Adam said, panting.

'I know,' Erica said. She pointed at a bare tree, on which a hawk was sitting motionless, watching the ground. 'Red-tailed,' she said.

'Yes,' Adam replied. 'That one I know.'

The path wound across the hillside, bringing them eventually to a junction on the hill's shoulder. Looking beyond it, Adam could see the I-5 narrowing in a glowing red-and-white snake of tail- and headlights, the mountains now dim and indistinct beneath the deep blue of the sky.

They turned right, walking under a stand of old eucalyptus trees, where the air was abruptly cool. Now, the top of Beacon Hill rose sharply a little way ahead. They climbed the short, steep path and emerged, breathless, onto its sandy top.

LA sprawled around them, a long way down. Before them were the towers of Downtown, the sluggish, firefly glow of helicopters, the bright bands of the cars' lights, the point-to-point vectors of planes heading into LAX, and the inky creases of the hillside. Behind the park, where the city would fade out into the ocean, the light was bright orange, the sun's disc dipping behind thc cliffs and ridges.

Erica turned to him, smiling, and they kissed again.

'I love to come up here,' she said. 'Look at it. In the middle of this city. It's so beautiful.' She was lit up with happiness, and Adam held her closer, pressing her to him and feeling himself infected by it.

* * *

They left Erica's car at her house, and made the short walk through Atwater Village to a restaurant called Madeleine. The place was dim and cosy, and they settled into a table in the far corner, away from the street.

'There's no real booze,' Erica told him. 'Just wine and beer. But they make Prosecco cocktails that're delicious.'

'Good enough,' Adam said.

When the drinks arrived, they clinked glasses. The cocktail was indeed delicious, though it failed to deliver the alcoholic tug that Adam favoured in an aperitif.

'Well,' he said. 'That beat my usual after-work walk.'

'No osprey though,' Erica reminded him.

'True.'

They ordered a bottle of wine and main courses, and got quite drunk.

When the waitress arrived with dessert menus, Erica asked for the check. She looked steadily at Adam while they waited for it, filling his head with small explosions of happiness and desire. After a moment, he felt her toes moving down the inside of his thigh.

* * *

In her room, she laughed and pushed him away. 'Let's shower first,' she said.

'Together?' he asked.

'No!' she said.

'Ladies first,' he told her.

While she was in the bathroom, he poured two glasses of red wine from an open bottle in her kitchen, and brought them through to the bedroom. He drank half of his quite quickly, his mind empty, waiting for Erica.

After a short while he felt awkward lying on her bed, like some ageing lothario, and he stood up and moved over to her bookshelf, scanning the titles. Her taste was different to his, but it was good. She had books he'd always meant to read, but hadn't got around to: Ferrante, Coetzee, Hilary Mantel and Jeffrey Eugenides. Prize-winning stuff, the popularity of which had perhaps stirred his contrarian instincts – which had the sole advantage of leaving good books out there for him to read one day. She had few of his great white Americans: Foster Wallace or Pynchon or Vollmann. Good for her.

Ten minutes later she emerged from the bathroom in a white towel and a swirl of steam. She sat on the edge of the bed and looked at him, shy now. Her hair was wet and flat against her head, very dark, and this seemed to emphasize the bright blue of her eyes. The blackness made the blue *pop* – was how Americans would phrase it.

They kissed for a long moment, and then she pulled away.

'OK,' she said. 'Your turn. There's a towel in there for you.'

In the shower, he ran the water very hot and let it scald his skin a little, burning off the day and the sweat of the hike. There was a bottle of shower gel, and he poured some out and lathered it over his skin. After a few minutes he heard Erica calling him.

'Adam,' she said, mischief in her voice. 'Don't be too long.'

'Coming,' he said.

She was lying on the bed, still in her towel, hands crossed atop her stomach. She smiled at him as he approached and lay beside her.

They touched their foreheads together, closing their eyes, and kissed deeply. After a moment they began to unwrap each other, moving their hands across warm, naked flesh, stroking and pressing and following the magnet pull from between each other's legs. Adam closed his eyes as her hand slipped around him, and he felt her moisture rise beneath his fingers.

Erica parted her legs wider, moaning softly. Adam pulled the towel away from her and lifted himself over her, kissing her neck and breasts, her stomach and thighs.

Her vagina was moist and splayed a little way open. He lowered his lips to it, closing his eyes and slipping his tongue into her. Her hand went to the back of his head, kneading his hair and pressing into his scalp, and he moved his hands to her thighs, pushing them wider and running his tongue further inside her. When he opened his eyes again, her smooth stomach was concave before him, she was writhing a little, rocking on her buttocks, her breasts and chin angled up, her brow and wet dark hair beyond them.

After a few minutes the taste and scent of her grew stronger, and his erection strained painfully. He sucked the lips of her pussy and ran his tongue over her swollen clitoris. The wetness from his mouth and from her vagina had spread out over her inner thighs and onto her buttocks, where she gleamed in the room's dim light.

Adam would have been content to kneel there before her forever, he thought. He lost track of time. There was just this beautiful woman in the semi-darkness of the room, the sound of her sharp breaths. Her pleasure seemed to fill him, too. To run through her and into him like a wave. It was like the first time he'd kissed her, on top of the mountain. The intimacy astounded him. There was no moment he could recall in which he'd been more alive than he was just then. He didn't want it to stop.

Finally, she moved her fingers to his chin and gently lifted it upward, pulling him towards her. They kissed again, and the thought of her taste running from his lips and tongue onto hers thrilled him.

It was only when she pushed him onto his back and began lowering her own head beneath his chin that something struck him: since he'd slept with Angelina, he no longer knew if he was clean.

The thought made his heart race. Erica was nuzzling his neck, moving downward to his chest.

Images of the sordid hotel room in Denver rose in his mind. He didn't actually know Angelina very well. As he'd never had sex with her before that night, he'd never even asked her the question he'd become accustomed to asking over his years of ill-advised sex. A cold fear leaked into his blood. I'll have to get checked, he thought. Either that or contact Angelina, ask her, see how certain she...

But what were the chances? They must be slim, surely. It wasn't as if she'd slept with him very easily, or at least, she hadn't done so very quickly. Perhaps it was OK. Perhaps it was fine to just forget it and move on...

There was something she'd said, though. Something that had bothered him... Striker, he realized. She and Striker had had different priorities.

He raised a hand to Erica's head, gently holding her to his chest. She kissed him there, apparently believing he wanted to prolong the moment. Further below, with a crushing sense of his own stupidity, he could feel his erection was faltering.

Sex, he thought. That would have been Striker's priority. Striker the notorious shagger, the archetypal booking agent. A sports-jacketed New Yorker who liked to talk about his artists crushing other people's, who had once assured Adam that one of his rivals, flirting with an attractive girl at a festival in Michigan, 'couldn't close that deal'. Who, he remembered now with a wave of nausea, Scott had once shared a house with at a festival, and who had kept Scott up all night, both nights, with his aggressively loud shagging of two different women.

That, of course, had seemed much funnier at the time.

Erica was moving her lips to his abdomen, lifting herself squarely over him. He'd prayed to get away with this so many times. He'd got away with it, time after time with Sofia and with others. Now, if he hadn't, wouldn't it be the perfect justice? To do something terrible to a woman, just as he fell in love with her? To have repeated a stupidity he'd thought banished?

He couldn't risk hurting her.

'Erica,' he said, holding her shoulders, stopping her descent.

She looked up, frowned. 'Yes?'

'Come back here.'

He felt her shrink away from him, clearly embarrassed, before she was lying beside him once more. There was a space between their bare skin now, and the air there felt cool.

'Don't tell me you don't like that?' she said.

'I do,' he told her. 'It's just… I want to take things slow with you. I can't explain it really.' He paused. 'I don't want to fuck it up.'

'OK,' she said.

After a moment, she moved closer to him again, closing her eyes and touching her brow to his cheek. Despite this, he could feel her uncertainty. The silence between them now was less than entirely comfortable.

Adam slipped his arm beneath her shoulder, and held her to him tightly. He wanted to tell her he was falling in love with her, but he didn't, and then the moment was gone.

29

Driving along Sunset at eleven o'clock the next morning, Adam's brain had gone numb with dread and panic. His penis kept itching, and he couldn't decide if the extent to which this was happening was normal. Some amount of itching surely was – but how much? Normally, would he even notice?

But what if it wasn't normal? What if he'd caught some sort of super-agent super-bug, brewed up in the bottle-service and breast-implant bars of New York City? What if Striker had crushed *him*?

He pushed his hand under his pants and gently scratched his dick. When a police car pulled alongside at a traffic light, he rapidly withdrew it and made his innocent citizen face.

It was very hot outside, the sun already bright in a cloudless, powder-blue sky. Traffic was sluggish as he crossed from Silver Lake into East Hollywood. The sidewalks looked hard and baking, the buildings ugly and unwelcoming. You're projecting, he told himself. Seeing the world through the lens of cock disease. You've been here before. Haven't you had enough of this?

He was outside the Vista Theatre – theatres in LA usually being cinemas, of course – when the phone rang, bringing up an unrecognized number. Grateful for the distraction, he pressed accept. The current affairs show on KPCC went silent, and his 'hello' sounded throaty and nervous in the car's abrupt silence.

'May I please speak with Adam Fairhead?' The voice was deep and slightly hesitant, but it sounded quite friendly.

'Speaking,' Adam said.

'Hi,' the voice continued, as though grateful to have got him. 'I'm Daniel Ledberg of *The Mammal*, in New York?'

'Ah, OK,' Adam said. 'Hello.'

'I'm calling to ask you about a, um, rumour, that seems to have surfaced on an anonymous messaging board recently.'

'Right,' Adam said, frowning.

'The rumour – well, actually, it's kind of an accusation. This messaging board, it's about employers and businesses. Kind of like a dark web version of a digital recruitment site?'

Adam's heart beat painfully.

'Right,' he said. His own voice sounded weak in the silence of the car.

'So like, people can leave anonymous information on there, when they had or have a bad boss, basically.'

'OK,' Adam said. He suddenly felt short of breath.

'And someone has written an entry that's rumoured to be about an executive at your company.'

Jesus Christ, Adam thought. Have I really been so bad that it's come to this? He tried to think which member of staff might have written about him. It could have been any, he supposed, with a wave of black despair.

'Hello?' the voice said.

'Hold on,' Adam replied. He'd stopped at another light, which had now changed to green. A jubilant cacophony of horns blared out behind him, and a grey Range Rover Sport with a plate that read IN0V8R roared past him, angrily, without using its indicators.

'Please take your time,' the reporter said, apologetically.

'I'm driving. Let me just…' Adam turned right into Rodney Drive, and pulled over. His pulse was thumping in his limbs and brow. Keep calm, he thought. Don't panic. He tried to remember all the excellent PR advice he'd heard – even given – over the years, and failed.

'Are you still there?' the voice said.

'Yes,' Adam told it.

'So I'm just looking for a comment, really,' the reporter said. 'To see if any of the allegations are true, or justified.'

'Allegations?' Adam said, feeling sick.

'Yes… I take it you didn't know anything about this until now?'

'This is the first I've heard of it,' Adam said. He cracked a window, needing air, but all that he got was heat, fumes and the sound of traffic. He breathed in through his nose and out of his mouth, remembering something he'd read about controlling panic.

'Well, the entry alleges that an executive at your company has been bullying staff there,' the reporter went on. 'Would you like me to give you some of the details?'

'Maybe you should call back, actually?' Adam said. 'I haven't seen this, er, website, and I'm in no place to comment. I might need…'

'What might you need, Adam?' the reporter said. Even in his panic, Adam recognized that the hesitancy had fallen away. Had it just been a technique?

'I need more information,' Adam said.

'That's what I'm trying to give you. You can choose whether to comment or not. There's no pressure. The way this works is that we give everyone time to respond.'

'The way what works?'

'Good investigative journalism,' the reporter said.

'Fine. Tell me then,' Adam said, unable to resist.

'So the entry—'

'Hold on,' Adam interrupted, a sudden little dose of anger reviving him, like smelling salts. 'You said "an executive". Is anyone actually named on this site?'

'No,' the reporter said. 'I think whoever runs it fears legal retaliation. But the type of company is closely described.'

'Well, there are lots of record labels,' Adam said. 'If we're not named, it could be any of them.'

'The rumour has expanded a little, on an industry message board.'

'Right…' Adam said, hope receding.

'But the original entry says that one of the senior executives at the label is transphobic.'

Transphobic? Adam thought. How could anyone possibly think I was—

'It's by a former member of staff at a music company, a transwoman, and her complaint is about an anti-working class, transphobic culture.'

'Working class…' Adam said. 'Hold on. Is this… Is this about our London office?'

'Yes,' the reporter said. 'The rumour is that Serena Miller is the executive in question.'

Adam slumped back into his seat and closed his eyes. A soft, warm sweat broke out around his nose and on his brow. Relief seeped into his veins like a drug.

'Fuck me…' he said.

'Excuse me?' the reporter said, irritably.

'Nothing, sorry…' Adam said. 'So what else does it say?'

'Can I take it from your reaction that this doesn't come as a surprise?'

'No you can't,' Adam said, anger rising again. 'Serena isn't a transphobe.'

Idiot, Adam thought. How could anyone think that of Serena, who'd been fighting the good fight since back when each battle was harder to win. The idea that this tricky reporter could come along and undo all that. Some nosey hack trying to give a moral veneer to his gossip hunting.

'But she's other things?'

'Yes. She's from a working-class background, for one thing. Not that that's for me to say, frankly. Have you thought about contacting her?'

'We've tried. Your London office is closed for the day.'

'What else does this… entry say?' Adam asked.

'It says that the executive suggested a drag ball theme for your Christmas party.'

'That's ridiculous.'

'That she presided over an anti-female atmosphere in the office, despite claiming to be a feminist.'

'An outright lie.'

'That she didn't attend this staff member's birthday drinks.'

'She's not much of a drinker!' Adam protested.

'That her moods and poorly managed stress inflicted anxiety and trauma on her staff.'

'You try keeping an independent music company going without getting a bit stressed!'

'So that part is true then?' the reporter said.

'No. Serena is a lovely person to work for. Don't quote that,' Adam said.

'Well then, can you give me a quote?'

'Who is the woman in question? The member of staff, I mean?'

'Can't you tell me that? It says in her entry that your label—'

'*The* label,' Adam said. 'You said no label was mentioned. This is all a bit much, isn't it?'

There was a moment of silence. Heather, Adam thought. The woman Jason had made Serena sack for trying to poach artists. It must've been her who'd complained.

'*The label* then, was only nine per cent BAME, and less than two per cent LGBTQIA and working class.'

'Do those last two get amalgamated then?' Adam asked.

'What?'

'LGBTQ and working class.'

'It's LGBTQIA,' the reporter said, icily. 'And no. I guess it's because you have less than one per cent of either.'

'What does the IA bit stand for?' Adam asked.

'Intersex and allies.'

'Right,' Adam said. 'Anyway, working class is very tricky to define. If you work at a record label you are by definition no longer in the working class. There are rather a lot of people in London who are middle class in denial.'

'She also writes that you have no one disabled,' the reporter continued.

'Our warehouse manager has a terrible lazy eye, does that count?' Adam snapped.

'Are you trying to be funny?'

'No,' Adam said, sighing.

'So, are these numbers an accurate reflection?'

'I don't know, I haven't counted,' Adam said. 'Our LA office is fifty percent female, which has always seemed a good thing. And Serena believes in positive discrimination.'

'Affirmative action, we call it,' the reporter said.

'Yes…' Adam told him. 'Listen, what exactly are you intending to print?'

'So far, I don't know. What are you going to let me quote?'

'This anonymous online accusation sounds as though it could be about any music company, and I can certainly tell you that Serena Miller is not in the least bit transphobic or anti-working class. Quite the contrary.'

There was a pause. 'I don't know,' the reporter said eventually. 'There's gotta be more to this. People don't make allegations like this for no reason.'

'Well, I can imagine more than one reason for writing them. Can't you?'

'That's dangerous ground,' the reporter said.

'I know,' Adam said. 'But in this case I think it might be a grudge.' Something occurred to him. 'You're looking in the wrong place,' he said. 'Far worse things happen here in LA. Far worse things have happened to… to…'

'To whom?' the reporter said, suddenly very interested.

A breathless tension filled Adam. Can I? he wondered. Should I? Toss Fischer the radio DJ under the wagon? Alicia, his producer, would be leaving soon anyway, he remembered. And she was the only person he liked on the show. Besides, Fischer was living on borrowed time. He deserved it.

'If I give you a story about something that's definitely true, will you research Serena's history properly, and check into whether this accusation comes from a sacked member of staff with a grudge?'

There was another pause, then: 'Yes.'

'And the information I'm about to give you, my name and the label have to be kept completely out of it.'

'OK,' the reporter said.

Adam took a deep breath. 'Have you heard of Brad Fischer?' he asked.

It took only a few minutes to give all the information he had, leaving out Meg's name.

'Thank you,' the reporter said, when he'd finished.

'Thank *you*,' Adam replied, and hung up.

* * *

Hollywood Presbyterian Hospital was a sprawling set of towers, just off Sunset in East Hollywood. It was here that Adam had decided to get tested.

Heart in mouth, he parked in the hospital's lot and found his way to the elevators. The place was white-walled, warren-like, with shiny beige floors that squeaked beneath his trainers. Twice he got lost, and on neither occasion did he dare ask anyone for directions.

When he finally found the STD testing unit, it was already very busy. There were four rows of seating in a smallish room, beyond which were an equal number of greasy glass windows, staff seated behind three of them. All but two of the chairs were full.

The room was otherwise windowless, the carpet tiles threadbare and the fluorescent light unpleasant. Purgatory, Adam thought.

Most of the people in the waiting room were men, and many of them apparently in couples. People stared at phones, talked in murmurs and slumped in their seats, bored.

A young heterosexual couple was giggling and whispering to each other, touching a great deal. The man wore a brown leather jacket and had a goatee, the woman long black hair and a roundish, pretty face. As Adam passed them, walking to the counter, he heard the man's American accent; the woman's was harder to place – Eastern Europe maybe. There was something a little manic about them; a false, over-egged happiness.

From behind one of the windows, a very fat man with dyed blond hair gestured Adam over, smiling warmly.

'How can I help you?' he asked.

'I'd like to get tested, please,' Adam told him.

'OK, great. Do you wanna get a full panel?'

'Um,' Adam said. 'What are the options?'

'Well, you can do urine for just gonorrhoea and chlamydia, but we also offer oral and anal swabs for those. Then we can do blood work for HIV and syphilis.'

'Right,' Adam said. 'I suppose I'll just do the lot.'

'Great,' the man said again, as though Adam had chosen excellently. 'So, I'ma have you fill out these pages, and sign where it's highlighted, OK?' He handed Adam a clipboard with a few sheets of paper attached, and a chewed Bic biro.

'Bring it right back to me when you're done.'

'Thanks,' Adam said. He squeezed onto one of the plastic chairs and began filling out the form. Over his right shoulder, he could feel that a hairy man in a singlet, beside him, was reading what he wrote.

How many times, Adam wondered, have I found myself in a place like this? More than he could count, that was for sure. Please let this be the last time, he begged himself. I'm getting too old for this.

It took a little over forty-five minutes for him to be called through. When he was, a friendly middle-aged woman took him through a security door into the rooms beyond, and seated him in a little space between two dividers.

'So, sweetie,' she said. 'Tell me what's going on.'

Adam did so.

'Well,' she said when he'd finished. 'The good news is, you don't need no anal swab.' She giggled uproariously, and ran him through the procedure for the other tests.

At least in LA, he thought, heading to the bathroom with his urine receptacle, even the STD clinics are friendlier.

He filled the plastic cup to the exact line, and placed it on a little sill above the sink.

Back at the cramped examination space, the woman swabbed his throat and drew his blood, cooing at him encouragingly as she did so.

'So you showing negative on the swabs,' she said. 'But you gotta wait seven days for the blood and the urine panels to come back, to know you in the clear. OK, sweetie?'

Adam nodded gratefully. 'Is that it then?'

'Sure is,' she giggled. 'What else you expecting?'

Back in London, there'd always been a painful penile swab. Adam remembered the first visit he'd ever made to a clinic, when he'd been twenty-one. An Indian doctor below him, struggling to insert the long plastic rod into his penis. Speaking calmly and philosophically in his musical lilt, the doctor had looked up, and told him that if he kept wriggling, it meant they were in conflict, and that was no good for either of them. There was, Adam reflected as he left the cubicle, a very fine line between experimentalism and degeneracy.

Back in the Los Angeles waiting room, the couple who'd been giggling and touching were now sitting quite still, in silence, their faces drained of colour. As Adam passed them, he saw the harsh fluorescent light from the ceiling reflect from the tracks of tears on the woman's face.

My God, he thought. What horrors must unfold in here. What sentences passed down.

Sorrow for the couple was tempered by the elation that always accompanied leaving these places, which flushed through him as he stepped back out into the corridor. Clean, he thought. Clean clean clean! Why was it that he always found himself thanking something, in these situations? Why was he, unlike other men – unlike the father who had raised him – so weak?

Still. He could always improve. For the second time that day, relief spread warmly within him as he walked down the corridor to the elevators and pressed the button.

After a moment, the elevator pinged. Its doors opened to reveal, wearing scuffed Dr Marten shoes and a white lab coat, hair tied back and a serious expression on her face, Erica.

'Adam,' she said, frowning.

'Hello,' he said, his voice breaking midway through the word.

Erica glanced over his shoulder, where a sign told disembarking elevator users that the Sexual Health Center was a short way down the corridor to their left.

Erica moved a hand to the elevator door to prevent it closing, her frown deepening.

'What's going on?' she said.

'I was getting a check-up,' he said.

'OK,' she said. 'Well, that's… sort of responsible of you, I guess?'

He couldn't bring himself to take her up on the opportunity to lie. The part of his brain that had once supplied these so easily was now, apparently, perished.

Her clever eyes were flashing, scanning his face, where he knew guilt was written.

'… I see,' she said. 'Something happened in Denver.'

Adam made no reply. His face felt tired, lifeless.

For a moment, it seemed that Erica might simply accept the news and move on. Her eyes had lost their focus on him as she processed this new knowledge. When they refocused, flashing with something else now, he saw how wrong he was.

'Stay the fuck away from me,' she said, very calmly.

She stepped back into the lift, jabbed a button, and was gone.

30

Can you do a pint tonight? Really need one.

There was only Craig left.

Tonight's not good, came the reply. *Tomorrow?*

Really need to see you tonight, Adam said. *Having a very bad day.*

Who cared if he sounded desperate – that was exactly what he was.

The little flow of ellipses told him that Craig was typing, typing, still typing. Typing and deleting, perhaps. Presumably thinking, deciding. Fuck you, Adam thought.

OK, the reply, unjustified by the typing, read when it came. *Early doors though like 5. Where?*

Great, Adam replied. *Long Shot.*

The sooner the better. He was already at home, had been since the hospital. The blind was drawn, holding back the blistering LA sun, preventing Stef from knowing if he was home.

It was four o'clock already. If he walked up the hill to Echo Park, he'd need to leave soon anyway. Time, time. Why, like the song said, did it go by so slowly? How was it to be filled? He poured himself a third, large glass of white wine and slumped back onto the couch.

He wasn't home, really. This wasn't home. The searing light of Los Angeles was alien and unreal, a world away from the cloud-stained skies and cool air of England. Hadn't he been more alive in England, with the spray of rain and grim reality in his face? He'd exiled himself on a different planet, one on which the relentless UV sun would eventually scorch everything into nothing.

Perhaps it was time to go home, after all. Otherwise, he'd become one of those expat Brits in LA, with a leathery face and a bad, loud shirt with a pointy collar. There'd be a row of vitamin tubs on his office shelf. He'd develop an awful transatlantic accent, his Ts crumbling to Ds. He'd become someone who habitually asked for the exciting bits to be excised from meals in restaurants.

He drank the wine quickly. Sure enough, it was time to leave.

He walked up Sunset slowly for once. Not really out of choice, but because a stocky woman was pushing a child's stroller ahead of him, bearing a car tyre, an unopened Amazon box and a half-unfurled street poster advertising a sneaker brand. It was very difficult to get past her. As she walked, she repeated, over and over: 'I pray for my little girl to die, Lord. I pray that she is raped, and thrown into a park or a lake. My little girl is not needed. By the power of the Father, the Son and the Holy Spirit. I pray for my little girl to die, Lord.'

Finally, atop the hill and able to speed up, Adam passed her. At the bar's door, a heavily tattooed, bearded young man with skinny black jeans and a chain wallet was opening up as Adam arrived.

'What's up,' the barman said, ushering him in and heading behind the bar.

The room was pleasingly dim and smelled of stale beer. Adam took a seat at the bar, trying not to look too miserable. The last thing he wanted was to be asked if he was OK.

'What's your poison?' the barman asked him.

'Hmm,' Adam said, considering. No more wine. Potency was what was needed now. 'Tequila soda, please,' he said.

'Coming right up.'

As the barman poured the drink, Adam glanced over at the bright portal of the open door. No sign of Craig. Just the wide expanse of Sunset Boulevard, a steep bank of litter-flecked, scrubby hillside beyond it. The finally mellowing, softening sunshine. An endless procession of cars and motorbikes scudding by.

'Here you go, man,' the barman said, and placed a brimming drink in front of him.

'Thank you,' Adam said, and knocked half of it back.

It was 5.20 before Craig arrived, and Adam had ordered a second drink. The barman, happy to have a customer, had appeared encouraging.

Craig cocked his head, making a sad face and extending his arms.

'Ah, come 'ere you,' he said, advancing across the bar in a pristine white, V-necked t-shirt, skinny jeans and boots. He threw his arms around Adam and gave him a bear hug.

'How you doing?' he asked, stepping back.

Adam grunted, embarrassed.

'I'll have what he's having,' Craig told the barman. 'Even if it doesn't seem to have cheered the silly fucker up.'

When the drink was served, they moved through to the back room, an even darker space in which wide, leather-covered benches surrounded a scuffed pool table. After the scorching light outside, the darkness felt velvety and luxurious.

'Thanks for coming out,' Adam said. 'What have you got on later?'

'A date, as it goes. And a show I need to be at. A combination of the two.'

'Work and pleasure,' Adam said. 'You're not supposed to mix them, are you? But everyone does here.'

Craig frowned gruesomely. 'Deary fucking dear,' he said. 'Not this nonsense again. What on earth's got into you?'

Adam told him.

'Shit,' Craig said when he'd finished, chuckling. 'That sucks. Then again, look on the bright side. Now you get into all sorts of new complications with new women.'

'I'm tired of complications,' Adam moaned.

'What about your friend Isa?' Craig said, watching Adam. 'She seems nice.'

'Oh, she contacted you then?'

'Yeah, I sorted her out a number.'

'She's a colleague,' Adam said. 'And anyway, we've got history.'

'Jeez,' Craig said. 'You need to stop fucking banging everyone.'

'Ha!' Adam said. 'Says you! You literally bang everyone!'

'Yes, but I'm good at it. You're not. In fact you're really shit at it.' He shook his head as though truly disappointed.

'We need more drinks,' Adam said, standing. 'Stay here.'

Craig glanced at his Apple watch.

'When is your date?' Adam asked him.

'Sevenish.'

'Wanker.'

'Cunt.'

The barman was seated in front of the bar now, staring at his phone. He got up and moved back around it as Adam approached.

'Two more of the same, please,' Adam said.

'Well, alright. You guys OK back there?'

'Excellent, thanks.'

The barman began work on the drinks. 'You guys are hittin' 'em up,' he said.

'That's right.' Adam flashed a grin, and carried the fresh drinks back to the table.

'Who's the date with?' he asked Craig.

'No one you know.'

'Fucking hell,' Adam said, sipping his drink.

'Hand,' Craig said.

'What?'

'Put out your hand.'

Adam did so. Craig placed a wrap in it, throwing a casual glance to the pool room's entrance.

'That'll cheer you up. But go easy, it's for my date.'

'Your business date.'

'Oh, fuck off. Who was it said that the bogs are the new boardroom? Go smash one before I fucking take it back.'

'Maybe I'm not in the right mood.'

Craig pulled another face.

'What happened last time, by the way?' Adam asked him. 'Was it all OK with Joel and your boss? About the drugs?'

Something flickered across Craig's features. 'Ah yeah, all fine in the end.'

'He never found out?'

Craig held his gaze. 'He did find out. But I told him you'd brought the coke.'

'Oh, that's just brilliant,' Adam said.

'It'll never matter to you, mate,' Craig said, his voice softened. 'For me it might have been my job.'

'You might have asked me.'

'Fair enough.'

Adam stood up, wobbling a little, and placed a hand on top of the bench to steady himself. 'So what happens if my bosses want to sign one of your artists? Your boss tells them no, because their employee knocked his friend off the wagon?'

'He's not gonna give a shit that you did it, mate. Why would he? He just didn't want *me* doing it.'

'It's my reputation though, isn't it?'

The atmosphere had soured. 'Don't come all careerist with me now, Adam,' Craig said. 'You go out of your way to show you don't give a shit about your job, so it's a bit fucking rich.'

'That's not true,' Adam said. 'Is it?'

'Go on.' Craig glanced at his watch again. 'Hit that shit and cheer the fuck up.'

Adam turned away, and walked a little unsteadily down the three steps to the corridor below. The gents was brightly lit, and the one stall, as usual, had bouncer-friendly gaps at the top and bottom. There was no flat surface. Through the psychic fog of misery, Adam had a flashing realization that he was about to make things worse.

He pushed away the unwelcome thought, unwrapped the cocaine and looked at it. Some powder, some big lumps, some smaller ones. Who cares? he thought. He dug his apartment key into it, scooping up and sniffing a satisfying bump. The lumps in the coke burned his nose, but he sniffed them all back, manfully, feeling the bitter drug smear down the back of his throat.

The familiar, jet-engine-kicking-in, floodlights-clunking-on feeling lit through him. He placed his foot on the toilet seat, balanced the coke on his knee and removed a receipt from his own wallet, quickly making a little wrap of his own out of it. When he had, he tipped a quarter of Craig's coke out into it, then a little more.

Back at the table, Craig held his drink up, and Adam knocked it with his own.

'Are we good?' Craig said, grinning again.

'Always,' Adam said.

He passed Craig the wrap.

'Drink up,' Craig said. 'I'll get us one more for the road.'

Adam heard him order the drinks and head for the toilet himself. As he was peering into the gloom of the pool room, trying not to think, a sudden glow from the table below him drew his eyes. It was Craig's iPhone, and a text had just arrived on it.

Adam's heart skipped a beat when he read the name. Angelina.

The phone went black, and Adam tapped its screen to wake it up again.

Runnin lil late like 7.45 c u there, it said, followed by a Martini glass emoji.

Adam felt his skin tighten coldly around his skull as the phone went black again.

This was the world he'd fashioned for himself. False and dishonest; his own grim psyche reflected back at him.

A couple of minutes later, Craig was back. If he'd noticed how diminished his stash was, he wasn't letting on.

'Alright?' he said, grinning his rodent grin.

'Yes, much better now, thanks,' Adam said, smiling back. There was nothing, after all, to redeem or reconcile. No point confronting any of it. Nothing real with Angelina, nor with Craig. They could fucking have each other.

'Listen,' Craig said as they started the fresh drinks. 'Try and chill out tonight. Things'll look better in the morning. You're in a city full of beautiful women, mate, it could be worse.'

Having dispensed wise words and bad medicine, he departed. It was only quarter past six, and Adam was on his own again. The barman looked at him cautiously as he took up a seat at the bar once more.

'Same again, please,' Adam said.

'Well, alright.'

'Back in a minute.'

In the toilet, he didn't bother crouching under the gap at the top of the door. With only a bit of Craig's coke to go at, it seemed more important to crush up the rocks. He did this with the flat of the key, pressing the wrap against the stall's wall. He'd finally raised a nice, fluffy bump to his nose when the door to the toilets flew open.

'I fucking knew it,' the barman yelled. 'Fucking cokeheads. Get the hell out of there.'

Adam sniffed the coke up, and did so.

Outside, the sun was dipping low, and the cars' headlights were on as they cruised up the Boulevard towards Dodger Stadium or Downtown. Adam's body was pulsing as he walked, quickly and purposefully down the hill, a light sweat on his brow, the mind behind it emptying of all but the thoughts of the home that wasn't home, of the drugs in his pocket and the booze in his fridge.

31

The river gleamed painfully in the late morning sun. Actually, it was hard to tell if the pain came from the gleam, or from the quickening throb in Adam's head. Crooked, was how everything looked. Slanted. Two words from the titles of Pavement albums. And over-bright, too. He felt very brittle and weak, his bones and the muscles in his legs aching. It was as though he'd just emerged, sore and hollowed out, from a period of hospitalization.

The day was very hot and sunny, and he was sweating heavily enough for his eyes to sting with it and his clothing to have dampened. It didn't matter. He was wearing his house-clothes: a very old, stained, shapeless pair of blue shorts and a faded, many-holed t-shirt with a hip-hop label's logo on it.

He didn't look good, he knew. He was unshaven and pale, with lumpy black bags beneath his swollen eyes. When he'd looked in the mirror, he'd remembered an old boss telling him one Monday morning after a heavy weekend that his eyes looked like piss-holes in the snow. They did again now.

Cyclists went by, most of them the serious kinds with the logoed Lycra and insect-like sunglasses. Most of them male. MAMILs, he remembered hearing them called. Middle-Aged Men in Lycra. They were intent on what they were doing, and few of them smiled. Certainly, none of them was Erica.

He had texted her twice the night before. He remembered that, but not exactly what he'd said. He hadn't been able to bring himself to check the messages in the morning.

He wasn't quite sure why he'd come to the river. To see something beautiful perhaps. To be where he'd met her, and to torture himself. To start once again, with new resolutions in this bleakly beautiful place, to make new promises to himself that in all probability, considering the ever-mounting evidence, he would fail to keep.

A cyclist scythed by and grunted something at him, and he realized he was walking in the centre of the bike path. Fuck it, he thought, and swung under the railing and onto the steep, dirty white concrete bank. This railing was usually the physical barrier between bum and regular citizen. Adam had never seen anyone altogether normal-looking wandering on the bank. Maybe the odd kid, smoking a joint and watching the water. Occasionally a fisherman or two. Certainly there would be no cyclists down here.

It was quite freeing. He let momentum carry him a few quick steps further down towards the water, its thick green smell rising up to greet him. Nausea rose, too, from his stomach, but he breathed and swallowed and it subsided. Still drunk, he thought. A little, anyway. The real pain is yet to come. One Sunday afternoon in London, still awakc from the night before, in a pub that smelled of stale beer and was pooled with dusty sunlight, a fellow straggler had raised his pint to Adam and said, 'Put the pain in the post, eh?' That was where it was again now.

Ahead of him, down the steep slope, trees and bushes and grass and reeds sprouted from the river. A mass of green, unmoving in the still air, sun bouncing off the blades and leaves in shades of gold. Abundant life. Beautiful.

A great blue heron was standing on a rock, very still, one leg raised behind it. It reminded Adam of the man doing t'ai chi in Ernest E. Debs Park, on the day of his first date with Erica. A mother duck, surrounded by ducklings, splashed in the sunny brown water a little further downstream. Something he couldn't identify flicked out of a tree, then disappeared back into its branches. Adam squinted after it. A green heron perhaps?

He reached the flat band of concrete at the bottom of the slope, which was half swamped with brownish water in most places. There was an old, disintegrating sneaker sat a little way from the river's edge. It was another world, down here. Hot and green and jungly and wild. Why had he not thought to walk down the bank before? It was easy enough. Much better to be away from the path, and the men with their logos and attitudes.

Swifts flitted low between the trees and across the water, ridding the air of some of the many insects, twisting and turning in the brightness. There were strands of rubbish caught in the trees, but not too many. Down here, nature seemed very much in charge.

Adam pottered along the bank, squinting in the light. He had left his phone at home, and his sunglasses. All he had were his keys, a sandwich wrapped in greaseproof paper – which he had made, for some reason, though he had absolutely no desire to eat – and the dregs of a bottle of water. He should have brought two of those.

Atwater Village stretched out on the other side of the river, sleepy and smart and well-to-do. Was Erica at home? What was she doing? He saw a vision of himself – as he was now – standing forlornly at the bottom of her driveway. He shuddered at the possibility.

A little way along, and above him now, was one of the huge outlet pipes that fed excess rainwater from the streets into the river. A slimy brown stain pointed down from it, like a bony finger. Beneath it, a respectable-looking man with grey hair and glasses was standing by the water, arms folded across his t-shirt. Adam stopped a little way from him, and the man turned.

'Hi,' he said, without smiling, and looked back at the water, frowning.

'Hi,' Adam said. His voice sounded thick and hoarse. It was the first time he'd spoken all day.

'I don't suppose,' the man said, 'that you've seen any frogs while you've been walking?' He looked at Adam again, longer this time, as though trying to figure him out.

'Frogs?' Adam said. 'No.'

'Shit,' the man said. 'Shit, shit, shit.'

'What's wrong?' Adam asked. Perhaps, he wondered, the man wasn't respectable at all. Just another Los Angeles whacko, with a unique brand of amphibian-focused psychosis.

'I think they're all gone,' the man said. 'The army has killed 'em all.'

'The army has… killed all the frogs?' Adam said.

'Yep.' The man lowered himself to a crouch, picked up a twig and twiddled it between finger and thumb as he watched the water. 'The Army Corps of Engineers. They've been down here trying to kill off an invasive weed. Using an industrial pesticide. I think they killed all the frogs too.'

'Oh,' Adam said, hoping the relief hadn't come across in his voice. 'I see.'

'It's a fucking tragedy,' the man said, looking at Adam again. Bright blue eyes behind his glasses. Like Scott's, Adam thought. Like a much nicer, kinder Scott. He was fairly confident that Scott wouldn't give a shit about frogs.

'They've been coming back. Just a few at first, but more every year. One of the last species native to the wetland here. Beautiful. That's why Frogtown is called Frogtown.'

'I don't know it,' Adam said.

'A little way downriver. Up-and-coming. All that shit.'

'Got it.'

'I take folks out kayaking on the river. See the frogs most days. The army was out two weeks ago, and I haven't seen one since. Lots of dead ones, but not a single one alive.'

'That's awful,' Adam said.

'We warned them…' the man said, standing again.

Adam searched his mind for something to say. 'Did you say there was a wetland here?' he asked.

'Oh yeah. The river always was a river. They just straightened it out, down here in the basin. Concreted it into a line.'

'I didn't know,' Adam said.

'1939. Roosevelt and the New Deal and all the infrastructure works. They did some good stuff, like making all the mountain trails, but a lot of bad too. The river always drained the mountains, just like it does now. But they had rail yards and all types of crap springing up. Meanders weren't convenient. So, the Army Engineers came out, poured concrete into it and made it straight.'

'Wow,' Adam said, ashamed that it was all he could think of.

'But it kinda grew back, gradually. There's deep ponds in it, where the concrete subsided, and guess what? – they're just where they used to be. Mother Nature tends to know what she's doing.'

Adam nodded.

'I was really happy about the frogs,' the man said.

'I like frogs too,' Adam said. 'I used to go to Scotland a lot, camping as a kid. I had a pet one once.'

'A pet frog?' the man frowned.

'Yeah. I found him in a boggy patch and kept him in my pocket. He was called Timothy, I think.'

'What happened to him?'

Adam thought back. The memory made him wince. 'Actually, I think he died. He just sort of… dried out.'

The man's frown deepened. 'Jesus,' he said.

'Well,' Adam said. 'If I see one around…'

'Sure, but maybe just leave it where it is?' The man shook his head. 'Nice meeting you,' he said, setting off past Adam and heading upstream.

Maybe if I wasn't such an idiot, Adam thought, I could focus on some really important stuff like that. Maybe it would be possible to earn a reasonable living, running a charity that looked after frogs?

He set off again, his legs tired, his thirst growing. A depth charge of sadness had exploded in his gut. His psyche had been scrubbed raw by the long night of drinking, leaving it alive to any gust of emotion. He didn't want to go back to the home that wasn't a home. A day of recovering on the couch, thinking of the past, resisting the temptation to drink. He swallowed the rest of his water, and wished again that he'd brought more.

The past was not a refuge. It was a seductive illusion, and a prison. Its siren call was a lure and a honeytrap. Give in, and you let yourself sink away from the present, from life. And each time you resurfaced there was a little less of you left. Just because things had been good once didn't mean they were OK now, or that they would be again. Just because *you'd* been good – been valuable – once, didn't mean that you still were.

The image of Erica's eyes kept coming to him, blazing and sad all at once, before the elevator doors had closed on them. Another loss. But he deserved it. Seven years since the great mistake he'd made, of letting go of Sofia, and he hadn't learned a thing.

He could still picture Sofia's eyes too, when it finally came out. They'd been to Lewes together, to see her parents over the first weekend in April. Adam had broken it off with Isa. Sofia had cut her hair into a fringe. Before they left the flat, he'd taken a photo of her, smiling – beaming – in the room they'd shared together. The last picture of her that he'd ever take. He could remember the fragile, doomed hope he'd had that maybe he could put what he'd done behind him and get on with life with Sofia.

When they'd arrived at her parents' house, her father told her she looked beautiful with the fringe, and he was right. They spent the weekend walking on the Downs, and driving south to Beachy Head, where the sea and the bright red-and-white lighthouse gleamed below them. They stopped in country pubs, talked of their friends and their plans. They were a normal couple, as far as she knew. He loved her. How could the horrible certainty of that fact not have become clear until after she was gone?

On Saturday, Isa had emailed him. *I thought you loved me?* she'd said. *How could you do this?* In his vanity, he didn't delete the email. Nor did he reply to it. It simply lurked on his phone, ready to read again when he had a moment, to feel the odd power of it as he did so, the little, fascinating pulse of pain.

On the Sunday morning, before they got on the train to London, Isa had texted him. Sofia saw her name on Adam's screen, and asked to see the text. He'd deleted it – with all the others – before she could.

They'd almost reached Hayward's Heath when he thought he'd persuaded her that Isa was flirty, that he may have been flirty back, that that was all it was. He was ashamed, he would never do anything like it again. Then, suddenly, she had grabbed his phone, was scrolling through texts, calls, then emails. She was so sad and so angry that he watched her scroll past the mail from Isa without noting it. When she reached the bottom of his inbox, she began to scroll back up, more slowly this time.

With a sudden, sick punch in his gut, he realized the futility of it, and he told her.

The train stopped at Hayward's Heath. She stood up, ran to the door. He grabbed their bags and followed her. She collapsed onto a bench on the platform and began retching, her beautiful face distorted, her eyes wide and black and flowing with tears. People staring at him like something foul, knowing him to be the cause of this.

After that, everything seemed to break into short, painful little fragments. Back on a train, telling her everything – or as much as he had to. Going numb with the pain of it all, like some psychic equivalent of passing out. On the Tube in London. Passing two of her friends – a couple who'd never liked him – her in tears, unable to speak, them looking at him, knowing, disgusted with him, thinking they'd known it all along. And probably they had, hadn't they?

Back at the flat, very briefly, then kicked out. A pub, two friends, oblivion, someone's couch. All the years that sprouted, poisoned, from this.

He sat down on the warm concrete bank and felt tears come. A little while after he'd lost her, he'd read her blog – the one that would germinate into the career she now had. She had written about what was happening to her, how art wasn't much on her mind 'when I feel heartbroken and sad like now my Adam has gone'. Why had he thrown her away? He didn't understand himself, and he was sure he never would. It was as though he could never quite see himself properly, like a landscape too wide for the camera's lens. If only he'd been able to fly above his life and see it all clearly.

Why did he have this need to be wanted, and to possess?

Standing up on his stiff, aching legs, he began to walk again. He passed under the Sunnynook footbridge, steaming around the pillars of which was a strong smell of urine. For a while, someone seemed to have been sleeping beneath the latticework of the bridge, atop one of these pillars. Living on a precarious perch only a few feet wide. There'd been a few possessions visible there, a sleeping bag, and above them some mad, sloganeering graffiti. Then, abruptly, whoever had been there had apparently gone.

Adam looked up now, but all he could see was the shadowy underside of the bridge. Something caught his attention as he lowered his eyes back to the river. A tall tree, a little way further along. That was where he'd seen the osprey, he realized, when Erica had first pointed it out. He stepped out of the smell of stale, condensed piss and walked a little faster, stopping again beneath the tree. Looking up, squinting in the light, he saw that its branches were empty now.

He sat down on the sloping bank again, the ache in his limbs worsening. He thought they must've been stiffened and over-stretched during his brief, tortuous sleep the night before. The water a few feet away gurgled and trickled, making him crave some of its sanitized form. Stupid, not to have brought more. He was a long way from the car now.

He let the vegetation distract him, running his eyes over it. So much of it. Amazing to think it had sprung back from being concreted over, to this. It had broken through, reasserted itself, bided its time.

Just then, taking him by surprise, he felt a small pang of hope. It rose in him like a weak flare, and was instantly distinguished by the blackness within.

Still, he thought. Life did quite obviously go on, didn't it? Whether you liked it or not. And happiness would probably grow back. In fact, his happiness had been a bit like a weed. Seemingly ineradicable, no matter how he mistreated it, how many chemicals he threw at it and how many of its roots he ripped up. Its resilience was almost obscene. It didn't matter what impediment he put before it, it would grow around, keep finding a way. Another little flare rose within him.

It was a bit like the creeper in the courtyard of the building in which he and Sofia had lived. Columbine, he thought it had been called. On countless weekends in spring and summer, a middle-aged blonde woman, the block's busybody, had been out there trying to kill it, and had never once succeeded. Within a few short weeks, its tendrils would be poking out once more, coiling themselves around the more welcome plants.

He'd thought that with each bad choice, the finite supply of happiness would be depleted. Now, he wasn't sure it worked like that. Happiness seemed to keep finding ways back to the light, too.

A growing noise from downstream distracted him. There seemed to be a lot of people gathered on the Glendale Boulevard bridge. There were shouts, and then a chant he couldn't make out. He stood up, walking a little way up the bank to get a better look. There were police vehicles up there, flashing lights atop them. He could make out the blue, hatted forms of a few cops, standing around with hands on hips. To their right, on the Silver Lake side of the bridge, was a large group of people, some holding placards, all of them apparently yelling at the cops.

Adam walked a little way along the bank, but the steep angle of the concrete was uncomfortable under his feet, so he dropped back down to the water. The voices grew louder. Someone was shouting through a megaphone.

'Where's your compassion?' the angry, high male voice said. 'Where the hell do you think they're gonna go?'

He walked a little way up the bank again. The cops, he could see, were clearing out the big homeless camp that had been set up along the river's opposite bank for as long as he could remember. The path there led to a dead end against the bridge, so its occupants had presumably thought they weren't bothering anyone.

'Move 'em on, make 'em go, where they'll end up, who fucking knows?' the voice behind the megaphone chanted. There seemed to be thirty or so protestors, a short row of grim-faced cops keeping them away from the camp. On the path and the bridge, ten or so more cops were issuing directions to the bums. Adam watched as the painfully thin, overdressed men and women, their hair long and matted or short and patched, walked dazedly around their tents, like dozy, sedated bees around a hive. The cops seemed to be on best behaviour, their movements calm and unhurried, their voices too low for Adam to hear.

Another van, parked up beside the cop cars and trucks, had a satellite dish on top of it. Adam could make out a man with a TV camera, a female presenter apparently speaking into it.

'Where are they gonna go?' the amplified voice screamed. 'They're just gonna set up somewhere else. Why are you doing this to them? How much is this costing?'

There were raised voices from the police side, and one of the men in the line stepped forward, pointing and yelling something at a protestor.

Adam was quite close to the bridge now. His car was parked on Glenhurst. Going back the way he came would mean a lot of extra walking. He was very tired, very hot and very thirsty. There seemed to be cars going over Glendale, so he assumed he could walk over the bridge on the other side from the protestors.

He carried on along the riverside, the protest going out of view above him but the voices much louder now. The shouts and yells blurred together. Only the voice from the megaphone, which was growing strained from overuse and emotion, was clear.

'How much is this *costing*? Paying your wages today,' it screamed, 'could house all these people for a week.' Then: 'Kick 'em out, move 'em on, who cares where they go, so long as they're gone.'

Adam had almost reached the bridge. The vegetation faded out before it, and he could see the camp on the other side of the river now. Tents were coming down, the homeless people were climbing up onto Glendale, dragging possessions, helping each other carry shopping trolleys stuffed with junk. A young woman, who Adam often saw on the river, was sitting atop the bank, clutching her head and rocking back and forth.

In the shade beneath the bridge, only a few steps away from Adam now, were a large Canada goose and her goslings, dabbling in the water as they circled her. She'd apparently come upstream under the bridge, and was heading towards him and away from the noise.

Adam looked back up to the camp. One of the homeless men was holding a dog by its collar, and a cop was poised in front of him, left hand held out warningly, right hand – out of Adam's view – apparently on his hip. God, Adam thought. Surely not resting on a pistol? Surely at worst a nightstick? The cop was shouting at the man, but his voice was drowned out by the megaphone.

After a moment, the man let go of the dog's collar. It ran straight down the bank into the water, heading across the shallows and towards the mother goose. The huge bird raised its head in alarm, then looked left, towards Adam. With a strange calm, he realized he was standing in the direction of her only aquatic escape route. As the dog approached, she spread her wings, hissed, and launched herself at Adam's chest.

The impact took the wind out of him. As he fell backwards, he felt a sharp pain below his left nipple, and realized she'd bitten him for good measure. Then he was lying on his back in the water, which momentarily covered his face, cutting out the world in a strangely peaceful moment of underwater silence.

As he raised his head, the goose climbed over him and slid off his brow into the water. The smell of her blossomed in his nostrils, a fusty, choking mix of oily under-feathers and wild water. As Adam raised himself on his elbows, shaking his head and sucking in breath, the goslings scrabbled past him to their mother, squeaking in alarm. He turned his head to see them moving upstream together, until they reached a band of reeds and disappeared behind it.

He sat up, reeling, soaking wet. Before him was the dog, a mongrel with big brown eyes beneath thick greying brows. Its head was cocked sympathetically.

'Hello,' Adam said. The dog stepped forward, and licked his face in long, generous strokes.

'Pmfff,' Adam said, twisting his neck and flailing at the dog to no avail. 'Fuckumpf.'

When the dog had finished, it stepped back and watched him, wagging its tail.

'Good boy,' Adam said automatically.

He got to his feet and looked down at himself. He was soaked through, the dank smell of river, dog and goose swirling around him. A thick green substance had smeared the back of his shirt and clothes, and he stank.

'Jesus,' he said. He raised his hands and waggled them in disgust. The dog was worrying at something, wedged behind a rock in the water. It was Adam's sandwich.

'You can definitely have that,' Adam said to the dog when it had retrieved the ruined meal. The empty bottle of water was nowhere to be seen. Just another piece of river trash, Adam thought, guiltily.

The dog stood where it was, gazing up at him and panting through its nose, the wag of its tail slowing. Adam looked back up at the camp. There was no sign of its owner. No one was looking in his direction.

He set off up the bank, his trainers heavy with water and smeared in the green-black slime. With each step, he left a wet footprint, and large drops of water fell from him and landed between them. His t-shirt was soaked through, hanging heavily from his back, and the water was dripping down over his brow. He smeared it with the back of his hand, which came away brown. I'm a fucking swamp monster! he thought. The dog, apparently excited to be moving, walked at his heel.

'Fuck's sakes,' Adam told it. 'For fuck's fucking sakes!'

He walked through the gate in the chain-link fence, and onto the sidewalk before the bridge. The protestors were blocking it. He'd have to work his way through them to cross to the opposite footpath.

Grimacing, he walked towards them. The people at the back of the group were fairly quiet, watching the action over each other's shoulders, shouting only occasionally. When one of them saw him approach, she turned, tapped another on the arm, and suddenly a path was forming between them. Adam only dared glance at them. His shame was too acute to look anyone in the eye. Hipsters, he saw. Of the angry, righteous, politically minded type. Vegans, PETA people. Oddly haired and pasty-faced, and with the cheaper type of hipster clothes, thrift-store stuff; the odd army jacket, faded, skimpy little slogan t-shirts. Lots of facial hair, some dreadlocks, bad jeans.

'Sorry, dude,' someone said to him. 'Stay strong, brother,' a man with shaven ginger hair and stubble and thick-rimmed glasses said. 'Can we help you in some way?' a voice said. 'Is there anything you need?' asked another.

A woman, who looked a little like Janis Joplin, thrust her head towards him. 'That's a beautiful dog, my friend,' she said.

Hipsters, Adam thought. I'm being nurtured by hipsters. The eco ones. The protesty ones.

'Make a path,' someone said. 'Look out behind you.' 'God bless you, dude.' A man was writing slogans on the sidewalk in bright, multicoloured chalk. Adam tried not to drip on his work.

Saved, he thought. Loved. Loved by… hipsters.

He was almost at the edge of the group, where he could cross the road, when he reached the film crew.

A short, tanned man with abundant, shiny black hair tapped the cameraman on the shoulder. 'Here's one,' he said.

The camera swirled around, facing Adam just a few inches from his nose. He could see his reflection in its lens. His awkward, bony neck and staring, frightened eyes. Suddenly, a very fragrant woman, who reminded him of the radio promoter in Denver, was beside him, frowning sympathetically – the presenter.

'Excuse me, sir,' she said. 'Could I speak with you for a moment?'

Adam gaped at the camera, in a state of abject terror. He was aware that his jaw was trembling. When he tried to speak, only a strange, strangled sob came out.

'I'll talk to you,' said a familiar voice. Adam glanced in its direction to see a man carrying a megaphone. He was tall and very thin, hair in a ponytail pulled back above a high forehead. He stood beside Adam and faced the camera.

'Look at the conditions these people are living in down here. This man has been driven into the filthy river water by the cops. You think this is acceptable? Look at him.' The man stepped aside and gestured. 'He's soaked through in goddamned polluted water and it just breaks my heart. This man hasn't harmed anyone.'

'What do you say to that, sir?' said the beautiful, concerned presenter.

'Um, well, I don't…' Adam said. 'I, ah, just came down for a walk. I don't actually…' He took a deep, shaky breath and gestured vaguely over his shoulder. 'I was talking to a nice man about the army killing the frogs, and then a goose knocked me over, trying to escape.'

'OK,' the presenter said, frowning and touching her earpiece. Adam lowered his head.

The camera was turned away, the presenter was talking, someone was offering him a blanket, someone else pressed a leaflet into his hand and told him there were places he could stay, and then suddenly he was walking – squelching – across the road and away. The dog peeled off as it did so, wagging its tail again, sandwich still held proudly in its jaws, apparently having sniffed out its real owner.

A few minutes later, he was walking down Glenhurst Avenue, partially recovered and a little bit drier. When he reached the car, he found he didn't want to get into it. It would be hot and airless, he knew, and he'd be able to smell himself, sitting in his sodden clothing. And even after that, where would he be? He saw himself in the apartment again, lying on the couch, recovering and stewing. He didn't want to be there, he realized.

In fact, there was only one place he did want to be.

32

Erica answered the door wearing loose trackpants and a UCLA t-shirt. Her hair was tied up at the back, and she didn't seem pleased to see him.

'Adam,' she said. 'When I said stay away, I meant it. You can't just show up at my house.'

'I need to talk to you,' he said. 'I can't just give up like that.'

She ran her eyes over him. 'What happened to you?'

'I fell in the river, basically,' he said.

'Good,' she said, nodding. She regarded him for a moment, apparently thinking.

'OK,' she said, finally. 'You can take off your shoes. And socks. In fact, just go around the back to the yard.' She pointed to where a path ran down the side of the house, and closed the door.

Adam made his way along the gravelled path to a wrought-iron gate. He was standing before it for several minutes before Erica reappeared to open it.

Beyond was a small, shaded yard with two fruit trees strung with fairy lights, and some chairs around a mosaic-surfaced table. A little hidden paradise that she'd made. Seeing this beautiful place in these circumstances made him feel horribly sad.

She removed the cushion from a rattan chair, and gestured to him to sit in it.

'You look awful,' she said, sitting opposite him.

'I feel awful,' he said. 'I was drowning my sorrows last night.'

'Look, Adam—'

'Erica,' he interrupted. 'I don't mean to be pushy, but please could I have a drink?'

'Oh, for God's sake,' she said. 'Fine.'

She walked back into the house, and re-emerged a few moments later with two glasses of white wine.

Adam sipped his gratefully. 'Thanks,' he said.

'I don't want to make a big deal out of all this, Adam,' she said. 'It's just not for me, OK?'

'I don't think you're being fair,' he said.

She cocked her chin at him. 'How do you figure that?'

'We'd just met each other, we hadn't made any commitments.'

'Yeah, but you still fucked another woman and then showed up in my hospital looking creepy. Or is there something I missed?'

'I'm sorry. I just wanted to make sure I was safe.'

'Good for you. I'm just not interested. I hope you get your life together.'

'Erica. You never even asked if I was seeing anyone.'

'Oh, come on. So I needed to do that, did I? Forgive me for assuming that you weren't seeing anyone.'

'I wasn't. Before you I was, then I crossed paths with her in Denver.'

'You know, I'm really mad at myself, not you. I knew that you being British or whatever didn't preclude you from being yet another LA asshole, but I let myself get sucked in anyway.'

'But I'm not an LA asshole,' Adam protested. 'I know I fucked up, but I tried not to make it any worse by sleeping with you and putting you at risk.'

Erica glanced over her shoulder, towards the closest neighbouring house.

'You keep your voice down, or you get out,' she said.

'Fine.'

'Are you seriously suggesting what you did was OK?'

'No. I'm suggesting you give me another chance, because if you and I actually get together I will never do anything like that again.'

'How can you be sure?'

'I lost my appetite for it.'

'Oh, fuck off,' she said, taking a deep sip of her wine.

'And I'm falling in love with you.'

'You're ridiculous,' she said, more quietly.

'I might be ridiculous, but I mean it, and I'm deeply sorry for what I did. And if you give me another chance I will never do anything like it again.'

Erica was looking over his shoulder. Her anger had dissipated, but now she looked miserable, which was worse.

'I knew something was up,' she said.

'What do you mean?'

'When you stopped me, in the bedroom. And I could tell you'd lied to me about why. When does a man ever stop a woman from doing that?'

'I meant it when I said I didn't want to fuck it up,' Adam told her.

'It's what my ex used to do,' Erica said. Her eyes had welled up. 'He didn't want to sleep with me.' She took a deep breath. 'That was how I knew he didn't want me to move away with him... That was how he told me.'

'I'm so sorry, Erica,' Adam said. He thought of Sofia. *Why don't you want to have sex with me any more?*

She dabbed away a tear as it ran down her beautiful face. 'I need some time to think about it all, Adam,' she said. 'Just leave me alone for now, please.'

* * *

Stef's screen door flew open as he climbed the stairs to his apartment, and smacked loudly into the wood frame of the house.

'Oh my God!' she yelled, standing in the doorway. 'What the hell happened to you? You were on the TV!' She gaped at him, then cackled uproariously. Adam was fumbling his key in the lock by the time she'd stopped.

'Sorry,' she said, grinning at him. 'It's just too wild.'

'It was horrible,' he said.

'Let me help you. Oh God, you poor kid.'

Inside the apartment, she helped him peel off his t-shirt.

'Go shower,' she said. 'Shall I make you, like, a tea or something?'

'Whisky,' he said. 'In the cupboard.'

'Right, yeah,' she said excitedly. 'Like a medicinal nip, right?'

Adam grunted, and padded into the bathroom. He showered for almost fifteen minutes, soaping and rinsing his entire body three full times.

When he'd finished, he dried off and dressed in a clean t-shirt and shorts. Stef was in the living room, sitting on the edge of the couch and flicking through channels on the TV. Beside her were two wine glasses with a large measure of whisky in each. The bottle was on the floor beside her bare feet.

Adam took a tumbler from the cupboard, sat beside her and poured his drink into it.

'Oh, sorry,' she said, glancing at him and smiling again. 'I didn't mean not to get it all proper for you, fancy-pants. I guess I got you confused with some type of bum.'

Adam necked the whisky, and poured himself another.

'Attaboy,' Stef said.

'What was that about the TV?' he asked, when the glow of the whisky had lit in his gut.

'That's what I'm looking for now. Oh my God, it was so cool.'

'Jesus,' Adam said. 'Was it a big station? Will people have seen it?'

'No, it's just the local news,' Stef said, flicking channels. 'Not so many people.'

'Shit,' he said, dropping his head into his hands. 'My colleagues.'

'Those kids?' Stef laughed. 'Those little fuckers don't watch TV, dude. Especially not the news. As long as you keep it off Instagram you'll be fine.'

'Yes,' Adam said hopefully. 'Yes, of course.'

'Shit. It's not on here. Let me get my laptop.'

She disappeared for a half a minute, and returned with Beans the cat, who sashayed around Adam's legs. He was allergic to cats, but, in his current state, his craving for affection outweighed the fear of the coming reaction.

Stef drained her glass, and typed excitedly into a browser on her MacBook. She pushed a strand of grey-blonde hair aside.

'Pour me another one, that shit's delicious,' she said.

Adam did so.

'Here!' she said. A video player had filled half the screen, the rest of which was made up of a bewildering array of TV logos, adverts and thumbnails for more news clips. Stef clicked play.

'There you are!' she said. Adam watched as the camera swung onto him. He grimaced at himself, grimacing and mumbling on the screen. It was over much more quickly than it had felt at the time.

Below the player was a comments section.

'Scroll down,' Adam said.

'Oh right,' Stef said excitedly. 'Comments.'

There were only three. A good sign, Adam thought.

Just because this guy is white and like a LIL bit betta lookin than most bums they pick HIM out for tha tv thats bs, said Bey420.

They go down there, someone calling themselves Sad_Liberal had said, *to prey on lost girls.*

wtf was that australian guy gonna do to a goose?! said Pepe666.

'Ha,' Stef said. 'You are good-looking. For a bum.'

'Well,' Adam said. 'At least it doesn't seem to have gone viral.'

'So, what the hell happened?' Stef said, turning sideways on the couch to face him.

Adam told her everything that had taken place over the previous, tumultuous days.

'Woah,' she said, when he'd finished. 'And I thought you were just the quiet dude who lived in my rental.'

'It's not always like this,' Adam told her.

'It's kinda rock 'n' roll actually,' she said. 'Apart from the falling in the river bit.'

'I suppose so.'

'The thing is, though, you didn't really do anything wrong, did you? I mean, has this chick dated in LA before?'

'I think I sort of sold myself as not an LA type of person.'

Stef laughed. 'Adam – an LA type of person would have let her give him head, then gone out for frozen yoghurt – not to the goddamn sex clinic.' She sipped her whisky. 'Am I allowed to use this in a script?'

'No you are not.'

'So what's the plan now?'

'I don't know.'

'Well,' Stef said, draining her glass. 'Then I guess this is the part where you wait by the phone.'

* * *

He did receive a call that evening, but it was from his sister. He answered it reluctantly, and largely out of loneliness.

'I had a call from the hospital,' she said after they'd exchanged pleasantries. 'Mum's getting worse. Or rather, she's already worsened.'

'Yes,' Adam said. 'I spoke to her again a couple of days ago.'

Elizabeth tutted. 'They never give me all the information. I take it it didn't go well?'

'No,' Adam said. 'She was very angry, and quite wired. I've never seen her like that.'

'You could've told me,' Elizabeth said.

'Sorry. I've been a bit caught up here.'

'Right,' she said, sceptically. 'Well, we might have some decisions to make.'

'Yes,' Adam agreed. 'I suppose we might.'

'I think one or both of us should go back. I mean, one is enough to help look after her, but if we want to have any sort of quality time with her, before the end…'

'Yes,' Adam said.

'Are you serious about making some changes?' Elizabeth asked. 'If you do move back, I suppose it wouldn't be to Somerset?'

'I haven't really given it much more thought,' Adam said.

'Well, I need to decide whether to turn down this job. I mean, I've already accepted it, but I can change my mind. And I'm the elder sibling after all.'

'It's not about that, though, is it?' Adam said. 'It's not just a question of duty.'

'Exactly,' his sister said.

'I've been thinking it would be nice to all be closer to each other again.'

'The three of us,' Elizabeth said. 'Barely qualifies as an "all", does it?'

'Not even three,' Adam said. 'More like two point five.'

Elizabeth laughed, a sound he loved. 'Ooh, dark,' she said, approvingly.

'I'll do some thinking,' Adam said.

'OK,' Elizabeth said. 'For what it's worth, I think I've made up my mind. The career can wait for a bit, and anyway, I can do translation work from anywhere.'

A wave of anxiety passed through Adam as the new reality crystallized.

'Might be a bit harder on you, workwise,' Elizabeth said.

'Yes.'

'You don't need to decide straight away. After all, she's probably still got years.'

33

On Sunday night, an email had come in from Roger. It was simply a subject line: **Call me as soon as you're in tomorrow.**

Now, as he walked to work on Monday morning, Adam began to abandon hope. There'd been no word from Erica. Roger's ominous message could surely only mean that Falconz were not going to stay on the label.

The office was already chilled when he arrived. Someone must have been in early.

On the upper floor, Beau, wearing headphones, grinned, winked and made pistol-cocking motions with his fingers. Kristen was hunched over her laptop, on which she quickly hid her Facebook page. Her sunglasses were perched on top of her head.

'Morning,' Adam said to her. 'How are you?'

'Like, exhausted,' she said.

Scott was also at his desk. He looked up, but didn't speak until Adam greeted him.

'Good weekend?' Adam asked him.

'Great,' Scott replied. 'Really great actually.'

'Excellent,' Adam said.

'Shall we, like, catch up?' Scott asked.

'Not just now. I have to call Roger.'

An anxious curiosity cleared the mists of happy weekend memories from Scott's eyes. They sharpened on Adam's.

'Should I be on that?' he asked.

'No,' Adam told him. 'I'm going to take it outside, actually.'

He couldn't stand being in the office any more. In London, he'd always felt excited to arrive at work. Happy to be around colleagues he liked. Potentially, he was some sort of cultural failure. Maybe just not a good manager of people. He assumed it wasn't normal to feel visceral hatred for the people who worked for you. Thus, the problem was him.

Outside, he paced the shady walkway that ran the length of the building, and which the day's heat hadn't yet colonized. Presumably it also wasn't normal to be afraid to make a business call. Why did he feel as though he'd been sent to the headmaster's office? This would be it, he was sure. Roger was going to take Falconz elsewhere, and Adam would have failed. It would have been better for the Autodidact to be first to know. That way, Adam wouldn't have had to tell him himself. Fuck, fuck, fuck.

He scrolled to Roger's number and hit Call with a brittle-feeling finger.

'Well hey,' the manager said, picking up immediately. There was something new in his voice. Glee, Adam decided.

'Hi,' Adam said.

'How you doing, sir?' Roger said.

Adam frowned at a tall plant which sprouted from a border running along the walkway. 'I'm OK, thanks. How are you?'

'I'm awesome,' Roger said, sounding very cheerful indeed. 'And I have some very good news for you, brother.'

Was Roger so demented that he thought a major label licence deal was going to come as good news?

'Exciting,' Adam said. 'What is it?'

'Well,' Roger said, 'Joel was going to call you himself, but I asked if I could break the news. Euphonic have come on board as exclusive national promoter, and they're gonna give us a big pot of marketing money as part of the deal.'

'Wow,' Adam said. The thought dawned on him that this was, technically at least, actually very good news.

'So really I just wanted to say thank you,' Roger said. 'Joel said it was the meeting he had with you that sparked this whole thing off. I didn't even know you knew the guy!'

'Oh yes,' Adam said, nodding at the plant.

'He told me you pitched him at his house?' The manager laughed, as though in approval of a well-executed extreme sports move. 'That's some next-level shit, bro.'

'Well,' Adam said. 'They say the bathroom is the new boardroom.'

'… Right,' Roger said. 'Well, this is the part of the picture that was missing, dude. There's no strings attached to the marketing money. We've got at least a million to do what we like with. And this way we keep it independent. No major label contracts and old-school licence deals.'

'Perfect,' Adam said.

'Honestly, brother,' Roger said, 'this is exactly the sort of futuristic thinking that Falconz is all about. No one's done a deal like this before, so we're making history. I'm gonna speak to *Billboard* this afternoon, and I want you to give a statement too.'

'Sure thing,' Adam said.

'It's so exciting, right? It's such a great feeling?'

'Oh yes,' Adam lied, thinking that there was something very wrong with him.

'And listen, Adam?' Roger said, his voice softening. 'I'm sorry if I pushed you. But I hope you see why now. I push everyone who works with us, but no one harder than myself. And in this case, look what it led to.'

Of course, Adam thought.

'Of course,' he said. 'It's absolutely fine.'

'Also, Marissa and Bret told me what you said in Denver, about me being a great manager? I appreciate it, buddy. That actually helped a lot. Things have been… intense.'

'I'm glad,' Adam said.

'Well, listen, man,' Roger continued, 'I gotta tell Bret and Marissa. And oh, by the way, you need to call Jason.'

'Jason?' Adam frowned.

'Yeah, I'm sorry, I already told him. I had a call scheduled with him before my workout, real early. I didn't think you'd be up. I hope that's alright?'

'Right, yes.'

'He wanted me to ask you to call him.'

'Right.'

'And Adam?'

'Yes?'

'Thanks for bringing your A-game for the team.'

Adam hung up, and walked back along the concrete path towards the stairs. Before he'd reached the door that led to them, it swung open, Isa framed within it.

She was dressed in trackpants and a faded grey t-shirt, struggling to get through the door with a handbag, a small, unzipped holdall evidently stuffed with sports kit, and a scuffed leather laptop case. She looked worried, the flesh of her face lifeless and drawn.

'Hi, mate,' she said, smiling.

'Hello.'

He held the door and took two of the bags from her, placing them by the entrance to the office.

'Thanks,' she said. She gave him a quick hug, pulling him to her quite tightly.

'You OK?' he asked.

'Been better,' she said. 'You off out?'

'Yes, I need to make a call. Thought I'd do it from the park.'

'OK.'

'What's wrong?' he asked.

'Nothing, really.'

'Something is, obviously. Just tell me.'

She puffed out her cheeks and sighed. 'I think I'm in trouble with Jason,' she said, removing her phone from a pocket and checking its screen, which was now cracked.

'Why? What's happened?'

'Well, I had a big night with those Vegas guys on Thursday,' she said. 'I called your mate Craig and ended up being out really late with them and getting all messy. I thought that was probably what I should do, since Jason really wants to work with them. Then on Friday I had a panic attack and missed a meeting he wanted me to take. And apparently that was more important.'

'A panic attack? Since when do you get those?'

She puffed out her cheeks again. 'Actually,' she said, 'since you dumped me.'

Adam's skin crawled with shame. 'I'm sorry, Isa,' he said. 'I didn't know…'

She looked him in the eye, sighed, and gave a strange, resigned smile.

'Let's talk when you're back?' she said. 'I need to get inside and sort a few things out.'

'OK, yes,' Adam said, opening the office door for her. 'We can definitely do that.'

* * *

The park was still quiet when he wandered into it. A few joggers and dog walkers, and the bums stirring in their makeshift beds in the shadows beneath the palm trees.

The benches at the lake's edge, beyond the statue of the Queen of the Angels, were all empty. Adam paused beneath the statue, and looked up at the tall, Art Deco woman, perfect in her symmetry, her palms raised beside the twin protrusions of her breasts, and above the slight swell of her belly. She had been sculpted, he knew, by a female artist. Perhaps that was why she seemed both imperiously mythic and physically, sympathetically, realistic.

He sat on the bench behind her, from which he'd called the Autodidact only a couple of short weeks earlier. At least this time he felt less sick.

Delaying the moment, he stared at the bright lake until his eyes ached. An egret was standing very straight and still, a little way into the water. In the crown of a tree on the birds' island, a flock of grackles was chattering and dive-bombing each other.

Putting off the moment no longer, he made the call to Jason.

'Hi, man,' the Autodidact said on answering.

'Hello,' Adam said.

'You in the office?'

'No, in the park actually.'

A man had seated himself on a mat on the lawn to Adam's left, raised palms resting on his knees, face upturned and eyes closed.

'It's just me and a meditator,' he said.

'Right,' the Autodidact said. 'Have you ever tried it?'

'Meditation? No. I probably should, I suppose.'

'I do it as often as possible. Would be daily if it wasn't for work. It's amazing, mate.'

'Right,' Adam said.

'I've got this book,' the Autodidact said, '*Tactics of the Titans*.' His voice had warmed up, as though he were a little boy showing off a prized possession in a playground. Christ, Adam thought. Are all of us just little boys at heart? Children, overendowed and made terrible with brainpower, insecurity and libido?

'That sounds interesting,' he told Jason.

'Yeah,' the Autodidact said. 'It's amazing how many successful people meditate. It really works. You should try it.'

I really should try it, Adam thought. But I never will. Not while people like you do it, and while there are jalapeño margaritas in the world.

'Anyway,' the Autodidact said, waking himself from this rare moment of small talk. 'Where do we start, eh?'

'Yes, big news this morning.'

'The Euphonic shit? Yeah, that's massive. Well done, man. That's a serious result you've pulled off there.'

'Thanks.'

'Well done on the Mammal thing too.'

'Shit, I haven't even seen it. Was it…'

'It was friendly, yeah. Rumours of transphobia unfounded. Strong history of activism on Serena's part. Liberal political outlook, all that shit. They referred to a potential grudge from a former member of staff.'

'Right,' Adam said. 'Good.'

'Sign of getting bigger I think, man,' the Autodidact said. 'Disgruntled employees and all that.'

'Yes,' Adam said.

He peered out at the water, which shone blue-white in the sun. It brought to mind the memory, as a youth, of going duck shooting in the Mendip Hills with his father. They'd lined up before dawn, and he'd missed the ducks flying over, because behind him had been a lake that shone like liquid silver in the moonlight, transmuting to gold as the sun rose, and he'd been unable to stop turning around to look at it. The beauty of the countryside his dad had shown him had almost terrified him – a raw, unfathomable beauty that he'd reeled from. He hadn't been able to stand it when he was younger. He'd had to get away from it.

'Anyway,' the Autodidact continued. 'Now we've got the deal sealed, we can get cracking on the album. Roger's ideas are alarming, frankly. I think we need to get in the studio with Marissa and Bret.'

'We?'

'Well,' the Autodidact said, 'probably you actually. You're tight with them. You should get to do it, I think. I mean, I'll send you all the A & R ideas and you can talk them through it, head up there and try and make it happen direct.'

Yes, Adam thought. I am a mere vessel. The power and the grace of others moves within me.

He pictured another flight, another studio, another set of someone else's notes for another record he hated, and the three days spent in windowless gloom, listening to it over and over again while its creators studied his face.

I just can't fucking do this any more, he thought. The realization quickened his pulse. He felt dizzy and hollowed out.

'… they need to rethink all the vocal ideas,' the Autodidact was saying. 'We need to get some real top-line writers in the studio with them. Pop people. I'm deeply worried about Roger's attitude to this stuff. If we're gonna get them to the sort of level he's thinking it's gonna take…'

Something in the sky above the lake caught Adam's attention. At first he thought it was just a gull, but something about the way it was flying drew his attention. He raised his left hand, shading his eyes. No, it wasn't a gull. It was too big. The shape was wrong. Standing, he began to move around the edge of the lake, closer to where the bird was circling. Adrenaline quickened his pulse further. Yes, he thought. It was an osprey.

'… pop type success,' the Autodidact was saying. 'Choruses. Hooks. Main stage culture. Really drum it into them. Probably take about a week of full studio days. I'll send extensive notes…'

Adam watched the bird as it circled over the lake, apparently hunting. It had to be a sign, didn't it? He'd never believed in them, but…

A vision of his father came to him, coaching him over some decision he had been struggling with as a teenager.

'Don't do anything,' his dad had said, 'unless it feels just right.' He'd made a circle of his thumb and forefinger, and a sound like a chime.

How he wished, now, that he could hang up the phone and call his father. Ask him for his advice once again.

'So, does that all sound good, man?' the Autodidact said. 'You feel happy with that?'

'Hold on...' Adam said.

Happy? No, he wasn't happy. Somewhere along the line he'd become unhappy, in fact. *I've become unhappy.* The realization sank through him and settled with horrible finality, like a bright coin tossed into a well.

'I don't know,' he said.

'I know it's hard work, mate,' the Autodidact said. 'To be honest, I was gonna send Isa up there to do it. Between you and me, though, I'm not sure it's gonna work with her.'

'What?' Adam said. 'What do you mean?'

'I think it might've been a mistake bringing her back. We might even have to let her go.'

'Why?'

'She's fucking all over the place, missing meetings. Defeating the purpose of being there. I don't think I can depend on her.'

Not submitting to the henpecker-in-chief, Adam thought, enraged. Not willing or able to be completely under your control.

'She's totally mad anyway, mate,' Jason continued. 'Doesn't know what the fuck she wants. You know she once told me you're the love of her life?'

Adam's jaw went stiff, and the osprey dissolved liquidly before he blinked back tears. The bird had reached the far end of the lake, was harder to make out. He took a few steps to the water's edge and squinted, trying to retain possession of it in his eyes. He thought it had gone, but then saw that it was circling, coming back over the lake towards him.

'Adam?' the Autodidact said.

'I don't think you should fire Isa,' Adam said.

'Right. Why not?'

'Lots of reasons. But mainly that she's good, and you're going to need her.'

His body felt light and fragile, as if a gust might blow him into the lake.

'Why?'

'Because I quit.'

'What? Why?'

'I've just had enough,' Adam said.

There was silence at the other end of the phone. Midway across the lake, the osprey suddenly contracted, and dropped towards its surface. It re-emerged seconds later, evidently having missed its target, curving upward to begin circling the water again.

'Mate,' Jason said. 'You don't want to make a decision like this without giving it a lot of thought.'

'I already have,' Adam said.

He thought of his mother, of standing at her funeral. Of how it would feel not to have seen her again, until she was lying dead in a wooden box before him. Of what it would feel like to hold her in his arms while he still had the chance. Of what it would be like to see her on another tiny screen one day, a lifeless avatar of the real her, six thousand miles away, and for her finally to have forgotten who he was.

When his father had died, he'd spent days walking around the streets, writing the perfect speech in his head. He'd captured his father's honour and honesty and charm and decency and even some of his failings in exactly the right words. Then, when the day came, he'd stood at the lectern and cried and been unable to say any of them. He'd failed his dad completely.

'I have to come back, I think,' he told Jason.

'Look, man,' the Autodidact said. 'This is a bit of a shock. We don't want to lose you. Shall I go get Serena?'

'No, I don't think you should,' Adam said.

'Well, at least just think about it until the end of the week. Will you do that?'

'… No. This is something that I need to do,' Adam said. 'It's been a long time coming.'

But after all, wasn't it a bit too late? Wasn't the time to go back long gone now, like his dad, like most of his mother? Like Sofia? He closed his eyes and saw her, beaming at him, beautiful and just slightly goofy in the sunny glow beneath white sheets; expectant, waiting for him to say something that he dearly wished, now, that he had said; her eyes alive with love, still his.

All of it was gone, scorched away. The house he'd grown up in, where year after slow year of love and life had passed. School uniforms and bullies and the sleepy relief of his mum driving him home. His sister's violin-playing filling the house; the fearful cacophony of municipal swimming pools and playing fields. His father's new cars and the buzz of being driven in them fast down country lanes. The one kiss his dad had given him, on a cheek damp with tears in the darkness of his bedroom, to which his father had returned after sending him to bed punished. The warm, wet patch on his trousers where another boy had turned at the school urinal to piss on him.

Aeons of time alone in his room, reading about musicians and playing records and dreaming of the life he wanted, a thousand virgin pathways stretching ahead.

Sofia, standing in an alleyway in east London with the wind in her hair. Walking ahead of him on a rainy mountainside, turning to look at him and smiling. Gone, all of it, sliding through his fingers like water, or his ring tumbling down a drain.

If he'd stayed with Sofia he could have poured it all into children, he realized. Kids that knew it how it was. He could have kept some of all this alive. Shown it to them so they could carry it on after he was gone.

Instead, he'd ruined everything. Failed to continue what his parents had started.

It doesn't matter if they're all gone, he thought. You still have a duty to do. And I want to, he realized. I want to go home.

'Adam?' Jason said.

'Yes?'

'What are you thinking?'

I used to work in the music industry, he heard his future self say, to a cheap-suited, sceptical colleague in a stifling office somewhere in the west of England. Wasn't this job the only thing he actually had left? Without it, he wouldn't be special. The idea frightened him. And how much harder, and more tragic, to pour scorn on something you weren't invited to any longer.

He wasn't sure he was cut out to be jobless. There was every chance that a different job would be much worse than the one he had. There were, after all, still a few records he did enjoy working on. The ones the Autodidact begrudgingly kept on for the critical acclaim they earned. The ones whose fans didn't own selfie sticks.

So stay? Win Erica back. Let his sister look after his mum. Make the best of the new world he'd created. Learn to enjoy success. Have some staying power. Don't throw away LA, like everything else. The apartment and the car and the woman he might still win. The mountains and the birds and the river. Was all of that enough? Was that the brave decision – staying power, all that – or was it the weak one?

He saw the strikingly clear image of his mum's face, her brave expression failing to hide her sadness, as he'd seen it in the rear-view mirror of a girlfriend's mother's car when he was eighteen. They'd just received their A-level results, and his mum had been proud and eager to be with him. Instead, he'd insisted on travelling with his girlfriend to the restaurant in which they planned to celebrate.

They'd been in front on the road, and every now and again he'd glimpsed his mother, alone in the car behind, waving and trying to smile, following them.

You can't run away any longer, he told himself.

The osprey dived again. A plume of water rose into the sunlight and broke apart into shining fragments. A wing thrashed. The bird fought its way back into the air, this time with a fish clutched in its talons. It turned the creature parallel to its body, to optimize its aerodynamics, and beat across the lake, away from Adam.

'Adam, you still there?' Jason asked. 'We can make some changes if you like. I didn't know you felt like this. We definitely want you to be happy.'

But how to be happy again? Do his duty and wreck his life in the process. Would doing that help him recover himself? He'd believed in something once, and those beliefs were like a wellspring of life and had drawn people to him. But was quitting his job going to bring that back?

Nevertheless, the decision *had* felt right. He saw his father again, smiling. He saw the gasping beauty of the West Country, and his mum rotting in a home. He knew he had to go back. Another path beckoned, pulling him in.

He thought of Erica, a kiss on the top of a mountain, and everything dissolved and swam into one.

'Adam?' Jason was saying. 'Look, just take some time. Just think about this until the end of the week. Will you do that at least?'

Adam sighed, the heaviness pouring back into his limbs. 'Yes,' he said. 'Yes, I suppose I will.'

The osprey had nearly reached the far end of the lake, when it somehow dropped its prey. The fish fell brightly through the sunlight and back to the water, like a tiny crystal, or the tear from the homeless woman's face.

This time, apparently defeated, the bird didn't circle back. It became a fleck against the sky, tiny, receding.

Adam wondered if it could still see him.

Author's note

For obvious reasons, music is extremely important to Adam – more so, perhaps, than his career. While some of his passion has faded as the novel opens, his obsession is undimmed. And like all music obsessives, Adam sees himself as having high, uncompromising standards.

This playlist loosely reflects Adam's path through the book. Pavement's 'Cut Your Hair' is a perfect slice of US indie rock, and an arch, searing satire on the industry and scene. 'Crash Bandicoot' by Wiley is 'only' a mixtape track, but it's a work of genius – a self-portrait in stream-of-consciousness east London slang, and an example of the sound and aesthetic that Adam loves most.

Nine Inch Nails' pulsing, writhing 'Closer' represents Adam's dark, compulsive side, while Depeche Mode's 'Never Let Me Down Again' relates directly to a scene in the novel. Adam loves the song as an ode to being high.

He sees Nirvana as the gold standard of the guitar music he's spent most of his career in – raw, poppy, accessible and dark all at once – and 'Lithium' is one of their best. By the same token, his love of hip-hop has waned in the face of the scene contemporary to the novel, and for him, Wu-Tang Clan's debut album represents the genre's high-water mark.

Coldplay's 'The Scientist' is the antithesis of everything Adam has always believed in – mild, middle-of-the-road – but it's irritatingly moving, and relates directly to the 'Coldplay crisis' scene in the novel. 'I Appear Missing' by Queens of the Stone Age is a piece of towering, existential, angsty hard rock that reflects Adam's low point in *The Edge.* Keen-eared listeners will detect a direct lyrical reference. (Incidentally, this song has a great coda, one of my favourite things in music.)

Continuing the LA rock theme, Guns N' Roses' 'Paradise City' is a blazing paean to the place Adam has come to love – its beauty, and perhaps its darkness too.

Finally, Small Faces' 'All or Nothing' – an apologia for being uncompromising, something that Adam still believes in – for better or for worse.

* * *

My old mentor in music and writing, Will Ashon, taught me that the ideal length for an album is forty-five minutes, or, as we used to think of it, one perfect side of a C90 cassette. I think he's right, and I kept this in mind when putting the playlist together. Unfortunately, I failed by one minute.

1 Pavement – 'Cut Your Hair'
2 Wiley – 'Crash Bandicoot'
3 Nine Inch Nails – 'Closer'
4 Depeche Mode – 'Never Let Me Down Again'
5 Nirvana – 'Lithium'
6 Wu-Tang Clan – 'Wu-Tang Clan Ain't Nuthing ta F' Wit'
7 Coldplay – 'The Scientist'
8 Queens of the Stone Age – 'I Appear Missing'
9 Guns N' Roses – 'Paradise City'
10 Small Faces – 'All or Nothing'

Acknowledgements

Thanks first and foremost to my editor, Jenny Parrott, without whom this book would never have been written. She has an uncanny ability to see what a novel could be, and I'm a very lucky writer in having met her. Thanks to Alex Christofi – once a tireless agent and now an excellent novelist – for all the help over the years, including introducing me to Jenny. I owe a huge debt to Will Ashon for his generous coaching – in both writing and the music industry – and for a couple of invaluable suggestions for this novel. Everyone should read his books.

Thanks to Harriet Wade, Anne Bihan, Paul Nash, Kate Bland, Hayley Warnham, Ben Summers and the incredible team at Oneworld, by whom I'm very proud to be published. Thanks also to Juan Gomez and Steve Hindle at the Huntington Library in San Marino, California, for facilitating my rewriting in such a beautiful place; to Felix and Jess, whose late-draft readings were invaluable; to Dan Reisinger for endless help and encouragement; and to Tamsin Shelton for copy-editing the novel.

Last but not least, thanks to my family: my uncle Ian – birder extraordinaire and true fictionhead; my long-suffering sister Shura, a brilliant writer, reader and editor, who is still seeking a specialized therapy for people who've read graphic fiction by their siblings; my wife Marie for standing beside me, sustaining me, and a great deal more; to my children for making me laugh – even when launching coordinated ram raids on my writing room; to my granny, for setting a wonderful example with her fiction habit; and finally to my parents, for more than I could ever say.